'It's .... rous situation.
. . . . wo years and he
writes about it with the kind of clarity and insight that puts
you right there with him'

—Jim Morris, author of *War Story*

'David Maurer's novel, *The Dying Place*, will open a lot of
eyes about the secret war in Laos, Cambodia, and North
Vietnam. As a recon team leader, I can say that Maurer will
put you on the helicopters and ride you into the hidden war'

—Fred Zabitosky, Congressional Medal of Honor
Recipient for actions in Laos, 1968

'David Maurer has written . . . about the little known and
still classified CIA controlled Special Operations Group of
the Vietnam War. No one is more qualified to write it.
Maurer served two combat tours as a recon team leader in
this top-secret reconnaissance unit. His writing skills are
such that he will make you a part of their deadly missions'

J. C. Pollock,
author of *Mission M.I.A.* and *Centrifuge*

THE DYING PLACE

David A. Maurer

CORGI BOOKS

To my godson, Talon

This novel is a work of fiction. Names, characters, places and incidents are either the product of the author's imagination or used fictitiously. Any resemblance to actual events or locales or persons, living or dead, is entirely coincidental.

THE DYING PLACE

A CORGI BOOK   0 552   12738 8

First publication in Great Britain

PRINTING HISTORY

Corgi edition published 1986

Copyright © 1986 by David A. Maurer

This book is set in 10/11pt Plantin

Corgi Books are published by Transworld Publishers Ltd., 61-63 Uxbridge Road, Ealing, London W5 5SA, in Australia by Transworld Publishers (Aust.) Pty. Ltd., 26 Harley Crescent, Condell Park, NSW 2200, and in New Zealand by Transorld Publishers (N.Z.) Ltd, Cnr. Moselle and Waipareira Avenues, Henderson, Auckland.

Made and printed in Great Britain by
Hunt Barnard Printing Ltd., Aylesbury, Bucks.

Acknowledgments

I would like to thank Len Sellers for all his support and help with the book. Fred Zabitosky for the time and trouble he took to get the book to the right people. J. C. Pollock and Al Hart for going to bat for me and the book. And of course, my friend and editor, Paul McCarthy, who did so much to make this book what it is.

Grateful acknowledgment is made for permission to quote excerpts from the following song lyrics:

"Who Put the Bomp (In the Bomp BA Bomp Ba Bomp)" by Barry Mann and Gerry Goffin. Copyright © 1961 by Screen Gems-EMI Music Inc. Used by permission. All rights reserved.

"Fortunate Son" by John Fogerty. © 1969 Jondora Music. Courtesy Fantasy Inc.

CHAPTER ONE

AT TWENTY-FIVE yards the front sight of the machine gun nearly covered the back of the reclining soldier's head. It was the only part of his body visible above the green lichen-encrusted trunk of a large, partially submerged snag.

Sam Walden watched through the rear peep sight as the black hair of the North Vietnamese soldier was ruffled by a gust of wind swirling down the stream bed that was between them. A moment later it swept up into the jungle tree-line where he and the seven other men lay. The ferns and thorn vines of the undergrowth rustled against each other as the small two-tone leaves higher in the trees fluttered green and silver.

Walden let the dull black barrel ease upstream, away from the target, past a clump of dwarf elephant grass to a small opening in the jungle wall in front of him. He again counted the seven other NVA squatting at the edge of the stream. They had filled their canteens and were now leisurely unlacing their rubber and canvas bata boots as they talked among themselves. Walden pushed himself up from the mattress of decaying leaves until he could see the brown wooden stocks of the AK-47's left carelessly on the rocks on the bank behind them. The high melodic voices merged easily with the sound of rushing water and the trill of birds flitting in the upper reaches of the trees.

A thick black beetle scurried over Walden's arm, dropped to the ground, and began picking a path around the green spears poking up between dead leaves. *Lucky bastard*. Walden watched the bug disappear beneath a brown chunk of bark. Laughter floated up from the tranquil setting below. Looking back down, Walden watched them wade into the cold mountain water. *They look like children*. They might have been boys on a camping trip. He found it unreal that he was going to kill them. Each of their movements took on a trancelike significance. In minutes they would all be dead. An odd sensation rose within him as the NVA moved through their last minutes on earth. Walden glanced at his watch. Three o'clock. He wished it were earlier.

Having watched for nearly twenty minutes, he was convinced the group was alone. The tension increased in Walden until it became a tangible thing. After five days and nights on the ground in Laos, his nerves were frayed raw. Walden felt the blood start to pound around his temples and his stomach grow thick with apprehension. The time had come. Turning his head slowly to the right and lowering it to the ear of Jerry Forrest, he whispered, 'We got to blow them away before we get extracted.' Forrest looked at him, nervously licked sweat from his upper lip, and nodded. Walden made eye contact with each of the six mercenaries scattered to Forrest's right. Each held a CAR-15 machine gun pointing toward the stream, except for Lap of course, who had an M-79 grenade launcher. With slow, deliberate motions of his gloved hand Walden signalled he would take the lone man. He paused for a second, looking into the ice sheen of Cuong's eyes. Cuong sneered briefly, silently telling Walden that he was going to enjoy it.

Fuck it. Walden sighed as he moved his head up and down to alert the others that the time had come. The man reclining against the snag had just lit a cigarette and a thin gray plume of smoke wreathed upward around his head. Walden's right thumb pushed down the steel nodule of the safety, sliding it silently into semiautomatic.

The skin around the corner of his eye began to twitch slightly as Walden squinted through the rear peephole and brought the post of the front sight squarely between the neck and head of the soldier. A small green spider ran down the outside of the barrel. Walden's finger tightened slowly

8

on the trigger. The soldier turned his head to the side, lifting it up as though to call to his comrades now standing on the rocks, shaking the water from their bare feet. His hand moved into view from behind the log to take the cigarette from his mouth. Walden would remember the gray shadow along the side of the head where the hair was cropped shorter than on top.

The loud crack from his weapon sent a jolt of adrenalin through Walden's body. Red erupted from the side of the soldier's head before it disappeared behind the log. Almost instantaneously, the others were firing into the group of men by the stream. The metallic sound of Lap's M-79 was nearly lost in the cacophony of machine-gun fire. Walden swung his weapon upstream toward the group just as the 40-millimeter shell exploded against the chest of one man. The body lifted from the ground; pieces of flesh and blood carried away by the force of the blast turned the gray smoke from the explosion into a dark-pink mist. Geysers of water rose around the flailing arms and legs of the stunned soldiers. One soldier, knocked down by an exploding 40-millimeter shell, rose to his feet. Holding one leg where a thick red was spreading down his pants, he looked up frantically and began to hobble toward the cover of the jungle behind him.

'I got him,' Walden said as the others stopped firing. The NVA, after stumbling a few feet, turned back toward them and yelled '*Khuông, khuông,*' his arms reaching up pleadingly. For a moment Walden felt pity. Then he remembered the Ia Drang Valley four years ago and pulled the trigger. The man spun in a full circle and fell spread-eagled onto the stones. The others on the rocks were motionless. The ambush had lasted no longer than five seconds. The roar of the shooting echoed down the valley. Bluish white smoke hung in the undergrowth like a fog.

Cuong took the point as they slid down the clay bank above the stream, grabbing branches and vines. Sharp thorns raked hands and faces, but they paid no attention as they broke into the open.

9

'Jerry, take Cuong with you and search the ones by the water. Pau, come with me. The rest of you cover us after you get across.' Walden was panting. The eight of them pumped through the knee-deep water, then the four that had been assigned to cover disappeared into the jungle. Forrest and Cuong went toward the sprawled corpses by the stream as Pau and Walden approached the snag, his finger tense on the trigger. He had seen too many dead people come to life to trust even a bullet through the head. The cigarette lay smouldering between two small rocks not far from the still, crumpled form.

Walden pushed against the soldier's right shoulder with his boot until the body flopped over onto its back. The salty, dry smell of arterial blood rose off the corpse. The jagged hole where the bullet had exited was still draining blood onto the ground.

'Shit-can his weapon,' Walden told Pau quietly. He grabbed the man's rucksack and dumped the contents out on the rocks. Pau picked up the AK-47 and threw it spinning across the stream into the brush on the other side. Walden began rummaging through the pile of items. A light-brown pair of pants and a shirt, a square rice-cake wrapped inside a green leaf, a tin cooking pot scorched black from use, and a towel. Walden shook out the towel. A toothbrush, a bar of lye soap, five small silver tubes of medical salve, and a book wrapped in thin oilskin. Walden jammed the book into his side pocket and began patting down the body. As he pushed up the ammo vest the NVA was wearing to get at the shirt pockets, Walden noticed that the skin was still warm. He avoided looking directly at the dead man's face. It was better that way. Less material for nightmares later. He knew about nightmares.

After satisfying himself that the soldier didn't have anything more, he and Pau jogged over to where Forrest and Cuong were finishing their search.

The area around the dead was littered with the rucksack's contents. Pieces of writing paper blew out over the water and settled like small white barges on the flowing stream. As the wind picked up, a pulp magazine lying on the rocks fluttered open, its pages flicking back and forth as though being thumbed. Walden looked over the blood-slick stones covered with the wreckage of the bodies. Years before, he and friends had been hunting and had come across twenty or so squirrels in one tree. The scene before him now was like that. Twisted bodies seemingly all over the ground, some lying on top of others.

The soldier hit by the 40-millimeter shell lay shattered on the rocks. The upper torso had been nearly severed at the waist. The chest yawned open, the stark white bones of the rib cage looking like the hull of an old beached ship. A sour stench of pepsin reached Walden's nostrils and he felt his stomach churn. His throat swelled as he gagged.

'Come on, Jer, let's get out of here.' Walden coughed as he began to salivate, and for a second he thought he might vomit. They hurried across the rocks to where the rest of the team had entered the jungle. Walden's left boot slipped on something spongy, and his leg went out from under him. He fell to the rocks, cursing under his breath as he looked back to see what he had stepped on. 'Oh Christ,' he groaned when he saw the red piece of scalp with the black bristly hair. He lurched to his feet, the image remaining in his mind as he scrambled up the clay bank into the jungle.

Walden was breathing heavily as he reached the place where the others had gathered. He knelt for a second to catch his breath and gestured to Cuong to start moving up the ridge. They moved out through the underbrush, scrambling and clawing their way up the steep incline. Walden tried to shake the guilt. He had never felt the exhilaration that some others professed to feel during an ambush. It always seemed like murder to him. It was never like the movies. The bodies were mangled, perforated, wet with blood. He pushed the thoughts from his mind. He couldn't think about that now. He had to think about getting the team out before other NVA, alerted by the gunfire, tried to kill them.

After thirty or forty metres Walden signaled a halt where

11

the ground flattened out for a short way before rising again. They dropped to the soft, mulch-covered ground. The wetness that had come to Walden's mouth down by the bodies had been drawn back into his skin and now his tongue felt parched and fat. He licked his cracked lips, feeling the flakes of dried skin and the sting of salt entering the split flesh. A high-pitched ringing ran back and forth between his ears as he fought to catch his breath, but the air didn't seem to reach his lungs. Waves of nausea rippled through his stomach and his head seemed to float above his shoulders. The bamboo and vine entanglement around them frustrated even the slightest breeze. The stifling heat not only pressed down on them, but radiated from the ground.

Forrest rummaged around in Walden's rucksack for the rod sections of the long antenna. Walden pulled out a canteen of water. Forrest unscrewed the short antenna together, and screwed it into the radio. Seconds after drinking the hot water, Walden felt his head clear and the strength come back to his body.

'Okay, Sam,' Forrest said when the radio was ready. Reaching into his fatigue shirt, Walden took out the black handset and began whispering into the mouthpiece.

'Covey, Covey, this is Star Machine, Star Machine, over.' He let up on the keying plunger and listened as a brief buzz of static came over the air and then silence. *Fuck me to tears.* He repeated the call. Silence. He glanced up at the others circled around him. Each team member was watching nervously, waiting for a hint that he had got through to someone.

'Goddamn it, you guys,' Walden hissed at them. 'Watch the jungle, for Christ's sake.' The little people turned their heads back to the jungle. Forrest hunched closer.

'We're in trouble if we don't get somebody,' Forrest said. 'Every gook in Laos heard that ambush.'

'Don't worry, Covey knows it's our last day of the mission,' Walden said. He winked reassurance, then repeated the call signs into the radio. *Come on, come on.* He glared at the handset and felt anger flowing up. He strained to keep from yelling into the mike. Then, the nearly inaudible crackling of a voice came over the air.

'Star Machine, this is Covey. Hear you. Weak. How me? Over.'

'Got 'em,' Walden whispered to Forrest, a smile spreading. 'Covey, this is Star Machine. We just ambushed eight Charlies, am calling a tactical emergency, over.'

'Ah, roger that, good buddy. Have ships standing by for your extraction. ETA is about three zero, over.'

Good old Pappy. No matter what was happening or how bad the situation was, Pappy always sounded as if he were calling out bingo numbers at a church bazaar. Walden had just brought the handset back up to his lips when an abrupt motion seen from the corner of his eye made him spin around. Pau had suddenly rolled over on his stomach. Twisting his head around to look at Walden, Pau looked frantic, his eyes wide. He jabbed his finger down the slope, mouthing 'VC, VC.' Walden felt the hair on the back of his neck bristle as the sounds of breaking brush and jabbering voices came up the side of the ridge.

Cupping his hand around the mouthpiece, Walden spit the words out as quietly as he could. 'Covey, this is Star. We got to move to the top of the ridge. A bunch of Chucks are coming up after us. Get them ships out here.'

There was no time to say any more. Forrest unscrewed the long antenna and screwed the short one back into the radio in record time. He kept mumbling, 'Fuck me to tears,' as he broke down the long antenna. 'Fuck me to tears.' The sound of the North Vietnamese coming up their back trail grew louder. The little people unconsciously tightened up the circle until their small shoulders were touching.

As soon as the long antenna had been stowed in his ruck, Walden motioned to Cuong to move up the slope. Rising to a crouch, team members began to push their way through the jungle foliage. It became nearly impossible to move quietly through the bamboo thickets interwoven with vines

13

which grew more dense with each step up the ridge. The Vietnamese voices were growing more distinct as the distance narrowed between the NVA and the recon team. The voices were angry and excited at the same time. Suddenly stealth was discarded for speed as the recon. team began smashing through the brush.

Oh, my God, I'm heartily sorry for having offended Thee. It kept running through Walden's head as he tried to remember the full prayer. His throat burned as the air rasped in and out. His legs were trembling from fatigue and fear as he pushed himself through a network of lianas dangling like ropes from the trees, which were growing shorter as they approached the crest.

Walden's foot caught an exposed root and he crashed to the ground. He cursed as he scrambled to get back on his feet but a vine had dropped around his neck. He grabbed and twisted it until juice ran out. 'Motherfuckin' son of a bitch,' he hissed. Forrest dropped next to him with his survival knife and cut the vine. Once on his feet, Walden mumbled the first line of the Lord's Prayer under his breath so a curse wouldn't be the last words he spoke on earth. His skin tightened as he anticipated the feel of bullets tearing into his back. The trees gave way to high grass, and the team groped and fought its way upward.

As they neared the crest of the ridge, the tall, sharp-edged elephant grass became nearly impregnable. It was too thick to push through, so Cuong would just fall forward, flattening the grass, stand up, and fall forward again. After a few minutes Walden saw that Cuong was exhausted. Moving up past Hung as if he were walking over the top of a haystack, Walden motioned to Cuong to fall in behind and took the point. The NVA voices below them had stopped and only the sounds of the team floundering through the wall of grass could be heard. It was as though, now, even the jungle was fighting them. Climbing the last twenty feet to the top of the ridge was like battering through a solid wall. Without the cover of trees the sun's rays became pounding heat. Gossamer veils of steam rose from their sweat-drenched uniforms.

The barrier of grass ended as abruptly as it had begun, and Walden emerged just where the ridge flattened into a glen of thirty-foot trees. He staggered forward through the trees for a dozen paces, then sagged to the ground, retching. Fatigue boiled through his legs and back, and then began to subside.

'We're getting pulled out right here,' Walden stammered. He squirmed off the ninety-pound rucksack as the others formed around him. Many times Walden had heard people say they were so scared they could run forever. He now knew it wasn't true. There came a point where dying was better than running, and the team had reached that point fighting through the elephant grass. A treed animal turning on its attackers, the team readied itself for the fight. The others began pulling Claymore mines out of their rucksacks, and Walden pulled two M-33 grenades out of one of his canteen pouches. He tore off the black electrical tape he had fastened around the levers as added safety. He twisted and pulled on the rings attached to the cotter-pin safeties. As soon as they were free, he lifted his thumbs from the arming levers and let them ping off. He moved down toward the grass wall with the grenades cooking in his hands and counted to himself. *One thousand one, one thousand two, three, four.* He threw them over the eight-foot-high grass, arcing them down the slope.

The grenades exploded above the elephant grass, sending shrapnel spraying downward. The explosions were sharp and crisp and Walden knew he had got the airbursts he wanted. He knew the grass would absorb the blasts if the grenades hit the ground. Walden never liked to put that much trust in the five- to six-second fuses, but once again he had got away with it.

He covered Forrest, Pau and Toan as they slid a few feet and set up two Claymores on the slope above the grass, in an arc facing downhill. Finished, they trailed the Claymore firing cords back to where the others were spreading grenades and magazines out in front of them.

Walden moved to where he had dropped his rucksack and dragged it behind a tree. The jungle had gone still after the grenades exploded. The only thing Walden could hear, it seemed, was the blood pounding around his temples. Grabbing the handset, he whispered, 'Covey, this is Star Machine, over.'

Instantly Pappy's voice came over. 'How you doing down there, buddy?'

'Not so hot. There're about twenty or thirty gooks coming up the north side of the ridge we're on.'

'Okay, buddy, just stay cool. We got some fast movers coming in right now. I need a fix on you, over.'

The drone of the airplane filtered down through the canopy of leaves. Walden waited until the sound was just over to one side of the ridge, then radioed the pilot to watch for a flare. Reaching into his side pocket, Walden pulled out the black pen flare launcher and inserted the fifty-caliber shell at the top of the stubby tube. A second later he pointed it up through the trees. In the hush that had fallen over the jungle, the report of the flare being fired sounded like a cannon. Jetting up through the branches overhead, it popped into a bright red star over the verdure of the jungle.

Pappy's voice came back over the air. 'Okay, buddy, we see the flare. Will make final pass for your mark-mark, over.'

'Roger that,' Walden whispered. He listened to the pitch of the engine change as the airplane began dropping toward them. It came in low over the tops of the trees, flying straight down the ridgeline. Walden waited until it was directly overhead, then said 'mark-mark' quickly into the mouthpiece. A moment later there were thick popping sounds of AK-47's firing from down the ridge. 'You're taking ground fire,' Walden said into the mike.

'No shit' was the only reply he heard as the jet's engine screamed and it banked out over the trees and began to climb. Seconds later Pappy's voice came back over the air, chuckling. 'By God, you do have some people after you down there.' Before Walden could reply, a businesslike, mature voice came over the earphone.

'Ah, Star Machine, this is Fast Mover Six. Understand you got a little trouble down there. What's your situation? Over.'

'Mover, this is Machine. We got gooks coming up the north side of the ridge right below us. Do you have us pinpointed, over?'

'Roger that, Star. We picked up mark-mark from Covey's pass. I'm going to amaze some of your friends down there, so keep your asses down. I'm rolling in hot.'

Walden looked at the team crouching around him and smiled. 'We got those fuckers now. Stay down, the jets are coming in on a hot run.'

As soon as the others heard him say that, they seemed to grow thinner as they squirmed deeper into the pungent humus. The whooshing of rockets mingled with the electronic whine of Mini-Guns began without warning. The rockets exploded barely fifteen yards in front of their positions, throwing dirt and debris into the air. The ground jerked beneath them as though flinching from the explosions scarring its back. The blast from the jet engines thundering over sent a rain of leaves fluttering toward the ground.

As though pausing in stride, the firing stopped briefly, and then began again, more intensely. The jets pulverized the slope, and the sounds of trees breaking and limbs crashing to the ground merged into an aching throb inside Walden's head. His mind went dark as the explosions climbed higher and higher up the ridge. Whirling shards of metal began flaying the trees around them. The exploding rockets were so close that the shock waves tugged at their uniforms. The team dug their fingers into the soft ground, trying to melt away.

They didn't fully realize when it ended, with the sounds rolling down between the valley walls. Smoke and dust rode the riled air currents, slowly sifting down the slope over the splayed and tattered thickets of grass and bamboo. Walden tried to clear his head, shaking it as he tasted blood in his mouth. He had bitten into his lower lip when the rockets were coming in. The handset was on the ground next to his head and he heard the voice as though he were listening through a long tube.

'Ah, Star, this is Mover Six. How was that? Over.'

'Are you sure you know where we are?' Walden blurted into the mike. 'There was shit exploding on top of us.'

'Sorry about that, buddy, but be advised you got Charlies running all over down there. Just a second, Star. Movers Three and Four, we got AA fire coming from the south side of the ridge.'

Suddenly the airwave was alive with excited voices as Walden heard the dull booming sound of 37-millimeter anti-aircraft guns. Forrest was cramped up at the base of a small tree. He looked at Walden, then crawled over.

'What's going on?'

Before Walden could reply, Pau and Cuong suddenly opened fire. Walden's body uncoiled as if he had been shocked, lifting him off the ground. His weapon began firing itself.

Through the smoke and dust NVA came stumbling through the grass near the top of the slope. Walden watched what was happening in complete calm. His nerve endings were dead from fear so great that it was not fear. The body functioned for survival. The words came to his mind clear and firm. *Shoot him, the others can wait. Good. Now, him. Now, him. Red tracer, change magazines. Quick, the one that's firing.* The voice went on, calmly, fear changed to not-fear. *Cuong is changing magazines, cover him.*

The firing became frantic as the soldiers blundered out of the elephant grass into the bullets that ripped and snapped around and through them. Walden watched puffs of dust erupt from the tan uniforms as the bullets smacked into twisting bodies. Some of the faces were black from the explosions. They looked dazed as they fought against the storm of bullets. They came on blindly, knowing that the closer they got to the team the better their chances were of surviving the next air strike. The lines of NVA wavered, as though caught in a heavy wind. Most of the NVA weren't even firing their weapons, as though they had forgotten what to do. Some of them were without weapons and seemed only to be running from the holocaust down the slope.

'Get down,' Walden yelled above the roar of the firefight. His hand grabbed the Claymore detonator forgotten in the hysteria. Flicking back the safety catch, Walden pushed the firing lever down hard. A flash of exploding light shook the skin on the sides of his face. The up-slope backblast slammed into him, knocking him off his knees. The voice inside of him didn't change. *You can see, you can feel, fire the other mine, make sure.* Walden stretched out his hand, grabbed the second detonator, and fired it. The backblast of the second mine was absorbed by a slight overhang of the slope, but the area directly in front and to the sides was devastated by the swarm of ball bearings that screamed out from the curved mine.

The NVA that had survived the team's fire were now blown back over the side of the ridge. One second they were there, the next all that remained was a haze of smoke clinging to the broken, splintered thicket.

Walden looked around to see who was dead or wounded. It was hard to tell at first, with faces black from the Claymore explosions and trickles of blood running out of noses. Then the team began moving about, slowly. Forrest crawled around, patting team members on the shoulders, asking with his eyes. It was impossible, but no one had been hit. Sweat glistened on their faces where the green-and-black camouflage grease was wiped away.

A dozen or so bodies were piled out in front of the team. A soft cry, an animal cry, came from a form lying on the edge of the grass. Before Walden could stop him, Cuong ran out to the man and fired several shots. He came sprinting back, fell down next to Walden, and grinned.

19

'*Fini* now.' He then nestled in the shallow depression he had clawed out of the ground.

Several voices were trying to talk at the same time over the radio as Walden lifted the handset to his ear. He keyed the mike a couple of times to clear the airwave.

'Covey, this is Star Machine. We got gooks coming out of the woodwork down here. Over.' He tried to sound matter of fact, but he didn't quite make it. His voice broke at the end.

'Okay, Star, take it easy,' Pappy said reassuringly. 'Cobras are on station. They're going to walk some fire in a three-sixty around you, then the fast movers are going to drop some two-fifty pounders on the south side of that ridge. We're going to get you out of there, no sweat. Keep your butts down.'

Oh, my God, I'm heartily sorry for having offended Thee. It kept running back and forth between the aching walls of his head. He and the others braced themselves for the next fire storm.

First the Cobra helicopters came in over the tops of the trees, using their Mini-Guns like fire hoses. Twigs and bark and leaves cascaded down as bullets tore branches into fibrous pulp.

That was preamble to the ground-tearing shocks felt when the jets came in, dropping the 250-pound bombs. Hot blasts of air carried by the shock waves lifted the temperature ten degrees. The team cringed against the ground. The world became one long scream as the light in Walden's head flickered, and faded, then came back into focus. The last stanza of the murderous aerial song faded away.

In nearly catatonic shock the team members looked around. Trees were broken and torn; black clumps of dirt were strewn like giant bird droppings. The bittersweet smell of cordite permeated the hot air. Walden lifted the phone to his throbbing ear and heard Pappy's calm voice.

'Star Machine, this is Covey. Taxi's approaching you. Guide them in, over.'

'Roger, Covey.' Walden felt a dull ache coming up into his stomach from his bowels. 'Taxi, this is Star Machine. Will talk you over our position, over.' A growl of static, then a different voice.

'Star, this is Taxi Two. Roger that. How about popping a smoke as we make our approach? Over.'

'Roger, Taxi. You identify smoke, over.'

'Roger. We're coming in over you now.'

Walden tore the canister of violet smoke from where he had it taped to his web-gear strap, pulled the pin, and tossed it a few yards away. It made a popping sound, emitted a brief spurt of sparks, then spit a plume of smoke out of the top of the can. He watched the smoke lift through the shattered canopy overhead.

'Ah, Star, this is Taxi. I see red, yellow, and violet smoke, over.'

'This is Star. Come in on the violet. Covey, do something about that other smoke, over.'

'Ah, Star, this is Taxi. Coming in on the violet.'

The team members peered up through the branches as the olive-colored belly of the Huey helicopter came into view. The blades popped the thin mountain air and the whine from the engine grew. Walden used the radio to direct the pilot, bringing him overhead. Forrest gathered Hung, Lap, Pau, and Nha to go out on the first ship. With the helicopter hovering just to one side, Walden called for the extraction rigs. A figure appeared in the doorway of the helicopter and dropped four McQuire loops attached to sandbags. The dirt-filled bags broke through the branches and slammed into the ground fifteen feet away.

Forrest moved with the four little people to the loops on the ground. He helped slip them in, and when all were ready he turned to Walden with a thumbs-up.

'Okay, take 'em up slow,' Walden said. The slack pulled out of the 120-foot ropes as the chopper rose. The ropes finally grew taut and the four lifted into the air. Walden's heart thundered as he watched the little ones squirming and wrestling the foliage as they were pulled through the

21

trees. The lift took a painfully long ten seconds and Walden sighed as the men cleared the tops of the trees and were gone with the fading rumble of the ship.

Forrest, Cuong, and Toan came running to Walden. The jungle began to murmur around them. 'At least we got half of them out of here,' Walden said. For some reason it wouldn't be so bad if some of them made it out. His ears were still ringing and the sounds of rustling leaves and his own breathing seemed oddly loud and yet removed.

Walden pulled the rucksack straps back over his shoulders as the second helicopter came in. He called for the rigs and the bags again broke open as they hit the ground. The four rushed to the heavy canvas loops, snapping their rucksacks onto the ropes. Walden pushed his left hand into the safety strap and pulled the sling up around his hips.

'You guys ready?' Walden yelled over the pounding sound of the chopper. They all nodded and Walden gave the command to lift.

The door gunners suddenly opened up with their M-60's and the empty shell casings began falling around the team. Walden felt the sling tighten around his hips as they were lifted into the air. Ten feet above the ground Walden looked down and his stomach lurched as he watched green tracers floating up. A thick smattering of khaki-colored uniforms flitted from tree to tree beneath them, most to the rear of where the team had been.

The hot shell-casings struck them on the heads and shoulders as the machine guns rattled above. Tree limbs tore past Walden's arms as he fired blindly downward. When his clip hit empty, Walden looked up and saw that only a few more feet of thin branches were laced between them and the open air.

As they broke clear, Walden heard a thwacking sound and turned to see a vapor of red burst from the back of Toan's head. *Jeez, how did he do that?* The slender body jerked and slipped out of the sling and hung by its left arm from the safety noose taut around the wrist. Without

22

thinking Walden lurched out, grabbed the heavy canvas sling, and pulled it to him. He stared at the blood gushing out of the wound as though it were part of the trick. The chopper rose upward in a sudden convulsion of power. The sling was torn from his hand as the wind ripped the rig away.

The remaining three clutched each other as the jungle fell away. The wind forced them out from beneath the helicopter until they trailed the ship, twisting slowly at the ends of the ropes. A scarlet wake widened behind little Toan as the wind blew the rivulets into a haze. Walden shuddered and looked away, looked at the horizon, which broadened as they lifted into the sky. He couldn't seem to move.

Mushrooming black clouds were erupting in the jungle behind as the jets dropped napalm into the green-and-yellow landscape. Boiling columns of liquid flames splashed through the trees. The ridge-line danced with the searing jelly. Toan's body swung back on a cushion of air, bumping lightly against them. Walden grabbed the rig again and pulled the lifeless form in among them. He pulled the green sweatband from his head and began wiping the blood away from Toan's face. He felt the cracked and broken bones around the hole beneath Toan's left eye as he drew the cloth over it. It was only then it really registered that Toan was dead.

'Oh, Toan, oh, man,' Walden whimpered in a voice he would never admit was his own. The others stared at the mountainous jungle three thousand feet below. Walden murmured to the body held close to him, comforting the boy as though he were only hurt. Walden trembled as his sweat began to dry in the thin wind swirling around him.

They held each harness with death grips as the terrain below began to level out as they crossed back into South Vietnam. They passed over the flat brown plains of Khe Sanh, then over the rolling hills that thrust up on the fringes. Walden squeezed his eyes shut, knowing that when he opened them again he would be home, waking from a dream. He couldn't be a soldier; he couldn't be holding a dead friend. It was not possible. It was possible, and closing his eyes wouldn't change it. Only Toan was dreaming; only Toan would wake in a different place.

Toan was dead, but the rest of the team was caught between the living and the dead, with no more hopes or dreams than could be fitted into a week of Saigon bars.

Nearing the launch site where the team had started five days before, the helicopter began to descend. Walden felt the air around him grow warmer. The reddish-brown roads weaving beneath them amid the patchwork quilting of rice paddies seemed like a different world. If looked at objectively, if looked at as if it were a magazine photograph.

Walden watched the barbed wire enclosure of the launch site coming up. His arms were filled with pain from holding Toan with his right and clutching the rig with his left. A thin stream of blood ran off the tops of Toan's boots as the chopper hovered over the perforated-steel-plate helipad and began to lower the men. Walden watched several men rushing about below, looking up, the emotion of the moment reflected in their gestures and cries. Outside the compound a truck full of Marines stopped to watch the strange scene.

'Ah, no, Jesus Christ.' A voice lifted, thick with shock and sadness. 'Get Doc over here. They're all shot to hell.' Toan's body twisted slowly away as Walden opened his cramped hand. The bandana that Walden had been holding, wet with blood, dropped fluttering to the ground. Just before the upstretched arms of the men on the ground touched the bottoms of their boots, Toan revolved facing them. His head was bowed, and his thin white arm, stretched over his head as he hung by his wrist from the strap, seemed to bid them farewell.

Walden felt the other world touching him, but there was a fog inside his head. He felt the strong, reassuring hands of his friends holding his body up, then laying it down. He tried to smile, to indicate he was all right, but he could only stare at the faces and wonder at the tears that were falling down Billy Slader's cheeks. Words jumbled together above him. Someone began to unbuckle his belt, and suddenly it all came back into focus. He pushed the hands away and fought the other hands trying to hold him down.

'I'm okay. I'm okay,' he said. He let the hands help him to his feet. The launch-site commander, Major Cane, embraced him.

'Oh, God. Oh, God,' Cane kept repeating as he rubbed and patted Walden's back, half-holding him up on his wobbly legs.

'Where's Jerry? Where's Forrest?' Walden asked, looking at the faces that reflected his numb, scared feeling. The major and Slader helped him to where Forrest was flat-back on the steel plating, clutching and unclutching his fist as a couple of the launch-site people massaged his legs, trying to work the blood back. Walden stumbled and was held up by Slader and Cane, and then followed to kneel next to his one-one.

'You okay?' Walden asked, pushing the hair out of Forrest's eyes.

'Yeah, Sam, I'm okay. I'll be fine in a minute. You all right?' Forrest looked at the blood-splattered face of the team leader.

'I'm fine. I'm fine.'

The little people clustered around the two Americans, touching them and speaking softly. Walden pushed himself to his feet when Pau and Cuong came over. They took him by the hands and walked him to where the frail form of Toan was being lifted and placed in the rubber body bag open on the plating. Helped by Lap and Nha, Forrest limped over to where Toan lay on the catafalque of steel. Pau squatted, whispering in Chinese, and untied the red piece of cloth from Toan's top buttonhole. Then he removed the cloth tied to the front sight of the weapon lying next to the body bag. The others remained silent as Pau moved his hands up and down in prayer.

After a few moments Major Cane whispered to Walden, 'I'm sorry you lost one of your men, Sam. I know how much each of them means to you. I'm real sorry.' Walden looked at the major and nodded that he understood. When Pau had finished, Walden bent down and zipped the body bag closed.

'Who were his next of kin, Sam?' the tall medic. next to him asked.

'We are. We'll take the body back to Da Nang with us,' Walden said.

An H-34 helicopter sitting at the end of the pad started to warm its engine, swirling the air around them. The major bent his head to Walden's ear. 'The Kingbee is going to take you back now.'

Shaking hands with the major and Slader, Walden and Forrest followed the little people carrying Toan's body to the helicopter. After his team was loaded in the chopper, Walden turned to the group of men standing behind them. 'Thanks,' he said.

He climbed inside the ship and sat down in the doorway. The engine revved up and the chopper lifted, spun around, and headed toward the ocean.

After a short time Walden scooted back from the doorway and rested against the bulkhead with his rucksack. He pulled out his last pack of cigarettes and passed them around to the team.

The Vietnamese door gunner grinned down at him and said, 'You kill *beaucoup* VC, huh?' Then he laughed, showing his mouthful of gold teeth. The wind ruffled Walden's uniform as he turned to look at the gunner. 'You kill *beaucoup* VC, huh?' the man repeated. Walden suddenly had a violent urge to throw him out the door.

'Yeah, I know you kill *beaucoup* Viet Cong. Hear on radio,' he shouted over the noise, pointing toward the two pilots in the cockpit. 'You guys plenty crazy,' he said, shaking his head.

'Shut the fuck up,' Walden yelled. 'Shut the fuck up or you're going right out that goddamn door.'

The Vietnamese looked shocked. Then he turned away

self-consciously and looked out over the barrel of the A-6 machine gun mounted in front of him.

Walden glanced over at Forrest. There was a darkness in Jerry's usually bright eyes as he smoothed his black mustache with his fingers. He nodded toward the door gunner and said matter-of-factly, 'I'll help you.' Walden smiled, then shook his head. He turned back to the door and watched the blond ribbon of beach below melt into the blue waters of the South China Sea.

Walden knew that the mission would be hailed as a huge success at Da Nang and at the puzzle palace in Saigon. It didn't matter much. The information gathered wasn't worth it, of course. But that wouldn't delay the next time. A chill ran down Walden's back.

CHAPTER TWO

CLOSING THE confessional door behind him, Sam Walden knelt down, then strained upward to put his head near the screened opening. He fidgeted in the dark, trying hard to think of sins to confess. There were so few. The booth was musty and held a strong odor of starch from the curtain behind the screen. He tried to listen to Keith, his classmate and best friend, mumbling in the opposite cubicle. He strained to hear what he was saying, hoping he might borrow a sin, then remembered what Sister Theresa had said in class: It was a sin to listen to others confess. *Have I just committed a sin? No, I stopped listening as soon as I remembered.* He concentrated then on the glowing crucifix above the window.

His palms were hot and moist by the time the wooden separator opened. The white curtain grew dark as the priest leaned against it to hear his sins.

'Bless me, Father, for I have sinned. My last confession was a week ago.' He paused to get his sins in order. 'I disobeyed my mother and father. I lost my temper three times. And I didn't say my bedtime prayers two times. These are all my sins, Father.'

'You must always say your prayers at night,' the priest whispered. 'If you died in your sleep without having said your prayers, you might go to hell. You don't want to go to hell, do you?'

'No, Father.'

'Control your temper. When you feel yourself becoming angry, say a prayer to the Lord. Obey your parents, as Jesus obeyed his. For your penance, say three Hail Marys and three Our Fathers, and now say a good Act of Contrition.'

He recited the prayer as the priest gave him absolution. The Latin was mysterious, frightening, as always.

'Go in peace and may God bless you,' the priest said, and slid the wooden separator across the opening.

'Thank you, Father,' he mumbled before leaving the booth. The thick air in the basement church felt almost nice as he stepped into the light. His classmates, waiting to go into the confessional, stood piously in a row, heads bowed. He felt a twinge of anger as he walked past Monty, the class bully, looking more holy than anyone. When around the nuns Monty was the perfect saint. When they weren't around, he was a real jerk. Sam offered a prayer to the Lord, trying out the priest's advice. He went to his class section of pews.

Genuflecting quickly, he tried to sneak into the row behind the large bulk of Sister Theresa before she spotted him. In his hurry his foot banged against the kneeler below the pew, and she spun around. Her thin, colorless lips pressed together as she glared down at him. Without a word she stepped out into the aisle and sternly pointed to where she wanted him to be – next to her. Without looking at her he moved into the pew and knelt down, next to Keith. They eyed each other as the sister moved back into the pew. Sam looked up at the altar and couldn't stop the distaste he felt as he saw all the burning candles denoting a high mass. Even worse, it was to be a funeral mass. A mass for the dead.

The church began to fill. The temperature rose, the air becoming stale and sour. While the sister's attention was drawn to the back of the church where the pallbearers were wrestling the coffin down the steps, Keith bumped a shoulder against his.

'What did you get?'

'Three Hail Marys and three Our Fathers,' Sam replied, just before the stiff hand of the sister banged against the back of his head.

'You know better than to talk in church, Samuel,' she snapped.

'Yes, sister,' Sam whispered. She became pious again, going back into her prayerful trance.

He turned slightly and watched the funeral directors and pall-bearers place the bronze coffin on the chrome-plated church truck and begin pushing it up the aisle.

They stopped right next to him. The priest who would say mass and the altar boys walked solemnly forward. The choir began to sing and Sam knew he was going to get sick again as soon as the first smell of incense wafted through the church. He felt a hot rush of nausea sweep through him as everyone stood up.

His mouth became dry and his ears started to ring as the priest, standing at the head of the casket, began the Latin prayers. Gray clouds of incense rose into the air as he swung the thurible back and forth. The ringing in Sam's ears became sharper. He felt faint. The sounds around him were distant and muffled.

'Sister, Sister,' Sam mumbled, pulling at the nun's habit. 'I can't breathe. I feel sick.' She grabbed his shoulders and pushed him down hard into the wooden pew. Roughly she shoved his head between his knees.

'You stay like that until you can stand up,' she hissed into his ear. 'You're going to stay right here in this church until the mass is over.' He listened to the blood in his ears, trying to breathe some air that wasn't filled with that sickening, sweet smell.

He tensed as he felt the vomit moving up out of his stomach. He stood up and tried to push past the nun. She was trying to force him back into the seat when he began to vomit. The yellow bile splattered the lap of her habit. With one quick motion she pulled him to his feet and dragged him out of the church as his classmates turned and gawked.

'You disgusting little beast,' she yelled once they were outside.

'I'm sorry. I didn't mean it,' he screamed as she yanked him across the street toward the school building and convent. He lost his balance and fell, skinning his knees on the asphalt. It felt as if his arm were being torn out of its socket when she jerked him back to his feet.

'Every time there's a funeral you get sick. Now you even throw up on me!' She pushed him through the school doorway. 'You're going to learn a lesson now.' She grabbed a fistful of his hair and shook his head from side to side. Pushing him into the classroom she ordered him to sit at his desk and wait until she returned. The bitter taste of the vomit lingered in his mouth. He felt helpless, and began to scold himself for getting sick. *Maybe I am a dirty little beast.* He looked out the tall classroom windows at the trees that were just beginning to leaf. Seeing a coffin made him sick, though. He couldn't help it. Even since that first time, with his cousin. People in coffins looked different, looked bad. They had told him that she was asleep, but he'd known it wasn't true. People didn't cry when you were only asleep.

CHAPTER THREE

THE SUN was just above the western horizon when the H-34 chugged around the rocky tip of Cap Tourane. The chopper shuddered as it began its southerly descent over Da Nang Harbor. Walden pushed himself away from the bulkhead, settling down in the open doorway. He dangled his legs over the edge. The wind carried with it a faint evening chill as it swirled around his pants. He looked down at the water. The glow from the sun filtering across the crests of the waves streaked the harbor with color, pink turning to red, yellow becoming gold. Out beyond the boats choking the harbor, Walden saw the looming hulk of the hospital ship.

The hypnotic pitch of the water gave way to white lines of froth as the waves broke over the sand shoals. The helicopter continued to descend, passing over China Beach and the sprawling equipment depots staggered along the waterline. Walden grabbed the aluminum leg of the door gunner's seat as he saw the POL dump approaching. The rows of fifty-five-gallon fuel drums looked like spools of green thread stacked neatly on the beach. The black tin roofs of the POW camp above the POL dump were just passing to the side of the ship when the pilot banked sharply to the right.

The jagged, pockmarked north wall of Marble Mountain swept into view to the south as the Kingbee roared west over the wooden hooches of the camp. Walden could make out through the side window to his left the faint outline of men, poncho lean-tos, and radio antennas on the summit. The mountain was a shrine, a holy place. It was also a marble anthill with a thousand different tunnels and passageways; a haven for local Viet Cong and NVA, it stood as an ironic reminder of what the war was like. The Americans held the top and the bottom simply because of their physical presence. The enemy held everything inside. Occasionally a sniper would fire a few rounds toward the camp from the mouth of a cave and then slip back into the labyrinth. No one was ever hit.

The helicopter, its blades popping and crackling over the compound, raced over the camp's northern perimeter to the landing pad. The silver tin roofs of the buildings, sandbagged against the wind, slid beneath them as Walden braced himself for the maniacal maneuver that was every Kingbee pilot's trademark. Fifty feet above the steel plating of the pad, the pilot stalled the engine and rolled the ship on its side. Walden and Forrest stared straight down at the ground as the chopper twisted in a small tight circle and began to plummet. The earth rushed up in a sickening blur of faces, barbed wire, and trucks. Just as Walden felt the centrifugal force that was pinning him and the others inside the ship begin to fade, the pilot lurched the ship back upright, barely twenty feet above the ground. The large balloon tires of the old chopper hit the pad hard. The ship bounced into the air, then finally settled, jolting the struts hard against the body.

'Stupid bullshit.' Walden felt his stomach lining slip back down his throat. Grabbing his weapon and rucksack, he turned to Forrest as the men that had been awaiting their arrival moved toward the ship. 'One of these times they're going to pull this shit and crash on somebody.' Then they were surrounded by their friends, getting thumped on the back and handed cold beer. Walden felt the handclasps and listened to the excited jumble of voices and let the anger go. They were home. Everyone was talking at once as they walked from the helicopter. The little people grinned as the Americans ruffled their hair and patted them on the shoulders.

They had returned from the dying place, all but one. And now, in ritual, they were welcomed back to life. All the

33

images the men used to cover themselves with during their stay in the storm disappeared in the brief euphoria of the meeting. Though they smelled of sweat, dirt, and dried blood, there was sweet joy in the air.

Major Jack Gleason broke through the throng gathered around the team and threw his large arms around Walden, kissing him on the ear. 'Don't you ever die, you sweet motherfucker,' he said.

'Shit.' Walden laughed. 'I'll be rallying troops on the front lawn of the White House before they get me.' Mike Workman, a grin spread across his thin face, punched Walden lightly on the chest. 'Hi, Mikie.' Walden grinned. 'Did you take good care of Giap?'

'That son of a bitch chewed all the straps off my rucksack,' Workman said. 'He hates me.' He grunted as he picked up Walden's rucksack. 'I got a jeep to take you to your hooch.' Workman looked at the body bag inside the chopper and paused for a second. 'Doc is bringing the ambulance down. Who got it?'

'Toan,' Walden said quietly as he watched the olive-colored truck with the large red cross roll up. Miles Keegan got out of the truck and walked to Walden. The little people began to load their gear into the back of a deuce-and-a-half. Keegan held out his hand.

'I'm sorry about your guy,' he said.

'Thanks, Miles,' Walden said, and the vision of the bullet hitting Toan jumped into his head. 'It was quick,' he added half-heartedly.

'Head wound?' Keegan asked.

'Under the left eye,' Walden said. He gestured to Pau and Cuong to help move the body from the floor of the ship. Lifting the bag out, Walden was surprised that Toan could weigh so much.

They carried the body to the ambulance. Keegan said, 'We'll keep him up at the dispensary tonight. I guess you have some plans for the burial.'

'Pau is handling that; we'll do it tomorrow,' Walden said. Toan's death was becoming real now as they put the body

34

bag on a canvas stretcher inside the truck. Walden felt sad and helpless. He turned away, feeling his eyes begin to sting. The doors slammed shut behind him; then he felt Keegan's hand on his shoulder.

'It's okay, Sam,' Keegan said softly.

'No, it ain't fuckin' okay,' Walden snapped, spinning around, his eyes burning. His voice lifted. 'Don't ever say it's fuckin' okay.' He stomped toward the truck where the rest of the team was standing and watching. By the time he had covered the twenty feet, the anger was gone. He turned to say he was sorry, but Keegan was already getting into the truck.

After Walden's outburst most of the people on the helipad drifted toward the club. The pad was soon deserted except for the team and Workman. The Americans helped the little people into the back of the deuce-and-a-half and were handing up the rucksacks when Walden heard running feet slapping across the plating of the strip. Though it was nearly dark, he recognized the shapes of the four team members that hadn't gone on the mission.

They were out of breath when they reached the truck, yet they started jumping around, giggling and grabbing Walden and Forrest by the arms.

'How you guys been doing?' Walden smiled, hugging each in turn as though they were his children.

'We stay Da Nang *beaucoup* boom-boom,' said Cricket, giggling, beaming, as the others laughed. His long, full face and small nose and big eyes had reminded Walden of Jiminy C. Baby-san, his soft, gentle features alight with excitement, was dancing around Walden as if he had to pee.

'No one tell us you come. We hear helicop and we know you come back.' He grinned, his white teeth shining in the fading light.

Walden boosted him up into the back of the truck. 'Go to the American mess hall with the others and Jerry and I will be down soon. *Biêt?*'

'Okay, GI.' Tang, at twenty the oldest of the four, laughed at his own joke.

35

Workman started up the jeep and Walden watched the faces caught in the headlights.

'Where Toan stay?' Tang asked, looking around at the glum expressions.

Ah, shit. No one told them. Walden felt the sharp pinch of nerves in his stomach. For an instant he saw his little cousin, who had been killed by a car, lying in the small white coffin. Death is just a step away. Close, breathing down your neck. The foul breath lingered with them now, and each felt their vulnerability.

'Toan's dead, buddy,' Walden said, looking up at the solemn faces. 'Cuong will tell you what happened.' He patted Tang's knee and gestured to the truck driver to take off. Tang nodded that he understood. The truck pulled away and turned onto the sand road that ran the east-west length of the camp. As soon as it was out of sight, Walden threw his arms up in the air in a gesture of frustration and anger.

'Why didn't anyone tell them we were coming in, for Christ's sake? What do these assholes think around here? Nobody bothers to tell them we're coming in. Nobody bothers to tell them we got somebody blown away. Nobody bothers to tell them shit.'

Workman just watched, used to the fact that Walden got angry each time he came back. He knew, as the others knew, that Walden always came off a mission mad as hell.

'Come on, Sam,' Workman said. 'Most of the guys are on guard down on the beach. They'll want to see you and Jerry.'

'Assholes,' Walden murmured as he sat down in the front seat of the jeep. Forrest climbed into the back.

'Here, man, smoke this,' Workman said, lighting a joint and handing it over. Walden took the joint and inhaled a deep lungful of the smoke, then passed it to Forrest.

'Hot damn, Vietnam.' Forrest chuckled, taking the joint and chopping its length by an inch with a single drag. He passed the number back to Walden and began to rub his one-zero's shoulders. Walden sucked a couple of hits and

36

passed it to Workman as they drove off the pad. The dark shape of the Kingbee faded behind them.

'You know, I shouldn't get pissed off,' Walden said, feeling better. He paused, then said, 'Fuck 'em.'

'Really,' Workman agreed, shifting the gears and playing stock-car driver. They rolled past the Headquarters area and up toward the southern perimeter, which faced the mountain. As they passed the twelve-foot hurricane fence surrounding the Tactical Operations Center, Walden drew the smoke deep into his lungs, feeling it expand and begin its shifting of his senses.

Workman turned left at the corner of the camp and headed for the beach. The twisted patterns of the barbed wire defenses looked like a maze of steel vines. The headlights cut through the umbra cast by the looming catacombed mountain, changing the color of the green plastic sandbags of the bunkers into a glossy black. The faces of the Vietnamese and Montagnard mercenaries on guard, standing and squatting on the tops of the bunkers, were lit in yellow hues as the jeep drove slowly past. The last five days broke away from Walden's mind like rotten ice as the smoke increased its effect.

'I'm blitzed already,' Walden said. He felt the silent buzzing working back and forth behind his eyes.

'After almost a week without, it doesn't take much.' Forrest giggled. The sand dunes they were riding over looked like clouds, the intricate design of dips and formations wind-woven. For a moment Walden forgot where he was, what he was doing, and just drifted.

The scraping sound of steel against steel made by a mortar being dropped down the tube jerked him back to reality. The report of the shell firing from the bunker next to Recon Company came next and Walden automatically began to count to determine how far away the shell was when it exploded. He stopped when he saw a small spark appear in the sky over the mountain, followed by a hollow pop as the illumination flare flickered briefly before bursting into brilliance. A bright, white light tinged with a

37

greenish glow fanned over the side of the mountain and the compound. A plume of white smoke followed the flare downward like the tail of a diving kite, and the slowly twisting light moved the shadows in a kaleidoscope. The flare faded out as they rounded the corner of the perimeter facing the ocean and continued north between the row of four concrete bunkers on their left and the rows of concertina wire on their right. Recon Company was responsible for the security along the ocean line of defense. Now they were back among their own people.

Shouts and yells from Americans and little people erupted from the bunkers as Workman stopped the jeep. Dark figures jumped from the bunkers and came jogging up to the jeep. Danny Jeffers, Ronnie Glenn, Pat Edgewater, Fish Simons, and half a dozen others crowded around, grinning and hugging. It was a replay of the scene at the helipad, except this one was special. All the men crowding around ran missions across the fence. Each knew what it was like. Each knew how truly easy it would have been to come back in a bag. Or not come back at all. The meeting was intense because there was never enough time. Now there was a little time, another parcel of days during which to smell and feel and be with each other. Then someone would have to go out again.

The conversations were held in the hushed tones of men speaking in the dark. When enough had been said, Walden, Forrest, and Workman took the jeep to the mess hall. After parking in front of the row of whitewashed rocks bordering the front, Walden picked up his and Toan's CAR-15's and led the others down the short cement sidewalk and through the front screen door into the brightly lit building. He looked across the empty tables to the back where the little people were chattering like a flock of birds. He warmed at seeing Coop, the mess-hall girl, returning his look. Her round, dark face went from joy to fear as she saw the black bloodstains on his uniform.

Walden walked forward, peeling off the fingerless handball gloves which he'd been wearing since the mission started and shoving them into his side pocket. Laying the two machine guns on a tabletop, he walked to Coop, holding out his hand.

In all the time he had known her, they had never kissed, never embraced. Her face looked flushed beneath the fluorescent lights as she took Walden's hands.

She gently squeezed his fingers, then stepped back. For a moment she just looked, then turned and scurried to the serving line for a plate of food. In a flurry of Vietnamese she explained to the cook how Walden liked his steak. Every few seconds or so she would look back as though to reaffirm that he had returned. She scolded the other girls for their teasing.

For the five days that the team had been gone, Coop had let no one sit in the chair where Walden now sat. His place was at the front table in the front chair against the wall next to the milk machine. It was his chair. It was his place. Over the months she had grown superstitious about it, having watched other Americans, those that did what Walden did, vanish. As long as no one sat in his chair, he would come back.

Forrest leaned back and smirked, smoothing his mustache. 'Man, that's love. You should marry her and take her away from all this, Sam.'

'Sure, there's a flight leaving every minute.'

The little people had stopped eating momentarily to watch the meeting between Walden and Coop. Cuong and Hung especially, but for different reasons. Walden knew Cuong watched because he would boast of making love to six different girls in an afternoon, and in that time would never see anything near the look that Coop had given Walden. Hung watched because he always tried to understand. Unlike the other mercenaries on the team, Hung had gone to college before he'd been forced into the war. He had served in the South Vietnamese Army as a lieutenant for three years before deciding that if he had to fight, he wanted to be with people who knew what they were doing.

He had deserted and come to the Special Forces camp. Now, three years later, Hung was talking about the odds running against him. Walden sensed that Hung saw him as an anchoring point, that he felt safe only with him. The Louisiana Team trusted Walden because he loved them. At least it seemed that way. Love, trust, certainty. Walden was always firm, sure. He wasn't a man of doubt. Walden always said he knew exactly why he was fighting. He was trying to free the oppressed, just as the Special Forces motto said.

Eldon Parrish and Len Michaels came into the mess. Grinning, they came to the table. Parrish pulled a chair from the table behind them and sat down. Michaels shook hands with Walden and Forrest by grabbing wrists.

'When are you going out?' Walden asked, the question like a tongue that can't stop probing a cavity.

'Day after tomorrow if the weather holds over the target area. We have to go up to the launch site regardless.' Parrish was matter of fact. His eyes locked on Walden's. 'And when you going out?' The polite laughter had an edge to it.

'We were just up at the TOC,' Parrish said softly, glancing over at the mess-hall girls as he pulled his chair closer to Walden. Lowering his voice further he said, 'We just saw some messages come across the teletype. They're going to arc-light the entire area where you were tonight. They think they got two regiments in a base area out there.'

'They knew that before they inserted us,' Walden said, and straightened up as Coop came to the table with his food.

'Well, it sounds like Saigon is real happy about the whole thing,' Parrish said, shrugging his shoulders.

'Great.' Coop placed the plate in front of him. He thanked her and reached for the ketchup bottle. She padded away, her rubber shower shoes slapping against the soles of her bare feet, to get him a glass of milk from the machine. Walden poured the ketchup over the steak, and suddenly thought of the stream. The hunger disappeared.

Coop put the glass of milk next to him and stood to one side. Walden slowly picked at the food. He put a french fry into his mouth without dipping it in the ketchup.

'You eat. You eat,' Coop said, with her small hands making a circular motion in front of her lips. Walden nodded, picked up his knife and fork. He cut into the meat.

'Fuck.' He pushed the plate away. 'I can't eat this. I'm going to take a shower.'

'Yeah, really,' Forrest said, getting up from the table. The little people also rose from their table.

Coop reached over and touched Walden's arm. He smiled weakly and patted her shoulder. He scooped up the two weapons from the table on the way out.

In the blue-tinged darkness Walden handed Toan's weapon to Hung and told him to take it to the hooch to keep for the replacement.

Hung took it silently, nodded that he understood, and with the others walked across the hard-packed company street. They single-filed down toward their hooch by the beach. Walden and Forrest slowly followed. They passed under the sign at the entrance to Recon Company: WE KILL FOR PEACE.

Walden listen to Giap whining and scratching at the door as he twisted the combination lock in the light of Forrest's Zippo. When the door opened, the medium-sized mongrel began jumping all over the two as they walked into the room and turned on the lights.

'How you doing?' Walden hugged the dog to him, ruffling the brown hair along his back. Released, the dog began running around the room in circles of excitement, barking. Finally Walden had to tell him to settle down. After a few minutes Giap went to his bed in the corner and happily watched from there.

Walden flopped down on his bunk. 'Oh, man,' he moaned as the soft, cool pillowcase folded around his face. He felt the weight of the past five days begin to slip away. Sometimes it was only a dream. Then the dream became real, then the reality slipped away again. It had become difficult to tell any longer, with the days and years melting together in one long roll of film. The fear, anger, pain, all left a flickering residue. He closed his eyes and wondered if going to hell was worth it.

Forrest's voice brought him back from the gates of sleep. 'You going to take a shower?'

Walden swung his legs over the side of the bunk and sat up. 'It seems weird, doesn't it?' he said, standing up and unbuckling his belt.

'The whole affair seems weird to me,' Forrest said. He looked around the room. 'Where the hell are my shower shoes?'

'On top of the refrigerator.'

Forrest dropped the shower shoes on the floor and pushed his feet into them. 'My nerves are shot to shit. I feel like I'm still on the ground. This war is becoming one long pain in the ass, Sam.' He suddenly sat back on his bunk. 'Toan's lying up in the morgue, my ears are still ringing, my hands are starting to shake, and I feel like I'm coming down with the drizzling shits.' Walden waited.

They walked out into the night, their arms around each other like two old drinking buddies parading down a late-night street. Giap jumped against their legs, in the intervals of running back and forth in front of them. As they stomped down the perforated-steel-plating sidewalk laid over the sand, the unspoken bond was simple: They had walked away from another one.

Walden walked into the shower building in front of Forrest.

'You got a basic load of leeches on your back, Sam.'

'Great.' Walden took the towel from around his waist and leaned against the sink. Forrest puffed his cigarette and began to push the burning coal against the flat black parasites dotting Walden's back and legs. As soon as the bright ember touched them, they fell to the concrete floor.

'You remember that picture?' Forrest asked. '*The African Queen*. When Bogart had all those leeches on him and he was coming apart while Hepburn took them off?'

42

'Yeah.' Walden had to laugh. 'He'd have a great time here.'

'That got it,' Forrest said as the last bloodsucker came loose.

'Let me check you out before you put out the cigarette.' Walden took the smoke from Forrest. After a moment he sighed. 'Shit, you don't have any. Why is it that you never have any, and I always do?'

'You should've seen me a couple of times when I was down in the delta with the A-Team. I'd have a hundred of those things on me.' Forrest wiggled his eyebrows.

'Just like Bogie.' Walden laughed and turned on one of the two showers that had good water pressure.

The hot water cascaded over him, washing the dirt and blood of the mission away. Walden felt the sting of the small scratches and cuts he had accumulated during the days on the ground. In the white flesh below his left hip, just where the dark brown tan ended, was the red bruise where he had fallen on the rocks. Closing his eyes, he let the water pour over his head. *You made it again.* He felt a hollow pang and something went loose inside his chest and stomach. The entire day began to whirl through his head and it came to him that if he let himself, he would cry. Instead he began to wash the streaks of camouflage grease from his face.

Afterward Walden went to the bank of sinks against the back wall to shave. Bending his six-foot frame to see in the low mirrow, he combed his fingers through the wet brown hair. The deep-blue eyes staring back looked tired. Pushing a hand around the angular features of his sun-bronzed face, he felt the seven-day growth of whiskers beneath the calloused palm. *And you used to be good-looking.* Stepping back he tensed the thick muscles across his chest, ran a hand over the knotted ripples of his stomach. *Lean and mean.* He sighed and bent to brush his teeth. After rinsing he smiled broadly, leaning in the mirror to inspect the even rows of teeth. *At least my teeth are holding up.*

When he finally shaved, he was slow and precise. Methodical people seldom hurt themselves.

Giap had waited for him, so he had company on the walk back to the hooch. Forrest had already dressed and was rolling joints on the desktop when they came in. A Dylan record was on the hi-fi. Walden crossed to his wooden locker and began to dress. The clean clothes felt good against his skin, after days of sleeping and crawling around in filthy jungle fatigues. Sitting down on his bunk, he pulled the spit-shined pair of Cocran jump boots from under his bed and laced them. He took the brown unpolished jungle boots he had worn on the mission and put them in his locker. He only wore them on missions. He never allowed any of the hooch mama-sans to polish them.

Forrest lit a joint and, after taking a toke, passed it. 'Victory,' he said.

'Unconditional surrender.'

Walden watched Forrest's chiselled features as he carefully rolled a replacement number. Everything Forrest did was careful and exact. It was one of the reasons Walden had chosen him over the others for the team. That, and the way his deep-brown eyes never seemed to stop moving behind the almost oriental curve of his eyelids. Walden had liked him from the first, liked the way his smile was controlled and confident. Forrest had *linebacker* written all over his thick five-foot-ten frame. He carried himself with the graceful ease of someone who knew exactly where he was going. Walden smiled as he watched him twist the black ends of the Fu Manchu mustache after tossing the new joint on the pile of others. *I sure wouldn't have liked to meet him out in the flats. He's just the kind that would enjoy tearing your head off.*

By the time they left the hooch, they were stoned again. With Giap running in front, they walked gingerly down the sidewalk, giggling, jostling each other. They journeyed across the sand dunes to the team hooches down by the beach. The stars were out. The rumble of waves pushing up against the beach drifted over the sand ruffles. The walk to the hooch seemed to take forever.

'I told you about smoking that marihoona shit,' Forrest said. Walden opened the door and let Giap in.

The little people called out as they entered the cluttered room. Double bunks lined the walls and a lone wooden table sat in the middle of the room. A tape recorder sat on a cabinet made of wooden ammo crates and in one corner a cooking area had been created around a portable stove. The room smelled of gun oil, wet hair, sandalwood incense, and the heavy, sweet odor of marijuana.

Walden and Forrest sat down at the table. Pau hopped over with a smoldering pipe. 'Hey, Walwon, you want smoke *consa?*'

'Just what I need.' Walden took the pipe, inhaled, and passed it to Forrest. The strong grass climbed quickly into his brain as he leaned back in his chair and relaxed. Pau went back to the stove and, after lighting a small chunk of C-4, began to heat a pot of soup over the burner. For the little people, eating was a constant thing. As long as food was available, they were eating.

The team was unusually quiet for having just come back from a mission. It was because of Toan, of course. Walden sighed. He couldn't help but grow close to them. He knew that most of the other Americans were interested in their people only when preparing for a mission or when actually on the ground. Walden and Forrest and a few of the others did it differently. They spent most of their time with the little people, rarely with the others in the American club. Walden thought it was the major reason the team worked so well together. They knew each other. They could move for hours through the jungle without speaking, without wondering what the others were up to.

Walden looked from one to another. *So different, so much alike. Sweet Lord, we're a strange group.*

Pau grinned broadly, his gold-lined teeth catching the light. His large eyes were distracting, and nearly made his round, homely face attractive. Then one noticed the discolored furrow of the knife scar that ran from below his left cheek, down through his thick lips, and off the end of his small chin.

Cuong's eyes were the opposite of Pau's, although they, too, were the most prominent feature. Cold, brooding, they belonged to a dangerous person. Ironically they made the smooth, doll-like features appear ugly and hard.

Hung, on the other hand, was wrapped in an easy, aristocratic air. The French blood showed in his light skin, high cheekbones, and the almost feminine lips. His straight, slender nose had no hint of the normal Vietnamese pug. It was easy to understand his many girlfriends.

Playboy was pretty and he knew it. He was the only team member with a mirror inside his locker. Walden had once told him that if he spent as much time on the firing range as he did in front of the mirror, he would be the best shot in the country. Playboy had merely smiled. He had as many personalities as smiles. He was a born actor. After watching James Dean in *East of Eden*, he had imitated the sulking actor for days. He stopped when they started to call him 'Jimmy.' He liked his original nickname much better.

Of all the team members Lap was the only one who really looked Vietnamese. His sepia-colored skin and flat nose were almost reassuring. Walden liked him because he was ordinary. And because he was damn good with the M-70.

Someone turned off the naked overhead light, creating a dazzling purple glow from the three black lights around the room. Several posters on the walls came to fluorescent life. Hung, Playboy, Cuong, and Nha sat down around the table as Lap and Tang flopped on the nearest bunks. From another bunk Giap watched and wagged his tail. Pau contentedly stirred his soup, pausing only to take the pipe when it was offered to him. Tang got up and helped Baby-san lace the *Sergeant Pepper* tape into the recorder. In a few minutes the music began to play and Walden felt content. The inside of the hooch was warm and cozy. It reminded him of one of those Rockwell paintings where people sat around a potbellied stove in a friendly place while a blizzard raged outside.

A soft knock rattled the thin door. 'It's me, Jeffers.'

Cuong got up from the table and unhooked the lock. Jeffers, Parrish, and Michaels came inside, soon followed by Workman and Mike Winston, each carrying a case of beer or sodas. Danny Jeffers patted Walden on the back. 'Everyone else is on guard,' he said.

Each found a place around the table and opened something to drink. Pau lit two red candles and placed them on the table. The flickering flames swayed with the rhythm of breathing. The room warmed from their bodies. The wind rose outside. When the tape ended, blowing sand could be heard brushing over the tin roof. Joints and pipes were passed around. The faces around the room were cast in black light, and conversation was quiet. Pau slid an old wooden grenade box next to Walden and sat down, putting his arm around Walden's shoulder. Tang, with Lap's help, slid a corner of a bunk over and sat down between Walden and Forrest.

When they were on their fourth beer, someone mentioned the mission. It was what they'd come for.

'How was it?' Parrish asked, lifting a can of beer to his lips.

'They were rookies,' Walden said quietly. 'If they had had their shit together, they could've nailed our asses to the wall.'

Michaels shook his head. 'Some of these targets are madness.'

'Not madness,' Walden said. 'Suicide. There's a difference.' In the glow of the room they each felt it, a shared understanding of a game gone crazy, of elements beyond their control, of changing rules.

'So what happened?' Parrish asked again.

'We came onto these dudes, around three this afternoon,' Walden began, and the room went dead quiet. 'For the first four days we thought we had gotten one of the fabled dry holes. Right, Jerry?' Walden looked at Forrest for verification.

47

'Really,' Forrest said. 'There weren't even any trail watchers, no woodcutters, nothing.'

'So today when we left our RON position, we started to hear all this shit, like trucks coming down the road.' He paused for a moment. 'I thought we had bought the farm for sure.'

'I experienced the same sensation more than once today,' Forrest laughed. 'We were walking against the red light 'bout then.' His laugh trailed off.

'These guys,' Walden said, 'took their boots off.' It was an unbelievable thing even to think about. 'Man, I can't imagine taking my boots off in Laos.' Then Walden remembered that it was different for the NVA. It was their sanctuary; they lived there. If they never removed their boots, their feet would rot off.

'So, anyway, we blew these eight guys away, and then the shit hit the fan when we were waiting for the choppers to extract us.' Walden suddenly felt that he didn't want to relive it, not now. He'd have to do it tomorrow during the debriefing session, God knows how many times. 'It's been a long day. I don't really want to get into it now.' The fatigue in his voice was real.

The other team leaders understood. They were disappointed, because there were so few ways to really learn, but they filed out of the hooch after saying good-night. Forrest and Walden sat in the candlelight as the little people got into their beds.

'You know,' Walden said, 'if it hadn't been for the fast-mover pilots, and the helicopter pilots, and the damn poor gunners, this whole team would be dead.' He shook his head. 'I don't know, man. I just don't know. That's a lot of people to depend on.'

They listened to the little people get comfortable in their beds. After a time Walden said, 'I don't want to die alone.'

'It's like we have always said, Sam. If you die, I die. That's the way it is.'

'It's shitty to die by yourself like Toan had to,' Walden said, twisting an empty pack of cigarettes. 'You know,

Jerry, I don't think I could come back here without you.'

'It's just a matter of time before we're killed,' Forrest said. 'It doesn't seem right, man. Here we are, half of our friends already dead, us going to be dead, and those people back in the States burning and pissing on the flag. I mean, why do we have to die?'

'They don't understand what's here,' Walden said. 'They just don't understand. They think because this country is twelve thousand miles away from them that what happens here won't affect them. They'll find out. Besides,' he added with a giggle, 'we can't take dying at an early age too personally.'

'Sorry, I guess I lost my head for a second.'

'Let's crash,' Walden said. 'This shit is killing me.' He put the joint out in the middle of the overflowing ashtray.

'Walk up to the dispensary with me to check on Toan?' Walden asked as they stepped out the door.

'Jesus, that's what I mean,' Forrest groaned, tossing his head back. 'I forgot all about Toan. Shit, I'm really getting callous.'

'How many times did you have to do this before I came on the team?' Forrest asked as they walked across the sand.

'I never had to do it before.'

'No shit.' Forrest was surprised.

'We could never get any of the bodies out.'

'God,' Forrest whispered. 'It's true, isn't it? There's no point in carrying a dead body on your back. I mean, what's the point, right?'

After putting the dog in the hooch, they headed toward the dispensary. The moon had a corona of white mist, looking cold in the still darkness. Walden's legs began to tire as they trudged up a sandy incline. The drone of the hospital's air conditioner could be faintly heard as they topped the rise. The shelf of sand the hospital sat on was the highest point in the camp. Across the river Walden could see the sparsely lighted streets of Da Nang. In different places over the city and around the outskirts, the yellow lights of flares could be seen drifting above the buildings.

Distant machine-gun fire sounded in the night. Walden paid attention, first hearing M-60's, followed by the faint crumps of M-79's as the 40-millimeter shells exploded somewhere. There was a smattering of M-16 fire, then quiet again. North of the city Cobra helicopters fired Mini-Guns; long, arching, solid-red lines of tracer bullets stood out sharply against the black sky. The electrically fired guns sounded like turbines revving up. The buzzing of air conditioners took over as they approached, and with its long sandbagged walls and domed sandbagged roof, the dispensary looked like a huge insect squatting in the sand.

Inside, the bright lights of the reception room made Walden squint. Miles Keegan was behind his desk, his feet propped up, reading a book.

'Hey, Doc,' Walden said. 'What are you doing still up?'

'Don't call me "Doc." This is only temporary, until I get back into Recon.' Keegan sounded tired of telling people that. 'You want some coffee?'

'Sure.' The three moved to the hot plate in the corner.

'I'm sorry about down at the helipad,' Walden said as Keegan handed him a cup.

'Forget it, man. It's cool.' Keegan poured the black, steaming coffee into the cups. 'We got some milk in the refrigerator in OR.' He led them across the polished lino-leum floor and through the swinging door. 'I have Toan in here.' He switched on the room light.

The first thing Walden saw was the glossy rubber bag on the operating table. The air conditioner was running full blast, belching frigid air into the small room.

'Jesus, it's cold in here.' Forrest rubbed his arms as he followed Walden and Keegan to the refrigerator against the wall.

'I didn't know where else to keep him,' Keegan said. 'We usually send all the dead down to the morgue, regular channels and all that crap. I knew you didn't want me to do that. You know, it's rare to have a body come back.'

Walden put his cup down at the foot of the stainless steel

50

table and walked to the head of the bag. It looked fresh and sinister somehow, with the odor of new tires. He didn't want to, but his fingers unzipped the bag and he looked down at Toan's face.

All the blood and dirt had been washed off, and he'd been dressed in a new uniform. A thick strip of white gauze covered the wound beneath the cheekbone. A green towel had been folded beneath his head. With the cocky sureness gone from Toan's features, and the smile turned into gray slack lips, the youth of the face was shocking. Walden shivered in the coldness. He wondered why he had never noticed how young Toan was. He closed the bag.

They walked from the room and Walden said, 'Thanks for having him cleaned up, Miles.'

Keegan turned out the light and shut the door behind them. 'I just, you know,' he said. 'You know, I mean, shit.'

Walden touched Keegan's shoulder. 'We're going to crash. We got the debriefing and all that other crap tomorrow. We'll see you at breakfast.'

Keegan waved as they went out the door.

After the cold of the OR the outside air was pleasantly warm. The clear night sky and the fresh breeze off the ocean allowed them to think of other things.

'You want to go to Saigon for a week?' Walden asked. They stutter-stepped down the slope to the hard-packed road running behind the supply buildings.

'Or we could go to Nha Trang,' Forrest suggested. 'I wouldn't mind seeing that girl that works at the Streamer Bar again.'

'I wouldn't either.' Walden laughed.

'She was great. We'll probably never find her again, though. It's been quite a while. Let's go to Saigon.'

'Okay,' Walden said. 'If we can get that debriefing and everything over with tomorrow, maybe we can catch a late Blackbird flight out.' He suddenly stopped in mid-stride and threw his hand against his forehead. 'Ah, shit, man. I forgot all about the book.'

'What book?'

'That Chuck I shot down by the stream. I took this book off him. It was in his rucksack. I forgot all about it. The headshed people are going to shit a brick when they find out.'

'Just tell them the truth. You forgot,' Forrest said. 'Hell, that's easy to understand.'

'I'll just tell them the truth. I forgot about it.' Walden sighed. 'Screw 'em if they can't take a joke.'

'Right.' Forrest held his lighter over the combination lock so Walden could see. As they entered, Giap eyed them tiredly and put his head back down on his paws. Walden locked the door behind them and went to the pile of field clothes in the corner of the room. Pulling the pants out, he patted the side pocket until he found the book. He walked to the desk, unwrapping the oilskin cloth.

Inside was a brown cardboard-covered book, about an inch thick. Walden sat down in the chair; Forrest pulled up the little stool. Opening the book, Walden stared at the handwriting.

'It must be a diary,' Forrest said, looking over his shoulder. 'See the dates above each page? There could be some really good stuff in there.'

Walden leafed through, looking at the carefully written words in the neat but flowing hand. 'After I turn this in, I'll probably never see it again.' He was matter of fact. 'Some Remington Raider will get a nice souvenir to take home.'

'Just tell them you want it back,' Forrest said softly. 'After they copy it and everything, there's no reason why they can't give it back.'

Walden yawned. 'Here, you want to check it out?' He handed the book to Forrest and went to his bunk. He started to unlace his boots when Forrest whistled.

'Check this out, Sam!' Forrest was holding open a slit in the inside front cover. 'There're photographs pushed down in here.' He was excited and eagerly wormed his fingers into the opening, pulling out photos.

There were seven in all, printed on cheap grainy paper. One was of a man in an NVA uniform, sitting with a woman in front of the painted backdrop of a lake scene. He held a pith helmet on his left knee, and the hand of the woman in his right hand. He looked pleased and proud in the picture, but the woman appeared cross and unhappy. Her lips were pursed together and her eyes stared directly out of the picture.

Walden was sure it was the man he had killed at the stream. The woman's eyes seemed to be looking at him. A crawling sensation passed over him and he pulled his eyes away from the photo.

The remaining pictures were of children and old people. Walden sat down on his bunk again and went back to unlacing his boots.

Undressed and lying between the clean sheets, he asked Forrest if he thought the decision down by the stream was a good one.

'It was the only decision you could make,' Forrest said flatly. 'We didn't have any choice but to blow them away. We couldn't go back the way we came. And we had to get on that opposite ridge to get pulled out.'

'I know,' Walden said, pulling the blankets up around his chin.

'Fuck the commie bastard,' Forrest said. 'That slope-headed motherfucker would've wasted any one of us sure as shit if he'd had the chance. You know that better than any of us.' He crossed the room and turned off the light. Walden listened to him pad back to his bed in the darkness.

'Good night, Sam,' Forrest said.

'Good night, Jerry. Maybe Saigon tomorrow night.'

'Really.'

'Think we got any mail?'

'I hope so,' Forrest said. 'Or else I'm going to kill Warner. I think he burns the mail so he doesn't have to bother handing it out.'

'Wouldn't that be a bitch.' Walden laughed quietly.

The wind blew around the corner of the hooch, whistling in the dark.

CHAPTER FOUR

THE LINE outside Father Ryan's confessional was much longer than that outside Father Daniel's. Sam didn't mind the extra wait. No one liked the grilling the younger priest administered. Sam had avoided going to confession as long as possible, but this was the last day of school and he had to go. He looked absently around the basement church. After going to mass six days a week for ten years, he knew every board, crack, paint peel, and warp in the place. If he went blind, this was the one place where he'd have no problem. When he was next for the booth, he tried to arrange his sins, not that it really mattered. It was rumored that Father Ryan couldn't even hear what you were saying. *Thank God for that.* He would throw in the jacking-off part between the stealing and the fighting.

Once inside the dark booth Sam thought how much he hated the process. Even though it was denied, he knew damn well the priest recognized each of them. You couldn't be around them your entire life without their knowing your voice. *Oh, no.* He heard the deep voice of Father Daniel giving absolution. *He tricked us. This is Father Ryan's confessional.* Sam was starting to leave when the wooden separator was pushed to the side.

With mind numb, and stomach churning, Sam began the preamble. 'Bless me, Father, for I have sinned. My last confession was a month ago.' He mumbled his sins as fast as he could, hoping the priest would miss the bad ones. 'I lied, I stole, I had impure actions, I fought, I swore, I missed the church on Sunday, these are all my sins, Father.' He squeezed his eyelids together and a cold trickle of sweat slid down his side.

'What did you steal?

Sam cringed. 'A record, Father.'

'You either take it back, or pay for it. Now, what do you mean by impure actions?' He seemed to shout it. Sam just knew everyone in the church had heard.

'You know, Father.

'I'm afraid I don't, young man. You'll have to explain.'

'Beat off, you know.' Sam felt every cell in his body twitch.

'Do you mean masturbation?' The words boomed.

'Ah, yeah.'

'How many times?'

'I don't remember.' He immediately knew that answer wouldn't do. 'Five times.'

'Five times,' the priest almost shouted. 'Did you do anything impure with girls?'

Sam wanted the booth to disappear. This wasn't fair. 'I, ah, well, I guess so. I mean, I touched her tit, I mean, excuse me, Father, breast, but only for a second.'

'What did she do?'

'Nothing.'

'Nothing?'

'She told me I shouldn't do that, so I didn't anymore.' *It's a lie and I've just sinned again. There's no way you can win.*

'These are very serious sins, young man. Mortal sins. Grievous sins. Do you realize that if you died with these sins on your soul, you would go straight to hell?'

Sam had a sudden thought that hell couldn't be all that bad. 'Yes, Father.'

'And you still carried these sins around with you for a month before coming here to confess?'

'I've been sick,' Sam lied again.

'I should say, young man, I should say. Missing church is very serious. I don't ever want to hear you tell me that again. Do you understand me?'

'Yes, Father.'

'For your penance I want you to say five rosaries, and now say a good Act of Contrition.'

Leaving the confessional, Sam wanted to die. He knew every eye in the church was on him. Pushing in next to Keith, he began to say his penance.

'What did you get?' Keith was smug.

'Five rosaries.'

Keith covered his mouth as he began to giggle. Sister Mary turned around in her pew, glowering, her tiny eyes narrowed. Sam glared at her, trying to make his eyes as hateful as he could.

That afternoon, before they were released for the summer, Father Daniel came into the classroom. The boys were instructed to follow the priest, while the girls remained in class.

'Here it comes,' Keith chirped under his breath as they were led into the gym. They were going to get the famous sex talk that came at the end of the sophomore year. The older guys only laughed about it, never giving out details. Now it was their turn.

Father Daniel led the group into the football classroom and shut the door. Sam avoided looking at him as he and Keith found seats.

'Gentlemen, what you are about to see is shocking. However, there is a good reason for it.' The stocky young priest paced a bit. 'You're at a stage in your life where you're going to be thinking about sexual experimentation.' A titter of nervous laughter ran through the class.

'Premarital sex is a sin!' the priest roared. The silence was instant. 'Some of you may think it's humorous, but I doubt that you will think it so funny after what you're about to see. Monty, will you please start the projector?' Father Daniel turned out the lights. 'This, gentlemen, is how God punishes those who commit this sin.'

The film hadn't been on two minutes before Sam was thankful it wasn't in color. The narrator's voice was cold and condemning as he pointed out the details of terminal syphilis. Each victim was more ravaged than the one

56

before. Huge draining sores, penises eaten away by infection, female genitalia eroded into large rotting cavities. Sam felt the same nausea as when the incense was lighted. *Please, God, don't let me be sick. Please, I'll be good.*

'That is what you'll have to look forward to if you have premarital sex.' Father Daniel actually smiled. 'Class dismissed.'

'Do you believe that?' Sam said as he and Keith walked home. 'People like that are better off dead.'

'Ah, it's bullshit,' Keith said. He didn't sound very certain. 'They're probably all actors.'

'What about that guy with his pecker gone?' Sam nearly yelled it.

'I don't know. Let's forget it, all right?' They walked on in silence. Before Sam got home, he had decided he wasn't ever going to have to know.

CHAPTER FIVE

Oh, no. Oh, please. Oh, God, no. Walden's upper body bolted upright in the bed, his fists clenching the damp sheets, his eyes staring at the darkness. A cold bead of sweat ran down his side as he shivered. His brain struggled for wakefulness.

Walden's sudden movement had brought Forrest awake, his hand automatically plucking his CAR-15 off the rack. A moment of frozen silence, then Forrest whispered, 'You okay, man?'

'Yeah, yeah, I'm fine, just a dream.'

'Shit.' Forrest pushed air softly through his teeth. 'For a second I thought we were back in the hole.' He hung his weapon back up. A few moments later Forrest's bedsprings squeaked as he eased back down, taking a moment to plump up his pillow.

Walden slid back under the covers, desperately wanting to turn the lights on. Instead he pushed his right hand under his pillow until he felt the coldness of the 9-milli-meter Browning High Power. He curled his right hand around the wooden handle grip and felt better. Afraid to close his eyes, he watched the first gloomy grays of morning start to outline the sparse furnishings of the hooch. He listened to Giap's nails clicking across the wooden floor as the dog came to the side of the bunk. Circling twice, the animal finally flopped down on the fatigue pants Walden had dropped. Slipping his hand over the side of the bed and patting the dog, Walden felt better as Giap's warm licks caressed his arm.

The bullets slammed into his body as he lay paralyzed in a hospital corridor. He couldn't see who was shooting him; he just knew he couldn't move and the lights were bright, and people were walking past not paying the least attention. He could only see legs. He was curled into a fetal position, his head ducked under his chest. If only they didn't hit him in the head, he would live. He was thinking it was odd he didn't feel any pain, only a distant ache each time the bullets hit. Curled up on the shiny wax floor, he felt his body begin to float in a warm fluid, and saw it was his blood.

The dream changed abruptly and he was swimming through the cold, pure waters of the old quarry hole. Keith waved to him from the top of one of the rock ledges. His best friend was wearing a white Navy uniform, and was rolling newspapers. Walden wondered why Keith was dressed up like that. He shouldn't be rolling papers now; they always delivered their papers before they went swimming. Walden tried to remember if he had delivered his papers, but he couldn't concentrate. The clouds above the swimming hole began to turn black as the wind picked up, and when he looked back, Keith was gone. He began to swim hard; it was growing darker around him. Leaves from the trees surrounding the quarry swirled down, piling up around him until he could no longer see where he was swimming. He felt cold, slimy things brushing against him as his legs tired and sagged deeper into the water. As he was sliding beneath the surface, the darkness blinked away and the sun was shining and he walked up the front steps of the house where he had grown up.

He was wearing his tailored khaki uniform. Before he went in the house, he paused to inspect himself. He looked at his jump boots and was pleased that they shone with the black luster that came from hours of rubbing polish. He bent over and arranged the creases of the pants over the tops of the boots. Straightening, he checked the left side of his chest and felt proud of the three rows of medals, the CIB, and the jump wings beneath. They would be proud, he thought as he entered the house. He heard his father's voice coming from the kitchen, then the voices of his brother and three sisters. He heard his mother laughing and his heart jumped into high gear. He walked into the kitchen. The room was empty except for his mother sweeping the floor. She looked up briefly and then went back to sweeping. Her lack of reaction made him feel dizzy, disoriented, as he stood in the middle of the kitchen floor smelling ginger snaps and linoleum. He tried to talk but found he couldn't. His throat had frozen shut. She didn't even say hello and he felt his face twist. Warm, fat tears began to run down his cheeks and he tossed his head. He knew that he was responsible for the blood that began to appear beneath the broom his mother was using. He watched as she began to sweep faster but only succeeded in smearing the blood. His skin began to twitch as the yellow broomstraws turned into wet, black, bristly hair. She began to weep. He stepped to her side, his voice finally breaking from his throat. 'I didn't mean it. Please, Mommy, please, I didn't mean to do it. I had to. Please understand.' She looked at him as at a stranger and began to back away, dropping the broom. 'I'm your son. Please remember me. Please don't be afraid.' He reached out, thinking that if he could only reach her, she would remember and not be frightened. But as he reached, she turned into the woman in the photograph. Her mouth twisted into a grimace, and her teeth were cigarettes. She grabbed at him, her fingers gleaming bone. He pulled away and fell over something behind him on the floor. It was the man by the stream. The corpse's skin was beginning to turn black with rot, and the stench of the dead wrapped around Sam like a blanket. The flesh slipped off the bones of the man's fingers. Large blue flies crawled everywhere. Sam wanted to strike out but he couldn't move. *Oh, no. Oh, please. Oh, God, no.*

The luminous hands on his watch showed ten minutes after six. Leaning over the side of the bunk, Walden rummaged around in his pants pockets until he found the lighter and his cigarettes. He lit one and watched the colors coming back into the room. As the light filtered through the cracks in the plywood walls, he admitted to himself that the dream hadn't been as bad as some others. He listened to the vague early-morning sounds of the camp as he smoked. A chattering of subdued Vietnamese words came and went with a group of camp workers walking down the road outside the hooch. The dull thumping of boots on the PSP sidewalk next to the hut made him smile. He knew it was Fish by the sound. He smiled because it made him remember home and how he always knew who was coming up the stairs by the way they walked. He put out the cigarette in the ashtray on the desk. He didn't close his eyes again until he could see the poster of Jimi Hendrix on the wall opposite his bed.

Sometime after seven o'clock a knock on the door woke him. Jeffers's voice came through the door. 'You going to sleep all day?'

Walden pushed himself down to the end of the bunk and unfastened the hook that screwed the door. Jeffers came into the room with Gunther Brunn following him.

'You guys better shake your ass if you want to eat breakfast,' Brunn said, sitting down in the desk chair. 'What's this?' he asked, picking up the diary and the pictures.

'I got it off one of the dudes we wasted,' Walden said, yawning. 'Hey, Jerry, wake up.'

Forrest grunted, then rolled over on his stomach, pulling the pillow over his head. Walden walked to the door and held it open for Giap, who stood in the doorway and slowly stretched. Walden looked down at the short-haired mongrel for a number of seconds. Finally he said, 'Move out, schmuck,' and Giap trotted down the steps.

A half hour later the foursome ambled into the empty mess hall. Mess Sergeant Burger eyed his watch as they filed up to the serving line. 'You guys know what time meals are served around here. This isn't a goddamn short-order café.'

Walden stared at the short, lumpy man, watching the beads of sweat on his forehead drip onto the grill. 'We were tired,' he said quietly. 'Last night was the first decent sleep we've had in five days.'

'Yeah, yeah,' Burger said, holding up his hand. 'How do you want your eggs?' He motioned to the Vietnamese cook to start frying. Normally Burger wouldn't serve anyone who came into the hall a minute after time. The mess hall was his domain and he had absolute power. But he never argued with Walden.

After breakfast Walden and Forrest gathered up the code books and note pads they had kept during the mission, along with the diary and photographs. Walden hated to give after-action reports. They always went on forever. The same questions over and over again. How tall were the trees? What type of soil? Were there any streams or prominent terrain features not shown on the map? Some of the questions were ridiculous. What kind of underwear did the team members wear? Did the team appear trustworthy? Did they bury their feces? Once, when asked that question, Walden had simply replied, 'They don't shit in the field.'

The sergeant had looked up from the form he had been filling out, with an incredulous expression.

'Are you telling me that you just spent five days on the ground and no one on your team took a shit?'

'We've gone for seven days before.'

'You're putting me on.'

'I'm not kidding,' Walden had said. 'Give everyone a Ply Mag pill first thing every morning. You don't eat that much out there to begin with, plus you burn a lot of it off. It's not like being around camp, you know.'

'Why?'

'The last place you want to be caught with your pants down is Laos.'

'God, it must be terrible when you finally do shit,' the

62

sergeant had moaned, and Walden had almost hurt himself in his effort not to laugh out loud.

Hung and Pau were waiting out in the company street. 'You sign pass, so we can go Da Nang,' Hung said, holding out the two forms to Walden.

'You going to take care of things for Toan?' Walden asked as he used Forrest's back to sign the passes.

'We go do now,' Pau said. 'You go debrief?'

'Yeah.' Walden handed the pass forms back. 'When you two return, wait with the others at the hooch. When Jerry and I are finished, we'll take care of Toan, okay?' Pau and Hung nodded, turned, and went up the road to the front gate.

The sun was already hot when Walden and Forrest reached the open stretch of sand that separated the Headquarters area from the lower portion of the camp. The puffing ocean breeze against their backs made the walk pleasant.

'Let's check the mail before we go into this thing,' Walden said as they approached the four rows of one-story wooden buildings where Headquarters personnel lived. The walkway became a corridor through one of the billets, went outside again, then passed through the latrine building built in the middle of the sidewalk. An old papa-san was wetting down the concrete floor by splashing water out of a number ten can he held in his bony hand.

'What's happening, Papa-san?' Walden smiled at him, bowing his head slightly. The elder grinned, bowing his head several times. Walden patted him on the shoulder. 'You do good work, Papa.' The old man seemed delighted by the unexpected praise. He reached out and touched Walden's arm gently.

From the latrine they continued toward the TOC. At the generator stack they saw George, the Filipino maintenance man, scribbling numbers on his log sheet.

'Hi, Sam, Jerry.'

'The King of the Generators in the flesh,' Walden said,

63

waving his hands in front of him like a magician casting a spell.

George chuckled, embracing Walden with one arm and Forrest with the other. 'I hear you guys had a bad time yesterday,' he said, stepping back and hanging the clipboard on a nail driven into a corner post.

'Nothing out of the ordinary,' Walden said. There was a moment of silence as he fished out a cigarette and lit it. 'How're your wife and kids?'

'Fine, just fine,' George said, moving back to his shack. 'Listen, you get time, come for dinner again.'

'Soon,' Walden said, looking up at the concrete TOC building behind the hurricane fence. They had dawdled long enough.

'I hope this doesn't take all day.' Walden showed the gate guard his pass. The gate was opened and they were escorted to the thick steel door that led into the operations center. The guard went back to the small wooden shelter next to the gate as Walden pushed the door buzzer. A moment later a voice cracked over the outside speaker box.

'Who is it?'

'Fuckin' Batman and Robin. Who the hell do you think it is?'

The sound of a steel bolt being slid open, followed by an electrical buzzing, came from behind the seven-inch-thick door. Charlie Horn stepped from behind the door as it opened, a large smile across his face.

'Peace, brother,' Horn said under his breath. 'Welcome to never-never land.'

'How you doing, Charlie?' Walden smiled. 'You better get some Visine in your eyes. They look like Japanese flags.'

'I only smoked half a joint,' Horn said defensively, pushing the door shut and bolting it behind them.

'The mothers of America would be proud of you.' They stood in the small vestibule as Horn went through the procedure for opening the second door.

'Sergeants Walden and Forrest for debriefing,' Horn said

64

into the speaker box next to the inside door. As they waited, he wrote down their names and the time in the logbook kept for all arrivals and departures. The inside door swung open silently and Walden and Forrest stepped into the cold air of the TOC interior.

Instead of turning left and going directly to the main room and reporting to Major Deacon, the pair walked down the opposite hallway to the mailroom. Bill Warner was sorting out the morning's outgoing mail when Walden and Forrest looked over the open Dutch doorway.

'Bill, you got any mail for us?'

'Sammy, you little cutie pie,' Warner said. 'And his faithful sidekick, Jerry.' Warner got up from the desk and unlocked the lower portion of the door. 'I thought you two were going to get killed for sure yesterday. I was all set to get your tape recorder.'

'We get any mail?' Forrest repeated, taking a bundle of letters from the desk and flipping through them.

'You both got some. It's over here in the deceased file.'

'You really do have them in the dead file,' Forrest said as he watched Warner pull the letters. 'Man, you're a morbid son of a bitch.'

'As many missions as you two run across the fence I figure it's just a matter of time. So when you're on an operation, I just put all your mail in the KIA box. One day it's going to save me the time. Know what I mean?'

'I'd love to take you out on a mission,' Forrest growled. He thumbed through the letters, looking at the return addresses.

'My mommy ain't raised no fool,' Warner said.

Walden and Forrest walked down the hallway, entering the main war room, and greeted the men sitting at the desks. Major Deacon, a man who seemed to have constant gas pains, came from behind his desk and extended his hand to Walden.

'Glad to see you two,' he said without conviction. 'I thought you guys were told to be up here at nine sharp.'

The major looked down at papers scattered over the top of the desk.

'We slept in,' Walden said.

'You know, Walden' – the major sighed – 'you have a bad habit of making up your own rules. Saigon's been on the horn all goddamn night and all morning bitching about not getting the AAR.'

'Does that mean we're going to lose the war?'

The major looked hard at Walden, his ruddy complexion deepening. He started to say something, but instead yelled across the room to Sergeant Nobel, who was sticking tacks on a wall map. 'Let's get this debriefing going.'

'We're going to get some coffee first,' Walden said, and walked to the coffeepot against the far wall. Above the field desk that held the pot and cups was a black-and-white poster, a picture of a dead Viet Cong lying naked on an operating table. Several parts of his body were missing and what remained hung in tatters held together by sinew. The caption across the bottom of the picture read: TELL HIM THE M-16 ISN'T EFFECTIVE!

'Do you believe this shit?' Walden said quietly, nodding his head at the poster.

'And they bitch about our stuff,' Forrest said, filling the cups.

Sergeant Nobel was still sticking glued triangles representing antiaircraft positions on one of the large maps of Laos.

'You can finish that later,' the major said tightly.

'Right, sir,' Nobel said, carefully placing back into the box in his hand all the tiny yellow markers he was holding. Dropping the box onto his desk, he grabbed a pile of forms and led the men into the debriefing room next to the war room. The room, painted institutional green, was empty except for a long table and several gray metal folding chairs.

'How about some ashtrays before we get on with this thing?' Walden asked, pulling out one of the chairs.

'I'll get the damn ashtray,' the major said. 'You start the debriefing.'

'What's his problem, anyway?' Forrest asked when the major had left. He and Walden tossed maps and notebooks on the table.

'He's uptight because Saigon has been on his ass to get this AAR,' Nobel said. 'He wanted to debrief you guys last night but the colonel told him to wait until morning.'

'He's an asshole,' Walden said. 'He thinks he knows everything and he's never been in a firefight in his life.'

'He's all right once you get used to him. He's under a lot of pressure up here.' Nobel arranged his forms in front of himself.

'He's an asshole,' Walden repeated. The major came back into the room with two ashtrays and a handful of Teletype messages. He dropped the yellow sheets of paper in front of Walden.

'I don't know if you know it yet, but Covey made a body count from the air yesterday after you got pulled, and counted seventy-eight bodies out in the open.'

'How nice.' Walden sighed, and flipped through the messages.

The major's smile faded. 'I don't know if you're a smart-ass or what, Walden, but I'm getting damn sick of your attitude.'

The two men stared at each other for a couple of seconds.

'So what's your problem, Walden?' the major asked, not wanting to drop it.

'I don't have a problem. I just get a little tired of seeing bullshit reports.'

'What the hell you talking about?'

'You tell me how someone could count seventy-eight bodies in the open when there weren't any openings.' Walden felt his blood pressure rise. 'I'll bet Lindell didn't make any report like that and he was Covey for us. So where does this bullshit come from? I mean, who's shitting who around here? I don't care what you tell Saigon, but don't try to feed me this crap.'

'Are you saying there weren't that many people killed in

67

that target area yesterday?' The major's voice had a threat in it.

'I'm not saying that at all. There were probably hundreds killed after they napalmed the goddamn place. But with the amount of fire coming up out of the jungle, no ship could have stayed around long enough to count seventy-eight bodies, even if they could see them. That report is complete hogwash.'

The major stared hard at Walden, then abruptly turned and left the room.

'Jeez, Sam, you never know when to keep your mouth shut, do you?' Nobel said under his breath.

'Let's get this thing over with, huh?' Walden fumbled in his shirt pocket for his cigarettes and lighter.

Nobel asked questions from the standard form in a monotone, checking the proper blocks as Walden and Forrest answered. What type of soil? Loam, hard-packed, clay, red, brown? Was it single-, double-, or triple-canopy jungle? The questions droned on.

Two hours later Walden and Forrest were relating the incident at the stream. 'And that's when I found this in the guy's rucksack.' Walden said, pulling the diary out of his side pants pocket.

'Oh, for God's sake, Walden! You had that all this time and didn't tell anyone?' Nobel reached over and yanked the book from him.

'I forgot about it,' Walden said.

'Just a minute. I've got to get the major in on this.' Nobel pushed his chair back and moved toward the door.

'There're some pictures too,' Walden called after him. Nobel stopped in mid-stride as if stabbed, then shook his head in disbelief and left.

Walden lit another cigarette and smiled across the table at Forrest. Forrest broke into a grin. 'Screw 'em if they can't take a joke.'

'Why didn't you tell us about this before?' the major yelled. The words came out angrily but with a touch of elation. 'How the hell could you forget something like this?

68

This could be really important.' He waved the book back and forth by the side of his face as though it were a fan.

'Look,' Walden said tiredly, 'a lot of things happened yesterday. Like we almost got killed, right? I forgot about it.'

'Okay, okay, no problem,' the major said, holding up his free hand for quiet. 'Saigon's going to love this. It could be a chronological record of his entire trip down through the root structure. I mean, this could be real good. I'm going to get an interpreter on this right away.' He left the room as if he had an overloaded bladder.

The debriefing continued. An hour later, wrapping up the details of the operation, Nobel asked if there were any streams, rivers, or terrain features not shown on the map. Walden and Forrest both began to laugh. Nobel lifted his eyebrow.

'You see the green color on the map?' Walden pushed the rumpled map across the table toward the sergeant. 'This map is green, the jungle was green, and that's where the similarity ends. This doesn't even show the stream where we ambushed those people, or the ridge where we got pulled out, or for that matter, the highway that ran right down the middle of the valley.'

Nobel shifted, getting ready to say something, but Walden beat him to it. 'Don't think that we're going to spend the next ten hours up here drawing a new map like the last time. You can forget that shit.'

'Come on, Sam, give me a break. That's the kind of thing they want to know in Saigon.' Nobel was apologetic. 'Just give me the main difference and how the road ran.'

Walden closed his eyes and the room was quiet. 'Make it short. We got to bury one of our guys today.'

CHAPTER SIX

LEAVING THE TOC, Walden breathed deeply. There were many smells, each mingling with, then separating from, the others. There were smells of new plywood, and exhaust fumes from the generators, and the dull pungent odor of burning feces coming from the cut-down fifty-five-gallon drums smouldering down behind Recon. There was the smell of the ocean, and of canvas, and the exotic fragrance of the country itself.

'I'll be glad to get away for a few days,' Forrest said, kicking sand as he walked.

Walden nodded. After a moment he had to say it. 'You know, that bullet that hit Toan missed us by no more than a foot.' They walked a little farther in silence. 'I can't get the picture of that bullet hitting him out of my mind,' Walden added. Forrest shrugged.

At the Recon Company office Captain Wells looked up from a map he had been studying. 'Hi, Sam, Jerry.' He smiled.

'We need the three-quarter to take Toan to the cemetery,' Walden said.

Wells took the keys from the board behind his desk. 'Here you go. Sorry about your losing one. You got a week stand-down time coming, starting tomorrow. You going to Saigon?'

'We were going to try to get out tonight, but there's no way now.' Walden tossed the keys to Forrest.

'You can catch a Blackbird flight out tomorrow. I'll call up the front office and get you on the manifest.'

'Thanks, captain. We should be back in a few hours.'

The little people were already sitting in the back of the

70

truck when Walden and Forrest climbed in the front. Forrest unlocked the padlock that fastened the two thick chains that ran through the spokes on the steering wheel and whose ends were welded to the frame. He started the truck and wheeled it onto the company road.

At the dispensary Keegan was waiting. 'He's all ready,' Keegan said, motioning to them to follow him around the side of the hospital. There, a row of steel supply containers sat anchored with sandbags. Keegan unlocked the door to the end container. Hot, stale air floated out of the improvised crypt. Walden flinched automatically when he saw the wooden coffin sitting inside. The coffin seemed more real than the body had the night before. He, Pau, Cuong, Hung, and Lap pulled the coffin from the crypt, circled the box, and lifted it by the nylon straps nailed to the sides as carrying handles.

Pau climbed into the front seat between Walden and Forrest as the truck headed down toward the front gate. The others sat quietly in the rear as the truck bounced and swayed over the dunes. Walden lit a cigarette and watched the camp pass. He felt as though he were playing out a scene from some stupid, melancholy drama. He caressed the side of the CAR-15 he held in his lap, gently, without thinking.

Once out on the paved road heading to Da Nang, he began to think of home. Everything would've changed again, he knew. Just like when he had gone home for the first time in the summer of 1966. He had discovered then that things were different in his hometown, and maybe within himself. Something unnameable had altered during the year he had served with the First Cavalry in the jungles and rice paddies of the Central Highlands. The memories of the Ia Drang Valley, Bong Son, Phu Cat, places that other people couldn't even pronounce, did not fade away. They didn't fade at all. No one had wanted to know what had happened in those places. He had tried to defend himself and his friends from the accusations that they were baby killers and pyromaniacs. Then he had just quit talking about it. He had naively expected a return welcome such as his father and uncle had received at the end of World War II, like in the movies. It hadn't happened.

There were some, of course, who'd gone through the patriotic motions. The VFW had given him a year's free membership. Walden had joined because his father and uncles had joined, and he had thought maybe there would be others like him. But only a handful from his hometown had been to Vietnam at all, and the VFW had been mostly World War II and a smattering of Korean War veterans. Growing up, he had listened to his father talk about not being able to buy a drink for a year after the big one. No one had ever bought him a drink at the VFW. But the big one was still paying off for the old-timers, because Walden bought them drinks.

Whenever he'd read about Nam in the newspapers, or seen it on the nightly news, Walden had felt slightly guilty for not being there. He'd missed his real friends. After nine months he'd gone back into the Army. And in time had tumbled all the way back to the war.

Now as they drove through the stretching shadows of late afternoon toward Da Nang, Walden felt a sadness, for he knew that even if he survived this thing it wouldn't make any difference. He would never really be able to escape.

The streets of Da Nang were a study in random activity. Chickens ran along the shoulder of the road; children scampered over piles of trash in open lots. Middle-aged women wearing black silk pants and blouses jogged by, carrying bundles on their backs. Slender schoolgirls wearing white sandals walked home from school in clusters. The truck slowed as it approached a throng of people crossing the street, and Walden watched a carpenter squatting in front of his dilapidated shop, chiselling a piece of wood. A dog, its skin stretched by hunger across its rib cage, wobbled by in front of the man, who threw a piece of wood at it. Walden lit a joint and passed it to Pau. It made the rounds to the other people and came back. Then two more were lit, and they settled back. By the time the truck had rounded the airfield road and started down the paved highway toward the military cemetery on the outskirts of town, they were stoned.

At the entrance to the cemetery stood a plaster building with a tiled roof. Forrest stopped the truck, and Pau and Hung went inside to talk to the caretaker. Walden for the first time looked over the expanse of white crosses and markers. It was big.

'Oh, man,' he exclaimed softly as he stared across the unending mounds of dirt, and the clusters of people here and there among them. A breeze blew fitfully across the open expanse, and with the sun now blocked by clouds, it was chilly.

After a few minutes Pau and Hung came out of the office building with a slight man. He was the curator, and looked the part with thin hollow cheeks and dull brown eyes that didn't do anything when his mouth smiled at Walden. Walden nodded to the man as he stepped out of the truck to let Pau back in.

'We close soon,' the man said, pointing to the watch on his wrist.

'I sure hope so,' Walden said, climbing back in and pulling the door shut.

Pau directed Forrest down a side road that ran along the edge of the cemetery, and signalled a stop when they reached the corner of the field. They gathered around the tailgate and slid the coffin off. The nylon straps creaked as the weight of the box came off the floorboards and rested in their hands. Pau motioned to them to follow him between the first row of white crosses and Buddhist mandara symbols marking the plots. Walden noticed the dates on the markers in the first row started at 1963. As they moved up through the rows, the years changed. Halfway through 1964 they passed a solitary woman kneeling on the hard clay before a grave. There was a small bouquet of fresh field flowers on the settled earth in front of the cross. Walden could tell the woman was crying because her shoulders trembled beneath the black peasant blouse. As he looked at the woman, the prayer began in his head again. *Oh, my God, I'm heartily sorry for having offended Thee. And I detest all my sins because I dread the loss of heaven and the pains of hell.* A sound like a kitten mewling came from the woman as they passed. The wind shut off the woman's sobs and the loudest sounds Walden could hear were made by bits of stones being pushed into the clay beneath his boots as they passed into 1965.

But most of all because I have offended Thee, my God, Who art all good and deserving of all my love. Walden glanced at Playboy walking beside him and saw a tear hanging in the lashes of his lower eyelid. He saw a reflection of light in it before it grew heavy and fell. *I firmly resolve with the help of Your grave to confess my sins, to do penance and to amend my life, Amen. Grace, not grave. Grace.* He shook his head to clear it as the end of 1965 approached and 1966 came nearer.

Because Walden had come to the war in 1965, the graves from that year on seemed more personal. When the little people began to weave under the weight of the coffin, Walden called a break. They gently lowered the box to the ground and rested between the graves of two men killed in November of 1965. Walden had nearly died that same month. A shiver ran down his back. He looked up toward the other years. Nineteen sixty-nine seemed a long way off. He looked down the slight slope they had just climbed. The early rows were deserted except for the lone woman still huddled over the grave back in 1964. The more advanced the years became, the more people stood around the graves. They lifted the coffin and moved into 1966.

An unnatural humming sound was coming from Playboy's throat as they continued. Playboy was biting down on his lower lip, and his small shoulders shook. He looked up at Walden, his large brown eyes wet. A tremor rippled beneath his left eye. Walden held out his arm and Playboy cradled himself against his side.

'He have no mother, no father,' Playboy whimpered. Walden drew him closer.

'It doesn't matter anymore,' Walden whispered. Playboy squeezed his hand until it hurt.

They passed through 1967 as small groups of people stared at them. Walden looked out over the barbed wire fence that surrounded the cemetery. The black new strands were woven in with the red rusted curls of wire that had been strung long before. Scattered among the graves were rotten sandbags.

New prayer words came into Walden's mind, words learned as he had studied to become an altar boy, words he hadn't remembered for a long time. *Mea culpa, mea culpa, mea maxima culpa. Ideo precor beatam semper virginem.* Through my fault, through my fault, through my most grievous fault. Therefore I pray ever to the Blessed Virgin. As the words popped inside his brain, he thought of Betty, his first real girlfriend. He felt the wind drying the sweat from the back of his jungle shirt. Betty disappeared as a jolt of the coffin suddenly reminded him of carrying artillery shell boxes back in 1965.

There were many more people among the graves as they moved into 1969. Though it was only half over, there were more graves already than in all of 1968. The last three rows were open, waiting for those not yet dead. A three-man crew of Vietnamese gravediggers stood leaning against their shovels, watching as the team turned left and headed for the far white cross that marked the grave of the last man buried. The three gravediggers grabbed the long canvas straps lying over a nearby pile of dirt and jogged up behind them.

One of the diggers yelled out, 'Five hundred piastre we bury.' Cuong turned on them and hissed, '*Di di mau.*' The CAR-15 hanging around his neck automatically centered on the lead man's stomach. The three stopped instantly. Seeing the expression on Cuong's face, they quickly retraced their steps.

They placed the coffin beside the first open grave, next to one with loose, fresh dirt mounded on top.

Walden tried to think of something to say. He looked to Forrest for help. Forrest was looking at the dirt. The little people sat or squatted around the coffin, waiting. Playboy brushed his small hand lightly back and forth along the top of the rough lid.

'Toan was a good man,' Walden said, out of desperation. He felt a hot, itchy wave flood up his back. 'In a war like this there are only good men and bad men.' Walden paused for a few moments. 'I loved Toan as you loved him. He's gone now, and we can't ever change that. He would want us to be happy and laugh, not cry, for him. Though right now it's damn hard. Hung, Cuong, you guys say something.' Walden quickly sat down next to Forrest.

First, Hung, and then Cuong, spoke. Walden could only understand brief words and phrases, but he could see that what was said meant something. A couple of times they laughed as Cuong related a story about Toan, gesturing with his graceful arms. The flowing movements caused Walden to think of the flocks of geese that would fly over his home in autumn. He stared across the open field in front of him where no graves had yet been dug, remembering the majestic birds descending into a cut-down cornfield, the shadow of their massed wings changing from white to gray to dark black as they changed directions in flight. He remembered how the honking seemed light and eager in the early fall. As the days shortened, there were fewer calls across the skies. Then would come the last cry of autumn. He would lie still in his bed and listen to the distant honking of a lone bird somewhere in the darkness. The sound was lonely and frightened, and Walden could remember one night crying for the bird because he could not help.

They buried the box by scraping dirt into the hole with their rifle butts. Very slowly the hole filled up. They stood back as Pau rewound the rope used to lower the coffin into the grave. Hung and Cuong placed a cross at the head of the grave. It had Toan's name printed on a card thumbtacked to the center.

Walden used his knife to carve an *I* with a *C* over the top on the upper branch of the cross. 'So we can find it again,' he said in explanation. They walked back to the truck in silence, and remained silent until they had driven all the way through Da Nang.

'You got a number on you?' Forrest finally asked.

'Yeah.' Walden pulled the plastic deck out of his pocket and lit one of the prerolled joints. He handed a couple to Pau for the little people in the back. After a few minutes Walden said, 'Forty trillion miles from home and not a star to steer on.'

'Say what?' Forrest peered at Walden over the tops of his sun-glasses.

'Just stumbling around in my head.'

The silence descended again until they turned the corner by the bicycle repair shop, marking the last half-mile to camp.

'We're common de-Nam-i-nators.' Walden chuckled.

'What?'

'You know,' Walden said. 'Delousing, denuding, demented, demeaning, de-Nam-ing.'

'Thanks, man. I'm glad I heard it from you first.'

As they were coming up on the Headquarters buildings, Sergeant Nobel came running, waving to the truck to stop.

'Oh, shit.' Walden groaned. 'Now what?' He started to get a headache as Forrest braked to a stop.

'The colonel wants to see you two right away,' Nobel said, avoiding looking straight at Walden.

'Fuck!' Walden yelled, kicking open the truck door.

'It's not my goddamn fault,' Nobel said, holding up his arms and jumping back a few steps as Walden came out.

'What's going on?' Forrest slid across the front seat and jumped down behind Walden.

Walden was high and his head hurt and he knew arguing wouldn't help. 'Hung, drive the truck down to the company and give the keys to Captain Wells. Okay?'

Hung nodded, and Walden headed to the TOC, Forrest and Nobel falling in behind.

Inside the TOC, Colonel Easton came right to the point. 'Saigon just called. They want you to take your team back into MA-12 and take a prisoner.'

'What? Are you crazy?' Walden blurted, amazement making his mind go numb.

The colonel pursed his lips. 'Saigon feels you're familiar with the area.'

Walden didn't say anything. *Goddamn, this isn't real.*

'Look, Sam,' the colonel said kindly, 'Saigon's got me by the balls.'

Walden stood in front of one of the few men in the camp he respected, and felt his stomach begin to churn. Easton was practically the only officer who knew what was real, and that made him important.

'Saigon says I'm getting too personally involved with the teams up here, and that if I can't produce, they'll get someone who can.' The colonel held his hands out, palms up, in a helpless gesture.

Major Deacon strode into the operations center. 'There you are,' he snapped, moving toward Walden.

'Take a break,' Walden spit out.

'Just hold on there a second,' Deacon began, but he colonel cut him off.

'Major! Do you have some letters to write?'

There was a frozen moment. 'Yes, sir,' Deacon replied, and spun on his heel.

'This is about par with the usual bullshit that comes out of Saigon,' Walden said, still dizzy with disbelief. 'That whole area is going to be crawling with gooks. It's going to be like shooting up a hornets' nest and then running over to it to see what happened.'

'You think it'll be that bad?' the colonel asked, pulling out his pipe and sticking it in the corner of his mouth.

'Jesus, going in there anytime for the next month is the same as suicide.' Walden thought he heard a whine in his voice, and that thought shocked him most of all. He straightened his back. 'Ah, goddammit.'

Easton pulled himself up to his full five feet eight inches and looked directly at Walden. 'Sam, I want this one.'

Walden glared at the ceiling. His jaw hurt. Two beats passed. 'I want my little people to get three days off in Da Nang,' he half yelled. 'We don't leave until five days from now. And when we get back, the whole team gets two weeks off.'

'You got it.' The colonel grinned. 'This one is really going to be rough, isn't it?'

'Two weeks in Saigon is two weeks in Saigon.' Walden tried to laugh and looked at Forrest.

'I don't believe this,' Forrest said, looking away. 'I just don't believe it.'

CHAPTER SEVEN

'YOU GOT any tape left?' Walden asked as he emptied the contents of a LRRP package onto his bunk.

'Here.' Forrest tossed a roll of black electrical tape across the room, then went back to crimping blasting caps onto short cuts of time fuse. Walden picked up the plastic pouch of dehydrated beef hash that had fallen out along with other items. Folding over the open top of the meal pouch, he taped it shut and put it into the bottom of his rucksack. After stacking in all the meals for a seven-day mission, he had the pack half filled. He looked at the other items lying on the floor that he had to carry: four Claymore mines, five blocks of C-4 explosives, two spare radio batteries, and the PRC-25 radio. He shrugged, removed all but two LRRP rations and two cans of C-ration fruit from the rucksack, then began placing the other items inside.

Watching Walden replace the food with Claymores, Forrest said, 'I guess you're not figuring on staying in very long.'

'When it's a matter of ammo or food, I always go for the ammo.' Walden tucked the radio in. He then lit a cigarette and leaned back on the bed.

'This is some shit.' Forrest snorted. He began filling magazines with bullets. 'Half the teams in this camp haven't run a mission in four months and here we're going back out damn near as soon as we came in. Some shit.'

'If you care enough to send the very best,' Walden said solemnly, then began to laugh. Forrest looked at him pensively for a moment, then chuckled. Walden smoked silently, listening to the vague sloshing sound of the waves falling on the beach. After a few minutes Forrest muttered, 'Some shit, though.'

Putting out the cigarette, Walden went to the stereo setup arranged between the two lockers. 'Request lines are open,' he said, thumbing through a stack of albums.

'How about some Creedence? We haven't listened to them since last night.'

'You got it. Off the charts but dear to your heart.' After putting the record on the turntable, Walden adjusted the sound and returned to his bunk. He began to fill magazines with practiced ease. He put eighteen bullets into each clip, making sure one of the last five was a tracer so he would know when to reload. The magazines were designed to hold twenty rounds, but had a history of not feeding properly when filled to capacity.

'How many magazines you carry for your CAR-15?' Forrest asked.

'Thirty-five,' Walden said, pushing bullets into yet another magazine.

'Goddamn, man,' Forrest exclaimed. 'That's, wait a minute, just a second . . . ' He grabbed a C-ration box and scribbled figures on the side. He nearly laughed when he looked up from his arithmetic. 'That's six hundred and thirty bullets, for Christ's sake.'

'You know I got this thing about running out of ammo,' Walden said as another clip hit the pile.

'The Ia Drang Valley trip,' Forrest said.

'I figure when the shit hits the fan like it's going to, it'll take the helicopters at least forty minutes to get to us, minimum. That's less than one magazine per minute and that isn't much when they're coming balls to the wall.'

A picture from 1965 slipped into Walden's mind. He tried to block it out, but the effort was too late and he was once again standing among the dead of the Seventh Cavalry. There were bodies everywhere, like empty beer cans strewn around a clearing after a high school party. Clearest in his mind was the boy spread-eagled in the grass, staring into the sun. An empty M-16 was clutched in his hand, dust cover open, the bolt cocked back waiting for the magazine. There hadn't been any magazines left, though, and that's when the boy had died. There weren't a handful of bullets left among the dead. Walden had moved to the perimeter as though sleepwalking. He hadn't wanted to be the one who had to remove the man's penis from where the NVA had placed it. For the first time in his life Walden had really wanted to kill someone.

After filling the magazines, Walden put them into the canteen covers on the left side of his web belt. He placed each so that the percussion caps of the cartridges were against his body, with the lead facing out. He did this so that if a bullet hit the magazine pouches they would explode outward. On the bottom of each were taped tabs so he could easily pull them up and out, even when his hands were shaking. On the right side he carried two canteen covers filled with M-33 hand grenades, and two pouches with 40-millimeter shells for his sawed-off M-79. The rear pouches carried water and his survival equipment.

Walden went through a mental checklist. He patted one of the side pockets on the rucksack, feeling the rubber bag of Ringer's lactate solution, and the thin IV tube and needle wrapped around it. Opening the top flap on the pack, he reassured himself that the rifle-cleaning sections were taped together; that was in case a round got jammed in the chamber of his weapon. He touched the .22 caliber pistol with the long black cylindrical silencer, and the extra clip of ammo next to it.

After a few minutes he was satisfied that he had everything in the pack. Cinching the straps shut, he checked the web gear. His knife was taped hilt-up on the left front carrying harness, with a strobe light taped to the sheath. Wrapped to the lower right front strap, where it wouldn't interfere with his aiming his weapon, was a violet smoke canister and a small squad radio for intrateam communications.

He then laid out the uniform he would wear the next day. In the top left pocket of the fatigue shirt, he placed the thick UR-10 survival radio, deliberately giving protection to his heart. In the right side pocket of his pants he placed the signal mirror, and the pen flare tube with ten flares rolled up in a bright orange-and-crimson marking panel. In his left side pocket he carried his map, ten quarter-gram syrettes of morphine, and a small survival kit. In the right top shirt-pocket he carried his notebook and pen along with a small Pen ES camera. After visually checking everything once more, Walden put on the web gear and hoisted the rucksack.

'Goddamn, this thing gets heavier every time I go out,' he muttered, biceps tightening as he heaved the pack onto his back. 'God.' He grunted at the ridiculous weight pulling down on his shoulders. 'This rucksack and web gear would've killed a Roman.'

'Don't forget nothing,' Forrest said with a grin, repeating a slogan used throughout Special Forces.

After settling the pack on his back, Walden jumped up and down to see if anything rattled or clanked. The only sounds were his boots against the floor and the dull squeaking of the shoulder straps protesting at the weight. Satisfied, he pulled the pack and web gear off and rested them carefully near the head of his bunk.

'Want to take a walk down to the beach and test-fire the weapons?' Walden asked, throwing empty cartridge boxes and cardboard hand-grenade tubes into an empty C-ration case on the floor.

'I need a break from this.' Forrest got up and turned off the stereo. The drunken voices of men shouting to one another drifted in from the club across the road.

'Quarter after four and they're fucked up already.'

'They were fucked up at one when I went over to get us a Coke,' Forrest said. He pulled a faded green T-shirt over his head.

'Drunk by one, Vietnam, doo dah, doo dah,' Walden sang. Giap rose from the folded Army blanket next to the

83

small refrigerator, stretched, and padded over as Walden picked his CAR-15 off the bed.

'Want to go hunting? Want to go hunting?' Walden teased. Giap yelped and dashed around in a circle.

'VC, VC,' Walden said menacingly. Giap began to snarl, crouching over his forelegs, his short brown hair bristling along the back of his neck. 'Good dog, good dog,' Walden cooed, patting his leg for Giap to come to him. The dog bounded over, his tail and rear end frantically wagging. Walden leaned down and rubbed the dog's head between his hands.

'Hunt 'em up,' Walden said, and Giap sprang out the door, flying over the steps and landing lightly on the sand in front of the hooch.

'It doesn't take much to psych him up, does it?'

'I wish I could get that enthused,' Forrest said, watching Giap dash back and forth.

They crossed the sand in the rear of Recon Company and neared the back gate. A row of concrete bunkers and barbed wire lined the oceanfront. A lone figure came into view, carrying a surfboard under his arm.

'Surfer Joe, check him out.' Walden nodded his head toward the muscular shape of Jim Milinger walking over the dunes. 'All he does is lift weights and surf. What a life. He's been on vacation since he got here.'

'It makes me sick,' Forrest said.

'I went through Training Group with him.' They walked past the Vietnamese gate guard, and down toward the water's edge. 'All he would talk about was how many VC he was going to grease. Once here he got a job at the message center up in the TOC and has been there ever since. He' never run one mission.'

'So what's his trip?' Forrest lit the joint Walden handed him.

'I guess he's just smarter than the rest of us.' Walden began to laugh.

They passed the joint back and forth as they headed up the beach. The sand bluffs shielded the POL dump and the

84

equipment depots, making it seem as though they were walking a beach in California. After a time they found a protected hollow in the sand bank, and sat facing the ocean. The sand still held the day heat and it felt good. Giap snuggled down between them, panting.

'I wonder where we're going to be this time tomorrow?' Forrest stubbed the roach out in the sand and took a fresh one from Walden. They smoked it leisurely, looking out over the waves rolling up thick and foamy along the shore. The light began to fade and the first hint of evening traced its way across the crest of the horizon. Giap lay quietly on the sand watching the joint go back and forth, sometimes tilting his head.

'Do you think it'll be bad news tomorrow?' Forrest asked as he lit a Pall Mall with his engraved Zippo.

'It'll be bad, way bad,' Walden said softly. 'But we're real bad too. Charlie got the guns, but we got the numbers.' They looked at each other, and then started to laugh.

'You know,' Walden said, 'tomorrow, when we're going in on that helicopter, nobody in the world will see us except a couple of pilots, and a couple of door gunners. We'll be hanging up there in the sky between heaven and the jungle and nobody will see us. I thought about that sometimes on night jumps at Bragg. It was, you know, like the finest moment, jumping out of the door into total darkness, like being born. And nobody would see you, not the people that were important. But I always knew that someone was watching it, someone was recording it.' Walden got up and brushed the sand off.

'I feel good about the mission. I think it's going to be all right,' Forrest said. They began to walk back to the camp. 'Even if we forgot to test the damn weapons.'

Standing on the helipad the next morning, Walden scanned the sky for the H-34 that was supposed to take them to the launch site. The little people sat bunched together on the PSP, leaning against their rucksacks.

'Look at this shit,' Walden growled, showing Forrest his

watch. 'Quarter to nine and those assholes haven't shown up yet. "Be down at the pad by eight o'clock," ' he quoted, savagely imitating Major Deacon's voice.

'Maybe they'll forget about us,' Forrest said.

'Nah. They'll fuck around and get us to the launch site around two and we'll get inserted an hour before dark.'

At nine o'clock, just as Walden was getting ready to go storming up to the TOC, a distant drumming of blades heralded the approach of the Kingbee.

It came in fast over the top of the garbage dump across the road from the camp, flared on its side over the pad, and corkscrewed slowly in a wide circle before it bounced on the perforated steel plating, then landed.

'Here we go again,' Walden mumbled, leaning over to pick up his rucksack. The noise from the helicopter covered the words. The little people jogged, bent over, to the ship, the prop wash making their fatigues pop and snap. Walden felt a cold knot forming in his stomach as he helped the little people into the ship. When they were all inside, he signalled thumbs up to the door gunner and the chopper lifted slowly into the air. In moments they were passing low over the POW camp. Walden looked down at the black pajama-clad prisoners milling about the yard. A number of them shook their fists at the helicopter as it flew over. Walden smiled and spread his fingers in a peace sign. Cuong spit, and both he and Walden watched the white string fall toward the ground.

Walden suddenly got a rush of euphoria as they flew north over the shanty-town squalor of the Da Nang outskirts. The sensation was unexpected, and Walden wondered why he now wanted to go. He thought for a moment. He could die, he realized, and he was ready. He had done everything within his power to ensure that they would come back. Now, though he had tried to stay awake last night to make the premission hours last longer, the time was upon him. It was beyond his control, and that was the fact that released him.

'We're going to kick some ass today,' Walden shouted

over the din of the engine. He smelled the hot stink of the fluids as they pulsed through the arteries of the ship. They were going to the world that few knew. Where only a limited number of travellers knew about the fear and the taste of bile and the triumph of survival.

'We're going to kick some ass. *Biêt?*' He smiled over his shoulder at the little people.

'We kill *beaucoup* VC, okay,' Pau shouted back.

Cuong leaned over and touched Walden's sleeve. 'We kill today for Toan.'

'Yeah,' Walden said. 'Goddamn right.'

The helicopter began straining for altitude as it neared the mountain line to the north of Da Nang. The old ship shuddered and swayed on the currents that swirled about the crags and up from the stream beds lacing the slopes. Walden looked down at the thick jungle pockmarked with bomb craters and dotted here and there by flare parachutes, white and shining in the morning wetness. The rise of the mountain from the foothills became steeper as the ship edged closer and closer until the tops of the trees swept by just beneath Walden's dangling boots. Looking straight out the door, all Walden could see were large banyan trees and rocks coming at them. For a second his hand reached out and tightened around the door gunner's seat leg when it seemed as though they weren't going to make it. His body unconsciously lifted, trying to relieve the chopper of his weight.

'Jesus,' Walden groaned just before the blue sky appeared above the trees. He looked down at tree branches being broken off by the wheels of the H-34 as it skimmed over the crest of the mountain. One moment they were about to crash into the trees and the next the mountain dropped away and they were three thousand feet in the air. Walden glanced at Forrest, who rolled his eyes and said, 'I don't believe this, man.' Then he giggled nervously.

The helicopter dropped like a broken elevator until they were a couple of hundred feet above the ground. The brown and green of the fields below made the basin a patchwork quilt. They followed Highway 1 along the ocean, heading for Quang Tri. The highway looked like a shiny black river twisted against nature as it ran parallel to the sea. Once past Phu Bai, the ground slowly turned from dark brown to red, then Quang Tri rose from the dusk like the Emerald City of Oz. A mass of radio antennas poked upward as they passed over a communications site. Military trucks and motorized mules replaced the cars and motor scooters on the roads. Clouds of red dust trailed behind the convoys. The native huts thinned out as they approached the Marine camp. On the edge of the camp, surrounded by barbed wire, was the launch site. The churning blades of the landing chopper sent clouds of red powder billowing into the six CP tents that made up the top-secret site. Seconds after they had disembarked and headed for the command tent, they wore the first layer of Quang Tri dust.

Billy Slader and Major Cane came out to the team as the chopper blades whined slowly to a stop.

'Hey, sweetie.' Slader grinned, shaking Walden's hand and slapping him on the back. 'You guys the only Recon team left in Da Nang?'

'The other teams were discontinued for lack of interest,' Walden said, then became quiet as they walked to the operations tent.

'It's a go for today,' the major said. 'The Hundred and first will insert you by slicks, and we have the gunships and Cobras laid on. The pilots will be here in a few minutes to get the briefing. You guys want some coffee?'

'Is Pappy up with Covey yet?' Walden asked.

'He took off ten minutes ago, so he should be out over your AO in about two zero minutes.' Slader poured coffee into cups.

'You realize we're going to be in a world of trouble as soon as we get on the ground, right?' Walden said matter-of-factly. Both Slader and Cane nodded.

'So the plan,' Walden continued, 'is to grab one of those little bastards as soon as we can and get the hell out.'

'That shouldn't take long.' Slader chuckled, nodding his

head. 'That whole area has been nothing but activity since you were pulled out last week. In fact, I'll be damn surprised if you get on the ground.'

'The only thing we got going for us is that they wouldn't believe we're dumb enough to go back in so soon.'

'Let's all hope so,' Cane said, the light tone gone from his voice.

Walden and Forrest were just finishing their coffee when the sound of Hueys coming in rumbled into the tent. As the ships settled down on the pad outside, the canvas walls of the tent began to pop and shiver. Dust drifted in and applied another layer of grit to the desk and typewriters.

'I don't know how you guys stand this all the time,' Forrest said, waving his hand in front of his face.

'War's a bitch,' Slader said. He began to pick up papers that had flown off the desks. 'Fun, though,' he added.

'You just love this, don't you?' Walden laughed, looking at Slader as the helicopter pilots started into the tent.

'It's a lot better than Korea. The weather's better, you know. Why, in Korea we'd call napalm in on top of our positions just to get warmed up.'

'Right.' Walden sighed. 'You're nuts, Billy, but I still love ya.'

'Only for my body,' Slader said, scratching the three-day beard on his deeply lined face.

'No, man, it's the real thing. I no bullshit you, GI.'

'What am I doing here?' Forrest asked, looking up at the canvas roof.

'Living a life of danger.' Slader crossed the room and began to set up the plywood board with the map thumb-tacked to it.

After the pilots were gathered, Walden began his briefing. 'Here's the trip.' He took the wooden pointer the major handed him. 'We're getting inserted here at Oscar Papa.' He gave the numerical coordinates. 'That's the primary LZ. If we get blown out of there, we'll go in three klicks away on the alternate.' He then went over the code words and radio frequencies. At the end of the briefing Walden laid the pointer down and took a breath.

'Some of you guys have been across the fence before, but for those of you that haven't, this is the way it works. When we're in the air, you guys are in charge. If we crash, I'm in charge. When we're on the ground, I don't want any debating. Just do what I tell you, and we'll make it through in one piece. Okay?'

The pilots all nodded, but some looked at each other uncertainly. 'I'm telling you this,' Walden said, 'because this target is going to be hot as hell. My team and I were just extracted from this area a week ago. So tell your door gunners to keep their eyes open going in. If we start taking ground fire, you get our butts out. Okay?'

The pilots nodded again and began folding their maps.

Minutes later, as the helicopters were warming up, Walden briefed the little people for the first time. He handed each a map and showed them the primary and alternate LZs and the escape and evasion route that he and Forrest had worked out. As they covered their faces with the green camouflage grease, Walden described the mission.

'We go in, I think we get in firefight right away. We grab prisoner and *di di mau*. If we have to lay ambush, then we will have the snatch team just like we practised. Everything be same. *Biêt?*'

Hung asked and answered questions for the team till Walden was satisfied that they all clearly understood.

'Okay, let's do it,' Walden said, swinging the heavy rucksack onto his back. The others followed suit and trailed behind him to the two Hueys. Walden, Hung, Pau, and Cuong climbed into the lead ship. Forrest, Baby-san, Tang, and Playboy got into the follow-up ship.

Walden leaned out the open doorway of the helicopter just as it lifted, and made eye contact with Forrest. He jabbed his thumb upward, then ducked back in as the chopper twisted around a few feet above the ground, sending up columns of dust. After completing a half circle the slick, its nose pitched downward, flew over the top of the concertina wire surrounding the site. Major Cane and Slader, along with a half-dozen others, stood in the dust and waved as the ships headed for the Laotian border.

The wind blowing through the open door grew colder as they rose far above the rice paddies. Walden could feel the adrenalin beginning to drip into his system. He breathed deeply through his nose, pushing down the fear that made his stomach feel hot and heavy.

He watched the countryside become hilly, then mountainous. Then there were no paddies and no huts left. Only jungle. Walden's stomach muscles tightened as he spotted the Cobra gunships circling lazily over the rendezvous point. They picked up the air support ships and crossed the border. Walden quickly said his prayers, ending with his usual plea: *Please, God, protect our team*. He tried to clear his mind as his finger wrapped around the trigger of the CAR-15. He felt as though a constant charge of electricity were running through his body. *This is just crazy*.

Walden pushed the handset of the radio against his ear and listened to Pappy Lindell talking to the gunships as they neared the landing zone. Twisting around, Walden looked at the little people squatting on the floor. Their faces, smeared with camouflage grease, were set in hard lines as they fidgeted with last-minute preparations. Walden smiled and yelled over the sound of the engine and the rushing wind, 'No sweat, *cum sow*.'

Walden glanced at the door gunner, who had a large white peace symbol on his flight helmet, as the man arranged two flak jackets on his seat. The door gunner noticed Walden watching and sheepishly yelled, 'I ain't getting my balls shot off.' Walden nodded and smiled. A few minutes later the gunner leaned over and said, 'We're about five minutes out; good luck, man.' Then after a pause he added, 'Don't worry, man. We'll come back and get you no matter what. Can you dig it?' He flashed a peace sign and then settled back behind his M-60.

CHAPTER EIGHT

BY EIGHT A.M. the oppressive Georgia sun had already turned the jump-school track into a skillet. After he'd twice circled the half-mile course, Sam's single purpose was not dropping out. That was all that counted. The pain in his legs told him to stop, the fire in his chest begged him to stop, and every cell in his body cursed him because he didn't.

'Number seventy-seven, stay in step, goddamn it. You're screwing up my whole formation.' *I'm seventy-seven*. Sam glanced at the burly jump instructor who had bellowed. *Christ, he isn't even sweating yet*. He skipped clumsily until his left boot was coming down in cadence with the others.

It had become agonizingly clear in the first week that jump school wasn't where you went to get in shape. You were supposed to be in shape when you arrived or you were in trouble. Sam was in trouble.

Only pride got him through that first week. Now, halfway through tower week, he could start to see the finish. Only jump week to go. After days of physical torture, merely jumping out of an airplane flying at a hundred and twenty knots, 1,250 feet above the ground, seemed minor.

'Goddammit, seventy-seven, if I have to tell you to get in step one more time, I'm going to terminate your ass. Now, get in step, puke!'

Sam tried to take his mind from the pain and his growing conviction that he was going to have a heart attack. *One more lap. Just one more*. He hadn't realized the toll ten months of civilian life had taken. Not until he started

Airborne training. The bill for trying to drink the war out of his head was coming due. *Airborne training. I guess the folks were right. The war did make me crazy.*

'Okay, girls. We're going to take an extra lap this morning and see if our hero from the First Cav can stay in step.' *Oh, God, no. I'll never make it around again.* Sam's legs felt as if they were being amputated with a hot butter-knife. It helped to see that the others were staggering too. Halfway through the last lap everyone was out of step, and four hundred eyes were glued to the finish line. *Everything has to end. Even if I die on this goddamn track, it has to end.*

'What are you?' the sweatless instructor screamed at them.

'Airborne!'

'How far can you go?'

'All the way!'

They formed back up after a third of the class had unloaded their breakfast. The sergeant yelled for their attention.

'Okay, girls, listen up. You see that man over there with the funny-looking hat?' He pointed toward a lone figure standing off to one side of the formation. 'He's Special Forces. If any of you shit-birds think you want to be snake-eaters, he's the man to see. You got ten minutes.'

Sam jogged over with half of the Airborne class. He got as close as he could. The man's tailored khaki uniform fit perfectly; his jump boots sparkled in the glaring sunlight; the beret commanded attention. Yet it was the casual confidence the man displayed that made Sam think of the one Special Forces soldier he'd seen in Vietnam.

It had been his first day in the Ia Drang Valley. Nightfall was approaching and he was at the command post getting ammo when the man slipped through the perimeter without anyone noticing. His face was covered with camouflage grease and he was carrying an AK-47. He strode up to the company commander and got right to the point.

'You'd better batten down the hatches, because you're

going to get hit by a battalion of hard-core regulars after dark. You got any salt?' They had given him all the salt packets he wanted. Then he'd simply walked back into the jungle. They had found out later he was Special Forces, involved with something called Delta Project. He had been right about the battalion attacking.

The man Sam was watching now didn't look as though he was often wrong either. 'Any of you interested in joining, we're giving the test at building T-5607, oh nine hundred, Saturday.' The man obviously couldn't have cared less. He turned and walked away.

Sam arrived an hour early. By the time the Special Forces man showed up, this time wearing a pair of cutoff jeans and a T-shirt, there were about a hundred applicants waiting.

The first test was language aptitude. The second was Morse code. Then it got strange. The third test contained the oddest collection of questions Sam had ever seen.

'If you are a bank security guard, and a robbery is taking place during rush hour with the area full of people, what would you do?'

A. Open fire immediately
B. Pull your gun, and order them to stop
C. Wait until they are outside before firing
D. Do nothing

Sam almost checked A, but after a moment's thought checked D. *Why not be honest? It's only money.*

CHAPTER NINE

WALDEN'S EYES watered as, leaning out the door, he watched the two Cobras nosing down toward a brown pinhole of open ground on the side of a densely covered mountain. High above them Covey circled in the light OV-10 airplane. Brown puffs of smoke appeared from the sides of the Cobras as they fired fleshette rockets into the LZ. Walden glanced quickly at the door gunner, who was intensely watching the jungle below, leaning out over the machine gun to see better. Walden took one last deep breath as the helicopter flared out over the LZ and dropped. His eyes scanned the trees and bending elephant grass as the rotor blades created a small tornado.

Four feet above the ground, as the ship swayed back and forth, Walden stepped down onto the skid, quickly surveyed the ground, and then jumped. He hit the ground hard, rolled over onto his stomach, and was lurching to his feet when the little people jumped out behind him. The chopper engine roared as it lifted the ship into the sky. A moment later the silence was absolute. The little people spread out around Walden, training their weapons up the side of the slope. Walden keyed the handset and told the second ship to come in.

Fat beads of sweat broke out on Walden's face as he hunched in the dry dirt, surrounded by elephant grass and brush, and watched the ship carrying the rest of the team. Dust and chaff exploded around them as the helicopter dropped, and hovered just above the ground. Walden squinted, watching Forrest climb out onto the skid. Seeing him search, Walden waved an arm, then Forrest and the others piled out. Moments later they were all together.

Walden quickly made sure everyone was okay, then moved the team hurriedly into the brush surrounding the clearing. Serrated blades of grass opened minute cuts on their faces as they moved farther into the smells and sensations of the jungle. After twenty or thirty yards Walden stopped the team. Squatting behind a large tree, he waited, waited and listened for any of the sounds humans made. The only noise was the leaves touching each other in the light breeze. Walden looked at Cuong, then at Forrest, to see what was in their eyes, to see what they felt. They shrugged. The little hairs on the back of Walden's neck moved. He did not like this. Finally, he brought the handset up, cupped his hand over it, and whispered, 'Covey, this is Freedom Son. Team okay. Over.'

A moment later Pappy Lindell's voice came back. 'Roger, son. Team okay. Check back at sixteen hundred. Out.'

Walden pushed the handset inside his shirt and gestured to Cuong to start moving up the side of the mountain. Cuong, crouching over, began silently pushing vines and bamboo stocks out of his way. The team eased up the slope. Flies buzzed around Walden's head and his ears tried to sort through the sound for something else. Sweat seeped through the green cravat he wore as a headband. Little beads ran sticky and wet down his legs and the loose fatigues bunched uncomfortably around his crotch as they moved. Through the trees they could see patches of sky, white in the late-noon heat. A bee darted back and forth in front of Walden's face, emitting a low drone. Already he could feel the grime begin to stick to his skin. Bits of grass pricked his neck, caught in the slick moisture. The jungle was too damn quiet. Walden could feel the NVA near, very near. His brain was flashing danger signals like a sputtering neon sign. He halted the team and motioned to Forrest to come up. The little people clustered around, tense and skittish.

'I don't like this worth a shit,' Walden whispered into Forrest's ear. Before Forrest had a chance to answer, a rifle shot shattered the silence. Screeching in panic, a flock of birds burst from the trees above them, their wings creating small thunder. For an instant Walden's brain was frozen in a bath of adrenalin. The first thing that broke through was relief that the silence was over.

'Curtain call.' Walden whistled. 'Son of a bitch.' The little people had reacted like startled cats, heads snapping around as they went to their toes, backs arched. Their faces were drained of color, eyes black smears of bloodless skin. Walden put his fingers to his lips and gently motioned with his left hand for them to get down.

He had heard signal shots fired before on missions. That in itself was not unusual. Normally the team would have moved directly toward the sound of the shot, knowing that whoever fired it would move. The signal shot was Walden's own favourite way of shaking pursuers. But instinctively he knew this one was different. No one would believe him, yet Walden would swear that he had fought so long he now knew how a weapon was fired, if it was angry, frightened, aggressive, searching, confident. The shot that had just been fired carried everything but fear. The echo was just fading when the clacking of bamboo sticks being struck together in unison began to the front and on both sides of them.

Without hesitation Walden grabbed the handset and keyed the mike. 'Covey, Covey,' he breathed into the mouthpiece, 'this is Freedom Son. Over.' He listened to the silence and knew that if he couldn't raise Lindell, they were dead. The color of the jungle changed, became more vivid as adrenalin flowed. The cadence of the clattering bamboo made Walden feel nauseous. He could smell the sour stench of fear around him as the circle tightened. Pappy Lindell's voice broke calm and clear over the radio and Walden's head went light.

'This is Covey. What's happening down there, buddy? Over.' The voice seemed almost happy.

'We got movement around us, bamboo signals. No contact yet, but I'm calling a Prairie Fire emergency.

We've got to get out of here.' Walden's whispers were urgent as he motioned to the team to begin falling back to the LZ.

'You got it, buddy. Stay cool. Ships are refuelling. We'll be on station in approximately five zero minutes. Over.'

'Roger that. We're being channelized back to primary.' Walden watched Forrest jam the metal spike legs of a Claymore into the soft mulch. A blasting cap, at the end of a short lead of orange time fuse, had already been inserted in the cap well. Forrest pulled the lighter ring. It popped as the fuse lighter detonated and the orange coloring began to turn black as it started to burn. Forrest adjusted the mine, aiming it uphill where the least amount of trees would obstruct the tiny ball bearings exploding from it.

Walden gestured to Cuong to head back to the LZ, then realized he was breaking a cardinal rule, that of never going back the way he had come. He didn't have any choice now, though; it was the only way out. Suddenly, as if on cue, whistles joined the clattering of bamboo, followed by the sounds of excited voices.

'Holy shit,' Walden groaned, and the team quit trying to be quiet, frantically beginning to fight the underbrush, lunging toward the landing zone. The brambles and vines, hanging from the trees and twisting over the ground, wrapped around them like fingers. 'Covey, they're blowing whistles and coming straight down the hill after us.' Walden gasped the message as he bulled his way through the brush. The crisp sound of the Claymore exploding behind them quickly died in the insulating jungle. Walden knew Covey was talking to him but he couldn't hear with his breath coming in short loud gasps. *God, my head is going to fly open. God, I don't want to die.*

When the team burst into the elephant grass at the edge of the LZ, the shouts and whistles and clacking bamboo suddenly stopped. The silence lasted two heartbeats, then came the disjointed rustling of leaves and snapping of twigs as the NVA began creeping down toward them. Walden hurriedly slipped off his rucksack and tossed the radio handset to Forrest.

'Talk to them,' he panted, then moved in a low crouch back up the slope a few yards to where Cuong and Pau were putting out Claymores, placing them in front of trees to protect the team from the back-blast. Other team members fanned out into a hasty perimeter, peering nervously uphill toward the sounds of the NVA moving closer. The helicopters were at least forty-five minutes out. Walden could smell death in the stagnant air. A part of his mind remembered the way the first attacking wave had sounded in the Ia Drang Valley, four years before. He heard the same sound now; different, but the same. He figured the team could hold the NVA off for twenty minutes if they didn't take any casualties during the initial assault. *We've had it. Right here is where the ticket gets punched.* He was so certain that he became calm. There was nothing left to do but make the bastards pay for it.

A few yards to his right, Baby-san was curled up behind Playboy, clutching his weapon and looking around wildly. When he saw Walden, his stricken expression shifted into a wide grin. Walden motioned to him to spread out, and pointed out a tree a few feet away that he should get behind. Baby-san bobbed his head in understanding, the smile frozen on his childlike face. Before Walden could move, Baby-san stood straight up and took a step. Walden saw the results of the bullet before he heard the shot. Bits of canvas blew into the air as the slug sliced through the shoulder strap of Baby-san's rucksack, penetrated his neck, and erupted out the other side in a stream of red. The small boy pitched sideways and slid headfirst down to Walden as a wall of gunfire exploded around them. Walden was paralyzed, staring into Baby-san's flickering eyelids. For an instant they stopped fluttering and opened wide as a spasm shook the body. The brown beautiful eyes filled with amazement, the mouth closed. Then there was only a corpse.

The jarring explosion from a Claymore slapped Walden's

mind back into place. Spinning away from the body, he blinked at a world completely in chaos. Pau and Cuong lay in a growing pile of shell casings, firing hysterically into the bobbing and breaking foliage.

'Waste the motherfuckers,' Walden screamed, flipping his weapon to automatic and firing at a cluster of muzzle flashes shaking the leaves just in front of him. Several bullets chewed up the soft tree pulp just above his head, spraying him with slivers of wood. Rolling behind a small deadfall, he huddled down, changing magazines as Pau, Cuong, and Playboy crawled up beside him. Playboy held two Claymore detonators in his hands.

'Blow the damn things,' Walden yelled, frantically pushing his CAR-15 over the top of the log and blindly spraying it back and forth. The exploding mines shook the ground, and created a rain of small branches and leaves. The volume of fire was suddenly reduced to sporadic chatter.

In the pause that the mines had afforded, Walden gestured to his group to fall back to Forrest and the others. Walden and Pau grabbed Baby-san's shirt collar as Cuong picked up his weapon. Playboy covered their retreat. They tugged and dragged the body through the brush to where the others were barricaded behind a large snag.

'Ah, Jesus,' Forrest groaned at the sight of Baby-san's bloody form flopping over the ground. It looked as though the group were coming out of hell, bringing the sour smell of cordite and dying with the hazy white smoke.

'Give me the radio,' Walden rasped, pulling Baby-san's body over the log. 'Get the map off him, and make sure he doesn't have any bad shit on him either.' Walden took the handset from Forrest. The little people spread hand grenades and magazines in front of them in anticipation of the next attack. Then they began to claw shallow depressions in the soft dirt.

'Covey, this is Freedom Son. We got one Soap Sud KIA. They're massing above us now for another attack. We need some air support bad. Over.'

'Roger that,' the reply came back instantly. 'Fast movers approaching your location. Stand by with shiny. Over.'

Walden looked up into the sky for a sign of the jets. He fumbled in his side pants pocket for the signal mirror. The only sound he could hear was the high-pitched ringing in his ears. The tension increased as the area sank into numbed silence.

'Why did I let myself flunk out of college?' Forrest whispered, pushing his lips into a faint smile. It was the way it came out that made it so funny, the way Forrest shook his head in disbelief. It struck Walden as one of the funniest things he had ever heard. He tried to muffle the laugh that squeaked between his fingers as he pressed his hand to his mouth, but that only made it worse. Forrest began to laugh right out loud. The little people spun their heads around and stared at the two of them, then looked at each other incredulously, then back at the crazy Americans. The unrestrained laughter rolled through the jungle, then slowly died away. The silence was complete, and for a long time nothing moved.

Both Cuong and Pau saw the NVA with the B-40 rocket launcher step from behind a tree. They fired simultaneously, the bullets hitting the birdcage-sized chest at nearly point-blank range. The soldier had only one rocket, the fact made obvious as his body turned completely around, arms twirling out like a dancer's. One end of the launcher bounced on the ground, then the weapon leaned against the tree as if propped there deliberately. The NVA flopped once.

The jungle froze again, and the silence was dazzling in its completeness. Then the drone of fat, shiny blue flies whirling above Baby-san's face marred the stillness. Walden untied the cravat from around his head and draped it over Baby-san's upturned face. The ground trembled, the tremor followed instantaneously by a deafening boom as two F-4 Phantom jets went streaking overhead.

'Hoooo shit, the cavalry has arrived,' Walden yelled, electrified by the sudden appearance of the jets. He handed the signal mirror to Forrest as he brought the radio handset to his ear. A jet pilot's voice came over the radio, calm and clear.

'Freedom Son, this is Fast Mover Six. We need visual on you. Over.'

'Look for shiny,' Walden whispered as the little people began pulling out marking panels and popping them open and closed over their heads. 'Panels too,' he added.

Forrest rolled over on his back, peering through the small window hole in the middle of the mirror and sighting on the green-and-brown camouflage cowling of one of the jets circling back.

'Okay, I see your shiny and panels,' the voice said. 'Where do you want us to start working? Over.'

'Mover, this is Son. Request air strike at One Six Five degrees from thirty yards above my position, or closer if you can do it without killing us. Over.'

'I give manicures with this baby,' the pilot said. 'Cover your ass, we're rolling in hot.' Then the air broke into screaming bits as the NVA attacked.

The volume of the assault told Walden it was the do-or-die attack he had been expecting. He tossed the handset to Forrest, took a deep breath, and lifted his head up from behind the log. Where the Claymores had blown tunnels through the brush, Walden could see soldiers coming down the slope. Some were only ten yards away. *The assholes are firing ten feet over our heads.* Bullets whirled harmlessly above them.

The team unleashed a murderous barrage into the descending line, then snapped back behind the log as the first bright flashes of jet cannon fire crinkled the air. A pounding roar went off inside Walden's head as the shells began walking up the slope.

Louisiana team huddled together behind the log as the second F-4 made its run. The cadence of the strike began in a sharp, crackling roar, then diminished in volume as the shells moved up the slope. Walden lifted his head again and peered over the log as the last shells were exploding high up the mountain. Branches hung by thin strips of bark in the haze. A sapling shifted quietly and fell like an old dance step through the thicket. Walden heard the chugging rumble of helicopters and jerked his head around to stare at two Cobra gunships swooping down on them. Brown smoke mushroomed around the rocket pods of the ships as they fired. Walden's eyes twitched as he watched the black streak of the rockets speeding toward them.

'Oh, God,' he said, as the rockets split the air overhead and detonated in a blur on the hillside. The blast shook the flesh on the sides of his face. Bile rose in his throat and he heard a moaning, hurt sound coming through a wall of bad-tasting chemicals. He realized that the sound was coming from him. His eyes fluttered open, then closed, then open, staring into the blue sky. A strong hand gripped his shirt collar. He struggled against it until his mind told him it was all right.

'Oh, man, oh, man.' Walden coughed, looking at Forrest's looming face.

'Jesus Christ,' Forrest screamed as the sound of the helicopters coming in on another run filled the air. Throwing himself over Walden, Forrest frantically waved a bright scarlet-and-orange marking panel over his head. The continuous roar of Mini-Guns, creating a blizzard of bullets that churned up the side of the wood line, was shattering. The trees and bushes, whipped by thousands of bullets, shuddered as several leaves and twigs showered down like confetti. Red tracers struck the rocks and rico-chetted in fragmented sparks into the green foliage. The Cobras lifted, rolling over on their sides to circle back. Walden untangled himself from Forrest, lurching to his knees.

'Get on the horn. Tell them to stop that shit,' Walden stammered. Forrest patted the grass around him, looking for the handset. Walden dizzily looked around. The slope was bathed in smoke and small flickering fires. Walden tried to suck air, then vomited.

As he finished heaving, he heard a faint gurgling from

103

the other side of the log. He quickly counted heads. Tang was missing. Rolling over the top of the log, Walden crawled to the sound. He found Tang on his back, half covered with dirt. A frothy stream of blood, mixed with bits of rice, ran out of the corner of his mouth. The front of his shirt was tattered and soaked with blood. His eyes were open. Walden tore the plastic wrapper off a field dressing and put it over the hole in Tang's chest. A tremor shook Tang's legs; his delicate hands, palm inward, twisted in spasms toward his forearms. His head began to lift and Walden moved his hand to keep him still, but Tang fell back onto the dirt, his eyes clouding over.

Walden dragged the body and weapon back to the log, then stripped the pockets of the map and other items. No one spoke or seemed affected as they watched Walden take the web gear off Tang as though undressing a drunk friend.

'The pickup ships are coming,' Forrest whispered urgently. Walden handed out the remainder of Tang and Baby-san's ammo to the rest of the little people.

They watched the jungle with renewed apprehension as the first slick, blades popping, came speeding down. Walden's leg muscles tensed for the sprint to the ship. At the moment the helicopter reached them, a hail of gunfire exploded along their right flank. It caught the chopper broadside, twenty feet in the air. It bucked and lurched and pieces of metal fell to the ground. The ship rose up on its tail and reeled backward. Slowly it twisted sideways and then fell, crashing into the scrub brush forty yards down the slope.

Walden felt his insides shiver while his outer skin went hot as he watched the helicopter drop out of sight.

'Call in some fire over there,' Walden said tightly, taking off his rucksack so Forrest would have the radio. 'I'm taking Pau with me. Keep the rest here with you. If there are any survivors, I'll fire a pen flare and you come down.'

Walden and Pau plunged through the eight-foot-high elephant grass. Before they reached the downed chopper, they could smell JP-4 fuel and hear hissing. They nearly fell

104

into the ravine holding the wreckage. The broken ship was on its side, resting among rocks and small bushes, the main rotor blade torn away. Looking through the Plexiglas windshield of the cockpit, they could see the two pilots hanging limp in their harnesses. Walden also saw wavering heat trails rising off the engine housing, and the crushed upper torso of one of the door gunners. Across the back of the flak jacket was grease-penciled, SHORT TIMER. Pau shook Walden's shoulder and pointed. Walden followed the finger, and there was the door gunner he had talked to on the way in. The man's legs were pinned beneath a strut, and Walden could see the large white peace symbol on the side of the flight helmet. He was starting down the ravine when Pau yanked him back. A gush of flames enveloped the tail of the ship. Walden's chest constricted as he saw the door gunner beneath the strut begin to move. The man started to pull at his legs, hopelessly flattened by the weight of the helicopter. His hands then tore at his helmet until it was off his head. The flames wavered a moment before they began to spread quickly around the magnesium cowling. The man began to scream as the flames, nurtured by the hydraulic fluids, rapidly moved toward the fuel tank. Walden stared. He knew the ship would explode. He knew the door gunner would be burned alive. The screaming grew into a hysterical wail as the rubber soles on the man's boots began to melt; Walden could see the blond hair begin to crinkle. Walden also knew what he had to do. First, the man had to hold still for an instant. At the top of his lungs, so that he could be heard above the mounting sound of the flames, Walden screamed, 'Hey, man. Can you dig it?'

The door gunner snapped his head around and looked up the side of the ravine. Walden had already sighted – he pulled the trigger. Pau pulled him away just as the flames ran down over the gas tank. Walden was almost crying as they stumbled and fell, moving back up the hill. Then the ground shook as the helicopter exploded, throwing a rolling fireball into the air.

The camouflage grease on Walden's face was streaked

and wet when they reached the team. He and Pau dropped next to Forrest as two Phantom jets streaked overhead, pounding the wood line with 250-pound bombs. Walden took little notice of the explosions as he took the handset from Forrest.

'All KIA on Apple Crate,' Walden said calmly into the mouthpiece.

There was a short pause, then Pappy Lindell's voice followed a brief rush of static. 'Roger. We got another ship coming in for you. Hang on, buddy. Over.'

'Also be advised one more Soap Sud KIA. Over.'

'Okay, we're going to get you out. Old Pappy never let you down before.'

'I'm going to get us a fuckin' prisoner,' Walden said, handing the handset back to Forrest. 'After all this we're going to have something to show for it.' He nudged Pau and in a moment they were up and over the log. The air strikes had done a job. As they moved up the slope, they saw bodies all over the ground. Walden caught movement out of the corner of his eye. Pau slipped sideways and quickly moved to a lone figure sitting against a tree. Pau kicked away an AK-47 as Walden caught up with him. The man looked up, his eyes glazed over and murky brown. His lower lip was bleeding where he was biting into it. He held his right leg, which was wet with blood. He began to mumble and toss his head from side to side. Walden reached down, grabbing a fistful of shirt, and yanked the man to his feet. A scream seemed to come out of the ground as the North Vietnamese twisted out of Walden's hand and fell back. Walden didn't blink when he saw the femur protruding from the thigh. He grabbed the man again and began dragging him down the slope. The prisoner vomited while they were pulling him to the log. They flopped him over the deadfall, then Walden rolled him on his side so he wouldn't strangle on his own vomit, and handcuffed him.

'We got one. We got one. Get us the fuck out of here,' Forrest said into the handset.

Walden threw on his rucksack and with the others crouched, waiting.

The second Huey appeared, flaring out just above them, both door gunners fired continuous bursts into the trees. Empty shell casings from the M-60 machine guns rained on the team as the tube skids on the chopper swung down to chest level. In a blur of motion the team was diving through the doorways, the prisoner being tossed on like a sack of feed. With full power the chopper rose into the air, banking sideways over the smoke rising from the helicopter wreckage. Walden let the cool steel plating on the floor push against his cheek as the gravitational force of the rising ship pushed him down. He felt he was being flown to heaven. He didn't move until one of the door gunners shook his shoulder.

'You okay, man? Jesus Christ, I never saw no shit like this, man. I mean, you okay, man?' Walden looked into the face of a kid. A faint downy mustache, all but transparent, graced the round smooth face.

'I'm fine. Thanks for bringing us out.' Walden lifted his arms out of the rucksack straps. The door gunners began moving among the team sprawled on the floor, seeing if anyone was hurt. No one was wounded except the prisoner. Walden moved to the NVA. The man was where he had been thrown, on his side, behind the pilot's seat. For the first time Walden noticed the blood on his back, and the black-edged hole. He rolled the prisoner over onto his back.

'Son of a bitch,' he said, when he saw the slackness in the face. He slid over to where Forrest was staring straight ahead and drawing deep breaths.

'The asshole is dead,' Walden said.

'Good,' Forrest said, drawing another breath then holding it. After a time he let it out slowly, then drew his legs up and put his head on his knees. He didn't look up again until they approached the launch site at Quang Tri.

CHAPTER TEN

WALDEN LISTENED to the whirling hum of the small cassette player as he rewound the tape for the fifth time. A moment later the first words of Bob Dylan's 'Just Like A Woman' came from the tiny recorder sitting on the sandbags. He leaned back against a post supporting the tin sheeting above the bunker and quietly began to sing along.

'Nobody feels any pain, tonight as I stand inside the rain.'
After a few bars he stopped singing and watched the waves roll onto the beach. Pau, sleeping on the concrete dome of the bunker, stirred, pulled the poncho liner tighter around him, then settled back down. Cuong mumbled in his sleep. Walden wondered why they never did that when they were on the ground.

He checked his watch and saw that it was time for the hourly situation report. He turned off the cassette player and picked up the radio handset.

'Sturgeon Renown, Sturgeon Renown, this is Key Graduate, Key Graduate, commo check. Over.'

'Roger, Graduate, hear you loud and clear. How me? Over.'

'This is me. Roger, hear you same. Nothing happening. Over.'

'Roger, Graduate. Negative further here. Out.'

Walden chuckled as he put the handset down. It was damn typical to get put on guard duty the night before they started their stand-down time. He didn't mind, though. The two amphetamine capsules he had taken a few hours before made his head feel pleasant and his mood warm. The camp behind him was quiet and dark. A breeze gusted off the ocean, tugging at the edges of the poncho liners the little people were rolled in. Walden switched the cassette player back on as Forrest clambered up the side of the bunker.

'I couldn't find the Iron Butterfly tape anywhere,'

Forrest said, tossing a handful of cassettes next to the machine. 'I think Michigan Team has it. You make the commo check yet?'

'Roger that. You get the j's?'

'Yup. You want to fire one of them up?' Forrest pulled cans of Coke out of his pockets.

Headlights splashed over the far corner bunker as a jeep drove slowly up to it. 'Wait a minute,' Walden said, pointing. 'Deacon is trying to catch somebody sleeping.' They watched as the lights went out, and the black silhouette of the jeep crept toward them. 'Can you believe this guy?' Walden reached over and turned the player off as the jeep neared their position.

'He's going to blind us with those headlights when he gets up here,' Forrest said dryly. They watched as the dark outline of the jeep crept closer. When it was twenty feet away, the high beams were turned on, illuminating the bunker and the men on it.

'Turn out those lights, you fuckin' idiot,' Walden yelled. He suppressed a giggle as the lights went off and the vehicle jerked to a halt. 'I love it,' Walden whispered to Forrest as Major Deacon stumbled over something in the sand and fell against the bottom of the bunker.

'What did you say?' Deacon asked crisply, irritation tightening his voice.

'Oh, it's you, sir. I didn't know you had guard tonight,' Walden said.

'Well, I don't,' Deacon answered defensively. 'I'm checking the perimeter. There have been reports that the R-20 Battalion is operating in the area.'

'What's new about that? They've been operating in this area since the French were here.'

'We have some hard intel that we might get hit tonight,' Deacon said. 'So just be alert.' There was a forced importance in his words.

'I wish they would hit us. I'd love to fight from a concrete pillbox for once.' Walden laughed. 'If you see any of those guys from the dread R-20 Battalion, send them over.'

'Tell them we've got an M-60 up here that just loves to play rock and roll,' Forrest added.

'You two are always so damn cool. Always ready with the smart mouth. Just keep your goddamn eyes open.' Deacon turned and walked back to the jeep.

'No problem, sir,' Walden yelled after him. Turning to Forrest, he said, 'Let's do a number.' He watched the jeep bounce down the perimeter road into the blackness. The inside of his mouth tasted sour.

Forrest lit the joint and turned the cassette player back on. 'Those green hornets are really nice, huh?' he said, smiling, referring to the amphetamines currently doing zigzags in their blood. He handed the bomber to Walden.

'Oh, yeah,' Walden said. 'The best drug we have is issued by the army.' They traded tokes a couple of times. 'There used to be a saying that all you got when you reported into Recon Company was a CAR-15, a thousand green hornets, and a body bag.'

'You ever take any when you've been on the ground?'

'No. It's strictly recreational.'

'Jeez, I can't believe they give us these things.' Forrest giggled. 'I feel like I could break the four-minute mile, like I'm going to start glowing or something any second.'

'Better living through chemistry,' Walden said. He took a deep breath and lit a cigarette.

'Do you think we'll really get hit?'

'Shit,' Walden said. 'If they tell you that you're going to get hit, forget it. The night I'm going to be sleeping on the bunkers is when they'll tell me we're not going to get hit.'

'What did they tell you last August when they did that number here?'

'Nothing,' Walden said, cupping his hand around the cigarette as he took a drag. 'We didn't know anything was happening until they started to push the air conditioners out of the windows and throw satchel charges into the barracks. When the guys ran out, they just shot them down.'

'Damn,' Forrest said, looking up into the black sky.

'What did you do?' He looked at Walden, then back at the night.

Walden shrugged. 'I was playing poker in the barracks up in the Headquarters area. It was like one in the morning and the game was breaking up. We heard this shooting by the front gate. Everyone heard it, but we all just kind of stood around looking at each other. We heard this pounding sound come from the other end of the building and then the air conditioner in the window falls out and this canvas bag comes flying into the room and falls on one of the bunks. Somebody, I don't remember who, had the presence of mind to throw it back out the window. Then it got really strange. This outrageous explosion goes off at the end of the barracks and everybody starts running out of the room, falling over each other to get outside, right? Man, you should've seen it.' Walden shook his head. 'Then the charge that was thrown back out the window goes off and blows in half the wall. I was partway to the hall door and these guys in front of me start falling down as soon as they get out the door. Everybody starts shooting guns through the doorway and all this shit is flying everywhere. I just ducked back into what was left of the room and went through this hole in the wall. All I could see when I got outside were these grenade flashes where our commo bunker used to be. With all these shadows running around, you couldn't tell who was an American or what.'

'Damn,' Forrest repeated. 'I was on the A-team down in the delta and we never heard a word about it. Like nothing. There were seventeen in-group people killed that night?'

'Yeah, the most ever lost at one time.' Walden turned to watch a flare pop above Marble Mountain. A machine gun rattled briefly, followed by silence. They watched and listened for more firing to erupt. After a few minutes Walden turned back and lit another cigarette. Forrest took the smoke and lit one for himself off it.

'Some funny things happened, though,' Walden said, and began to laugh. 'This guy Steele – he got killed before you got here – was in his hooch, the one where Maine Team is now.

He hears all this shit going off, and he kicks open his door and throws a grenade out.' Walden started to laugh harder.

'So what happened?' Forrest was interested in a story he hadn't heard before.

'There was this sapper coming up the steps, just when he throws the grenade. Steele, man,' Walden said affectionately, 'hit that little fucker right between the running lights. He told me later that the gook dropped like he had been poleaxed.' They both began to laugh. 'The best part, though,' Walden gasped, 'is that Steele forgot to pull the pin.' They had to hold each other, the laughter was so hard.

They quieted slowly and just looked over the beach. After a bit Walden said, almost to himself, 'These green hornets really make you talk a lot.' He took the can of Coke Forrest offered.

'Let me make the commo check. Okay?' Forrest asked.

'Knock yourself out.' Walden stood up and carefully stepped over Pau and walked to the edge of the bunker. 'They make you piss a lot too.'

Forrest was just finishing the radio check when Walden walked back. 'Tell them we're going to fire a jack-off flare,' Walden said, picking one up from a pile next to a crate of grenades. As Forrest informed net control of the firing, Walden prepared the hand-held illumination round. 'I love these little suckers.' He giggled. 'Here we go.' He struck the bottom of the tube with the palm of his hand. The flare whooshed up into the dark sky, a trail of sparks marking the trajectory.

'Far goddamn out,' Forrest yelled as the flare popped into life above the breakers, lighting the perimeter wire and the beach with a yellow-green tint. Pau sat up, his weapon in his hand, twisting his head from side to side.

'It's okay, Pau. Just play. Go back to sleep.' Walden made his tone comforting.

'You want to sleep, I be on guard?' Pau asked sleepily.

'No, it's okay. I took a couple of hornets.' Walden patted Pau's shoulder. Pau smiled and nodded before lying back down.

CHAPTER ELEVEN

THE TEAM caught the late-afternoon Blackbird flight to Saigon. When they climbed up the rear ramp of the C-130, Walden saw the metal container holding the prisoner they'd brought back. The container was fastened down with red cargo straps that reminded Walden of the red strips of cloth Pau would tie on the front sight of the weapons and in the top left buttonhole of their fatigue shirts when they were on a mission. Walden and Forrest sat down opposite the coffin container. The little people chose seats away from it.

'That's the dude?' Forrest asked, nodding toward the box.

'They're going to do an autopsy on him in Saigon. This major told me that they can find out all kinds of things from a body. Science and technology.' Walden closed his eyes.

The black airplane rolled onto the takeoff apron, revving engines. Walden fastened the seatbelt across his lap without opening his eyes. He covered his ears and leaned forward toward the bulkhead as the engines screamed. The plane leapt forward as the pilots dropped their feet from the brakes. With his eyes closed Walden felt he was riding a dragster. The plane lifted from the runway and Walden opened his eyes to watch the ground drop away through the half-open tailgate. The cream-colored control tower with the red-checkered belt painted around the bottom receded. As they gained altitude, he could look over the entire airfield. Gray antirocket barriers separated the F-4 Phantom jets and helicopters. Heat waves rose off the blacktop runways. An expression Walden had heard a year or so before popped into his mind as he watched a C-123 lift from the shimmering tar lane below them: War is our business and business is good. He closed his eyes again.

After a brief stop at Kontum the Blackbird delivered the team to Saigon. Walden gathered the little people in front of the Air America terminal as a black pickup truck pulled up to the lowered plane ramp. They watched the gray box loaded onto the back of the truck. No one said anything. *We should have left the man to die in the jungle.*

Pau and Hung stood to one side as Walden gave instructions to the rest of the team – Cuong, Playboy, Cricket, and Lap, the quiet one, who looked like Little Beaver, Red Ryder's sidekick. 'Don't screw up. Be back in Da Nang on the fourth.' They grinned and shuffled around like schoolboys being turned loose on their first class trip. Walden looked at Cuong's grinning face. 'I'm putting you in charge of these guys. So have a good time and don't go AWOL.' They all nodded very sincerely. 'Okay, make it,' Walden said. They grabbed up their rucksacks and began jogging toward the gate, each one turning and waving. 'You got their stuff?' Walden asked Hung, even though he could see that he did. 'I hope they don't mess up,' Walden said to Forrest.

'They'll be all right.' Forrest glanced at Walden. 'They don't have any guns, do they?'

'What do you think, man?' The noise of the street grew as they approached the gate. Forrest looked apprehensive.

'Ah, hell, they'll be fine,' Walden said. 'I just hope they didn't bring any grenades.'

Outside the gate Pau waved down a taxi. It wasn't far to the Chinese area of Cholon, to the families of Baby-san and Tang. Hung gave the driver directions as Walden and Forrest settled back on the plastic-covered seat in the rear. The street boiled with evening life as the cab swerved and jostled its way block by block through the city teeming with people. They passed French-style buildings, the wrought iron balconies giving an ironic flair of elegance to the cracked and peeling walls. In places the plaster had been pockmarked by machine-gun bullets. Shops sat dark and quiet behind accordion steel gates. Shards of glass set in the cement cap on walls glimmered beneath pale streetlights. *Even the walls have thorns.*

The French architecture wavered and lost its place in the last blocks before the dark, squalid alleys of Cholon. Faces of children were caught in the headlights as they crept over the rutted lane. Shacks made of flattened sheets of beer cans and plywood bordered the passage. The sound of children and barking dogs, the smell of fish and urine, flowed into the cab.

'There is Tang's house,' Hung said, pointing at a mud-brick hut with tin roof. The cab stopped next to a drainage ditch. Walden paid the driver and told him to wait. The smell of stagnant water and cooking food filled Walden's nose as they walked to the flimsy plywood door. A streak of yellow light leaked under the door. Pau rapped his knuckles lightly against the door, stepped back, and waited. A wet, gurgling cough came from inside, followed by a brushing of feet across the floor. Hung leaned toward the door and said something, the only part of which Walden understood was Tang's name. The door opened slightly and the face of an old woman peered out.

'He has been wounded, yes?' Her eyes begged for confirmation. Walden glanced at Pau as the woman's face disappeared behind the door. He pushed the door open slowly and walked into the hut. A kerosene lantern sat on a table, and in the thin yellow light Walden watched a skeletal man sit up on a sleeping pallet along the wall. The woman was bent over, clasping and unclasping her hands as she turned in a small circle. The man cleared his throat and spat into a can next to the pallet. He immediately began to cough again. Walden turned to Hung, indicating with a movement of his eyes that he should tell them. He watched the woman start to shake, beaten by each word from Hung. A cry like that from dying squirrels shuddered through her body. She stumbled toward Walden, then lunged, sobbing, grabbing the front of his uniform. He couldn't move as she slid slowly down until she rested at his feet, her small fists

115

beating against his legs. Her husband came off the pallet, wheezing. Leaning over, he drew the woman to her feet. The man spoke to Walden and Forrest in broken English.

'He was last son. We have four. All gone now.' He sounded as though he had resigned himself to this moment long before. Walden and Hung helped him move his wife to the wooden table. The oily smoke from the lamp was making Walden's eyes water.

'Your son was a brave man. He was our friend. We are all sad from the loss. I have money. You take it, his pay, insurance.' Walden felt guilty holding out the thick bundle of piastres. Tang's father lowered his head, avoiding the eyes around him. Walden self-consciously placed the bills on the table. He then put his hand gently on the man's shoulder. 'We must go now. I'm very sorry.' He didn't know what more to say. The others had their eyes either on the floor or the walls. 'Come on, let's go,' he whispered, turning his back on the old couple. The others were outside the door when Walden stopped. 'He didn't suffer. He died quickly. There was no pain.' The words echoed inside the small dwelling. The old man looked up at him, his twisted face shining and wet. He looked so very tired.

'Let's get this other one over with,' Walden said, climbing into the back of the taxi. The driver was sombre now that he knew what they were doing. No one spoke except for Hung giving directions.

The cab stopped in front of a similar hut. Walden could hear a baby crying, and the cries became louder as they approached the shack. When they'd gathered around the door, Hung called out a name, then knocked. The baby stopped crying and Walden could hear voices and small children laughing inside. A young, pretty Vietnamese girl opened the door slightly. She smiled as she recognized Hung and pushed the door open wide, looking around.

'Tot, Tot?' she called playfully, as though Baby-san were hiding. Then she saw their faces and a look of fear flooded through her, washing away her youth.

'Ma, Ma,' she screamed to a woman sitting on the floor

116

holding a baby. The visitors stepped inside. The air was heavy with smoke and the smell of cooking. Hung put down the package containing Baby-san's things and moved to the crying girl. She screamed at him when he tried to put his arm around her.

'You are to blame,' she shouted in English. 'And you,' she said, pointing at Walden. She began to cry in great gulps as she ran to a sleeping pad and threw herself across it. The room filled with crying, shaking voices tumbling over each other, some asking questions Walden couldn't understand. A middle-aged man rose from a cushion by the fireplace. He had only one leg, and hobbled over to Walden on crutches. Specks of saliva flew off the man's lips as he began to curse in Vietnamese. Walden stood before him, his teeth chewing at the inside of his lower lip. The man's voice rose higher and higher and suddenly he swung one of the crutches at Walden, losing his balance and falling partway before Walden caught him. He twisted out of Walden's grasp and fell the rest of the way to the hard, dirt-packed floor. The man looked up, his face contorted with rage. He began to shout again, then broke down, his crying rising until it became a wail. The single light bulb dangling by a frayed cord from the tin ceiling became bright and then faded back as a power surge from a generator rode through the lines.

'Hung, give somebody this money and tell them I'm sorry,' Walden said. He and Forrest quickly strode out, leaving Hung and Pau to try to calm the relatives.

'Goddamn,' Walden said weakly when they got to the taxi. He put his arm on the cab roof and cradled his head. Forrest draped an arm over Walden.

'There wasn't anything you could do, Sam. There wasn't anything any of us could do.'

'You never think of this part,' Walden said. His voice trailed off as he rolled his head back and forth on his arm. Forrest patted him on the back and moved out to the middle of the road. A group of children gathered around, begging for cigarettes and food. Forrest shook the cigarettes from a pack and passed them out as they jumped up and down, grabbing.

'You number one, GI. You number hucking one,' they yelled.

'You bet,' Forrest said, throwing the crumpled pack into the ditch. He began to untangle the small arms and legs that clung to him. 'No have any more, no have,' he shouted as they began trying to get into his pockets. They continued to grab. '*Di di mau*,' he finally said, pushing them away. They scurried off a short distance and then began to yell.

'You number ten. You number hucking ten, GI.'

'Grateful little bastards,' Forrest said, coming back to the cab where Walden was now leaning, arms folded across his chest.

'Let's get drunk,' Walden said, glancing at his watch and then at the hut. Just then a sheet of light spread across the rutted road. Hung stepped out of the hut.

'You can go now. We stay here awhile. They are very upset Baby-san sent them money, you know.'

'I'll see you back in Da Nang,' Walden said, and he and Forrest climbed into the cab. 'Tu Do Street,' Walden told the driver. The car jerked away from the hut and slowly bounced down the narrow road.

'Let's go to the Sporting Bar first.' Forrest rubbed his hands together as if he were trying to start a fire. 'Hot damn Vietnam,' he exclaimed, fighting the dark mood that had fallen over Walden. The taxi drove along the waterfront and then turned up Tu Do Street. Neon lights glowed purple and red, turning the people churning over the sidewalk the color of raw meat. Soldiers, sailors, bar girls, pimps, prostitutes, money changers, beggars, old women selling flowers – all mingled together in a dirty stream that overflowed into the street. Young men whizzed through the traffic on motorbikes. There was a hurried intensity to the movement along the sidewalks and street. They seemed to Walden to be searching, looking for something important.

He wished he hadn't come. He didn't want to talk to anyone. He especially didn't want to go through the rituals in the bars, with the conniving bar girls trying to fleece the last Saigon tea from lonely, drunk GIs, playing their femaleness against the urgency of fear. With a continuous flow of tea one could forget. What Walden disliked most was the masquerade that each had to play in order to make the encounter something other than an embarrassment. It was like the false fronts of a Hollywood prop town, where everything looks real until you walk through the door. With tea girls there was always an empty lot behind the door. But one went through one door after another.

The cab idled next to the line of cars against the curb. Walden got out and Forrest paid the driver. A middle-aged woman, her face caked with make-up, stepped out of the people stream and touched Walden's arm. Walden looked at the dyed hair that somehow had become orange, at the mouth smeared a bright red, at the hollow, empty eyes.

'Forget it,' he snapped, pulling his arm from the woman's grasp. He didn't look back until he could feel her move away.

'God, what was that?' Forrest asked, watching the orange fuzz of the woman's hair floating back into the crowd.

They pushed their way through the flow until Walden saw the neon sign over the door of the Sporting Bar. Flying bugs battered the glowing red tubing, dazzled by the light and heat. The front door of the bar was propped open by a chair, exchanging the stale cigarette smoke and smell of spilled beer for the exhaust fumes of the street.

Several girls sitting on a bench against the wall jumped up and raced toward them as they came through the doorway.

'You buy me drinky?' they all shouted at once, grabbing and pulling on them from different directions.

'Stop it,' Walden flared, pulling his arms from the clutching fingers. The girls stepped back, smiles fading, eyes clouding over.

'What matter with you?' one of the girls asked accusingly, placing her hands on her hips. 'You crazy?'

Walden stared at her for a second, then turned to an empty booth against the back wall. Forrest slid into the opposite seat and looked at him.

'Sam, we're supposed to be down here to have some fun,' Forrest said. 'Come on. I'll buy you a beer.'

Walden spread a smile across his face. 'You're right. Sorry I screwed up a romance for you.'

'Well, the night's still young.'

'I don't like people pulling on me,' Walden said, and ordered beer from a girl that had ventured to the booth. 'I got half a notion to catch a flight back to Da Nang tomorrow. I'm getting tired of paying money so someone will talk to me.'

'Give me a break.' Forrest laughed. 'How many teas have you bought in the last six months?'

'Not very damn many.'

'That's what I mean. They're always swooning over you anyway.'

'Sure, you give them money and they fall in love.' The girl brought the beers and Forrest paid, giving her a hundred-piastre tip. They both swallowed deeply from the brown bottles, and before the girl had moved very far, Forrest ordered two more.

'What about Coop?' Forrest asked. 'I've been in country a long time, too, and I've never seen anything like that.' A real smile formed slowly on Walden's face. The girl returned with the beer. Forrest paid again and told her to bring four more. The girl stared at him for a moment then hurried off.

'Unconditional surrender,' Forrest toasted, lifting the bottle and clicking it against Walden's.

'Total victory,' Walden laughed.

An hour later Walden was peeling the label off his seventh beer while trying not to listen to 'Tiny Bubbles' being played for the tenth time on the jukebox at the front of the barroom. There was no pretence of drinking for enjoyment. They were drinking to get drunk. Walden tipped the bottle to his mouth and froze. He slowly put the

120

bottle down, still staring at the girl who'd just walked in and sat down.

'There you go, Jerry, the queen of the hop.' Walden nodded toward the girl. 'You better police her up quick.'

'Oh, my God, I've been hit,' Forrest moaned when he turned to look. He was up and out of the seat before Walden could say anything more. He moved as if someone had dropped a live grenade on the table. Walden watched as he eased up next to the girl and began talking. After a few minutes he led her back to the booth. Walden's eyes took in the tight, faded blue jeans and the red-and-white checkered blouse tied in a knot across her front. *Damn. This one is something.*

'My name is Dominica,' she said, smiling down at Walden. Her English carried only a faint accent. Walden stared as she and Forrest slid into the booth. 'What is your name?' she asked softly, her eyes direct on Walden's face. Her beauty, her certainty, made Walden feel vulnerable. He didn't say anything. She watched him for a second before she turned to Forrest. 'What's his name?'

'Sam,' Forrest answered. 'He doesn't talk much.' He kicked Walden under the table.

'How you doing?' Walden said, pained into speech. 'Been in Vietnam very long?'

She began to laugh. It was very pretty. 'I stay now twenty-two years,' she said.

'Oh, you're with Special Forces too,' Walden said, and Forrest broke up. The sight of Forrest shaking with laughter triggered Walden too. When his stomach began to hurt, he realized that he hadn't really laughed for weeks. Forrest was trying to catch his breath. He would just manage to get himself under control, then look at Walden and start all over. Walden started to wonder if he himself would ever be able to stop as his stomach muscles tightened painfully. Finally the laughter ebbed, and they sagged weakly in the booth. The relief was exhausting. Walden ordered more beer.

Hours later Walden was leaning against the side of the

121

seat, slowly working on a whiskey and water. The girl and Forrest had been talking intimately for the last half hour, cuddled up across from him. Walden didn't want to think about anything. He didn't want any complications.

'Hey, Jer,' he said thickly. 'I'm going to split. I'll see you over at Tommy's Bar tomorrow. Okay?'

'You all right?' Forrest asked, briefly turning away from Dominica.

'Sure, I'm fine. I'll see you tomorrow.' He nodded to the girl as he got up from the booth.

Outside the crowds had thinned. He walked a short way before stepping into an alley. He swayed into the darkness until he felt comfortably concealed, then lit a joint. Finding a broken wooden crate, he propped it against a brick building and sat down. The night felt soft and warm around him. As he slowly toked on the joint, he looked back to where the walls met the street, which seemed to be glowing. Walden smiled and took another hit. He watched a figure of a man dart into the shadows of the entrance and throw up. Another form came up next to the sick man.

'You okay, Jimmy?' the voice asked, amused.

'Just gimme a minute,' the sick man stammered, then started to vomit again. After minutes of retching and cursing the two men staggered back into the light and were gone.

'Weird,' Walden said to the darkness. He looked up along the canyon walls of the buildings and saw the night sky. Even in the haze of the lighted city the stars could be seen. He thought of the nights on the ground when he would look at the sky through the leaves. His mind tightened automatically when the thought formed. He pushed himself up from the makeshift couch and took a last drag from the joint. He looked at the light at the entrance, dropped the butt, and put it out with a pivot of his boot. '*Nobody feels any pain*,' he sang under his breath as he staggered back out. '*Tonight as I stand inside the rain*.'

The late night streets had taken on a mercantile sexuality. Walden watched the prostitutes standing in small

122

clusters chanting at passing GIs. Their tightly clothed bodies swayed deliberately in the milky glow of the early-morning street. Walden debated a few minutes as he surveyed the girls on the sidewalk. He didn't want to have to worry about catching something. He headed down the street, ignoring the calls from the whores, and turned into the first entrance that had a massage and steambath sign over the door. Once inside, he stared up a dimly lit flight of stairs that ended in front of a closed door. Walden changed his mind several times as he climbed the steps.

An old mama-san, leafing through the magazine, sat behind a field desk. A white sheet covered the doorway behind her.

'You want massagie?' the woman asked.

'How much for a blowjob?' Walden asked as he pulled out his wallet.

'Two thousand piastre, ten dolla GI money,' she answered. Walden hesitated for a moment, then handed the woman the money. The woman yelled over her shoulder. A moment later a second woman, wearing a white cotton blouse and shorts, pulled back the sheet and indicated with her finger that Walden should follow. She led him down an aisle between two rows of cloth screens. It reminded Walden of a hospital ward. As they walked past the openings, a single bed inside each cubicle could be seen. Walden felt a slight drumming in his head as the woman turned into the last slot against the far wall. It was like the others: a single army cot with a white sheet thrown over it and a flattened pillow lying at the head. A couple of towels and a glass of water had been placed under the bed.

'This is a class operation you got here,' Walden said, unbuckling his belt. The woman looked at him, a vacant gaze clouding her eyes, and motioned to him to lie down. Her expression did not change when Walden pulled the .22 pistol with the silencer out of his waistband and tossed it on the cot. He lay down, staring at the ceiling. The woman, with robotic motions, tugged the fatigue pants down over his hips. She tossed her black hair back over her shoulder and lowered her head. *She's like a zombie.* He felt the warm wetness of her mouth close around him. The cobwebs and shadows on the ceiling swirled and swayed. A horn honked down on the street. Someone yelled and then all was quiet save for labored breathing coming from beyond the partition. At the far end of the room Walden heard a Vietnamese girl's angry voice.

'Goddamn it. Gimme a break, will you?'

Walden closed his eyes and hoped it wouldn't take long. He thought of Betty, thought of her holding him, but it didn't work. It was too much of a fantasy. He thought of a girl he had spent the night with in Da Nang a couple of months before. He remembered the feeling of their sliding together in the perspiration of the evening, of her body, smooth and firm beneath the touch of his hands. The orgasm rushed from his loins and he was relieved it was over. He opened his eyes and looked at the woman bowed between his thighs as the tremors subsided. She lifted her head, turned, and nonchalantly spit the sperm against the wall. Stunned, Walden looked at the wall, and for the first time saw the number of wet trails that had run down and collected in small pools on the dusty floorboards. He almost knocked the woman over as he swung his legs off the cot. She spit again as he quickly pulled his pants up and fastened his belt. A queasy, disgusted feeling lined his stomach as he watched the woman take a drink of water from the glass and spit that into a tin can he hadn't seen before. He replaced the pistol, and for a split second thought of the favour he could do the woman. He heard her gargling more water as he walked down the corridor. Back on the street, he hailed a cab.

'Take me to a hotel,' he said. He hoped the empty feeling inside would go away soon.

CHAPTER TWELVE

THE NEXT DAY Walden sat in Tommy's Bar, sipping beer and watching the dust particles float in the sunlight flooding through the open doorway. The girl next to him was giggling and playing cards across the table with the bar mama-san. She discreetly fondled Walden's crotch beneath the table. A sudden turbulence sent the dust motes into swirling flight as Forrest stepped through the doorway. He tipped his head forward, lowering his sunglasses to the tip of his nose, and peered into the shadows of the bar. Walden just sat and smiled, watching Forrest squint and probe into the corners of the bar for a sign of him. After a few moments Forrest finally spotted him.

'Sam, you've got to come with me,' Forrest said, with excitement in his voice. 'That girl, Dominica, the one I was with last night, well, she's got a sister.'

'Hey, calm down, man. I got a sister too. It happens,' Walden said dreamily. 'Sit down. Let's get fucked up.'

Forrest shook his head. 'You don't understand, man. She has a sister, and she wants to meet you.'

Walden looked up at Forrest and tried not to look bored. 'I got her,' he said, nodding at the girl whose hidden hand was groping him.

'Forget her!' Forrest was getting a bit shrill. 'Come on, you've got to meet his girl.' Walden looked at his table partner, then back at Forrest. Shrugging, he stood up.

'Where you go?' the girl yelped, looking at Walden with real dislike.

'Hell if I know,' Walden said, dropping lighter and cigarettes into his side pocket. 'This better be good,' he warned, following Forrest out of the bar.

Stepping out into the sunlight, Walden convulsed, throwing his hands up to cover his eyes. 'Oh, my God, we're being nuked.' He bent over and covered his head.

'Come on. Quit screwing around,' Forrest said, obviously getting angry. Walden elaborately fitted the beret on his head, standing in the middle of the sidewalk, as people flowed around him. He pulled down on the flash, centering it over his left eye. Two people, not used to someone's blocking the sidewalk, bounced off Walden, then were caught up in the colorful current again.

'Come on, Sam. Knock it off. They're waiting for us now.'

'Okay, okay.' Walden gave in. 'But I'm thinking, what the hell am I doing leaving a perfectly good bar that doesn't play "Tiny Bubbles" every other song, coming out into this furnace, people knocking into me, just to see some broad in another goddamn bar.'

They crossed the street and Forrest looked Walden up and down. 'How much you been drinking? You're totally screwed, huh?' Walden's giggle answered the question better than words. 'Ah, man, not now,' Forrest grumbled, steering Walden as they moved down the sidewalk to the Sporting Bar.

'You told me we were down here to have fun. I'm having fun,' Walden said, as he tried to light a cigarette and keep pace with Forrest at the same time. 'Besides, it's almost two o'clock.' Walden stopped in the middle of the sidewalk, lit the cigarette, and then yelled after Forrest, 'You want to smoke a joint?'

Forrest whirled and came back to Walden. 'Sam, this isn't what you think. These aren't regular bar girls.' He talked very slowly and quietly, as if he were explaining football to little girls. 'This isn't jungle rules time, Sam. It's like the senior prom, man. Remember that.' Forrest paused. 'You're not going to believe this,' he said, putting his hand on Walden's shoulder. 'You're just not going to believe it.'

126

'Well,' Walden said, throwing his arms up in dejection, 'I'm screwed.'

Forrest looked at him nervously as they walked into the bar. 'What do you mean?' he asked, glancing at the rear table and then back at Walden.

'I never made it to the senior prom, man,' Walden said, and took the beret off. 'I almost made it to the junior prom, but at the steps, I met Connie Hanks and Karen Slone. I can't tell you what that night meant to me. A case of Grain Belt beer, a heater in a fifty-two Ford, and Karen telling me she loved my spit curls.'

As Walden walked toward the back of the room, he felt he knew who she was even though he could only see her shiny black hair bunched up over the back of the booth where her head was resting against the seat. Dominica smiled at him from the opposite side of the booth as they approached.

'Sam, this is Hoa,' Forrest said. Hoa turned her gaze from her sister and looked at Walden. A sensation swept over him like that when he heard the helicopters coming to get the team. His chest muscles contracted as his eyes took in her bronzed face, the high cheekbones, the curve of her faintly smiling lips. A nearly overwhelming impulse grabbed at him, making him want to bolt from the bar. He needed to find a place to hide until he could regroup. Her beauty flat scared the hell out of him.

'You sit down with me,' she said softly. Walden slowly eased into the booth, his eyes never leaving her. He felt old feelings being stretched and pulled inside of him. His tongue had grown fat and thick inside his mouth.

'Last night at our home, Jerry talk about you. I think then I want to meet you,' Hoa said, a flicker of a smile going on and off. The smell of her filled him. There was the musk of warm skin, the scent of an expensive perfume.

'Ah, Sam. Sam, you want a beer?' Forrest asked, clearing his throat. Walden turned and looked at him as though he had just come in.

'I'll have a beer.' Walden looked back at Hoa. She was

still there, with that soft look in her eyes. Her hands reached over and covered his where it lay on the table. Walden kept looking at her, not directly, but having her fill the edges of his eyes. After a few minutes the women asked to be let out of the booth for a minute.

'We be right back,' Hoa said as Walden got up. When she caught the look in his eyes, she touched his arm. 'You no have to worry.'

'I just want to talk to you,' Walden said quietly.

'You pretty,' Hoa said, and the faint smile turned full force. Walden didn't answer. When she walked to the rear of the bar, she looked back over her shoulder and smiled again. Walden sat back down.

'Oh, my God.'

'I told you, man,' Forrest said, smiling a fat-cat smile. 'Wait until you see where they live.'

'She's beautiful,' Walden almost whispered. 'I'm not used to this. I'm going to blow it. I know it. I'm used to whores. How in hell am I supposed to act? I couldn't even talk.'

'Just be yourself, Sam.'

'Don't say that,' Walden said seriously. 'I'll blow it for sure then.'

When the girls came back, they suggested the group go to their home.

'Come,' Hoa said, taking Walden's hand. 'You like very much.'

'You want me to come with you?'

Hoa and Dominica began to laugh.

'Why you think we come here today?' Hoa teased, wrapping her arm around Walden's. 'We come here to find you.'

'I don't believe this,' Walden said as they walked toward the door.

'What you no believe?'

'Long story,' Walden said, smiling at her for the first time. Hoa said something in French to her sister. They stopped on the sidewalk and Forrest waved down a taxi.

'You're beautiful,' Walden said.

'I think you beautiful too,' Hoa answered, her brown eyes shining in the sunlight.

Once they'd piled into the taxi, with Hoa and Sam in back, Hoa gave instructions and the driver pulled into the thick traffic

'You smoke *cânsa?*' Walden asked as he pulled a joint out of his top pocket.

'I like to smoke, if you like to smoke,' Hoa said. She wiggled closer. He felt her jean-covered leg warm against his, her firm braless breasts pushing against his upper arm. He lit the joint and handed it to her. She took a couple of tokes and passed it to her sister. Walden looked out the windows at the street and the people. They seemed happy today. It was hard to find someone in the crowd who wasn't smiling. Every time he looked back at Hoa, he felt like grinning himself.

'I feel like I've known you for a long time,' Walden said after a while. He didn't look at her when he said it. *God, this is unreal. It's like some movie. Please don't let it stop.*

The taxi ride was a long one, and by the time the cab finally stopped, Walden and Hoa were talking easily and smoothly. When they got out, Walden saw a high cream-colored wall with an elaborate iron gate fastened by chain and padlock.

'What is this?' A guard with an M-2 carbine stepped out of a wooden rain shelter, quickly unlocked the gate, and swung it open. 'This is it?' The words popped out. They walked through the gate and into a garden of manicured shrubs and tall trees. A small reflecting pool caught light coming through the overhanging branches. Birds fluttered above them as they passed, while others pecked and strutted over the close-cropped lawn. A white two-story French villa proudly dominated the grounds. For the second time in as many hours Walden was stunned.

'This is our home,' Hoa said proudly as she eased her arm around Walden's waist. They stopped next to the pond while Forrest and Dominica continued up the stone walkway to the house. Hoa smiled and pointed at the multicoloured fish swimming through the clear water.

'Later you can feed. Over there by rocks,' she said, bending over and pointing to a cluster of gray stones at the far end, 'one big fish stay.' She looked at Walden, her eyes merry, her smile making him feel like something other than a soldier. A tingle he hadn't felt in a long time floated through him.

'I'm dead, right?' he said as they continued the walk to the house.

'No, no, you not die,' Hoa said. She softly rubbed her face against Walden's shoulder. A simple understanding flowed between them, something easy and open and far different from what Walden had known before. As they walked through the front door, the image of his mother crying over a simple Mixmaster she had received for Christmas came into his mind, and he smiled.

Inside, the house more than matched the grounds. It felt warm and friendly, yet maintained an understated elegance. Walden stopped to look at a carving of an eagle, set upon a pedestal entwined with green climbing ivy. The spread wings shone with a lacquered clearness.

Hoa led him through the vestibule and into the living room to join Forrest and Dominica. A low, polished table, surrounded by multicoloured pillows, centered the room. There was stereo equipment and a television set, and on the walls were oil paintings. An intricately carved desk stood in one corner next to a large wooden chest. A round mama-san pattered into the room and put a platter of cut fruit and cheeses on the table. Hoa spoke in Vietnamese and the mama-san smiled and bowed to Walden. Walden nodded politely. Hoa said something else, and shortly after Walden had sat on a cushion next to the coffee table, the maid returned with a glass and a bottle of beer. Hoa pulled pillows from around the floor and propped them behind Walden.

'We have our own room, so I'll see you later. Okay?' Forrest asked, squatting down next to Walden. Walden nodded as music began to play from four corner speakers. Forrest was just leaving the room when Walden sat up.

'Just a minute. Wait a minute.' Forrest and Dominica stopped at the doorway. 'There's something strange here.' Walden was dead serious.

'Look, buddy,' Forrest said, walking back to Walden. 'I know what you're thinking. I was thinking the same thing, but believe me, it's okay.' Walden looked at Hoa, standing quietly with her hands behind her back, looking down at the floor. Walden suddenly knew he didn't give a damn. He wasn't going to question this.

'Just enjoy it, Sam. You deserve it,' Forrest said.

Walden ran his fingers through his hair. 'Right.' Forrest and Dominica left the room and Hoa came to sit next to Walden.

'You think maybe we VC?' she asked. The way she said it was flat and disappointed.

'Yes,' Walden muttered, looking away to where a warm breeze was ruffling thin curtains on a far window.

'Why you think that?'

'Because I'm still alive, and I've stayed alive because I don't trust anything.' Walden tightened as he thought of the contradiction apparent to him. 'Why should you bring me to your house?' Walden nervously tapped a cigarette out of his pack. Hoa picked up the lighter and lit the cigarette for him.

'Last night Jerry tell Dominica and me about you. I think for long time that I don't need someone. But I think maybe you and I can be together. I don't know why I think this. I wait long time. Today, I know. I feel you.'

Walden knocked the ash off the tip of his smoke. 'I can't tell you anything. Don't ask me about what I do.'

'I no care what you do,' Hoa said. 'I want you to stay with me. I no want to stay alone.' Walden heard a catch in her soft voice, heard a sad, frightened tone. 'You wonder how we can live in house like this? How we can have car?'

'I didn't know you had a car too,' Walden said. 'But yes, I wonder.'

131

'This is our parents' home. They live in France. My father French, my mother Vietnamese. I show you letters.'

'Look, Hoa,' Walden said gently, 'I believe you. It's just that I don't trust. I can't trust many people. I'm sorry.'

'You no have to be sorry. Maybe you not believe, but you and Jerry first Americans ever come to our house. It be true that we sometimes work in bar for GI to buy tea, but we no make love for money.'

'It doesn't matter,' Walden said.

'I think at first, not good to do, but so much money,' Hoa exclaimed. 'Some day can make more than one hundred dollar easy.'

'Hey,' Walden said, closing his eyes and exhaling. 'I don't care. I've done things in this place I would never have believed. The war changes everything. I don't even know who I am sometimes.' He paused for a minute. 'I have to go back to Da Nang in less than two weeks. I want to be with you for what time there is left. But I just want to know why us, why me?'

Hoa smiled as she slid her leg across Walden's. 'I think maybe it was time,' she whispered.

That evening Walden and Hoa sat on the patio furniture arranged on top of the flat roof of the villa. The wavering resonance of a heavy machine gun came from far away. A mental picture of the muzzle flash, how it would look as the gun fired, came to Walden's mind. A parachute flare blossomed over the river in mid-distance. Hoa pulled Walden's hand over and used his cigarette to light her own. She leaned back in the wicker chair and was silhouetted by the drifting flare.

'Sometimes you seem very far away,' she said.

'I'm sorry. I guess I haven't been talking much.'

'I think maybe you no like me.'

'No, no. I'm sorry. I'm still adjusting.'

'Why you no kiss me, then?' Hoa asked bluntly. 'In bar, GI buy me one drink, then want to make love. You stay here, eat with me, hold me, but you not even kiss me. Why?'

Walden started to speak, but stopped and pulled another beer out of the ice chest below the table. After popping the top he put the opener back on the table and took a swallow from the bottle. He tried to speak again but only said, 'Ah, man.'

Hoa reached over and took the beer from him and brought it to her lips, her eyes not leaving Walden's. After a swallow Hoa asked, 'What you say?'

'Ah, man.' Walden sighed as he lifted his right hand for a moment and then let it drop back down to the armrest. 'It's one of those things that you can't tell, because if you do tell, then . . .' His voice trailed off. He leaned back in the chair and tried again. 'I'll tell you why I haven't kissed you, if you really want to know.' He smiled and then grinned, watching her face become firm as she waited for the worst. Walden began to laugh. He looked away from her and then he looked back and began to laugh again.

'Why you laugh at me?' Hoa said, in a voice both hurt and angry. Walden reached over and dragged her chair next to his and hugged her. 'I wasn't laughing at you. But you were chewing your bottom lip just like Mary Mosley did when I'd talk to her in the sixth grade.'

Hoa tilted her head to one side in exasperation. 'I want you to tell me why you no kiss me.'

'I'm afraid you'll bite my tongue off,' Walden said, still chuckling.

'I no bite your tongue,' Hoa cooed, wrapping her arms around him. Walden looked into her eyes and touched the side of her face with his hand.

'It's because with you I have something to lose,' Walden said before he thought it. He heard the words like an echo. It was suddenly clear to him why he had felt so frightened by her, why he had been dancing around it all afternoon. He watched her eyes change and he felt her hand caress his cheek. It was warm and soft.

'I guess it doesn't matter too much,' Walden said, after a

133

time. 'It's funny, though. I'm worried about a future and I don't have one. Except for a week and a few days it looks like darkness out there.'

'We can be something together,' Hoa said, straightening up. 'We have time now. Not tomorrow. Tomorrow has nothing.' She looked away quickly, out across the river. She worried her hands down between her legs and tightened her arms as she looked into the darkness.

'Hoa,' Walden said, reaching for her, 'come here by me.'

Tears ran down her cheeks. A sound, quiet and uncertain and surrendering, came from her as she let Walden draw her to him. He felt the tendons on her wrist bunch as she grabbed him. He felt her fingernails dig into his back as her head pushed and rubbed against his neck. He felt the tears, slow, tepid drops, falling into the hollow of his neck. Walden closed his eyes as he cradled her head against his chest with his hand. The image of the woman in the graveyard came to him. He squeezed his eyes tighter until all he could see were dancing lights and sparks inside his head. He hadn't noticed that his own hands had become tense on Hoa's back until she moaned and pushed closer against him.

'You, you,' she whispered as she crawled onto him. Her cheek, slippery and wet, slid over his lips. Slowly, their lips moved to each other. As they met, Walden knew a warmth and joy that was past memory and part brand new. With movements slow and feather soft, her lips traced over his eyelids, his cheeks, then back to his mouth. He felt her tongue touch his own, lingering, pushing. Walden felt as though he were floating. Her arms held him as he had always wanted to be held. He also felt alive. Very much alive.

On the morning he had to leave for Da Nang, Walden woke before it became light. He lay still in the darkness of the room, feeling Hoa's warm breathing against his chest. The time had passed so quickly; he felt cheated. Hoa murmured as she pushed a leg over Walden and cuddled closer. He kissed her forehead as he felt her soft pubic hair push against his leg. Being with her had simply been the happiest days of his life. It seemed they had been together for years.

The gray morning light climbed up to the bed and Walden wondered how long he would have to be gone. They'd get targeted for a mission as soon as they got back. *A week to get ready, a week on the ground. Another week for the unexpected. Three weeks, a month at the outside.* Then it hit him that it was very possible that he would never come back, that he would be killed. He smiled, but the smile faded quickly when the thought popped into his head that the days with Hoa had been a going-away present, a way to balance what was coming. He shook the thought out of his mind. Hoa stirred and looked up at him. She smiled and even in the grainy dawn light, he could see her eyes shining. She leaned up and they kissed. She eased herself onto him.

'I love you,' she whispered. 'I no want you to go from me.'

'Come on, Hoa,' Walden said quietly, brushing a stray hair out of her face. 'We went through this last night. It almost killed me. I gotta go back. That's it. That's it.'

'I know. I not talk about. I want to go airport with you.' She was pleading.

'No,' Walden said. 'I never want to say good-by to you. Not like that. You stay away from the war.'

'I love you, Sam. You come back.'

'I love you, too, babe. I love you too.' Walden closed his eyes and saw a jungle. A bright blot of leaves stretching into a blue sky. Then he saw her face and he felt as if he would die for wanting her, and now he was missing her even before they were apart. 'Just hold me for a little while, Hoa.'

CHAPTER THIRTEEN

COVEY SHOULD be along soon. Walden's eyes searched the jungle for a place to spend the night. The sound of bulldozers coughing into life filtered up the slope from the road below. Walden stopped the team and looked at his watch. He made notations in his notebook, then motioned to Cuong and Playboy to continue along the top of the ridge. While moving through a patch of leafy bamboo, Walden decided it would be a good place to get extracted the following day. One large tree stood in the middle of the thicket. He took a guess at how much C-4 it would take to blow it.

The team moved out of the stand of bamboo into denser cover of trees and ferns. Walden saw Playboy stagger. After four days of climbing in and out of ravines and steep valleys, the team was dead tired. The shock of the trucks coming just as they were planting the sensor devices along the road had sapped what energy they had left.

Walden remembered cursing the incredibly bad timing when the first of the trucks had slowly rumbled down the road. The thinnest veil of brush had separated the team from the troops riding in each truck. At first the team had been near panic. But everyone had frozen and Walden had thought of the way chickens stood stockstill when the shadow of a hawk passed across the chicken yard. Afterward, listening to the sound of the trucks fading in the distance, he'd felt totally drained. Being frightened took a lot of energy.

A short way out of the bamboo stand, where the ridge narrowed and there were large trees for protection, Walden stopped the team. He made a circular motion with his left hand. The team members began pulling Claymores out of their packs for night defence. Shrugging off his rucksack, Walden motioned to Forrest to set up the long antenna. He picked up the six Claymore detonators that went with the mines being planted in a circle. He dropped them into his large side pocket and signalled for Pau to follow him for a quick recon before the team settled in for the night.

Before slipping into the shadows Walden made eye contact with each of the team members to make sure they knew he was going. Satisfied that they wouldn't be shot on their return, Walden and Pau quietly circled twenty feet out, taking their time and learning the area. Once completely around the RON position, they crept back inside. As soon as they were inside the perimeter, Forrest motioned to Walden to take the radio. Holding the handset, Walden swirled two fingers of his free hand in front of his mouth, signalling that the team should eat.

'Covey, this is Fig Leaf. How do you hear me? Over.' Walden whispered into his cupped hands.

'Roger, Leaf, this is Covey. Hear you Lima Charlie. How about a RON position? Over.'

'Roger, Covey, wait one.' Walden looked at Forrest, who began to encipher the coordinates. After a few minutes Forrest handed Walden his notebook and pointed at the code words he had written. Walden gave the message to Covey, then waited to make sure it broke correctly.

'Okay, good buddy, got you covered,' Pappy came back a minute later. 'Also request update on Whiskey Wind. Over.'

'Roger, Covey, we have Alpha, Alpha six five on that. Over.'

'Roger, Leaf, Alpha, Alpha six five. Good show. Will see you tomorrow for Bravo X-ray. Have a good night.'

'Hear from you tomorrow. Out.' He put the mike down and gave a thumbs-up to the team. The little people went back to eating rations.

One more night to survive, then home. The heavy smell of a LRRP ration invaded his nostrils when Forrest slid up. He was glad a breeze was blowing that would sweep away the smell of the food.

'We're getting extracted tomorrow?' Forrest stirred water into the dehydrated meal.

'Yeah, thank God.' Walden began to fasten the Claymore wires into the detonators. After hooking them all and double-checking which detonator would explode which mine, he settled back against his rucksack and lit another cigarette off the coal of the first. *Last cigarette*. He drew the smoke deep into his lungs, and with it came the taste of the dry fish and rice the little people were eating.

'That road was a bit much,' Forrest whispered, wanting to talk some before it became dark. Walden trailed some smoke out of his mouth and nodded. Forrest handed his half-eaten ration over.

'One more night and we're home free.' Walden spooned up a half-dozen mouthfuls of the ham and scalloped potatoes before handing it back. Forrest finished the meal, folded the pouch up, and stuck it back into his rucksack.

Walden watched the leaves of the trees above them quickly darken. The leaves turned gray, then black. For a few minutes the little people rustled about, rolling up in their poncho liners for the night. They left their web gear on, taking off only their rucksacks to use as headrests.

A root pressed into the small of Walden's back as he stretched out on the ground. He didn't move to find a new space. The root would be his insurance against falling into too deep a sleep. He put his CAR-15 on his chest, his finger wrapped around the trigger. He silently fluffed his poncho liner out over the top. Pau cuddled up to one side of him, then Forrest did the same on the other.

Walden's sweat-soaked fatigues were cold at first, then warmed as his body generated heat inside the poncho liner. He closed his eyes, dreading the long hours of darkness. The night could be both friend and enemy. Mostly it was enemy.

It grew even darker, layer upon layer of black paint being brushed over the jungle. It was in the jungle that Walden had experienced degrees of darkness that before would have been unimaginable. Only the bodies pressed against his, and the ground against his back, gave him a sense of being anchored to the earth. He brought his left hand up and pressed the palm against his nose. He couldn't even see the outline. Walden closed his eyes and thought it seemed lighter.

It ended and started where it always did. He could see the doctor as they stood apart from the others in the tunnels of the discharge area in Oakland. He could see the partitioned offices, the numbers painted on the pillars that they would follow, station after station, like school children reciting the Way of the Cross during Lent. It was station twelve. The crucifixion. The euphoria of surviving a year in Vietnam, the plans, the joy of becoming a civilian again, destroyed by the doctor's three words.

'You have syphilis.' It was said calmly. Walden felt as though he had been hit by a baseball bat. The doctor had been kind, reassuring, explaining it was easily cured, that Walden was lucky because he had just contracted it recently. The next day he would go to Letterman Hospital, the doctor said, get his shots, and be on his way home.

'Tell me I have cancer. Tell me I have leprosy,' Walden remembered saying. It was syphilis, though, and he could imagine people looking at him for the rest of his life as if he were unclean. The nun had told the class that venereal disease was a curse from God. The nun had said that you would go crazy and die a horrible death. And the film, the draining sores and rotting bodies, that was the ending God had picked for him.

The lies and cover-up started then. He remembered the phone call to his parents, saying his records were messed up, so he wouldn't be home when he'd said; the lie he told his buddies, that the blood test showed he might have malaria, and he had been put on medical hold.

Once home, he was choked with fear that his mother would somehow discover his secret. There was the fear of a letter from the health department, opened by mistake. There was the fear of not being completely cured, despite what the doctor had said. There was the hopelessness of not being able to confide in anyone, of not being able to tell of the shame and guilt. There was no confessional.

He couldn't tell Betty, of course, and he knew it was hopeless as he fell in love with her. There could be no children, no opportunity for God to strike him again, and there could be no marriage. His shame was a constant hurt, yet he lingered in the light of her, like geese letting themselves be fooled by warm autumn days. When he loved her as much as he could, he knew he had to go. The last time he saw her, he told her he didn't want to marry anyone, that he had to leave so he could breathe. Then he sat on the hill overlooking the Mississippi River and hoped the pain inside would kill him.

He had come back to the war. He would keep running missions as long as he could, fighting as hard as he could. Suicide was a sin, but it was beyond his control if the odds finally caught up. Only it couldn't be his fault. It had to be in God's hand.

In the darkness of Laos, Walden felt lost all over again. He had allowed himself to fall in love once more, so now he would hurt someone again. He had killed so often to die only once, and he didn't even have heaven to look forward to.

It could have been that village in 1965. Each thatch roof burst aflame like the head of a match. There was screaming and wild shouts as the Viet Cong were flushed out and shot in their attempts to reach the jungle. There was the bent American, vomiting up blood as he clutched his exposed stomach. There was the smoke and distorted faces in the gushing flames. Then the figure in black pajamas jumped from the spider hole clutching something. He fired before the shape could turn and shoot him or the others.

Later, when the wounded were Medevaced out by the dust-off choppers, he returned to the hole. The body had slid back down the lip. There was no way he would outlive

140

the memory of the dead mother still holding the dead baby to her. That could have been the sin he was paying for.

Sleep came and went in brief skips. He would doze, then be instantly awake, ears straining for a sound that didn't fit. Pau snuggled closer, head pushed against his side. The movement made part of Walden's blanket slide off. He shivered as the cold air touched him, until he rearranged the liner.

At first Walden thought he was dreaming. The faint sound of a helicopter was there in his ears but it didn't make any sense. He felt Pau shift as he awoke. Walden's hair began to bristle at the nape of his neck.

'You hear that?' Walden whispered.

'It's a chopper,' Forrest squeaked.

'It doesn't sound right.' Walden listened carefully. It sounded almost like a Chinook, but there was something missing. He thought for a second it could be a Huey or a Cobra, but discounted that as the aircraft came nearer. *It's too big*. He ducked his head beneath the liner and lifted the tape covering the face of his watch. The luminous hands showed it was quarter to twelve. He replaced the tape and stood back up, pulling the handset out of the front of his shirt. Before he had a chance to request it, Forrest had fumbled in his rucksack to turn the radio on. He pulled the poncho liner back over his head and cupped his hands around the mouthpiece.

'Hickory, Hickory, this is Fig Leaf, Fig Leaf. Over.' A few seconds later a shallow voice wavered in the static, coming from the radio relay site on the border.

'Fig Leaf, this is Hickory. Hear you weak and broken. How me? Over.'

'This is Fig Leaf. Hear you same. Listen, are there any helicopters flying around out here tonight? Over.'

A long pause followed before the voice came back. 'Ah, Fig Leaf, this is Hickory. Wait one.' A quick popping sound, something like a stick being drawn along a picket fence, grew as the helicopter passed almost directly over the team. Walden felt Pau's head push under the blanket.

141

'Helicop come?' Pau smelled of the fish and rice.

'Shssss,' Walden warned.

The voice from the border came back, at first faint, then stronger. 'Fig Leaf, be advised there're no helicopters out there.' The voice could have been informing them that there wasn't any snow on the sun either.

'Bullshit,' Walden hissed into the mouthpiece. 'This big motherfucker just flew over us.' Another pause and then the voice.

'Fig Leaf, this is Hickory. Are you sure it's not thunder? Over.'

'For Christ's sake, it's a goddamn helicopter!' Walden fought to keep his voice muffled. He was about to ask someone else to come to the radio when he felt Forrest shake his shoulder. He lifted his head and then dropped his mouth. The trees far below were lit up as the helicopter started to land.

Walden keyed the mike. 'It's not one of ours, because the sonofabitch is landing.' A second later the light was gone. He wondered if he was dreaming again. Forrest's lips touched his ear.

'That thing just landed,' Forrest croaked. The sudden sound of truck engines jumped the valley wall. Then came the sound of another helicopter.

'There's another one,' Walden groaned into the mike. 'Jesus, what is this?'

'Fig Leaf, this is Hickory. Are you sure? I say again, are you positive a helicopter just landed? Over.' It was a new voice, and more businesslike.

'Ah, shit.' Walden was exasperated. He paused to collect himself. 'Yes, I'm sure, and there's a third one coming in. Over.' The sound of the first helicopter lifting mingled with that of the second and third ships. It sounded like Tan Son Nhut at high noon.

'Fig Leaf, this is Hickory. Can you identify type? Over.'

'Oh, for God's sake, man.' Walden was trying not to scream. 'It doesn't sound like a shit-hook and it sure the hell isn't a Huey. I don't know what they are.'

'Fig Leaf, stand by.' Walden kept the silent phone to his ear, watching the jungle light up again as the second ship landed.

'Are you believing this?' Forrest said quietly as the third ship passed over. Walden felt he was watching a fleet of flying saucers invading earth.

'Now the bastards got helicopters too.'

'They got a whole lot of trucks too. Listen to that.' Forrest tried to laugh. 'Sounds like a drive-in after a racing movie.'

The team watched the third helicopter land in a brief burst of light and then they heard the relief ebb of the blades as it idled in the dark.

'Fig Leaf, this is Hickory. We have fast movers heading out to your position. Request confirmation on World Series. Over.'

Damn. Walden had forgotten about the code words that would bring out the Seventh Air Force. 'Roger that, Hickory. World Series. Over.'

'Roger, Leaf. Activate Mini-Ponder. Over.'

'Roger, Hickory. Stand by.' Walden slipped his arm out of the rucksack straps and twisted around to reach inside. A tingling raced around inside him as another ship approached the landing area. He could feel the little people squirming around when he pulled out the small black homing device.

'Hickory, this is Fig Leaf. Activating ponder. Over.' Letting up on the keyer, he cradled the phone against his ear as he ran his hand over the face of the box until he felt the switch. He clicked it upward.

'Roger, Leaf. Movers will home on signal. Switch to secondary frequency. Over.'

Walden heard a distant thunder approaching from the east. He pulled the rucksack back on as Forrest twisted the dials on the PRC-25. Bursts of static came over the radio and then stopped in a jumble of voices. Walden keyed the mike several times to clear the air before he broke in and identified himself.

'Fig Leaf, this is Fast Mover Six,' a voice said. 'Have you locked in, looking good. Give me degrees on approach. Over.'

'Roger, Mover.' Walden looked at the glowing numbers and arrow of his compass. 'Six hundred meters, one niner, zero degrees. If you hurry, you got at least one on the ground. Over.'

'Roger that, Leaf. Damn,' the pilot said eagerly. The sound of the helicopter on the ground faded, and the truck began to shut down too. *They got radar.* The activity in the valley stopped.

'Mover Six, this is Leaf. They know you're coming. Over.'

'No problem. No problem.' The voice considered it incidental, a minor inconvenience. He talked to the other Phantom pilots, giving instructions. Walden stared into the darkness, knowing it was now out of his hands.

The attack began with pale heat lightning flashes, followed by explosions glued together as they erupted along the valley floor. The air-cracking boom of the jets came last.

'Drop three hundred. Drop three hundred,' Walden said into the mike.

'Roger, Leaf.' In the lull, as the jets circled for another pass, Walden heard the helicopter begin to rev and the trucks chug back into life. The helicopter engines strained as the throttle was twisted wide open. It lifted into the air. Streaks of light touched the foliage around the team as the jets began firing again. A fireball mushroomed into the night sky, followed by a heavy explosion.

'Got him! Got him! Goddamn, I got him, sonofabitch.' The voice was sheer joy. 'Mover Six, be advised I just shot down what looks to be an MI-6 Hook Soviet helicopter. Over.'

Another voice broke in. 'Trucks in the open on the road. Christ, look at that sonofabitch burn.'

'Mover Four, this is Six. Negative, I say again, negative on Soviet ship. Clear airway. Switch to secure voice.'

'Fig Leaf, this is Mover Six. Hickory will relay.

144

Switching to secure voice. Out.' The radio relay site operator came back over the air.

'Fig Leaf, this is Hickory. Be advised, ah, disregard last transmission.' A short pause followed. 'Um, Fig Leaf, ah, disregard message about helicopters. Over.'

'Roger,' Walden said. The air above them filled with the scream of attacking jets. Strobe flashes stabbed through the darkness as the valley shook.

'Sweet Jesus,' Forrest said, watching the lightshow below.

'We're going to be in for it tomorrow.' Walden sighed. The smell of dust and smoke drifted through the trees. Red streams of tracers pinstriped the night, and bombs went off in firecracker strings. He could feel it coming, the crescendo approaching center stage. He didn't know what would happen or how, but he could sense it building in the snapping fury created below. Then it was there, the finale.

'Holy shit.' The first canisters of napalm belly-flopped into the jungle. The trees around him glowed red, dancing in black shadows. The rush of sucked air shook the leaves. The little people came into focus, images on a developing photograph, as more and more canisters of molten jelly joined the river of fire. Walden could see a sheen of perspiration on Forrest's cheeks. Finally the storm abated, lessening as the jets peeled away into the night. When the last one was gone, there was only the futile booming of a 37-millimeter gun firing into the empty sky.

The team silently listened to the crackling of burning trees and brush as the flames slowly died. Walden finally dozed off again, dreaming of autumn and burning leaves. Near dawn he dreamed of himself and Keith walking down a sidewalk in his hometown, singing. *'Who put the bop in the bop she bop, who put the ram in the ram a lama ding dong? Who was that man, I'd like to shake his hand, he made my baby fall in love with me.'*

The graveyard below smoldered all night.

Morning came with the stinging jab of a mosquito on the side of Walden's face. He brushed it against the rucksack

145

strap and for a second wondered where he was. Then he lifted his head from beneath the poncho liner. The team lay around him, sleeping, rolled in their blankets. It reminded Walden of kindergarten and the rugs used for naps. He remembered milk and graham crackers and the tom-tom he had made from a Quaker Oats box. He couldn't remember what his teacher had looked like; just another nun.

He watched the team wake, and it felt like Sunday. They would be pulled out today. It was the day looked forward to. The dawn was beginning, touching the trees with a cold gray. Walden shivered, feeling the clammy morning dew on him. Without a word the team began packing their sleeping gear. Thin white trails traced their breathing in the crisp mountain air.

'I think we can get pulled out back in that bamboo stand,' Walden whispered to Forrest. His teeth chattered. He gently opened and closed the bolt on his weapon to make sure it hadn't sealed shut with condensation. Forrest nodded agreement as he painted a new layer of camouflage onto his face. Walden saw the toll the five days had taken on the team. Eyes were puffy and red, uniforms torn and ragged, dirt matted into their hair. He was glad it was the last day, and that it felt like Sunday.

An hour passed and the sun began to dry the foliage. Forrest looked at his watch and turned on the radio in Walden's pack. The little people were spread out in a circle, watching and listening. The distant drone of the OV-10 finally came and Walden keyed the mike.

'Covey, this is Fig Leaf. Commo check. How do you hear me? Over.' A few seconds later the voice of Pappy Lindell came clear and sweet.

'Roger, Fig Leaf. Hear you loud and clear. Over.'

'Covey, this is Leaf. Request extraction. Over.'

'Leaf, be advised we are putting another team first. We'll pull you next. Over.'

'Roger, Covey. Will be standing by. Out.' Walden unkeyed the mike and pushed it back inside his shirt. 'They're pulling another team first, probably Oregon.'

146

Forrest nodded and shook a cigarette from a crumpled pack, offering one to Walden. They relaxed against their rucksacks, smoking and basking in the morning sun. They watched the little people preparing PIR rations.

Forrest leaned over to whisper in Walden's ear. 'You ever hear of them bringing in troops with helicopters before?'

'No, it's a new one on me,' Walden answered softly. They let it drop for the moment and quietly finished their cigarettes. A nagging feeling pulled at Walden's brain, an out-of-reach annoyance like a bottle rolling around the floorboard of a car. It was an irksome vagueness, and he cleared his mind to see if it would solidify. Then it registered in living color. He saw the soldiers they'd killed by the stream. It was the warm sun, the feeling of completion, the tranquil jungle and the casual atmosphere. Walden cursed as he realized the dangerously reckless mood that he had allowed to come over the team.

He hissed to get attention and motioned the members around him. Cuong and Playboy sashayed over. The six little people squatted, grinning and jostling each other. A cold shot of fear crinkled up the inside of Walden's stomach. He had allowed this.

'Cut the shit,' Walden hissed, the anger clear. The little people stiffened as though slapped across the face. 'We got some real short memories, don't we? We better get serious or we'll never get home. And this ain't home.' Cricket's dark face jerked and for a second Walden thought that he was going to cry. Cuong and Pau instantly knew the mistake they had made and jumped when Walden pointed to where he wanted them to be. Walden grabbed his own rucksack and dragged it over to the edge of the slope. The jungle was silent, but he felt a strong apprehension. He had made two bad mistakes. The first was in not moving away from the RON position. The second, even worse, was that he had let the team forget where it was.

Long minutes passed. Walden pulled out his last LRRP ration of spaghetti and ate as he listened intently. He forced down the last bites of the ration so he wouldn't have to mess with a partly filled pouch. He had just shoved the empty pack back into his ruck when he heard a twig snap twenty yards below. He looked back at Forrest, ten yards away. The sound of someone slipping and falling, climbing up the slope, almost made Walden gag. Quietly he unsnapped the cover of the canteen pouch where he kept grenades.

There was another sound of rustling brush. Walden caught Cuong and Pau out of the corner of his eye bracing themselves behind a tree.

Three quick shots jumped from Forrest's CAR-15. The scream of birds startled Walden more than the shots. He wished he hadn't moved so far away from the others. The way the team pushed down behind the roots told him that they had seen someone coming down the ridgeline. Having forgotten about the movement on the slope, Walden was half turned around when he heard a sound like a rock hitting the ground in front of him. He pulled the pin from the grenade, trying to see some movement in the thick brush. A flashbulb burst inside his head, making him reel backward. There was pain in his neck. His left hand reached out to steady him as the scalding hurt almost made him shut his eyes.

His only thought was to get rid of the grenade. He lobbed it over the edge of the slope and then brought his fingertips up to the side of his neck. He pulled them back and looked at the bright smear of blood. The grenade exploded with a thick crump. Walden grabbed the radio and dragged it back toward the team.

The side of his neck was on fire. Forrest reached out and grabbed him as he lurched into the slight depression, and Walden saw the look in his eye.

'They blew half your neck off,' Forrest blurted, then ducked as Playboy and Cuong opened up. Walden kept his weapon pointed along the ridge in the direction the little people were shooting, but his left hand crept up and touched the wound. He stared at the thick red blood that suddenly covered his entire forearm and began dripping off his elbow. His neck felt swollen, becoming larger than the rest of his body. It came to him that he was bleeding to death.

Not now, goddammit. Not now. His legs kicked at the ground, pushing him against the base of a tree. He felt faint, nauseous. The firing stopped abruptly. His eyes dropped to his chest where the blood ran down the soaked fatigue shirt. Darkness gathered at the periphery of his vision. He watched Forrest working on him through a narrowing tunnel. He felt him tear the cravat from his forehead and then the distant ache as it was pushed against his neck.

'Please, please,' he heard Forrest say. Hung stepped into the mouth of the tunnel. He looked far away as he unwrapped a field dressing. The words came then. *Say a prayer, Sam. Say the prayer and everything will be all right. You'll go to heaven. Walden knew he had to concentrate on being alive or it would end. The words were so hard to remember. Oh, my God, I'm heartily . . .* It was too hard. He couldn't think of the rest and still listen to the rushing sound that was lifting him off the ground. It didn't matter. He felt tired. Hung's face hectored him, keeping him awake.

Under the pressure of the thick cotton dressing he stopped bleeding. Hung reached out and pulled him back when Walden lurched over onto his side. The blood puddled in the wrinkled material bunched above his web gear spilled into the dirt.

'I need some water. Give me some water.' Something inside was pushing him awake. Hung lifted a canteen to his lips. It came too fast at first, running out of the corners of his mouth. Hung levelled the canteen and Walden gulped. He had never been so thirsty. The water brought strength with it. The darkness slowly drew away. He slid his hand down over the bloody weapon in his lap until he could wrap his finger around the trigger. He smiled and gave the team a peace sign with his left hand. He saw the relief, and Hung smiled down at him.

'You no bleed now,' Hung said, inspecting the dressing

149

on Walden's neck. Walden turned his head, trying to breathe air that didn't have the odor of his own blood in it. Minutes passed, and Walden felt himself grow stronger. He pushed himself up from the stained leaves and motioned to Forrest.

'What's going on?'

'We got some ships coming for us, about five minutes out.' Forrest patted Walden's leg.

'Leave Cuong and Pau with us. Put the rest on the first ship.' Walden slipped his arms back through his rucksack straps.

'No way,' Forrest said flatly. 'You're going out on the first ship.'

'I don't intend to argue with you. Cuong and Pau stay with us. The rest go out on the first ship.'

Forrest looked away briefly, biting his tongue. 'Okay. Does it hurt much?'

'It's not so bad now. It just burns. You'd better stay on the radio.' Walden gingerly turned his head from side to side. He couldn't turn it much to the left without feeling a stabbing pain in his neck and back.

The surrounding area remained quiet. There could only have been a few NVA or they'd be attacking. But the sound of the gunfire and grenades would let others know where they were, and that's what bothered Walden.

Forrest flinched noticeably while listening on the radio. He twisted around and dragged himself the few feet to Walden.

'They just shot up one of our ships and they had to turn back. They're going to try and pull us with one Huey.'

'We've got to blow that tree back in the bamboo, then. They can't pull eight of us out with strings.' Walden pushed himself into a kneeling position. He felt light, almost weightless, as he gave instructions to pick up the Claymores in front. The team dropped down past the other mines below, reversing them as they moved down the slope to the bamboo thicket. Stopping twenty feet from the large tree, they pulled pound blocks of C-4 out of each other's rucksacks.

'Make sure it goes on the first shot.' Walden lifted the handset to his ear. He watched Forrest and Cuong move to the tree, arms loaded with explosives wrapped in olive-drab wax paper.

'Covey, this is Fig Leaf. Over.' He had to smile when he heard the normally calm voice of Lindell come over the airway sounding happy.

'Leaf, this is Covey. How you doing, sweet thing? Over.'

'Getting ready to blow LZ. Over.' Just hearing Lindell's voice made him feel better.

'Roger, Leaf. We'll get mark-mark on you when you blow it. We're heading in now. Stand by. Over.'

'Let us know when you want us to detonate. Over.'

Forrest and Cuong crawled back through the bamboo, stringing out Claymore wire behind them.

'We have to move back some more. We had to put a half ton of shit on that tree to drop it,' Forrest said.

'We can't go back very far. We can get behind that.' Walden pointed to a tree at the edge of the bamboo.

As the little people squeezed down behind the tree, Forrest handed Walden the detonating device. 'You think this is far enough?' Walden asked.

'Borderline.' Forrest had his eyes glued on Walden's hand.

'Covey, this is Leaf. Any time now. Cover your ears, and open your mouth,' Walden said to Hung, nodding to the others so Hung would interpret.

'Okay, Leaf, any time you're ready,' Lindell said.

'Watch for flash.' Walden pushed down farther behind the tree and forced his breath out of his mouth. He pushed the firing lever down and immediately knew they were too close. The shock wave tore branches off the tree they were behind. Dirt and smoke enveloped them instantly. Walden didn't know how long Covey had been calling before he heard him.

'Fig Leaf, Fig Leaf, this is Covey, Covey. Come in,

151

dammit.' Walden didn't move as he listened to the pitter-pat of wood and dirt raining down. He struggled to draw some air into his lungs, but they seemed flat and unwilling. Just when he was becoming frantic, his lungs opened like an inflated balloon and he began to cough. He looked around as his head cleared. Cricket lay behind him, his small legs churning as though he were riding a bicycle, his hands still over his ears.

'Shit.' Forrest coughed.

'Bring them around. The ships are coming.' Walden squinted through the smoke and dust, keying the mike.

'Covey, this is Leaf. Did you see it? Over.'

'See it? See it? It looked like a nuclear explosion, for Christ's sake,' Lindell shouted.

'We are moving to LZ,' Walden said. Forrest poured water on Cricket's and Playboy's faces. The smoke clung to the ground as the team stumbled to where the tree had been. The ground around the trunk of the tree looked freshly plowed. Large, jagged slabs of bark were strewn everywhere. The tree itself had fallen nearly to the ground, yet was partially held up by smaller trees.

'Fig Leaf, this is Stately Wonder. Am making my approach. Over.'

Walden looked at the figures bunched around him in the half-light of the smoke and dust. 'Stately Wonder, this is Fig Leaf. Am going to blow three Claymores to your east. Over.'

'Roger, Leaf. Good idea. Over.'

Walden grabbed the two detonators from where Playboy had placed them, and nodded at Forrest to fire the other. They went off almost simultaneously. The sound of Cobras strafing the sides of the ridge followed the booming echo of the mines. Within seconds the deep thunder of the Huey descending reverberated through Walden. The downdraft blew the smoke into the woodline as bits of bark and dirt whirled around.

The Huey dropped, its nose pitched upward. Its skids were four feet above the ground when Walden heard weapons firing. He began tossing the little people into the seesawing ship. The door gunners' fingers locked back on the triggers of the mounted M-60 machine guns. Walden and Forrest leaped onto the skids, grabbing onto the floor edge as the helicopter lifted higher. Then it lowered again and Hung and one of the door gunners grabbed the rucksacks, dragging them into the ship.

'Go, go,' Walden screamed above the roar of the helicopter and the firing of the other door gunner. His hands clawed at the waffle steel flooring as the Huey shot into the air and banked to the left. The tilting of the ship helped them to slide into the helicopter. As soon as they were in, both Walden and Forrest turned to the doorway and began firing magazine after magazine into the green-and-yellow canopy of jungle below. They began to giggle and then laugh. Heat waves rippled off the hot barrels and shell casings piled up on the floor. As the Huey climbed, Walden unfastened his sawed-off M-79 from the snap-link and began popping 40-millimeter rounds downwards. After firing six rounds he flopped backward.

He was breathing a sigh of relief when he looked at the door gunner nearest him. The man was talking frantically into his mouthpiece. Walden noticed for the first time that the helicopter was swaying and dipping. The door gunners began running back and forth through the small area, flipping the cord attached to their helmets around like stage performers. One of the gunners inspected the ceiling, then squatted next to Walden.

'You okay? How bad you fucked up?' The gunner's tanned face told Walden he had been around for a while.

'I'll make it. You guys have balls to come in and get us. Thanks.'

'Us, my ass.' The gunner looked away for emphasis and then back. 'You guys were down there. I mean, I don't believe that.' He patted Walden's shoulder, then scurried about again. The ship sounded funny. Walden wished he had asked him how bad they had been hit. Pau and Cricket reached out and took his hands. The team gathered tighter

153

together, each holding hands with another. They were calm now, a certain serenity covering them as they waited to see what was in store.

Walden hoped they would make the border at least. Even hostile Vietnam seemed like a refuge after Laos. Hope rose as he watched the plains of Khe Sanh pass below. Walden listened to the beat of the blades. He thought of the helicopter carrying seven of his friends that had gone down two years before. It had been hit at six thousand feet by antiaircraft fire. It had exploded in the air and then fallen, end over end, like a flaming torch. When it had hit the ground it had exploded again. His friends were still carried as Missing in Action.

Walden reached the red clay of a Marine artillery base come up in jerks. The faces of his team reflected the feeling in his gut. He knew they were in serious trouble when he saw the reception committee of Marines start running for foxholes and bunkers. Just before the Huey hit the ground, Walden and Forrest locked eyes.

Walden hadn't noticed that he had stopped breathing until an involuntary gasp filled his lungs when the chopper slammed against the ground.

'*Di di. Di di*,' Walden yelled. The little people began diving out of the ship as dust billowed up. They looked back at Walden to see if he was being helped before they began to sprint away from the ship. Forrest and Pau grabbed Walden by the arms and jumped out the doorway. The gunners in a flurry opened the pilot's door and helped them out. Walden's unslung CAR-15 fell to the ground as Forrest and Pau dragged him out. The pilots raced the gunners away from the hissing chopper. Walden had stumbled a dozen yard before he realized his weapon was gone. He twisted out of Forrest's grasp and ran back to the ship.

'It's going to blow. Goddammit, Walden, it's going to blow,' Forrest screamed after him. The rifle had been passed down to him from the leader of Louisiana team long before. He couldn't let it burn. Pain seared through his neck when he bent over and plucked the weapon from the

154

ground. The rotor blades slowly turned as he stood up triumphantly and held the weapon over his head. He grinned. Forrest put his hand over his eyes and shook his head.

A Navy corpsman ran up to Walden when he reached the edge of the pad.

'Damn, you really bled some,' he drawled. He inspected the dressing. 'You'd better get to the hospital in Quang Tri.'

'Screw Quang Tri. I'm going home.' Walden lit a cigarette. 'When is another ship coming in?'

'You'd better get to a hospital and have that taken care of,' the medic insisted. 'You guys Marines?'

'Shit.'

The medic snorted and walked away. A gathering crowd of Marines gawked at the group. The little people gathered around Walden.

'*Beaucoup dau?*' Pau lifted himself on tiptoe to look at the side of Walden's neck.

'It doesn't hurt. Much.' Walden squeezed Pau to him. They stood watching the lonely helicopter cool down. After twenty minutes the door gunners eased gingerly back. They inspected the cowling and blades, then brought out a couple of rolls of green masking tape. Setting up a ladder, they began to tape over the holes blown through the blades. Walden looked up through one of the holes, seeing the honeycombed interior.

'When's another ship coming in?' Walden asked.

'We're going to fly this one back. It's all right. We just got to patch it up a little. We got to get back to Da Nang for new blades or we'll sit here forever.' The gunner pressed tape over a jagged gap.

'You're crazy if you think I'm flying anywhere in this,' Walden blurted. 'Look at this.' He pointed at a puddle of fluid created by a steady drip from the bottom of the ship.

'Ah, no sweat, man.'

'Bullshit,' Walden yelped. He stormed over to where the pilots were sitting on unused sandbags.

'Well?' Walden was not smiling.

'It's okay. The engine is fine,' one said, waving his hand. 'We'll be over the ocean most of the way.'

'Oh, that's great. That's all right, then,' Walden said, turning back and forth. 'Does it matter that the damn thing is leaking?'

Twenty minutes later the pilots climbed into the ship with the same bored expression bus drivers wear. Walden mumbled a lot as he helped the little people in.

On the way back the door gunner on Walden's side hung the barrel of an M-79 out into the slipstream. A high-pitched whistle ran through the craft. The team jumped and looked around frantically, grabbing anything handy. The gunner began to laugh, giving himself away. Walden looked at him tiredly. The gunner quieted into a series of giggles.

They banked right off the ocean and flew directly over Marine Team hooch, its tin walls yellow and shiny in the setting sun. The little people shouted and waved at people in the camp who'd stopped to look at the arriving helicopter.

As soon as the skids touched, the PSP people jumped into the ship, grabbing the team and slapping them on the back. People lifted Walden out of the ship as if he were a litter case. Miles Keegan yelled for them to take it easy.

'I can walk. I can walk,' Walden said, pulling himself back down to the ground. He moved over to the front of the ship where the pilots were climbing out.

'I told you she'd make it,' the one said.

'Thanks for getting us out. I mean that. Thanks.'

'Our pleasure.' Both pilots reached out to shake hands, then left to find their gunners.

Colonel Easton waded through the crowd and embraced Walden. 'You and your people did a damn fine job, son.' Beer cans were being passed around. Walden took a swig from one and felt instantly drunk. 'You'd better get to the hospital and have that taken care of,' the colonel said, ushering Walden through the crowd.

As Walden walked with the colonel, a tingling weakness started working through his legs. The drone began inside his head again. He crawled into the back of the jeep and flopped down on the seat.

'We can get an after-action report from you tomorrow. We've been briefed by the launch site.' The colonel paused. 'We can get the rest from Jerry if you're still in the hospital.'

'I'm going to the hospital with you.' Forrest slid into the front seat.

'But someone has to take care of the little people.' Walden thought the beer was going to make him sick.

Pau climbed over the back of the jeep. 'I go with you.'

'Sure, sure.' Walden shut his eyes. He listened to Workman starting the jeep, then felt the swaying as they headed for the road running outside camp.

Along the stretch between the camp and the hospital, the wind blew by so fast that it carried no smell. But as they slowed to make the turn into the Naval Medical Station, Walden could smell hot rubber, asphalt, and sweat. He concentrated on not being sick. He felt Sister Theresa pushing his head down.

Walden opened his eyes when they parked outside the large brown tent. They lifted him out and walked him past a CONEX container and then through a large entrance leading into an open area. The floor was gray gravel that crunched beneath their boots when they walked into the gloomy tent. Walden sat down on a wooden folding chair and Workman went off to find someone. It was a large cavern inside, smelling of alcohol and canvas. Stacks of stretchers stood along one wall; silver stands to hold IV and blood bottles stood in a cluster, waiting. Walden began to feel much better. Once when he had walked into a dentist's office, his tooth had stopped hurting.

'How you feeling?' Forrest squatted in front of Walden. 'Guess business is kind of slow,' he said, looking around the empty tent.

'I'm going to screw up their whole day.'

157

'Want a cigarette?' Forrest fished in his pocket for a pack. He lit two, handing one to Walden. He tossed the pack to Pau, who stood to one side of Walden, holding his CAR-15.

The smoke entering Walden's lungs tasted sweet and dry, almost nauseating. The second drag was better. There was the sound of crunching gravel as Workman and a Navy corpsman came in.

'We'll take some X rays here to see what we've got,' the corpsman said. 'But then you'll go down to the surgical Army hospital to get operated on.' He ushered Walden into a boxed-off room. He laid a sheet over the top of the X-ray table and told Walden to take off his shirt. As Walden unbuttoned the blood-starched jungle shirt, he thought of Hoa. He felt the cold of the metal creep through the sheet as he stretched out on the table. The medic took his pictures and twenty minutes later returned with a large manila envelope, which he handed to Forrest. Walden was suddenly invisible as the medic explained to Forrest and Workman.

'It's a pretty fair chunk,' the medic began. Walden turned and walked out of the tent with Pau. He didn't want to hear about it.

They sat together in the jeep. 'You go Saigon now?' Pau asked.

'I go after I get out of the hospital.' Walden patted Pau's knee. They sat silently.

'We have to take you to the Army hospital now,' Forrest said, climbing into the jeep with Workman. 'The medic said you were lucky. He said if that piece of shrapnel had been an inch or so closer you'd be dead or paralyzed.'

They drove back onto the highway. Workman flicked on the headlights as small shacks took the place of the equipment depots. Walden smelled the exotic odor of Vietnam, the scent of sandalwood and cooking spices and oils. He wondered at his heightened sense of smell. They continued north past one of the Monkey Mountain Marine facilities. After a mile Workman slowed the jeep and turned down a short dirt road. He turned off the lights as he approached a gate with an American guard. The guard let them in and told them to stop while he secured the gate with a large chain. He walked to the jeep.

'You have to check your weapons here,' he said, looking at Pau.

'Forget it.' Walden climbed out of the jeep. 'These weapons are classified. We don't surrender them to anyone.' He started leading the others toward a long Quonset hut.

'Wait a minute,' the guard said angrily. 'I said, you check your weapons here, or you don't get on this compound.' He put his hand firmly on Walden's shoulder. Walden pulled away, and the tension was immediate.

'Hey, take it easy,' Forrest said, keeping his voice quiet. 'What he says is true. Call our commander.'

'All they are is weird-looking M-16's,' the guard said defensively, pointing at the weapon slung over Walden's shoulder. Walden lifted the weapon to the guard's face, pointing to the spot where the serial numbers normally were. Only a silver swirling pattern was there, the numbers having been expertly removed. The guard knew the difference.

'You want to call our commander or not?' Walden asked.

'I guess it's okay for you guys, but we sure as hell don't allow any armed Orientals in here.' He looked Pau up and down.

'Four hours ago I was lying out in a jungle a million miles from here and I trusted him then. Don't tell me I can't trust him now.' Walden suddenly felt sorry for the guard, but he was too tired to be nice.

'Fuck it, man. Do what you want to.' The guard stalked back to his gate shack.

They walked through the front screen door of the tin-and-plywood building, and an Army medic wearing a green T-shirt and carrying a clipboard confronted them.

'Who's Walden?' he asked, peering through a pair of thick glasses.

'I am.' The medic looked at him and then at the others. He looked as if he were going to say something about the weapons, but then thought better of it.

'I need your full name, and address of next of kin.' He waved the clipboard, indicating that Walden should follow him. 'The rest of you have to stay in the reception area.'

'We're going with him,' Forrest said, and there was no debate in his voice.

'This certainly isn't procedure,' the medic said, but led them down a corridor through a set of swinging doors. They walked in on a nurse and doctor leaning against an operating table, drinking coffee and joking. The doctor looked irritated by their arrival. He whispered something to the nurse and she giggled. He straightened up and came forward.

'No, no, Cooper, don't tell me. Let me guess.' He flourished the coffee cup in his hand, talking as if he were playing twenty questions. The medic looked exasperated.

'You're from that hush-hush Special Forces camp down the road, right? You give nothing but your name, rank, serial number, and date of birth, right? You can't tell us where you were when you were wounded. You wouldn't tell us what unit or outfit you were with. You can't tell us what state you're from. Am I right?'

'I don't need a fuckin' comic.' Walden turned to leave. Pau instinctively pointed the barrel of his CAR-15 at the doctor. Workman rolled his eyes and looked away.

'For God's sake, tell him to point that thing somewhere else,' the doctor said, stepping back.

'What kind of asshole are you?' Forrest asked, motioning to Pau to lower the barrel. 'You got a wounded man here, goddammit.'

'I was just kidding, for Christ's sake.' He motioned to Walden to come to the table. Pau relaxed slightly. A priest came into the room as the doctor unwrapped the dressing.

'Oh.' The priest laughed. 'I thought you might need the last rites. The report said you were Catholic.'

'Stick around,' Forrest said blandly.

160

'Oh, yes.' He fumbled with a black leather case he held in his hands.

'No, Father. I don't need you.' Walden was respectful.

The doctor, stiffened by the priest's presence, changed tone again.

'You're going to have to wash that grease off your face before I can do anything. Cooper, give him some soap and a towel.'

The medic handed the towel and soap to Walden and pointed to a restroom.

'I wish they would let us have some of the ones you have to fight to save, instead of all these flesh wounds.' The nurse's voice carried into the bathroom. For five minutes Walden scrubbed at his face. When he was finished, most of the grease was still there.

'Take off your shirt and lie down on the table,' the doctor said, arranging instruments on a clean white towel. Walden watched the doctor pick up a stainless steel probe.

'You going to give me anything before you stick that in?'

'We never give anything to the Marines. You guys are supposed to be tougher than they are. Right?'

'Christ,' Walden mumbled.

'Now, son,' the priest said scoldingly.

'Father, will you please get the hell out of here?'

'Don't worry. It won't hurt,' the doctor said, almost kindly. Walden listened to the footsteps of the departing priest. He stared down at the shiny metal tabletop as the probe icicled into the hole in his neck. He listened to the doctor make noises.

'You got real lucky,' the doctor said, putting the probe down. 'You can sit up.' His voice became professional, the wisecracking manner gone. 'You have two choices. You can stay here and we will operate tomorrow morning to remove the piece of shrapnel, or we can leave it in and hope that it doesn't move.'

'Leave it in,' Walden said immediately, sliding off the table.

'You'll have to get a tetanus shot.'

'I'll get one from my people.' Forrest helped him put his shirt back on.

'Don't put your shirt back on. I have to redress the wound,' the nurse said, laying out bandages and tape. Walden thought she was almost pretty for a round-eye.

'I'll try to get hit more seriously the next time,' he said, when she began dressing the wound. She avoided his eyes. When finished, she quickly left the room. Cooper stood with his clipboard, a permanent part of his hand.

'Make sure you change the dressing every day, and keep it clean,' he said. 'And don't forget to put in for your medal.'

CHAPTER FOURTEEN

IN THE dim cast of a quarter moon Walden and Forrest sat on the front porch of the team hooch, drinking beer and watching an occasional flare drift down over Marble Mountain. Inside, voices and laughter merged with the music of the Doors. Walden spoke as though talking to himself.

'Have you ever noticed how peaceful it seems back here? Like they could be attacking with five hundred troops and it wouldn't bother me. After the shock of being in Laos wears off, it seems really safe back here at base, like it's neutral ground.'

'Sure.' Forrest looked across the deserted sandlot that separated them from the hooches in Recon Company. 'Except there isn't anyplace in this whole country that's neutral.' He slapped a mosquito on his forearm, then took a long swallow from his can of beer. Walden tossed his empty into the case at their feet and reached for another. A grimace etched his face for an instant. His right hand went reflexively to the side of his neck.

'You said your neck wasn't bothering you anymore.' Forrest got a beer out of the case and handed it to him. Walden opened the beer without answering.

'Well?'

'Well, what?' Walden said. 'It's only been a week or so since I got hit.' He wiped the wetness from the sweating can onto his pants.

'Two weeks, almost three.'

'Don't worry about it. It'll be fine by the time we get back from extension leave.' Walden slowly turned his head back and forth to relieve the cramp.

'Hot damn, I keep forgetting that we're going back to the States for thirty days. It's not real.' The music ended inside the hooch. The voices of the little people were subdued in the sudden quiet.

'Thirty days to get old and shaky,' Walden said, rolling the beer can slowly between his palms. 'You start thinking about it. You can't smell it anymore, you can't touch it, but you're still here, because you know you have to come back.' He leaned forward, resting his arms on his knees. 'I've been home on extension leave before. That's why I want to go to Saigon this time.'

'You can't go fishing in Saigon, man,' Forrest said.

'Bullshit.' Walden laughed. 'I could catch that big one in Hoa's pond a couple of hundred times in a month.'

'Ah, man.' Forrest blew the smoke of a fresh joint over the wooden railing. 'Thirty days to do what I want. No smell of burning shit every morning. No Charlies trying to put my dick in a bag. No goddamn missions.' He looked at Walden for a sign of confirmation, but there wasn't any. 'What's the matter? Don't you want to go home?'

'It isn't that I don't want to go back, it's just that I don't see any point,' he said tiredly. 'You go back, and you start seeing friends who work for something worthwhile. They have wives, kids, a future.'

'You've been bummed out about this leave since they told us it was approved,' Forrest said. 'I mean, you've been here longer than anyone, not to mention the year you spent with the First Cav. Take a break, for Christ's sake.'

'Why?' Walden threw his arms in the air. 'When I was home the first time, after the Cav, I wanted just to slip back into it. But the more I tried to forget the war, the more I thought about it. I couldn't seem to stop talking about it. My friends got tired of it real quick. They would say, "You're not going to get off on that again, are you?" Or I would get asked to a party, but only if I promised not to talk about the war.'

'They sound like assholes to me.'

'No. They were my friends, most of them since grade school. I don't blame them. They just didn't want to know.'

'But from some of the stuff you told me about the Ia Drang Valley and those other places, I'm surprised you didn't go crazy with no one to talk it out with.'

'I kind of did,' Walden said. 'A couple of weeks after I was home, I started to have these dreams. Guys that I had known in the Cav, guys that had been killed. This one dream I must have had a dozen times, about this kid I had known from another platoon. He was killed outside the church I've told you about, the one in Bong Son.'

'Where you killed those gooks behind the altar, and the crucifix was blown off the wall?'

'Yeah. Anyway, he would look just the way he did when they took him away. He had been killed by this explosion. I don't know what it was. He was all wet with blood and his uniform had been pretty much blown off. I remember how he used to hate to get wet, how you could always hear him bitching when we came to a stream or when it started to rain. In this dream he would be crying and telling me that he didn't have his jacket anymore and he was cold. He would beg me to go back and get his jacket. Then I would wake up.'

'Jesus.' Walden noticed the shiver that shook Forrest.

'I had that dream every night, until I took my field jacket out in the woods and burned it. I got drunk and burned this field jacket and I told him it was for him and it was the only way I could think of to get it to him. I never had the dream again.'

'Goddamn, that gives me goose bumps.'

'That was one of the good dreams. I could live with that. It was the other dreams, night after night. They were worse than the real thing. This one, I was up to my neck in shit. There were all these parts of bodies floating on top. Then faces of dead gooks started to swim toward me. From all sides I could see them. I woke up and couldn't go to sleep anymore. I turned on all the lights in my room, and sat on my bed and tried to cry until I had to go to work. It seemed as though if I cried it would be all right, that I would be forgiven. I couldn't, though.'

'You can go fishing.' Forrest had had enough. 'You're always talking about fishing in Minnesota.'

'I want to go to Saigon and see Hoa.'

'You can see Hoa when you get back.'

'A half a million dudes would give their left nut to go back to the States. All I want is a damn extension leave to Saigon and they won't give it to me.'

'It'd take you two months to recuperate.' Forrest unconsciously began tapping his boot against the flooring as 'Fortunate Son' boomed through the plywood.

'They're playing our song.' Walden grinned. It was like a Scottish soldier suddenly hearing the pipes.

'Ain't it the truth?' Forrest rasped in his best W. C. Fields voice. He pulled another joint from his pocket, bit the paper twist off the end, and lit it. He took a deep drag, began to cough, and handed the joint hurriedly to Walden. 'Send my remains to Philadelphia.'

Walden listened to the words yet again. '*And when you ask them how much should we give, they only answer more, more, more. It ain't me, it ain't me, I ain't no fortunate son.*'

They listened to the end of the song. Walden sighed. 'What the hell, I can go and check out the craftmobile.'

'The craftmobile?' Forrest raised his eyebrow. 'Do you think you can handle that? What the hell is the craftmobile?'

'It was this van that would travel around to school parking lots during the summer and sell crafts. Plaster of Paris plaques and statues you could paint. They had this one plaque of an Indian chief. I just loved it. They had fishes, horses, little dogs, which were cheap. The Indian was the most expensive. It cost maybe three, four bucks. I always thought of it as something grown-ups could buy. Little kids could buy the bead stringing kits, and the plastic billfold kits, but not the Indian chief. I sure wanted that Indian chief.'

Forrest waited. 'Well, did you ever get it?'

'Get what?'

'The goddamn Indian chief.'

'Oh.' Walden was distant.

'Well?' Forrest bent over for another beer. After a time Forrest said, 'Look, tell me you got it even if you didn't. Okay?'

'I got it,' Walden said. He took the beer from Forrest.

166

Forrest reached for another. He sat back up and twirled his mustache. 'You never did, did you?'

'I'll get us each one when I'm home,' Walden said. 'You want one?'

'Sure,' Forrest smiled. 'Don't forget the paint.' He abruptly stopped as a large shiver ran through the ground, making the hooch creak. There was a distant rumble, filtered through miles of air.

'Big time,' Walden said. They got up from the chairs and went to the corner of the porch. In the distance a pulsating glow danced behind the mountains, lighting up the sky in a weird yellow.

'Arc light, you mother,' Forrest shouted, shaking his fist toward the mountains. Walden pictured the B-52's, forty thousand feet up, dropping tons of bombs on a place they couldn't see. The strobe-light effect of the large bombs exploding behind the mountains made the night flicker like an old movie. Then it was over, the mountains fading into darkness, the thudding sounds erasing out over the ocean.

'I'm glad to be going back to the States, even if only for thirty days,' Forrest said.

'What's the point? It's all crazy. That stupid movie star goes to Hanoi and has her picture taken sighting down the barrel of a thirty-seven goddamn mike-mike at one of our own jets. This war is like a cereal box: you reach into the sonofabitch and wonder what kind of a prize you're going to get. And all you get are surprises.'

Walden thought of his bed at home, of how it had looked when he was small, and what it had become when he went back. At the end it had a bedspread of nightmares, the dreams of war invading the place where he had dreamed of children's things. Night after night the war screamed through his head. The dark mud speckled on the windshields of the Hueys. The faces of the dead, the dying, merging with the cold dust clouds of An Khe. The blank, staring eyes that lifted and rose on the shadows of the wind.

'Let's go inside,' Forrest said, getting up from the chair.

'Sure,' Walden said. 'It's getting cold out here.'

CHAPTER FIFTEEN

WALDEN FELT the isolation that came from being with strangers. *Cam Ranh Bay, going home, waiting for the freedom bird.* The words didn't feel as though they belonged to him. The holiday atmosphere of the others waiting to go home pushed him farther into the dark mood that had been with him since he left Da Nang. For a second he thought again of walking out the gate and going to Saigon. It was his leave, his time, they were taking away.

He rolled over on his side, elbowing up from the bare mattress, and lit his fourth cigarette in an hour. The last rays of sunlight spread along the screened windows of the transit barracks, casting purple shadows across the walls and bunks. The billet smelled of cheap PX cologne and sweat, along with that odor everyone in Vietnam had.

Walden's head snapped around as the lights came on and two drunk GIs stumbled into the barracks.

'We're not short, we're next,' one of them yelled, staggering down the center aisle. He accidentally kicked over a butt can. Walden watched the brown sludge of decomposing cigarettes and water spread across the floor. People cursed and grabbed their bags from the path of the stinking water. The kid who had kicked the can was frozen in place, waiting for something to explode. He stared at the puddle, not moving. Walden rolled off his bunk and went to the door.

Standing on the steps outside the billet, he heard a Beatles tune drifting from a gathering of nearly a hundred GIs. Walden pushed his beret down into the side pocket of his fatigue pants. The smell of marijuana hung over the

168

crowd. In the twilight Walden could see smoke rising from around faces like air strikes.

It was the last night most of them would spend in Vietnam. As the darkness set in, they joined together in celebration and to smoke up the last of their Nam stash. Even the few MPs milling around the edge of the crowd seemed to understand. They knew they weren't going to bust anybody who had been out in the bush for a year and was going home the next day. They knew it and the grunts knew it. They were the survivors, the ones who hadn't died, hadn't gotten maimed, the ones who could walk away. They gathered for a last time on a barren depression between barracks and latrines.

Walden felt he could tell the difference between the infantry types and the clerks. The grunts looked rumpled and used, the dirt of a year still deep in their pores. They looked out from somewhere far behind their eyes. The clerks were the bored ones, the overweight ones, the ones wearing new fatigues with everything on them. The grunts usually didn't have anything sewn on their jungle shirts, and their boots had turned the color of the area they'd fought in, the black dye having worn off. The clerks wore spitshined boots.

Walden moved into the gathering and a tall GI handed him a long, fat joint. Walden looked into the angular face with a pair of granny glasses perched on the end of a long nose. The flop-hat he was wearing, decorated with a white plastic C-ration spoon and a dozen grenade pins, made Walden feel at home. He took the joint and Flop-Hat giggled.

'Made the dude special,' he said, watching Walden take a toke. As soon as the smoke hit his lungs, Walden knew he had taken too much. He began to cough, the smoke coming back feeling as if it were dragging razor blades with it.

'Damn,' Walden gasped when he could talk again. 'What the hell you got in that thing?'

'Made the dude special,' Flop-Hat said proudly. 'Cured the sonofabitch. That's the secret. Cured it. Carried it

169

through War Zone fuckin' D, man.' He nodded his head hard. 'It's been wet, dry, I don't know how many times. Never took it out of the bag, though. Saved it just for tonight.' He took a long drag from the smoldering bomber and Walden waited for him to start coughing. He didn't. He grinned as the smoke poured out between his teeth.

Handing the joint to someone else, Flop-Hat said, 'This is Moon-Pie,' and pointed at a form on the sand. 'Me and the Pie came over together.' He bent over to pat the guy on the back. 'He's from I-o-way. Going back now, though.' He ruffled the man's hair. Moon-Pie didn't answer. He took the joint handed to him, but didn't say a word. Minutes later, as Flop-Hat and Walden were talking about their tour, Moon-Pie spoke up.

'I'll get back home in time for the harvest,' he said, the words wandering a bit. His head was bowed, and he talked into the sand. 'I'll help Daddy with the crops, then I'll get my winter job back at the feed store in Grundy Center.' He recited the words as a litany. Walden saw the pained expression pass over Flop-Hat's face. He shifted his weight uncomfortably from side to side, then saw Walden's eyes watching. He moved closer and whispered so Moon-Pie couldn't hear.

'That feed store burned down, six, seven months ago. He showed me the letter.' The rumble of machine-gun fire on a distant perimeter ended his explanation. The entire mass of soldiers froze. The music quickly ended as the GIs turned off the cassette players to listen. The firing chugged to a stop, then flared again like the dry heaves.

'Gooks in the wire. Gooks in the wire,' voices whispered to one another. Walden listened carefully. Intermixed with the shooting was the dull crump of M-79 shells. *Somebody has for sure seen something.* The firing wavered, almost died, and then erupted anew. *How the hell am I going to get a gun?* He was angry for having allowed himself to be still in-country without one. An image of himself lying dead in the middle of one of the largest bases in Vietnam popped into his head. At CCN it wouldn't have bothered him, even if

170

they'd been in the wires; he would've known the people on the perimeter. But here he didn't know anyone.

He was getting ready to tell Flop-Hat that he was going to hit it before the rockets started, when the cheer began. At first it was just a few lone voices, but it quickly became a roar. 'Fuck you, Charlie. We're going home,' a voice yelled, rising above the other shouts. As though on cue every cassette player in the area was turned back on full blast.

'Rock and goddamn roll,' a shadow near Walden yelled as the opening sound of Iron Butterfly exploded like a bomb.

Walden grinned as two smoldering joints were passed to him. He, too, had been relieved from the war. He, too, was going home. For the first time in a long time it wasn't he who had to fight, had to lead, had to keep everyone alive. For this night someone else could do the job. He suddenly felt peaceful, as if he had taken three green hornets. He was going home. Even if it was only for thirty days, he suddenly wanted it. The queasy sensation of being homesick ran through him. He saw quick images of tulips poking through the snow and mud beside his grandmother's house, hot bread and dripping butter in a warm kitchen, the watch he'd gotten for his twelfth birthday. The pictures ran on top of each other. The firing ended.

'I can't go home. I can't go home now,' Moon-Pie stammered. Flop-Hat knelt and put his arm around him. There was a lost sound to Moon-Pie's voice that made a shiver lace along Walden's spine.

'It's okay, buddy. It's okay,' Flop-Hat said. He rocked Moon-Pie back and forth. Walden looked down at the bowed heads. Feeling like an intruder, he looked at the faces around him, lit by illumination flares hanging in the night. *They could easily be the dead ones.* The ragged figures, many of whom had been in the jungle the day before, were apparitions swaying back and forth in the swinging light. *They could all be dead. I could be dead. I should be dead.* Moon-Pie sobbed quietly.

The sound took him back to the launch site a year before where the team was waiting for the target area to clear so they could get in. Jimmy Jensen had taken California Team in that morning. The insertion had gone fine. Then an hour later word came back that Jensen had been killed. A branch had pulled the pin out of the white phosphorus grenade Jensen had been carrying and it had exploded before he could get it off his web gear.

He saw again the Huey, blades drumming as it flew over the bare rolling hills toward the helipad, with a dark bundle dangling from the end of the 120-foot rope. The ship hovered overhead, slowly lowering the bundle. The wind had loosened the hastily wrapped poncho, making it flutter around the charred corpse. He had braced himself and jogged to where Miles Keegan was frantically trying to find the snap links that were hidden in the black-and-red furrows of the split skin. Walden had cut the rope with his knife and then signalled to the door gunner that it was loose.

Not looking at the body, he'd helped Keegan place it in a rubber body bag. As the bag was being zipped, he realized that he was holding his breath. He turned and walked quickly to the edge of the pad. When he couldn't hold it any longer, he sucked in slowly, as though he had broken ribs. The odor of the cauterized flesh was on his hands, his clothes, in the air around him. His stomach heaved and he knelt in the weeds and vomited. He thought of the man he had shaken hands with that morning. He heaved again.

After he'd heard the ambulance drive off, he'd gotten back up. He found the helipad deserted except for the kid who took care of the radio and paperwork at the launch site. He was standing where the body had been, staring at the steel plating. The kid said something that Walden couldn't make out, but the tone made him walk over.

'Jim? Jim?' The words were repeated over and over. Walden then saw his face. The stare was that of someone who had stepped out the back door of his mind and was

172

gone. Walden took him to his friends then. For three days the boy sat on his bunk and stared at the canvas walls of the tent, sometimes sobbing. Finally they saw that the kid wouldn't come back on his own, so they put him through channels and Walden had never seen him again.

Moon-Pie had that same voice, the same look. Something had gone wrong inside of him, too, and Walden didn't want to know what he had seen.

Part of Walden wanted to stay with the crowd, and another part told him to get away from it. The things he had learned, the things that had kept him alive, nagged at him. *Don't stay in a crowd. Don't go anywhere without a weapon. Always know where to go if it hits the fan. Always leave yourself a way out.* The adrenaline started to drip into his veins as he realized how many of his rules he had broken already. It came to him that he was a lot more stoned than he should be.

The faces looked gaunt and tired as he moved to the edge of the crowd. To be alone, just to regroup, seemed important. Once outside the throng, he quickened his footsteps. He walked past the huge, open-ended barn with the deserted processing tables standing stark and white. He headed for the shadows away from the floodlit gravel area. He walked between wooden barracks and smaller shacks until he came to a road, which he followed until the lights of the area fell behind. In the wavering light of a flare he saw a sandbagged bunker off to one side. He turned toward it, the sight of the sandbags making him feel better. He climbed up and sat on the top. He didn't realize that he had been sweating until a puff of wind flowed over him.

Alone on the bunker he began to feel calm again. The pounding of his heart quieted as he looked back at the lighted area. He thought of his family back in Minnesota, and then he thought of Hoa in Saigon.

An hour later he walked back to the barracks, having decided that he wanted to go back home, just one more time.

173

The next morning they stood on the gravel in the assembly area and joints were passed around again. By the time the buses arrived for the airfield, Walden was stoned. His eyes felt as though they were glowing when he got on the bus and found a seat next to the wire-mesh windows. He watched others struggling with duffel bags and Montagnard crossbows. Cameras banged off seats, swinging back and forth on sweating necks. Walden touched the briefcase between his legs and was glad he could travel light. He had only the khaki uniform he was wearing, a few gifts, and his toilet articles. He'd thrown away the fatigues he had worn from Da Nang. He smiled as the bus pulled away, the tires crunching the sparkling gravel. The fatigues hadn't been in the wastebasket a minute before someone had seen the arrowhead of the Special Forces patch and picked them out of the trash.

The bus stopped at an intersection. Walden saw a crowd of newly arrived soldiers being issued steel pots. They filed past the wooden bins and old, dented helmets were tossed to them like footballs. They looked so white, so young, their jungle fatigues glossy with newness, their faces stiff with uncertainty. He looked away from the shuffling line as the bus started to move. No one on the bus made catcalls or taunting remarks. The fresh soldiers were their replacements.

Walden remembered himself when he was first about to put foot on Vietnamese soil, crouched with the others in the landing craft as it bucked through the waves toward the beach of Qui Nhon. That morning for the first time he had been issued ammo that was intended to kill. He remembered looking at the amber lead crowns of the bullets differently. As they'd waited for the front of the LST to drop onto the sand, he'd thought of his uncle and the beaches of World War II. Now it was his turn, his war. Then they were there, moving across the beaches. The first Vietnamese he'd seen was a little boy trying to sell them Cokes. White plaster houses stood among palm trees and they were intact, unblemished. It was not Saipan or

174

Tarawa. Officers and NCOs had dashed about, collecting their people, as groups of soldiers who had arrived long before shouted and jeered.

The TWA airliner was waiting for the chain of buses. The unloading and loading went quickly because no one was playing dragass. Walden felt a slight shock as he stepped past a pretty blond stewardess who smiled and greeted the soldiers. She dropped the professional smile when she eyed the green beret and the rows of medals. Her eyes lifted to his, but he avoided her stare and turned down the aisle to find a seat.

He found an empty row and sidestepped to the seat against the window. As soon as he'd placed the briefcase under his seat, he closed his eyes. Movement churned around him, yet he kept himself in darkness, feeling the lids of his eyes vibrating as he squeezed them together. He hadn't planned on ever going home again. Now that it was happening he couldn't help feeling that something would happen, something would go wrong. He listened to GIs sit down in the seats next to him, but didn't open his eyes. Something terrible had happened at An Khe in sixty-five. A military airplane loaded with people going home had slammed into the side of a mountain after taking off. Walden and others had gone in that night by helicopters and by foot to search the wreckage for the living and to bag up the dead. A thick fog had shrouded the mountain. Soldiers had been arranged around the wreckage for defence, while others had moved through the small fires. Some had started to cry, and had had to be sent to the perimeter and replaced. Walden's mind had frozen shut. He couldn't even remember exactly what he had done.

And there was Khe Sanh in February of sixty-eight. The C-130 had careened in a ball of fire down the runway, exploding ammo blowing out large hunks of the plane. Walden had watched them pinwheel through the air.

He tightened his seatbelt as the TWA engines began to roar. His jaw muscles twitched when the jet leapt forward.

175

One thousand one, one thousand two, one thousand three. The acceleration pushed him back into the seat. He listened to the clunking sound the tyres made rolling over the tar seams of the runway. Then came the lift. As though they had been practising, the soldiers and sailors began to cheer at the top of their lungs. The roar was so loud and shrill that it hurt his ears.

The plane strained for deep air over the bay and Walden sagged deeper into his seat. *Oh, my God, I am heartily sorry for having offended Thee*. His forearms and fingers began to hurt as he gripped the armrests as hard as he could and fought back the tears.

CHAPTER SIXTEEN

WALDEN PUSHED himself up from the leaves and spit. The inside of his mouth tasted of gun oil. For five minutes he had stared down the barrel of the .44 Magnum, heavy steel resting against his bottom row of teeth. The hammer had been cocked back, his finger near the trigger. Now he felt the same exhilaration as when coming back from a mission. During the past three weeks at home the edge had slipped farther and farther away. To be this close now, made him feel alive.

He listened to a squirrel running through the upper boughs of the tree he was leaning against. He aimed the .44 at a nearby tree and pulled the trigger. The recoil slammed his arm upward and fat splinters of wood exploded off the oak. Again he fired as the first shot echoed back across the lake. Again his finger pulled the trigger back and another chunk of bark blew from the tree. And again, a flame shot out a foot from the barrel. His arm and shoulder muscles tensed as the pistol kicked toward the sky before dropping back on the target. Again the boom and flash, and Walden breathed the smell of gunpowder. He fired the last round, then let the pistol drop, dangling from his hand.

The haze drifted away, then the pounding in his hand ebbed, then the ringing in his ears quieted. Still he did not move. Finally he shook himself and walked back to the house.

'Was that you shooting?' his mother asked, nervously drying her hands on her apron.

'Yeah.' He headed for his room in the basement.

'The neighbours around the lake don't like it when there's shooting,' she said, pushing a stray hair off her forehead. 'Especially that thing you have. It sounds like a cannon.'

Walden didn't answer, but turned down the steps into the coolness of the basement. Inside his room he closed the door and tossed the pistol onto the rumpled bed. He stiffened at the sight of his reflection in the dresser mirror. The past three weeks had been far worse than he'd anticipated. The family had tried so hard to make him feel at home, but the more his parents tried to make him happy the more he'd stiffened and pulled away. It was always there in his mind, that good memories would make it worse when he died. And he had to create it so he could look forward to going back to the war. He listened to the ceiling squeak as his mother walked above him. He didn't want to hurt them any more.

He walked to his bed and sat down. He reached into the nightstand and picked up a crumpled pack of Pall Malls. Squeezing it gently, he searched for the cigarette he knew wasn't there. He threw the empty pack into the wastebasket. It hit the beer bottles mounding over the top and fell to the floor. He opened the Styrofoam lid of his beer cooler, reaching into the melted ice for a beer. After opening it, he looked through the heaping ashtray for a long butt. He found one that had been bent over, straightening it out, then lit it. Leaning against the headboard of his bed, he smoked the butt and stared at the closet door.

He felt like crying. Everyone had been so nice. But the longer he stayed at home, the more he saw the hopelessness of it all. Each day crumpled up like the pages of a small book, a thirty-day book that would end with his going back to purgatory.

He dropped the butt into an empty beer bottle and felt a yearning to be held that approached physical pain. Hoa could hold him, coo against him, her warm breath against his face. He could look into her eyes and see that she knew him, knew what he did, understood. Now, here, twelve thousand miles away from the country he would die in, there was alien life going on around him. He thought of the

178

girl he had met three days before, the one with fresh open eyes, a deep tan, and an angular beauty.

He had been at the bar in Bess's Place. She'd come into the bar with a couple of her girlfriends, and a half a dozen college guys made room for them around their table. He'd tried not to look at her. The night had stretched out, and around midnight she'd come up to the bar and ordered popcorn.

'Hi,' she'd said, looking sideways at him. 'It's not good to put salt in your beer. It can cause kidney stones.' He'd looked at her, and then smiled. Kidney stones would be a relief.

'Thanks. I'll remember that.' He'd looked at the Hamm's Bear behind the bar, then nervously back down at his hands spread flat around his beer glass.

'Do you live here?' she'd asked. Bess had slid the basket of popcorn across the bar top.

'I was born here. I'm on vacation now.' He'd looked back at her, wondering.

'Where do you work?' Her slender fingers had pulled the basket slowly to her.

'It's a long story. Your popcorn will get cold,' he'd said softly, wanting her to stay next to him more than anything.

'If you buy me a beer, I'll share my popcorn with you.' She'd cocked her head to one side and looked straight into his eyes. He'd bought her the beer.

She went to the college in town, her name was Heidi, she lived with roommates. He'd said he had never known anyone with the name Heidi, but that he had liked it ever since reading the book. She'd said that everyone told her that. They'd laughed, and found reasons to laugh again. Then she'd again asked what he did for a living and the shield had dropped back down. She'd seen the change in him. The darkness had had him by the throat and wouldn't let go. He'd felt so alone as he'd watched his dour attitude erase her smile.

'I gotta go,' he'd said. He'd stood up from the barstool,

179

said good-night to Bess, and mumbled a good-bye to her. She'd looked a little surprised as he left.

He had to get out of the house. He drained off the beer, then slowly walked up the stairs, trying to be quiet. His mother was in the kitchen and saw him as he headed for the door.

'You're not going out?'

'I'm out of cigarettes. I'm going to get some.' He removed his jacket from the wall peg next to the door.

'I have cigarettes,' she said, opening the kitchen drawer where she kept her dish towels and Winstons.

'I just want to go for a drive in my car.' He avoided her eyes.

'You've been drinking again, haven't you.' She wiped her hands together in front of her. 'You didn't eat hardly any breakfast.'

'Come on, Mom,' Walden said defensively. He picked up her open pack of cigarettes and shook one out.

'It'll be suppertime soon,' she said, as he went to the refrigerator and took out a beer. 'Your father will be home soon. You can have a nice lunch with him and then go fishing. I have a beautiful roast for tonight.' She walked to him and put her hand on his shoulder, lighting his cigarette with her floral-designed lighter. She dropped her hand to his and held it. He felt the warmth and the love that she was trying to show. He wanted her to hold him.

'Sam, do you have to drink so much? We're decent people, Sam. It's not right that you should be drinking all the time.'

He recoiled. 'Leave me the hell alone.' He pulled his hand away.

'Sam, you know better than to use that tone of voice with me.'

'You're worried about tone?' He turned away from her. 'I've been killing people for the last three years and you tell me I have to watch my tone.'

'Sam, you've been drinking,' she said, as though it explained everything.

'Drinking? Drinking? What the hell else am I supposed to do, for God's sake? I'm going back to that scum hole in a week and you're telling me not to drink.' He stomped to the door.

'You were mad at the world when you were five,' she yelled. 'I think it's time you woke up and smelled the coffee, young man.' She planted her hands on her hips. 'If this is the way you want to act when you're home, maybe it's better that you stay with those savages you always talk about. We're decent, Samuel. We didn't raise you to become a drunk.'

She was crying as he walked out of the house, the screen door banging. He knew that she would still be crying when his father got home.

'Fuck,' he yelled as he twisted the ignition key and listened to the souped-up Cobra engine explode into life. He ran his hand softly over the dashboard, feeling closer to the car than to anything he had touched since he'd been home.

'I love you. I love you,' he whispered, caressing the steering wheel. He slammed the Hurst shifter into first gear. The engine screamed as he himself wanted to just before he popped the clutch and fishtailed out the driveway onto the road that led to Highway 52.

The sound of the engine was intoxicating, the sensation of speed soothing. He was going into fourth gear when he saw his father's car come over the railroad tracks nearly a mile up the road. His first thought was to slow down, but he kept the pedal to the floor, watching spears of sunlight reflect off the approaching windshield. In a slash of air they passed, too fast for Walden to see the expression on his father's face. He let up on the gas then, milking the gears back down slowly as he approached the highway. He pulled up to the stop sign and felt under the front seat for the deck of joints. He pulled one out of the plastic wrapper and silently thanked Jerry for having mailed them. After lighting up he pulled out and swung into the right lane, sliding up to sixty-five before turning on the radio.

181

He patted the dash affectionately and relaxed as Otis Redding came on. He puffed on the joint, then twisted the volume up as he watched the white lines flick by. *'Looks like nothing's going change,'* he sang along. *'Everything's going remain the same.'*

He glanced at his watch. Quarter to two. No place to go except Bess's Bar. The only car in the lot was Bess's old Cadillac, its left rear tyre sagging into one of the chuckholes. Walden finished the joint, listening to a disc jockey give an intro to a song he said had been a monster hit in sixty-five. Walden had never heard it before.

The bar smelled the way rummage sales look. He walked past the pool table and Bess looked up from behind the bar.

'Hey, good lookin',' she said, her chubby red face breaking into a smile. He slid onto one of the barstools.

'How's it going, sweetheart?' Walden dropped his lighter onto the bar. 'How about a pack of Pall Mall and a beer.' She tossed him the cigarettes and turned around to draw a Grain Belt.

'You're early today. I'd think you'd be out fishing.' She pushed the glass of beer in front of him.

'I've been fishing for the last three weeks,' Walden answered as she went back to washing beer glasses. 'It's not as much fun without Keith.'

'He should be getting out of the Navy pretty soon.'

'He has about a year. I was talking to his mom the other day and she said he's in the Mediterranean now.'

Bess folded the drying towel neatly before putting it on the drainboard. 'It doesn't seem like a moment has passed since you would deliver me paper and have a pop.'

'You were the best customer I had.' Walden smiled. 'You always paid on time.'

'You were always polite – reliable too.' Bess patted Walden's hand. Walden looked down at the soft, fleshy hand on his own. Bess stepped back and said, 'Damn, why don't you play some music, boy? This place is like a church at midnight.'

'Got any requests?'

182

'Anything but B-5.' Bess chuckled. The scene came back to Walden's mind as he went to the old Wurlitzer standing amid faded yellow advertisements of polka bands. The winter of sixty-seven and he was drunk, being a soldier again. It had been a Saturday night, he'd been at the bar, talking about the rain forests of the Central Highlands. A drunk woman had stumbled up to him, and asked if he had a request for the jukebox.

'B-5,' he'd said, then watched her wiggle off. In a moment she'd returned, scowling as she pushed herself up against him.

'Do you know that song you asked me to play?'

'Yeah. It's "Baby, Let Me Bang Your Box,"' he'd answered matter-of-factly. She'd taken a swing at him. Her boyfriend or husband had rushed over and the fight had broken out. The woman had ended up on the floor, screaming for someone to kill him. He and Danny Redman had punched their way to the door. Once outside, he'd run to the car and brought out the gun. The shadows massing around the door had pushed a balding farmer out onto the wooden porch. Walden had cocked back the hammer of the .44 and held it for a second on the thin form. Then he had lifted the sights to the Hamm's beer sign lighting the parking lot and pulled the trigger. The sign had shredded into a hundred pieces of plastic, the boom of the shot turning heads in Joe's Drive-in a block down the street. The farmer had thrown himself to the ground and hurriedly crawled back into the bar.

The next day Bess had called him to tell him it would cost him two hundred dollars. 'The goddamn beer sign is all over the parking lot,' she had yelled. Now it was a funny story.

Walden looked down at the numbers and letters on the selector panel of the jukebox. He pushed buttons that made up old target designators. Each time he pushed a new set, the target would appear in his mind. *A-5. Late-afternoon insertion. Too late. Quarter after four, fifteen minutes after being on the ground, two helicopters shot down, four dead, two wounded, and he and Jerry.*

'Tango six,' he whispered, pushing the buttons. *T-6, a vacation for three days and then the end of the world.* For some reason a withered leaf that moved back and forth in the heat of the napalm.

'November third.' *N-3. POW camp. Laos. Dying. Late morning.* The sound of the helicopter crashing after dropping them off. That old puking feeling in his gut. Rocks, concrete bunkers, an NVA flag. The smell of soup in the air.

'A Shau four.' *Sweet Jesus. A Shau four.* The place where you could die, come back to life, and die again all in the time it took you for lunch. *The A-Shau-for-lunch bunch.* He walked back to the bar.

'Buy you a beer,' he said.

'Why not?' She pushed her glasses up with the back of her hand, then waddled to the beer tap and drew two fresh ones. 'Here's to you, Sammy.' She lifted her glass to his. She took a drink, then padded to the far end of the bar and began filling the Copenhagen snuff canister. Walden watched her slipping the silver-topped cans one at a time into the green dispenser as if she were loading a magazine. Her dog barked outside the back door. He thought of Giap. Bess flicked a fly off the Hav-A-Hank display and came back.

'I can't stand letting something go that I know I have to do,' she said. She planted a third of herself on her stool and took another sip of beer. 'When you going back?'

'About a week. I felt like going back a week after I got home.' Walden looked out the near window and across the street to Hook's gas station. The jukebox stopped, and the silence hung in the air with the dust.

'Not getting on at home?' Her voice sounded as if coming through a confessional curtain.

'Oh, jeez.' Walden sighed. 'My mother is on the verge of a nervous breakdown. My father is counting the days until I'm gone, and I can't see where I've done anything wrong

184

except leave the boat motor out on the dock.' The first days had been wonderful. The barbecue in the backyard and his father acting like an old friend. They'd drunk beer and eaten steaks. His father had wrapped an arm around him, and told everyone within shouting distance that he was his boy. 'And damn proud of him, too, I'll tell you that.' He had beamed. At last they had become father and son, Walden had thought.

He looked at the amber color of the beer before him, and noticed it matched the grainy spears of light that floated off the end of the bar by the window. Bess sat patiently on her stool.

He drained off the last of the beer and handed the glass to Bess for a refill. He fumbled a cigarette out of the pack as she put the glass in the sink and picked up a fresh one. 'I was home about a week. I was drinking with my dad, and the conversation came around to the war.' He paused, trying to find the words. He held his hands up before him like a doctor after scrubbing. 'I thought that they should know. They're my parents.' He let his hands drop back to the bar. Bess touched his hand, and he looked at her widow's ring.

'I told them what I do,' Walden said quietly. 'I told them that if they got word I was missing in action, they should know that I was dead. That's what I told them.' Walden looked at Bess's old face and felt as though he were inside it. He looked at the frayed, erupted veins around her cheeks. The sad tilt to her lips that her second stroke had brought. 'I told them that I, ah, practised in South Vietnam. That I go in with four or six mercenaries, and one other American. That, ah, a lot of people get killed, a lot die.' Bess pushed her glasses down on her pug nose and looked directly into Walden's eyes.

'So?' She fiddled with her cigarette.

'So my mother told me that she couldn't believe it and I must be lying.'

Bess's eyelids opened like a yanked windowshade. 'What?'

185

'It's no big thing.' Walden held his hands up. 'She just doesn't know. She doesn't understand.'

'By the Jesus,' Bess said, slamming her hand down on the bar.

'They don't know what goes on over there. They don't want to know.'

'Sam, you listen to me now,' Bess said, tapping her stubby fingers on the bar for emphasis. 'I'm old, and that means I'm going to die soon.' She held up her hand like a traffic cop as Walden started to speak. 'I've known you since you were real small. In all that time I've never known you to tell a lie. Sure, you've raised hell, but you were always a good boy.' She pulled a white handkerchief out of the top of her blouse, looked at it for a second, then bunched it up in her hand.

'I pumped my first beer in Veternsville, Minnesota, in nineteen and thirty-two. I've been pumping beer ever since. I thought I was old back then.' She pushed a stray hair back onto her head. 'I've seen a lot of people where you're sitting now. Seen a lot of soldiers. Seen the has-beens from the First World War getting drunk and trying to make people remember. Then we got World War Two. We really lived then, Sam. We really lived.' She fluffed up the corner of her apron and then folded her hands across her lap. 'I guess we thought we had saved the world. Then we got Korea,' she said, the last part of the sentence trailing off. 'I saw 'em all go away, and I saw some of them come back. But they weren't like you. I've watched you go off to war, what is this now?' She looked at the ceiling and sniffed. 'Three times. Three times I've watched you go.' She fumbled with the hem of her apron. A long moment passed. The old floor creaked. 'I've seen you go three times, but I haven't seen you come back yet.'

She started to cry then. Quiet sobs. His nose began to sting.

'Would you do me a favor, Bess? Would you put your arms around me and give me a couple of hugs?'

CHAPTER SEVENTEEN

THE C-130 Blackbird dropped through the turbulent air currents coming off the South China Sea, and began its approach into Da Nang. Sullen gray clouds hung over the city. Walden peered through the window, searching for the twin summits of Marble Mountain. He found them, far past the deserted beaches, shrouded in the mist. The familiar combination of dread and excitement ran through him.

The tin shacks and cardboard hovels bordering the approach lanes to the airfield lifted into view. Turning from the window, Walden fastened his seatbelt. He watched the nervous fumbling of the young Special Forces soldier next to him. The man smiled self-consciously.

'You've been here before, I see,' he said, nodding at the blue-and-silver CIB above Walden's jump wings.

'Yeah.'

'How is it?'

'It's fun,' Walden said. 'You'll love it.' The kid smiled, fingering the green beret he was holding.

'Who are you assigned to?'

'Command and Control North,' Walden answered.

'Jesus. Everyone says that's the last place you want to be assigned.'

'Depends on what you're looking for,' Walden said. The plane hit the runway. The half-moon corrugated steel shelters where they kept aircraft swept by the window. The plane taxied quickly to the special area. Walden wished the new arrival luck and went down the rear ramp of the airplane. The black CCN bus was parked next to the Special Forces Air Liaison office. Walden wondered what the new people thought when they saw the bullet-scarred bus.

'Welcome back, Sam,' Carlos Gurrería said, stepping out of the bus. 'Any of these other guys going to our place?'

'I doubt it,' Walden said, looking to where the other Special Forces people were gathering.

'Any of you guys going to CCN?' Gurrería shouted.

'Only if you tie me up and drag me there,' a grizzled master sergeant yelled back. The others gawked at the shot-out windows and the bullet holes in the metal.

A jeep wheeled up next to the bus. 'Hey, guy.' Forrest grinned. Danny Jeffers, sitting next to him, was singing, '*Get back, get back, get back to where you once belong.*'

Walden put an arm around Forrest's head and kissed him on the ear.

'How was it?' Jeffers asked, climbing into the back.'You get laid?'

'I didn't want to take the chance of catching anything.' Walden climbed in.

'Who am I supposed to drive back?' Gurrería hollered as the jeep pulled away.

Once outside the airfield Jeffers lit a joint. Walden took in the smells of the city as they drove along the river. He felt more at home than he had on the streets of St. Cloud.

'Giap was hit by a truck. He's dead,' Forrest said quickly.

Walden looked at him for a moment, then sighed. 'It was only a dog.'

'And they got us targeted for a mission.'

'Sweet Christ, any more good news? Where is it?'

'Golf Nine, wiretap.' Forrest looked at Walden out of the corner of his eye.

'Fuck me.' Walden threw his head back.

'Tell me about it,' Forrest said. 'Potter's team went in two weeks ago and they haven't heard from them since. Like they disappeared into thin air. No nothing.'

'Jimmy Williams and Pete Sutton were on Potter's team?'

188

'Yeah. They're gone,' Forrest said quietly.

'Home sweet home.' Walden watched the approaching entrance to the Da Nang bridge.

'Better stub the joint,' Jeffers said. 'Charlie tried to blow the bridge again a few weeks back, so these jarheads have become even bigger assholes.' Walden put out the joint as they crept to the sandbag bunker where two Marine guards were checking carts and vehicles.

'Let's see your trip ticket,' a pin-faced Marine ordered, leaning into the jeep and looking around.

'Let me see here.' Forrest rummaged through empty beer cans and crumpled up copies of *Stars and Stripes*. 'There that little bugger is.' He handed the rumpled form to the guard.

'There's nothing on this. It's blank.' The guard turned the form front and back a couple of times.

'I'll fill it in.' Forrest held out his hand. 'What do you want me to put on it?'

'A wiseass.' The Marine scowled. 'You can't go anywhere in Nam without a trip ticket. Where you from?'

Forrest reached into his pocket for his wallet. He pulled out a small laminated card. The Marine looked at the card for a long time before handing it back.

'Can you really carry concealed weapons with silencers?' he asked in a small voice.

'Right. You will also notice that it says we're not to be detained.'

'Go ahead,' the Marine said, waving them on.

'These walk-on-water passes really come in handy,' Forrest said once they were on the bridge.

'It almost makes it worth being at CCN to get one.'

'Tell him, Jer,' Jeffers said, bringing out another joint.

'Now what? I've had enough for today.'

'No, this is good.' Forrest grinned. 'I brought some hits of LSD from the States.'

Walden looked at Forrest and then back at Jeffers. 'You guys take any yet?'

189

'I took a trip the other night.' Jeffers giggled. 'You're not going to believe it, man.'

'The first time I took it back home,' Forrest said, laughing, 'I saw Dracula come through the window of my bedroom.'

'I don't need it,' Walden said. 'I read about that stuff. People flipping out and jumping out of windows thinking they can fly.'

'No, man, it's beautiful,' Forrest said eagerly. 'You have to take precautions, like having someone straight watching out for you. But relax, you have to try this. It's spiritual, mystical.' Forrest was excited. 'It's not like you take it just for a kick. There's something that happens in your head.' The jeep swung into the camp.

'Maybe I'll try it when we get back from the mission,' Walden said. The jeep pulled up to the hooch. He looked at the WE KILL FOR PEACE sign above the entrance to Recon Company, and knew he had never really left.

The opening of the door woke Walden from his nap. He rolled over as Forrest came in.

'There's a weird guy from CCS over at the club. Said he's a friend of yours. Wants to see you.'

'What's his name?'

'He didn't say.'

'What does he look like?' Walden began lacing on his boots.

'About six four, blond hair, crooked teeth, eyes that look like he would kill you for the hell of it.'

'You know who you just met?' Walden strapped on his pistol. 'You just met the legendary Mad Dog Banner.'

'Jesus. That's the guy the NVA offered twenty-five thousand dollars to leave country?'

'That's the boy.'

Walden and Forrest hadn't taken two steps into the club before a voice boomed out, 'Hey, jerk-off.' Banner stood up from a table and waved them over.

190

'I heard you were killed last month,' Walden said as they shook hands.

'I'm always getting killed,' Banner sneered. 'Come on, let's get fucked up. I have to get back to Ban Me Thuot tomorrow.'

'This is my one-one, Jerry Forrest.'

'Yeah,' Banner said, looking at Forrest. 'You're lucky you're not dead.' Then he laughed. 'Have a beer, Forrest,' he said, taking one out of the open case on the table.

'What are you doing up here?' Walden asked.

'Ah, they tried to blow my shit away again. I was taking a goddamn shower and some sonofabitch tosses in a grenade. I got the little puke. Messed that motherfucker up, Jim.' He laughed again.

Walden could see that Banner was even more insane than the last time he'd run into him. The pale-blue eyes looked dead. The tallow-colored skin stretched over his bony face looked like the belly of a fish.

'I figured I'd do a little visiting,' Banner said. 'Let it calm down back there.'

'What did you do to the guy?' Forrest asked.

'Spare yourself, son,' Banner said, lighting Walden's cigarette. 'You remember Adolf, my German shepherd?'

'How's he doing?'

'My goddamn little people got mad at me, and fed me the sonofabitch. Didn't tell me until the party was over. Little bastards,' he said affectionately.

'Oh, man,' Forrest said, looking away. Banner thought that was funny and started to laugh again.

'What's wrong, Forrest, don't you have a sense of humor?'

Back in the hooch Forrest flopped on his bunk. 'That man is insane.'

'Sure he is.'

'What are they going to do with him when he gets back to the States?'

'They don't let that kind go back.'

191

CHAPTER EIGHTEEN

AS WAS his habit on the morning of a mission, Walden woke before dawn. It was the last hour he would have to himself until it was over. The cold air in the dark room made the warm press of the covers feel especially good. Reaching over the side of his bunk, he patted the floor for his cigarettes and lighter. He half expected to feel Giap's coarse hair and wet tongue. He found the cigarettes and lit one.

With the covers back over his chest he watched the Beatles poster next to him appear and disappear as he dragged on the smoke. *Golf Nine*. The words were synonymous with bad news. It was the hottest target area they had. Three teams had been lost there already. Now it would be their turn. Before, it would have been just another chance. Now, with Hoa waiting in Saigon, it was all different. Now he would do it because it stood between Hoa and him.

He thought of Hoa as the first tracings of light appeared. A warm pang swirled around his stomach. He pictured her face on the pillow. He closed his eyes to see better the arch of her cheekbones, and the straight line of her nose. He suddenly felt anxious to get on with the mission. The sooner it was finished, the sooner he could be with her.

Throwing back the blankets, Walden got out of bed. He shivered as he shuffled to the light switch. Forrest mumbled and pulled the blankets over his head.

'It's time to wake up and smell the coffee.' For a moment Walden saw his mother standing in the kitchen, looking disappointed. He rubbed his arms as he sat on the edge of his bunk.

Forrest groaned, sat up, rubbed his eyes. He pulled the

blankets around him like a cloak before swinging his legs off the bed. He lit a cigarette. 'You think we'll go in today?'

'It's Sunday,' Walden said. 'Louisiana Team always goes in on Sunday.'

'I was afraid you would say that.' Forrest flicked an ash off his cigarette. He stared at the floor, as though meditating on the tiny gray ashes. Walden could hear him drawing in long, slow breaths, then exhaling. After a number of minutes he threw back the blankets from his shoulders and stood up.

'Okay, I'm ready.' He grabbed a towel off his locker door. 'Let's do it.'

That early in the morning the showers were always hot. Walden adjusted the temperature until he was just able to stand it. The heated water rose in a white vapor around him. He stood in the burning spray, purifying himself. His muscles tensed, then relaxed, tensed again, then relaxed again. He squeezed his eyelids shut. His resolve stiffened as his body prepared for the day.

Oh, God, please protect us. He stood for several more minutes before turning off the shower. They never washed with soap during their last shower. In the jungle the perfume of soap could be smelled a long way. He towelled off quickly. He was ready.

Back in the hooch Walden put on a clean pair of underwear, and a clean T-shirt. He put the leather necklace with his amulet around his neck, slipping it under his T-shirt. He and Forrest were dressing in silence, like matadors preparing for the bullring. Walden pulled on his jungle fatigue pants, the side pockets sagging with his survival items. Sitting down on his bunk, he powdered his socks and feet before slipping on the jungle boots he wore only on missions. He pulled the socks over his pants legs before lacing them up. With a roll of black electrical tape he taped the tops of his boots and the tops of the socks to keep leeches out.

The fatigue shirt already had the URC-10 survival radio in the top left pocket, with the other pockets full of items he wanted to have on his person if he had to dump his rucksack and run. The shirt sagged heavily on his shoulders. 'You ready?' Walden asked.

Forrest looked around his area, making the check to see that he had everything. 'Lead the way.'

The little people were dressed and waiting when they got to the team hooch. Without a word they rose and put on their web gear and rucksacks. Weapons in hand, and with Pau carrying a chicken under his arm, they walked toward the shrine.

'You think maybe we die today, Walden?' Hung was nonchalant as he took a puff from a smelly cigarette.

'No way,' Walden answered without hesitation. 'A lot of people may die today, but not us.'

Hung kicked at a ripple in one of the sand dunes. He smiled.

'What kind of cigarette are you smoking?' Walden wrinkled up his nose.

'Ruby Queen, French cigarette,' Hung held it out in front of him, inspecting it critically. 'Smell bad, huh?'

The shrine was just a small wooden rain shelter, open in front, with a small statue of Buddha on a table inside. Pau tied the chicken to the side of the temple with a piece of string, then handed everyone incense sticks. Each in turn would kneel in front of the Buddha, clap his hands together twice, then bow his head in prayer. Walden waited until everyone else had made peace before performing the ritual.

The chatter of the mess-hall girls ended abruptly as the team walked into the dining area. Coop walked shyly up to Walden when he sat in his reserved place.

'You go today?'

'I go today,' Walden answered. 'You no worry. I always come back.' She went to get his breakfast, and during the meal kept finding jobs around Walden. First she polished the milk machine, then she pretended to chase a fly hidden in the window curtains next to the table. Walden liked her being near. During breakfast before an operation his stomach always seemed to be right behind his mouth. He could never eat very much, mostly drinking coffee and smoking.

He said good-bye to Coop, then led the team out of the mess hall. Other teams would use a truck to take them down to the helipad, but Walden and Louisiana Team always walked. It had become one of the team's rituals. It seemed to loosen them up, and it also gave Walden a chance to listen for anything clanking that could give them away once on the ground. It was the little things that shaved down the odds. Dying was one thing. Dying stupid was something else.

The little people waited outside the TOC while Walden and Forrest went inside to pick up the wiretap equipment, code books, and maps. Colonel Easton was sitting on the edge of his desk drinking coffee. His thin, weathered face looked drawn and tired. In the moment before the colonel noticed them Walden saw in the dull stare what this last tour had taken out of him. He looked up when he heard them. Walden couldn't help but see the anguish in the colonel's expression.

'I want to tell you I think this operation is beyond what anyone should rightfully ask,' the colonel said. 'I want you to know, too, that I told Saigon that. Of course, it didn't make any difference.' He glanced at his watch as he walked around to his chair behind the desk. 'The helicopter won't be leaving for a few more minutes. You have time for a cup of coffee with me,' he said, gesturing toward the coffee table in the corner.

'Yes, sir.' Walden felt something different in the colonel.

After getting the coffee they sat in front of the desk. Walden waited.

'I don't think Saigon is very happy with my attitude any longer.' The colonel's lips moved slightly as he tried to smile, then stopped, the tired expression returning. 'It's the same old story. They seem to think that I have a private army up here. You understand that this war is changing,' he said evenly. 'It already has changed. A new type of soldier is coming in now, a new type of command. The flagpole boys.' He took a drink from his coffee cup. 'What I'm trying to say is that I'm being sent back to the States soon. You may not be back before I leave. I wanted to tell you that I'm damn proud of both of you. You've been one of the teams that has carried the burden. I remember when you ran five missions in a month. I just wanted to say I'm glad I soldiered with you.' There was a silence. 'I guess it's time you should be off.'

At the helipad the Vietnamese pilots and the door gunner were trying to start the H-34 Kingbee that would fly them to Quang Tri. The engine would sputter, cough, catch for a moment, and die again.

'Oh, shit,' Forrest muttered as they watched the small door gunner scrambling around the ship. They listened as the batteries began to wear down.

The gunner pulled a ball peen hammer out of a metal toolbox under his seat. 'I fix,' he said, waving the hammer.

'I don't believe this,' Walden said. The gunner opened the front engine covers at the nose of the ship, and proceeded to bang on the engine. After several hard blows he stepped back and motioned to the pilots to try again. For a few seconds the engine ground before it caught. It chugged slowly into life, backfiring and missing, but not dying.

'Okay, okay, we go now,' the gunner said proudly, fastening the doors back together with the metal latch.

Walden motioned for the little people to start loading into the ship. The engine began to sound stronger as it warmed up, settling the nerves of the team. After five minutes the ship lifted in a slow, lazy arc over the power lines and headed out over the POL dump.

Walden watched the POW camp sweep past. Seeing no prisoners in the yard, he checked the time. *Five after eight. With a minimum amount of bullshit we can be on the ground by noon.* He knew it would be better to get in before noon, before the road crews stopped working to take the traditional two-hour *pok* time. The team would have a better chance of getting in undetected if the road repair crews were working and the heavy equipment was running and making noise.

Once over the countryside surrounding Da Nang, Walden looked down at the serene outlying villages and cultivated farmlands. The farther north they went, the more the land began to look tattered and hurt. *It's changed so much since sixty-five. It's changing faster and faster. We're making it all so ugly. It can only be excused if we win. No, when we win. When.*

Roger Tillis was waiting for them with a three-quarter truck when they landed at Quang Tri.

'How you doing, buddy,' Walden said, shaking hands. 'How does it look for going in today?'

'I think it's a go for sure.' Tillis helped them load the little people and rucksacks into the back of the truck. 'You heard about Potter's team?'

They climbed into the front of the truck. 'They must have gone in too damn close to that road,' Walden said.

'That's where the wire is.' Tillis shrugged as he started the truck.

At the CP tent Walden noticed a small crowd of soldiers gathering around a portable wooden altar in a field outside the compound.

'We can go church?' Hung asked, pointing to the priest preparing for services.

'Go ahead, but be ready to go when I call you.' Walden went to the operations tent. Slader and Major Cane were studying a map when he came in.

'How you doing, Sam?' Slader was normally cheerful. Today he seemed worried.

'There've been some changes,' the major said, pointing at the terrain map of Laos.

'Now what?' Walden looked at the yellow triangular stick-ons that denoted antiaircraft positions. The target area was full of them, along with red squares that stood for truck parks and equipment dumps.

'MOONBEAM was up over your area last night,' the major said, referring to the C-130 equipped with sensor reading devices. 'They picked up heavy traffic along the road. Actually the entire area was bustling. The consensus is that they're grouping for a push across the border.'

'Why don't you arc-light the goddamn place if you know all these people and crap are in there?'

'We don't know what stage they're in.' The major was patient. 'If they're halfway through the buildup, and we nail them now, we only get half. That's what we have to find out.' The major paused for a moment, rubbing his face as if washing it. Walden looked at the heavy bags under his eyes, and the deep lines around the corners of his mouth. The war was grinding him down too. The major stared at the target area as if to will it away.

'A couple of weeks ago Nixon announced that they were going to withdraw an additional thirty-five thousand troops. During August twenty-five thousand were withdrawn. Ho Chi Minh died last month. The target area, for that matter the whole damn root structure, has had a steady increase in activity. Like nothing before, even during the siege of Khe Sanh, which I'm sure you remember.'

'If they're going to launch this offensive within the next few weeks, we have to hit them now and hit them damn hard,' Slader interjected. 'We're spread so thin up here that a couple of well-equipped divisions could push us back to Da Nang, maybe farther.'

'That's not to mention the casualties if they hit these support units,' the major continued. 'Most of these support people haven't thrown a grenade since basic training. There are seven damn clerks for every soldier on the line. So the bottom line is that we have to find out. The wire looks like our best bet.'

'Can I go to church first?' Walden sighed. The words broke the heaviness in the room.

'After considerable debate last night and early this morning, it's our opinion, Bill's and my own, that the area is too congested with troops to make a walk-in feasible.

198

From these photographs of the area' – the major stepped to his desk where a number of photos were spread out – 'we think we've figured out something that just might work.'

'Now we're getting somewhere,' Walden said. 'We've gone from "impossible" to "just might work."'

'The wire when last located ran along this road.' The major pointed out a long groove in the tops of the trees. 'Now, we know that there are two main elements, one here, and one here.' He tapped the photos with the eraser end of a pencil. 'The back of this ridge has an old bomb crater that we can insert you on. We make a false insertion here.' He pointed at a place on the other side of the road. 'We hope this will distract them long enough for you to come in from the opposite direction. This ridgeline should hide you from the valley and road area.' The major looked up from the photos to see if Walden and Forrest had been following.

'Okay. Then what?' Walden bent over the desk to study the pictures.

'You move up and over the ridge, then straight down to the road. You find the wire, tap it, record what you can, then move back up the ridge. There's a small slash-and-burn area about two hundred meters from your insertion LZ, here. Tomorrow morning oh nine hundred, we send in one ship to pull you out.'

'So that's the deal?' Walden looked from the major to Slader.

'Not quite,' Slader answered, and for the first time he smiled. 'We figure that the key to pulling this off is making them fall for the false insertion. We're going to have the gunships work over the area just as if we were inserting a team. A helicopter will drop down, but instead of putting a team in, we drop off a device.'

'A device?'

'That's right.' Slader motioned for them to follow him to the back of the tent. 'This, my friend, is what's going to trick them.' Slader pulled a poncho off the floor. Walden stepped closer, looking down at a four-by-four foot pad covered with what looked like M-80 firecrackers coated with a hardened liquid plastic.

'The Nightingale device,' Slader said as though announcing the atom bomb.

'What the hell?' Walden squatted down to inspect the pad more closely.

'It's a firefight simulator,' Slader said eagerly. 'Here is a time pencil. It'll go off ten minutes after we drop it in.'

'The idea,' the major said, 'is to make Charlie think some of his troops have found you guys and a firefight is happening. They'll send troops up there, away from you, which will give you time to get down and tap the line.'

'Of all the dumb crap,' Walden said, shaking his head.

The major held up his hand. 'I know what you're thinking, a bunch of cherry bombs isn't going to fool Charlie. Well, we set one of these things off the other day and it sounded like another world war had started. I'm telling you, it sounded like a damn good firefight.'

Walden looked at Forrest, who was staring down at the device and frowning. 'How long before the pilots' briefing?'

'About half an hour.'

'There's a priest saying mass just outside the wire. I think I'd better make my peace with God,' Walden said.

CHAPTER NINETEEN

THE CHURCH services were half over when Walden and Forrest moved in among the little people. Several GIs stared at them. A steady breeze ruffled the priest's vestments and two soldiers held down the altar cloth. The priest recited the offertory. Normally at this point Walden's insides would be in knots, but the serene manner in which the priest was saying the mass made him feel safe, and a calm settled on him.

After the priest had given a general absolution, Walden, along with Hung and Cuong, received communion. Afterward, walking back to the operations tent, Walden felt light and easy. Forrest noticed.

'Nothing like going to church, huh?' He smiled.

'Nothing like having God on your side.' They walked into the operations tent where the pilots were assembling.

'Did you enjoy the services?' Slader asked.

'Very pleasant, Mr Slader, very pleasant,' Walden said. 'They give general absolution in war when you're a Catholic. Perhaps I could interest you in our conversion package.'

The briefing began. Fifteen minutes later the mission was a go. The helicopter pilots, from the 101st Airborne, shook hands with Walden and Forrest as they filed out.

Walden was surprised at how calm he felt. On this mission, when the odds were higher than ever before, he felt composed, almost arrogant. It struck him, as he climbed into the front of the truck that would take them to the pad, that this was the first mission he had ever gone on in a state of grace. According to the Catholic church, if he died he would go to heaven. He was stunned at how much knowing this helped.

The team applied the black-and-green camouflage grease to their faces as the helicopters that would make the false insertion lifted. Walden briefed the little people and handed them the maps for the target area. They made final adjustments to their packs and weapon slings. They slid the bolts back and forth in their CAR-15's, making sure they were loose. Lastly, as their helicopter was warming up, they wrapped cravats around their heads for sweatbands. Pau tied the red bits of cloth that the Buddhist monks had blessed to each man's shirt buttonhole, and to the front sight of their weapons. The hot exhaust from the Huey made Walden's stomach tense. He associated the sweet smell with danger.

Minutes after the decoy ships had departed, they climbed in. Slader, the major, and Tillis stood off to one side and gave the thumbs-up gesture as they lifted off. Walden and the others returned the signal, then settled in the doors as the group dropped away. Soon they were out over the rolling red plains.

'Easy Dare, Easy Dare, this is Whiskey Fever, Whiskey Fever. Commo check. How do you hear me? Over,' Walden spoke into the radio handset. He watched the foothills become steeper, the foliage become thicker.

'Fever, this is Dare. Hear you loud and clear. Will begin insertion, one five minutes. Over.'

'Roger, Dare, hear you same. Keep in touch. Out.' Walden pushed the handset back down inside his shirt. Standing up, he moved until he could see through the front windshield of the helicopter. He watched as the mountains of Laos drew near, thinking of the first time he had heard of the country. It had been in a book by Dr Tom Dooley, *The Night They Burned the Mountain*. He didn't remember much about it.

'I hope this works,' Forrest shouted over the wind whipping through the open chopper.

Walden moved up behind the starboard pilot seat and

202

squatted down in the doorway. He let the weight of the rucksack pull him over slightly as he hung his legs over the edge.

'Five minutes,' the door gunner on his side of the ship shouted, indicating with an open hand the time left before they hit the LZ. Walden nodded to show he understood, then chambered a round into his CAR-15. He looked around, making eye contact with each team member as they also chambered a round. Their faces were tense, locked into the expression they alway had before insertion. They were ready.

The helicopter dropped down to treetop level, riding up and over the mountains like an automobile in hilly country. Walden had never approached an LZ in this manner and was caught off-guard by the blur of the trees passing below.

'This bastard is really cooking,' Forrest yelled, his eyes jumping. The door gunner jacked back the charging arm of the M-60 and smoothed the belted rounds down over the C-ration can the belt rolled over before being chambered. Walden's eyes teared when he stuck his head into the air current and watched the decoy ships and Covey swooping like tiny bugs down to the false LZ. Then the trees hid them as his ship dropped even further into the valley to make the final rush to the small brown crater.

'Do it fast. Do it fast,' Walden yelled over his shoulder as his muscles began to swim in adrenalin. The helicopter skidded through the air as the pilots lifted up the nose and flared out over the tiny opening. Walden hung on to the side of the pilot's seat and slid out until his feet touched the skid. He held his CAR-15 in his right hand, his finger on the trigger, as his eyes scanned the jungle around the clearing. The skids were hovering five feet off the ground when Walden jumped. The others followed as though they were attached to a rope. Before Walden had a chance to spit the dirt out of his mouth, the chopper was gone.

They skittered into the jungle surrounding the bomb crater. Walden listened intently to the sounds of the area. He knew they were playing the outside limits on this one.

He listened to the booming sound of 37-millimeter anti-aircraft guns from across the valley.

Walden broke squelch three times over the radio, pushing, then releasing, the keying plunger. He paused for a moment, then whispered, 'Nickel, Nickel,' the code word that told Covey that they were in and momentarily okay. The birds began to caw and cackle as the area settled down. Birds were always the first to pick up on bad vibes. The swiftness of the return to normalcy reassured Walden.

They quickly moved the fifty meters to the ridgetop. Before they crossed over, Walden stopped for a break. He checked his watch.

'Any minute now,' he whispered into Forrest's ear. They waited to hear the Nightingale device go off. A minute passed, then two. Then it began. First came two distant sounds like rifle shots, then the eruption of a full-scale firefight. Walden grinned at Forrest. The noise rose and fell, sputtered almost to a stop, then began anew, sounding just as though two enemy forces had made contact.

'I bet those little Chucks are going ape-shit down there,' Forrest said. Walden pictured the NVA rushing toward the fight and away from them.

'We should do this more often,' Walden said. 'Let's get down to that wire.' They were up and moving, Cuong leading them over the ridge and down the steep slope. The Nightingale device kept going for at least five more minutes as the team moved through the boulders and vegetation toward the floor of the valley. Halfway down, Cuong stopped abruptly. The gurgling sound of a small stream could be heard. Walden moved up, following Cuong's hand signals. He picked out several spider holes, along with a long trench line, dug into the side of the mountain. It appeared deserted. Walden debated a moment whether to move straight through it, or skirt around. *Screw it. If there was ever a time to take a chance, this was it.* He motioned to Cuong to keep moving. Once past the trench line, they saw animal pens and the residue of campfires. Trails crisscrossed the area. They hurried for the shelter of larger trees.

The vines and vegetables became thicker and more difficult to navigate as they neared the stream. Even though it was hard going, Walden was glad to have the cover. Slowly the slope levelled out. Cuong moved as though he were walking on eggs. Then, in one blur of motion, Cuong was down on his stomach. Walden then heard the voices. He motioned to the others to stay where they were, then squirmed up next to Cuong. Together they crawled forward. Prickly heat ran up Walden's spine and across his sweating face. He looked through the grass and vines at several thatch huts concealed from the air by a thick jungle canopy.

Several dozen NVA stood around in the centre of the encampment, obviously waiting. Walden saw an NVA flag flying from a tall bamboo pole in the middle of the camp. Then he heard the sound of trucks. His chest constricted and he fought down the urge to turn and run. He watched two ZIL-150 Soviet trucks drive into the circle of huts. He thought of the camera in his side pocket, but didn't want to move to get it. The troops climbed onto the trucks, laughing and yelling at each other. Once loaded, the trucks turned in the quadrangle and went out the way they had come. Walden began to breathe again as he watched two remaining NVA, trailing a small white puppy, stroll back to a cooking area at the far side of the camp.

He and Cuong crawled backward not taking their eyes off the huts until the vines and brush hid them. Once back with the others, he stood in a low crouch and without a word began moving away from the area. After moving several dozen meters Walden stopped, easing himself to the ground. The little people and Forrest huddled close. The tart smell of sudden sweat was biting and sour. Walden cupped his hands around Forrest's ear and Cuong did the same with Hung.

'There's a bivouac area back there with a goddamn NVA flag flying over it,' Walden whispered, his breath catching.

'A load of troops just pulled out on two trucks. There's a skeleton crew left.' Hung was shaking his shoulder.

'Cuong say he hear they go across stream to find team,' Hung said very quietly, an excited glint in his eyes. Walden glanced back at Forrest to see if he'd heard. Forrest slowly blew air out of his mouth as though releasing pressure from inside. He cradled Walden's face next to his.

'Did you see the road?'

'The sonofabitch runs right through the village. It's probably about fifty meters from here. The stream is on the other side, so at least we don't have to deal with that.'

'I'll bet you anything the wire is right next to the road,' Forrest said. 'You want to go for it, or get pulled out?'

'Go for it,' Walden said without hesitation. 'They think we're across the stream. I've got a feeling that this is our day. We can really fuck over these little bastards.'

Forrest smiled and nodded. The confidence was contagious.

They kept close to the ground, carefully handing the vines from one to the other so as not to make noise. Almost before they realized it, they were next to the road. Walden caught a glimpse of the brown, hard-packed dirt through the brush when Cuong stopped. Walden sat down, shrugging off his rucksack. The little people made a tight circle. Reaching into the rucksack, he grabbed the black recorder and the two black wires. Forrest was beginning to take off his ruck when Walden stopped him.

'You have to stay here with the others,' Walden whispered. 'If anything happens when we're down there, split.' Forrest tilted his head to one side, his expression a definite argument.

Walden held up his hand. 'That's the way it has to be, Jerry,' Walden whispered. Forrest finally nodded.

Walden and Cuong slithered out of the trees and into the waist-high brush along the edge of the road. A small pathway paralleled the road. Along the side of the path were six separate doublestrand wires. There was no way to tell what was what, so Walden grabbed the nearest wire and

206

planted the pointed metal tips of the recording wires. He played out the wire as they crawled back into the higher brush. If someone happened along, he only had to give the wires a yank and they would pull out of the tapped line. Drops of sweat dripped onto the black box as Walden turned it on. He eyed the gauge and the needle that would move back and forth when someone was talking. Long minutes passed as Walden stared at the dead needle. He had begun to think that he should try another wire when the needle started to jump.

Switching on the recorder, he listened to the faint hum of the cassette. As soon as the needle stopped moving, he switched the recorder off. Every few minutes the needle would jump again and he would repeat the procedure. By the time the first hour tape was full, it was after five o'clock. Walden inserted a fresh tape and told Cuong to go back and tell Forrest that he was going to record another tape. Cuong looked as though he had misgivings, but crawled back to the others without a word. A few minutes later he was back at Walden's side.

The traffic on the line picked up as the shadows stretched towards the treetops. It was a few minutes past six when the tape was full. Walden considered trying for a third hour. *No, we've pushed our luck a long way already. The road will become active as soon as it gets dark.* He yanked the wires from the main and couldn't help but smile at the look of relief that swept over Cuong's face. Back with the others, Walden stowed the recorder back into his ruck, then slipped the two cassette tapes into his side pants pocket. With a flick of his hand he signalled the team back up the slope. Darkness came quickly. Before they were halfway up the mountain-side, it was pitch dark and each man had to hang on to the pack in front of him.

It was after eight when Walden felt the ground under his boots begin to level off. They stumbled onto the crest of the ridgeline and flopped down heavily. Walden counted heads by touching each of them. He searched for Hung by feeling the faces.

'Hung?' he whispered hoarsely.

'Here, here,' Hung said softly, though still breathing hard.

'We stay here tonight. No one is to move from the circle. Forget the Claymores. I don't want to take the chance of losing somebody now.'

'Okay, I tell team.' Walden felt bodies shuffle as Hung began to whisper in Vietnamese. He felt the heavy bulk of Forrest's body lean against him, then Forrest's hand patting his chest as it searched to find Walden's head.

'You get anything on the tapes?' Forrest breathed into his ear.

'We got two hours.' Walden was unable to hide his exhilaration.

'Oh, sweet Jesus, I hope we can get out of here with that.' Forrest's voice began to rise.

'Shhhhh,' Walden whispered. 'There are more gooks in here than I've seen since the Ia Drang Valley. I think they all stay pretty close to that stream and – ' His words were cut off by a firefight erupting down in the valley. Walden froze at the sudden bedlam booming up at them. The distant sound of mortars firing mingled with the other firing. Walden had only counted to five when the rounds started to explode on the opposite ridge.

'They ran into each other and think it's us,' Walden squealed, trying to hold back the giggles that began jumping into his throat. Everyone seemed to understand what was happening at the same time. Short little laughs were suppressed with a quick hand as they listened to the firefight rage. Walden lifted the tape from his watch, looking at the time so he would know the duration. His heart pounded as the minutes went by and the thick popping of AK-47's and RPD machine guns continued to rip the night. *Die, you bastards*. Walden remembered September of sixty-five when Charlie had sucked them into doing the same thing. They had died and hurt each other then. A bunch of nervous, green kids trading shots across a dry creek bed, shooting hell out of each other because a

208

couple of gooks had slipped between and fired a few rounds. Now the sound coming up from the valley was music to Walden. Sweet music.

When it was over, the resonance of the firing echoed and hung in the trees. Walden thought of wounded animals as the sounds diminished.

'Nine minutes,' he whispered to Forrest.

'I was hoping they would keep at it all night,' Forrest said. They were just rolling up in their poncho liners, preparing for a long night, when the NVA opened up on each other again. It sounded even more intense.

'Goddamn,' Forrest exclaimed. 'They're really going for it this time.'

Walden checked his watch. *Keep it up. Keep it up.* As each minute passed, he savored the taste of revenge. Ten minutes passed without a let-up. Fifteen minutes, and the firing became sporadic. Finally it stopped.

'Seventeen minutes.' The silence came back except for a faint wail, and that quickly trailed off. They curled up with each other for warmth. Walden felt a strange contentment as he closed his eyes. *God, they're going to feel dumb when they find out.*

Throughout the night Walden slept in the space below consciousness, and above real sleep. It was a place that sometimes caused confusion. As it neared dawn, he thought that he was with Hoa, dreaming about being on the ground. It was so real that he tried to wake, succeeded, then felt cheated. He remained awake then, watching the gray fog drifting in the first light. The dew sharpened the smell of the ground and the growth. Oddly, it reminded Walden of the sweet odor of July corn after a rain.

By the time it was light enough to see each other, the team was packed and moving toward the slash-and-burn area. They moved until the fog began to burn off. Walden called a halt and made a rolling motion in front of his mouth to tell the team to eat.

'We can stumble around out here forever trying to find

209

that slash-and-burn area,' he said in a low voice to Forrest. 'It looked big as hell from the air when we were coming in.'

'It has to be around here,' Forrest said. 'Why don't you climb a tree and see if we can locate it?' He looked at Walden matter-of-factly, chewing a mouthful of shrimp and rice.

'Why the hell didn't I think of that?' Walden looked up at the nearest tree and saw that the numerous branches would be as easy to climb as a flight of stairs.

Slipping out of his rucksack and web gear, Walden stood, grabbing one of the lower limbs. He pulled on it, testing for strength before swinging up. Soon the team was lost below the leaves and branches. Once beyond the secondary growth, he was able to see the blue of the sky. Farther up, before the spread of the triple canopy thickened, there was an open spot where he had a panoramic view of the surrounding valley. The blackened area was fifty meters below them. He slipped and almost fell twice in his rush to get back down.

'It's right below us,' he whispered excitedly to Forrest as soon as his boots touched. 'Come on, let's go.' He quickly put his equipment back on. The little people gobbled the remaining portions of their meals and the team moved straight down the slope. In minutes they were at the edge of the LZ.

It was twenty minutes to nine when they huddled in the high, dry grass. Walden cocked his ear to try to hear the drone of Covey. There was only the wind in the grass.

'Screw in the long antenna,' Walden whispered to Forrest, pulling the handset out. As soon as it was in, Walden heard Pappy's voice making a long count. As soon as Pappy was finished, Walden keyed the mike.

'Rolling Dare, Rolling Dare,' Walden began, then remembered that it was a new day and the call signs had changed. 'Stand by, one,' he said, grabbing for his code book. After a few seconds he found the new call signs and returned to the air.

'This is Graphic Circus. How do you hear me, shit,' he

mumbled, tracing a finger down the list before finding Covey's new call words. 'Gypsy Rejoin,' he said hurriedly when he found it.

'All right, Circus,' Pappy's voice came back. 'Hear you Lima Charlie. Do we have a Mike, Alpha Ten?' he asked, referring to the code that meant the team was at the extraction LZ.

'Roger that. We're right where we're supposed to be,' Walden said.

'Outstanding. We have Swirling Joy on the way, approximate Zulu, X-Ray zero five, Tango Foxtrot,' Pappy said as though he were reading off a sweepstake number. Walden quickly went to the code book to decipher. A few seconds later he understood that the helicopter had been launched and would be at their location in five minutes.

'Gypsy Rejoin, this is me. Roger, I'll have panel out.'

'Okay, good buddy. I'm going to mind my own business now, and stay out of the way. Good luck.'

Walden turned to Forrest and grinned. 'Pappy launched the pickup ship already. It'll be here in a few minutes.' Forrest unscrewed the long antenna and replaced it with the short one. Walden listened for the helicopter. A few minutes later the drumming of the blades could be faintly heard as it slipped over the eastern ridge. Pulling the bright-orange panel out of his pocket, Walden crawled to the edge of the clearing.

'Come on, baby, come on,' Walden whispered, watching the growing speck of the Huey race toward them. Crawling out into the gray soot of the LZ, Walden began to pop the panel open and closed. He laid the panel down and pulled the handset out.

'Swirling Joy, this is Graphic Circus. Do you see us? Over.'

'I got you, buddy. Let's make this quick.'

Walden rammed the handset back inside his shirt, looked back at the others squatting behind. He jerked his thumb into the air and they tensed for the sprint to the ship. A cloud of black powdery dust blasted up around the

211

ship as it flared over the LZ. It came in so quickly that for a second Walden thought it was going to crash. Bursting out of the brush, the team dived for the open sides of the chopper, a scrambling mass of arms, legs, and rucksacks.

'Go, go,' Walden screamed as he jumped up from the ground and got a foot on one of the skids. He was still half out when the ship banked sharply to the left. Hands grabbed at him and pulled him in. Once inside, spread on his stomach, Walden began to breathe heavily. He didn't move until the jungle had dropped far away.

'The first time, the first fuckin' time,' Walden shouted. He rolled over, pulling his arms out of the rucksack straps as though it were on fire.

'Wow-eeeeeeee,' Forrest howled. They grabbed each other and the little people piled on top.

'The first fuckin' time, the first fuckin' time, everything went the way it was supposed to,' Walden yelled. The two door gunners were whooping it up right along with them. Walden got to his feet, stumbling over rucksacks in his haste to get to the pilots.

'That was great, just great,' Walden shouted as he moved up between the two seats. Commander Lynch leaned to the side and slapped Walden on the back, his big toothy grin seeming to fill his flight helmet.

'You did good, Sam. You were right where you were supposed to be, at the right time. We didn't take a round.'

Walden just smiled. It settled in that they were out and heading home. Suddenly he felt as though he were going to throw up. He turned away and was ready to hang out the door, and as quickly as it came the nausea passed. He remembered then he hadn't eaten since the morning before. He pulled cans of fruit from one of the pockets on his ruck. He tossed them around to the little people, keeping a can of pears. After cracking it with his P-38 can opener he lifted the can to his lips. The cool, thick syrup ran over his tongue and down his throat.

'Oh, God, taste this,' Walden said, passing the can to Forrest. Everyone started rifling their rations. Soon it became a ten-course meal. Cans of ham and eggs, peaches, spaghetti, fruit cocktail, were passed around. After wolfing down an odd combination of food, Walden leaned back and lit his first cigarette since they had left the launch site. He smoked silently, watching the plains of Khe Sanh drifting far below. He thought of the thirty days he had spent at home. It was like a dream now. It was a different world back there. It might as well be in a different galaxy. Yesterday, lying on the fringe of the village, that was reality. He patted his side pocket where the tapes were. They made him feel as if he were carrying a magic scroll.

A crowd was gathered on the helipad to welcome them back.

'I told you it would work. Didn't I? Didn't I?' Slader shouted. He helped Walden out of the ship and hugged him. Major Cane rushed past people in his hurry to get next to them.

'Good goddamn show, Sam,' he said, shaking hands briskly. 'What did you get?'

'Two hours, solid.' Walden grinned.

'Wheeeee,' Slader hollered. 'That's what we wanted. That's what we wanted.'

'I prayed my ass off on this one.' The major sighed happily. 'A Blackbird is being dispatched from Da Nang to take you right to Saigon.' They began walking to the trucks. 'We don't have time for an impact report. They'll want to debrief you in Saigon, but I do need to know what went on in there.' He pulled a notebook and pen out of his pocket.

'Right down from the ridge they have a bivouac area. Maybe twenty hooches. I got the impression that they were as thick as fleas all along that road. I saw two Soviet trucks come into the village and pick up a couple dozen NVA. The road is large enough for two-way traffic, but you can't see it from the air because of overhead cover. The wire was right where you figured it would be. Six double strands.'

'Do you think that it would be feasible to try it again? Put another team in there?'

213

'No goddamn way,' Walden said emphatically. 'They got into two hellish firefights last night while looking for us. They'll know how we did it now.'

'Okay. At least we got one on them this time, and got out clean.' The major smiled. 'You'd better load up and start for the airfield. I'll send a message to Da Nang to relay to Saigon that you're on your way.'

Once the little people were loaded on the truck, Walden and Forrest climbed into the front with Roger Tillis.

'Wow, they're taking you guys right to Saigon. Called in your own private plane and everything.' Tillis chuckled. 'You finally made the big time.'

'Did you bring any joints with you?' Walden asked.

'I got a deck. You want to smoke one?' Tillis reached for his side pocket.

'I want to wait until Saigon is over. I want them for after.'

'Here.' Tillis handed a plastic deck of ten to him.

'I still can't believe it.' Walden put the joints in his pocket. 'Everything went just like it was supposed to. I'll bet that never happens again.'

CHAPTER TWENTY

BY THE TIME the C-130 landed at the Tan Son Nhut airbase, the adrenalin had long gone and Walden was tired. The plane taxied over the tarmac before stopping in front of the Air America terminal. The little people and Forrest had slept almost the entire trip, and they groggily grabbed their weapons and equipment. A black Econoline van backed up to the lowered tailgate. The two back doors swung open and a sergeant first class wearing a baseball cap motioned to them to get in. A colonel sat in the front passenger seat, watching as they climbed into the back of the van.

There was a sour smell in the close confines of the van. Walden realized it was coming from the team. They were filthy with the dirt and black soot of the extraction LZ, and still had the camouflage grease on their faces.

'Ah, sir,' Walden said, 'do you think that we should clean up a little before we go to SOG headquarters? We smell pretty rank.'

'You smell like war, son. They'll love it.' The colonel laughed.

Walden sat down, running his tongue over the film on his teeth. He felt sticky and hot, but mostly he just wanted to brush his teeth. He lit a cigarette and looked at the team dozing off again. The jarring of the van as it hit potholes didn't seem to bother them. *I guess no one got very much sleep last night.*

He jumped awake when the coal on the cigarette began to burn the top of his leg. He brushed off the sparks from around the burn hole, then stubbed out the smoke on the floor of the van before closing his eyes again. The next thing he felt was Forrest shaking him awake.

The interior of Special Operations Group Headquarters was air conditioned. The hallways were freshly waxed and it smelled like the inside of a school building.

They were escorted into an inner office and the colonel instructed them to wait. Walden was shocked to see a pretty American woman sitting behind a reception desk. From the look on her face she was just as surprised.

'Would you gentlemen care for some coffee or something?' she asked, obviously uncertain of what to say.

'I could use about a bucket of it.' Walden lowered his rucksack and web gear to the floor. She got up from behind the desk and went to a coffee maker in the corner.

'What would you like in it?'

'A little cream would be nice,' Walden answered. She stirred a spoon of powdered cream into the cup and brought it to him. She gestured toward the machine, letting the others know that they could help themselves.

'You must be Walden,' she said, watching him take a sip. 'My name is Marilyn Rush. I work for the State Department.'

'I didn't know they had round-eyes working here,' he said.

'Do you call all American girls round-eyes?' She plainly didn't like the label.

'I didn't mean anything by it,' Walden said tiredly. The last thing he wanted was to get into a discussion of terminology.

'You're from Minnesota, St Cloud, right?'

Walden knew it was no question. 'What else do you know about me?'

'You'd be surprised.' She laughed. 'Nothing bad,' she quickly added, seeing Walden's face. 'As a matter of fact you're quite well known back in Washington. You have quite a following among the people that analyze the after-action reports. There are people there who follow your mission like a television serial.'

'They should enjoy this one,' Walden said. 'You don't

happen to have a toothbrush, do you?' He wanted to change the subject.

'I'll see what I can do?' She left the room. A few minutes later she was back with brushes and a number of small complimentary tubes of paste.

'Is there a bathroom or something around here?'

'Right down the hall and to the right. The guard will have to escort you.' She motioned to an MP to follow them.

After brushing his teeth Walden felt better. As soon as they were back in the office, Colonel Tesler, the Chief SOG, walked into the room and began shaking hands.

'Let's go into the debriefing room,' Tesler said. 'We have lots to talk about.'

Walden was impressed with the war room. Two large maps had electric lights blinking where teams were on the ground in Cambodia and Laos. Teletypes chattered in a far corner, and people scurried back and forth. Walden pulled out the two tape cassettes and handed them to the colonel.

'Let's see what we have here,' Tesler said eagerly. They sat down at a long conference table. He slipped a tape into the player set up on the table. A two-star Vietnamese general walked into the room just as a voice came over the speaker. After a few minutes the general began to chuckle.

'What is he saying?' Walden asked Hung, who was snickering along with the others who could understand.

'He say to move troops up onto far hill where they shoot last night. The man say, if can, they should capture them.' The voices kept changing.

'They say now to double guard at POL supply area,' Hung translated. At one point Tesler played back a portion that dealt with trucks and an ammo site.

At the end of the first tape they were surprised to hear Vietnamese music. The second tape was all music, some of it American rock and roll. Walden stared at the tape player. Part of him wanted to laugh because he had risked everything to tape an hour of music. Part of him wanted to smash the tape. He rubbed his face tiredly as Tesler stood up.

'We can work with the first tape,' Tesler said, handing

the two cassettes to a sergeant. 'I want the entire transcript of both of these tapes put on paper, though, music, the whole ball of wax.'

'I can't believe it,' Walden said.

'Our analyst boys can get quite a bit of intel from these tapes,' Tesler said. 'Just the fact that they feel so safe, and are so well set up, that they can pipe music over a commo line tells us something.'

'I suppose,' Walden said, looking away.

'You did a damn fine job, son. Your whole team did.'

'I could've stayed in Da Nang and taped the goddamn AFRN.'

'The segment where they're discussing their POL supply and ammo site could be worth the entire mission,' Tesler said. 'Let's reserve our opinion until we've had time to study it.' He motioned to one of the sergeants.

'Get these boys debriefed so they can get some sleep,' he said. 'I'll want you to be available for the next few days,' he said to Walden. 'You can stay at House Ten.' He was referring to the Special Forces safehouse used by SOG personnel passing through Saigon.

'Sir, if it would be all right, Jerry and I have girlfriends in town here. We'd be at their house. I can give you a phone number where you can reach me if you have to get in touch.'

Tesler screwed up his face, not liking the suggestion. But he finally nodded. 'Just be damn sure you stay close to the phone.'

'Yes, sir,' Walden replied. 'How about a week's pass for my little people? They deserve it, and they all have family here.'

'Okay,' Tesler agreed. He waved to a first lieutenant and the process was started. Two hours later the debriefing was over. Walden collected the maps and classified code books and handed them in. As he was writing down the phone number of Hoa's home, he realized they didn't have any identification or money. When he mentioned this to the lieutenant, he was told to wait. After a short time the lieutenant returned with ID papers for each of them.

'How much money do you want me to issue them?' The lieutenant nodded toward the little people as he produced a thick bundle of piastres from a briefcase.

'Give them each a hundred dollars' worth,' Walden said, not really sure if he could get that much, but figuring it wouldn't hurt to ask. The lieutenant thumbed out six stacks of bills, and then handed one to each of the little people.

'Okay, guys,' Walden said sternly. 'I want you here at this address at seven in the morning one week from today so we can catch a flight back to Da Nang. I'm going to let you keep your weapons, but remember I know what each of you has. So don't come telling me you had stuff stolen. If you lose anything, you have to pay for it. And I don't want to hear about your throwing grenades around bars either.' He waited for Hung to translate for him. They all indicated they understood. He handed each a slip of paper with the address and phone number of Hoa's place.

'You guys did real fine. Have a good time, but please, don't fuck up.'

'No buck up, no buck up,' Pau said.

After the team was gone, the lieutenant asked the Americans how much money they wanted.

'A couple of hundred each,' Walden said, catching on to the strange procedures. Without a word the lieutenant counted out two stacks of MPC and pushed them across the desk along with ID and pass forms.

'Do you want me to sign something for this or what?' Walden asked, looking at the expressionless face.

'No, just turn in all the ID and pass forms to your people at the TOC when you get back up north.'

'You guys don't have much red tape here.'

Once on the street Walden quickly hailed a cab. The first cab driver that stopped took one look and pulled back into the flow of traffic.

'Asshole,' Forrest yelled after him. The next driver didn't seem to care, asking to see the money first.

They put their rucksacks in the trunk and climbed into the backseat. After giving the driver the address, Walden pulled one of the joints out of the deck and lit it.

'I almost cried when that music came on,' he said. 'Those bastards were playing the Cream. God, this war is getting weird.'

CHAPTER TWENTY-ONE

THE TAXI pulled up in front of the iron gate and Walden and Forrest stepped out. The gate guard almost fell off his stool in his haste to get to the carbine leaning against the shack.

'Take it easy. Take it easy,' Walden said, holding his hands up in the air. The guard tilted his head forward to get a better look. Walden walked around to the trunk to get the rucksacks. 'Tell Hoa or Dominica that we're here.' The guard stood frozen in place, the carbine in his hands.

'Well?' Forrest asked, nodding toward the field phone inside the guard shack.

'If we'd wanted to kill you, you'd be dead already,' Walden purred. The guard rang the crank on the phone. He waited a few seconds, then started to whisper. Walden heard his name. Before the guard put the phone back on the cradle, there was the sound of feet running toward the gate.

'Sam? Sam?' Hoa yelled.

'It's me. It's me.' Walden grinned as she rushed up to the gate. He reached through the bars and pulled her to him.

'Open the goddamn gate,' Walden said to the guard. Hoa nodded. The gate was only partially open when she squeezed through and threw her arms around Walden's neck.

'Where you come from?' she asked, drawing her head back and looking into his eyes. It made him feel weak and warm at the same time. She placed her hands on his face and kissed him.

'I love you. I love you,' he kept repeating.

A tear ran down her cheek. 'I think you never come back. I think you forget about me.'

'I never forget you. Don't cry. Why you cry?'

'I happy. I cry because I happy. I love you.' She sniffled, smiling. They walked to the house arm in arm.

'You can stay long time?'

'I can stay one week,' Walden answered as they closed the door behind them.

'I want to go Da Nang with you,' Hoa whispered. 'I want to make house for you, cook for you.' More tears came, making her face shine.

They kissed and slowly sank to the floor, the CAR-15 hung around Walden's neck pressed between them. It didn't seem to matter. After many minutes Walden sat up.

'Hoa, I just got to take a shower.'

'Come, I wash you.' She walked him into her bedroom, unbuttoning his fatigue shirt. When she pulled the sour-smelling T-shirt over his head, he heard her take a quick breath.

'Oh, Sam, you hurt.' She stared at the deep thorn-cuts along his arms and shoulders. He glanced at the crusted blood.

'It's nothing, just from the brush.'

She sat him on the bed and began to unlace his boots. After he was naked, she turned her back so he could unzip the loose dress she was wearing. With a shrug of her shoulders she made the dress slide down her body and fall to the floor. Late-afternoon sunlight came through the open window, and her body glowed.

'I think we better hurry up with this shower,' Walden said. She began to giggle. From her dresser she took two large Turkish towels. She fastened one around his waist, then the other around herself.

'We go.' She smiled, her eyes bright. As they walked outside, Walden heard Forrest laughing upstairs.

Next to the house was a small brick shower. She turned on the shower, adjusting the temperature. Walden jumped as the hot spray hit the cuts.

'I make you better.' Hoa began to wash him gently, slowly lathering soap onto his body. It took many minutes

222

just to get the camouflage grease off his face and from the inside of his ears. She shaved his face, stopping every few seconds to kiss him. When she was finished, they stood under the water as it became lukewarm and then cold. Walden nuzzled her neck, smelling her wet hair and feeling the warmth of her smooth body against his own. Her arms squeezed him to her and he thought of new things. There were times to come; there was a future.

In the bedroom Hoa pulled back the quilt and sheet, crawling to the middle of the bed to fluff the pillows.

'Oh, man.' Walden sighed, crawling between the clean white sheets and the heavy bedspread. 'This feels almost as good as you do.' She pushed his hands away.

'I go tell mama-san to make supper first.' She patted the blanket around him and quickly slipped from the room.

The rays of morning touched his face, waking him. He tensed, unsure of where he was. Then he felt Hoa's warm body next to him. She burrowed tighter against him as she felt him awake.

'Good morning,' she whispered, rubbing her face against his.

'Morning? I slept all night?'

'I come back one minute, and you asleep. I see you very tired. I think you should sleep.'

'I guess I was.' Walden softly rubbed his hand over her back. She pushed her loins against his, and ran her fingers through his hair.

'I no can tell you I be virgin when we meet. But I can say I never make love before you.'

Walden held her tightly, afraid that something would come and take her away. They collapsed into a world of murmurs and shivers.

All during breakfast they touched and stroked. Every time Walden looked, he thought she was more beautiful. The small alcove where they sat was cozy and warm. The leaves of an ivy plant hung before an open window,

223

dappling the cream walls with sunlight and shadows. The breeze and slivers of sun, subdued by the broad palms outside, wrapped around them. She took a sip from her iced tea, then leaned forward and kissed him. As their mouths opened, he felt the cool sweetened liquid run over his tongue. He felt it all the way to his feet.

They had sliced fruit and meat rolls. They smoked cigarettes and sipped coffee. She leaned against him, sometimes speaking French. He didn't understand what she said, but he seemed to know what she meant.

'You want some coffee?' Walden asked when Forrest walked in.

'No, thanks. We had some already.' Dominica came bustling in and crawled over Walden to sit next to Hoa.

'We go shopping for some clothes. You want to come?' she asked.

'I have to get some civvies. My fatigues are in a bad way,' Walden said.

'I have mama-san clean for you,' Hoa said, getting up and moving into the hallway. She called out in Vietnamese, and a few seconds later the maid came shuffling into the room.

'Jesus,' Forrest groaned.

Walden felt he had been hit in the stomach when he saw the field boots the maid was holding.

'I shine for you,' Hoa said proudly. Walden stared at the polished boots, a cold jolt going through his spine. The jungle boots were never to be touched. Everyone in camp knew that.

'What wrong?' Hoa said, grabbing his hand.

He recovered. 'Jerry make joke. He never see my boots shined before.' He laughed. 'It's all right, honey. It's only joke.'

'You look funny,' Hoa said, her voice wavering.

'They just never shined before,' he repeated. He felt her relax a little as they got up. *It's just a stupid superstition.* He walked into the bedroom to get dressed. *I'm getting as bad as the little people.*

224

The days that followed were the happiest Walden had ever known. They took long walks through the park near the university, and down through the marketplaces. They went to movies, caught some nightclub acts, ate at restaurants where only natives went. They stayed awake nights, talking and making love, not wanting to sleep and lose time.

The morning of the day Walden had to report back, they stayed in bed, talking.

'As soon as I can find a place for us to live, I'll come back for you.'

'I want to go with you now,' Hoa said.

'You can't come now. You must wait.'

'Why can you not send me letter when you find house, and then I can come to you?'

'I don't want you travelling up there by yourself,' Walden explained for the tenth time. 'You'll be safer here in Saigon than in Da Nang. I'll come to get you as soon as I can.'

'How long before you come for me?'

'I'm not sure. Maybe one month.'

'I miss you.' Hoa leaned her head against his chest.

'Just remember, this will be the last time we're ever apart from each other again,' Walden said softly.

'I wait for you to come to me,' Hoa said. 'I wait forever.'

CHAPTER TWENTY-TWO

THEY HAD just stepped off the bus, blinking at Marble Mountain, when Jeffers started the story.

'Manning's team went into A Shau Six last week while you were in Saigon. Their second day on the ground, they make contact, and Manning radios back that they have dead and wounded.' Walden felt his stomach stiffen.

'We didn't hear anything for like three days,' Jeffers continued. 'I thought for sure that it was all over, man.'

'Yeah, well?' Walden started for the hooch, trying not to be angry.

'This morning, Pappy is out over the area and he sees somebody popping a panel from inside a bomb crater. It turns out to be Andy. He's been running and hiding out there for three days. They sent in a Bright Light team and helicopters and got him out. They're bringing him here by ship now.'

'Damn, that must've been a nightmare.' It took Walden two tries to get the lock on the hooch open. 'Was he the only one that got out? Tibbens and Holly were on that team.'

'From everything we've heard so far, it was only Andy,' Jeffers said.

'Our supply of friends is slowly dwindling away,' Forrest said quietly. A moment later he slammed a book against the wall. 'Shit, fuck,' he shouted. 'Fuck, fuck, fuck.'

Walden remembered Manning reporting in to Recon Company, limping with two duffel bags toward the operations shack. Walden had offered a hand, and Manning had been really grateful. He was an old man compared to the rest of them; Walden had wondered why he had asked for a team in the first place. Thirty-eight years old, two years left before retirement. It didn't make sense. A wife he was always talking about. Three kids, a dog. A nice house outside of Fayetteville.

'Damn, I'm glad he made it,' Walden suddenly said.

He and Forrest put away their gear, then picked up a case of beer at the club and headed for the helipad. Almost everyone from Recon was already there. The party was in full swing. Colonel Easton came over, a beer in his hand.

'Great mission. How was your vacation?' He shook hands.

'Beautiful,' Walden said. 'How would you feel about my getting a house downtown so I can bring my girl here from Saigon?'

'Jesus Christ, Walden, you're as blunt as a rock. Don't ask me shit like that. I'm supposed to be the last to know. And I don't want to know.'

'Yes, sir.' Walden quickly opened a beer. The colonel walked away.

Walden was on his fourth beer when the cry went up.

'Here they come. Here they come,' people began to yell, pointing at the Kingbee flying down the beach. Before it had settled to the ground, people were cheering and rushing toward it. The short, stocky form of Manning was dragged from the helicopter and hoisted onto shoulders. He struggled, flailing his arms until they let him down. Walden could see how tired the man was. His face was sunburned and peeling; the crow's-feet around his eyes and mouth were deeply etched.

'I just thank God I'm home.' Manning coughed. He rubbed the back of a bruised hand across his eyes as tears began to well up. He tried to say something more, but then shook his hand nervously in front of his face.

'We're going to have the damnedest party this camp has ever seen,' Easton shouted. 'We're going to do a quick debriefing, then we're going to be down at the club. Drinks are on me until we get there.'

Everyone cheered and began heading up the sand road to the club. Mike Workman suggested to Walden and Forrest that they take the long way to the club so they could get high first. They divided the beers left in the case and headed for the ocean bunkers.

'I think 1970 is going to be a good year,' Jeffers said as he passed a joint. 'My mom is sending me one of those fake Christmas trees and lights. It'll be just like home.'

'I'm already home,' Walden said, taking a drag. 'Everything I ever wanted or needed is right here in this country, right now. I'm gonna stay here and eat rice balls and fish heads for the rest of my life.' Walden saw Manning's eyes, lost and hurt. *I don't want to die. Please, God.*

The club was packed with people when they walked in. It seemed as though everyone was drunk already. The air was thick with sweat, spilled beer, and smoke.

'How would you like to walk into this place sober?' Walden asked as they squeezed up to the bar.

'The animals are out in force tonight,' Forrest said when a beer can went flying through the air. Jim Dansworth, standing at the far end of the club, caught it, then stood on a chair waving his arms and shouting for more. He caught the first few thrown, but then there were too many and not as accurately tossed. The cans began to fall among the people sitting at the surrounding tables. Shouting, and scrambling out of the way, they began to throw cans back as though it were a snowball fight.

'You dumb sons of bitches, you're supposed to drink them, not throw them at each other,' Charlie Pepper bellowed at the top of his lungs. The club became stone quiet, but in a few seconds it was back to normal.

'These people are crazy,' Jeffers said.

'It's party time.' Parrish shrugged. 'We finally get something to celebrate. God knows that doesn't happen often.' The group moved to the end of the club and found a folding table and some chairs stacked against the wall. Len Michaels dragged his chair over from another table and shook hands with Walden and Forrest.

'Golf Nine, man.' He snickered. 'You'll be the last team ever to run that target.'

'I wouldn't take any bets on that,' Walden said. 'They sent us in there knowing full well how hot it was.'

'I'd like to send Major Deacon in there,' Jeffers said. There was real anger in his voice. 'While you were gone, I was down at the beach with the little people and the gate guard locked us out.' He paused, looking around the table to see if anyone was listening.

'Well?' Walden asked.

'Well, we climbed through the perimeter wire and Deacon comes along in his jeep and arrests us.' The table started to laugh. 'The prick has seen me a thousand times. Anyway, he says we're under arrest for breaching camp security.' The laughter grew louder. 'Twenty-five indig, and one American, me, were thrown into Deacon's CONEX-container jail. What a riot. There were Chinese, Vietnamese, Montagnard. God, what a gathering.'

'So what happened?' Forrest asked.

'He let us out around supper and I had to go see him the next day. He couldn't really do anything, since everyone was laughing about it.'

'That guy is such a puke.' Walden sighed. 'Always trying to screw someone over.'

Parrish added, 'He's lucky he's not with one of these grunt units around here. They'd frag his ass for sure.'

'I'd just love to see him go across the fence,' Walden said.

The beer kept coming and the barbecue sauce was readied for the steaks. After an hour the colonel and Manning arrived to a turbulent welcome. Walden and the others left the club to smoke a joint and let it calm down.

Outside in the twilight Walden breathed in the smell of barbecue smoke. It reminded him of home. He walked over to the piss tubes at the side of the club. Pepper came staggering over.

'How you doing, son?' Pepper slapped Walden on the back. Walden had to take a step forward to keep his balance, then a quick step to the side to keep from peeing on his boots.

'Just fine, Charlie. How you doing?'

229

'I'll be fucked up by the time this is all over. I'm just getting rid of some excess fuel right now.'

Walden buttoned his fly. 'This is the first time I've talked to you during the last couple of months that you haven't given me a mission to run.'

'Don't press your luck, kid.' Pepper belched, swaying back and forth, hitting the tube briefly on each pass. 'Me and the Dai, we figure you and your team need training, so we're sending you to Monkey Mountain for a week.'

'Thanks, Charlie.'

'Don't mention it,' Pepper said, waving as he headed back to the club.

'You hear that?' Walden asked the others. 'We get to go to Monkey Mountain for a week.'

'Lucky bastards,' Jeffers said, acting angry. 'You guys always get the good deals.'

They went to the barbecue pit, where Coop stood next to a massive pile of raw steaks, waving a fan back and forth to keep the flies off. Walden said hello. She ignored him, a pout on her face. Walden shrugged and had begun to walk away when she called after him.

'You come back soon. I cook for you,' she said.

'Okay, I be back *tê tê*,' Walden said. She went back to her job as though she hadn't spoken.

'Boy, she's really pissed about something,' Forrest said.

'Somebody told her something.' Walden looked at the others. Parrish and Workman looked away.

'All right, what did you guys say?'

'We didn't know she was listening,' Workman said. 'I mean, me and Eldon were just talking over coffee a few days ago in the mess hall, and I mentioned you and Jerry were having a good time in Saigon. She shit a brick. Started to scream that you were supposed to be in the field. I didn't know.'

'She got really uptight,' Parrish admitted.

'Damn,' Walden said. 'I never wanted her to get hurt.'

'Just explain that you had to go down there after a mission,' Len Michaels said.

230

'That's not the thing. I'm bringing Hoa up here to live with me. How the hell do I explain that?'

The team hooch was empty, so they went to the tin hooch farther out on the sand where Maine Team stayed. They walked through the screen door and found Edgewater sitting on the porch stripping down an AK-47.

'How you doing, Ed?' Walden asked as they all sat down. 'They're barbecuing steaks down at the club.'

'Those people are idiots.'

'Good old Ed,' Parrish said. 'Nobody like you to put things into perspective.'

'Hell, I like Manning as much as the next guy. I'm glad he made it out, but that doesn't take away from the fact that there are still seven dead dudes out there. This big fuckin' to-do about one person getting back. Shit.' No one said anything. Edgewater had been close to Tibbens, a drinking buddy.

They got wasted sitting on the porch, drinking beer and smoking grass, then they headed back to the club to get a steak. Stumbling across the dunes, Walden said he felt like taking the LSD.

'You have to be straight before you take it,' Forrest explained. 'It's not like cranking up on some speed. It's like launching a mission in your head. You don't want to be fucked up.'

'Give me a break,' Walden said. 'I've taken a lot of pills, man.'

'You haven't taken anything like this,' Forrest said firmly. 'It's like getting arc-lighted by God.'

Later that evening, when the party was breaking up, Walden finally ran into Manning.

'Hey, Sam.' Manning was very drunk. 'I haven't had a minute to talk to you since I got back.' He put a hand on Walden's shoulder.

'That's okay, Andy. You're a celebrity now.' They walked outside and in silent agreement turned for the hooches. 'I'm real sorry about your team,' Walden said.

'God, Sam, you're the first one to say that.' Manning

231

staggered against him. 'I don't know why I should be here and they're all dead. I just don't understand it, Sam.' He began to cry.

'Come on, Andy, I'll help you to your hooch.'

'I got pretty drunk, I guess.' He sniffled. 'Here I am crying like a kid. I can't seem to help it. Every time I think of my guys.' He wiped at the tears running down his face. 'Big tough Green Beret bastard, huh?' They reached the door of his hooch.

'You got the key?' Walden asked, holding the lock in his hand.

'It doesn't need one. Just yank it.' Inside, the thick smell of mildew filled the empty room. Walden thought of dead flowers and funeral parlors. The silence had grown along with the dust balls and cobwebs.

'They let me call Marlene in the States. I talked to my kids, too. I'm going home, Sam. I've run my last mission.' Manning flopped onto his bunk and slowly closed his eyes. Walden pushed at the light switch and looked back. Manning's arm was dangling over the edge of the bunk. The hand twitched.

Walden woke around noon and immediately wished he hadn't. The hair on the back of his neck was matted to his skin in a sweaty smear. His head throbbed. The inside of his mouth felt burnt. He had been dreaming of water. He sat up, and the ache in his head sharpened.

'Oh, my God,' he moaned, falling back onto the damp sheets. Forrest didn't stir from where he was sprawled on his bunk. A surge of nausea rippled through Walden's stomach. After a few minutes he sat back up. When he was ready, he stood up and went to his locker for his shaving kit and towel. He pulled on his fatigue pants and slowly eased out into the bright sunlight. With his eyelids almost closed to cut down on the glare, he shuffled toward the shower. He was turning the corner when Workman sprinted across the sand, panic in his face and spittle flying. He was half yelling incoherent sounds.

'What the hell is going on?' Walden yelled.

'He drowned. He drowned,' Workman stuttered, then began to cough as his throat contracted.

'What are you talking about, drowned?' Walden grabbed Workman by the front of his shirt.

'Manning. Andy Manning. He just drowned down at the beach.' Workman's eyes were huge behind his glasses. Walden's hand slid down the shirtfront, fingers flopping like dying fish.

'Oh, my God,' Walden finally murmured, and began running toward the beach. His feet churned through the sand, heavy, dragging. *It's not possible. God wouldn't do that. No one could live through that, then just drown. It's not fair.* He had almost convinced himself by the time he reached the group of people standing at the water's edge. He didn't want to look, but he couldn't not look. He pushed his way through the outer circle and looked down.

'Oh, Andy,' he whispered.

'We gave him mouth to mouth. We tried.' Parrish was almost crying. 'He just didn't . . . I mean, it was like a door closed.'

'How did it happen?' Walden knelt and brushed wet sand off the face. The eyes were open, but the expression was relaxed.

'We swam out to the raft,' Parrish said, pointing out to the planked-over drums floating offshore. 'We caught some rays and then started to swim back to eat. We didn't notice anything wrong; he didn't yell for help or anything. We were almost to shore before we noticed he was missing. We swam back and dived for him. Found him right away, but he was already dead.'

The ambulance came up behind them and stopped. Walden closed the eyes, but as soon as he removed his fingers they opened again. He didn't realize that he had walked away until he found himself far down the beach.

CHAPTER TWENTY-THREE

DAYS PASSED before Walden's depression lifted. Early one evening a practice alert was called. The entire team was sitting on one of the bunkers next to the ocean, waiting for the all clear. Forrest left the bunker for a few minutes. When he returned, he held a hit of LSD in his hand.

'Take this, brother. May it serve you well.' Forrest held it out for Walden to take. Forrest placed the tiny orange pill on his upturned palm. 'Put it under your tongue and let it dissolve.'

'This thing is so small you'd better give me two,' Walden said.

'One is plenty, believe me.' The all-clear siren went off.

'Okay, take the team back up to the hooch, and I'll meet you at ours.' Alone on the bunker, he held the pill up and inspected it in the moonlight. *What the hell.* He dropped it under his tongue. A bitter taste filled his mouth, making him shiver as the tab began to melt. He started to swallow it, then changed his mind. *I might as well do this right.* He felt the pill becoming smaller, then it was gone. He walked back to the American hooches.

His hooch was empty when Walden dropped off his weapon and web gear. He walked to Parrish's hooch, where he had seen a light. He went up the wooden steps and pushed open the screen door, expecting someone inside. The tape recorder was playing 'Martha My Dear' from The Beatles' *White Album*, but the hooch was empty. He sat on Parrish's bunk. The music was soothing and he stretched out on the bed. He pulled out a pack of cigarettes and his lighter and put them on the nightstand. *Nothing's going to happen. I knew I should've taken two.*

Then something stirred inside his head. The room became brighter and he sat up. Across the room the dark grains in the plywood wall were beginning to move in slow waves. The graceful undulation of the wall sped up.

He pulled his eyes away. The music grew louder. *Do something natural and it'll go away*. The words echoed inside his head. He reached for the cigarettes and lighter. He stopped his hand, staring at the trails of colors flowing from it. Shades he had never seen before, floating, swirling, came off the back of his hand like liquid plastic. He drew his hand back and looked at his palm. It was aglow with red sparks. Walden felt the first touch of panic. It hadn't been twenty minutes since he'd taken the pill.

'What the hell is going on?' Walden asked when Forrest and Workman came into the room. 'Colors are coming off my hand.'

'It's cool, Sam. It's cool.' Forrest was soothing.

'Far out, man.' Workman chuckled. 'Didn't take you long to start tripping.'

'Damn.' Walden looked around the glowing room. 'I don't like this.'

'Don't fight it, just go with it,' Forrest said, sitting down next to Walden. 'I'll be right here, no sweat.' A new song came over the speakers, riotous and shrill. What was around him was still there, but it was changing. Workman's face became multidimensional, made of painted panes of glass.

'Jerry, this is real strange,' Walden said, then he realized he hadn't really said it, only thought it. When he tried again, it was gone, the words falling off the side of his tongue. He stood up, the music confusing him. The air, the room, the inside of his head, were humming with the song of a million crickets.

I got to get to my hooch, got to get to my hooch to stop this. Forrest followed him into the night. The air outside was whining. Walden paused at the bottom of the steps, bits and pieces of words flowing past his ears. Bright flashes of light, red, green, yellow, began appearing around him. He

235

looked down at his boots and they were a hundred feet below his head. He felt he was losing control. He slowly made his way up the steps to his hooch. Forrest flicked on the overhead light. Walden jumped as though a bomb had exploded.

'Take it easy, buddy. Take it easy,' Forrest cautioned. Walden looked down at the wooden floor and watched a lace pattern change and expand. Colors ran down the walls. The room surged and swelled.

This isn't real. Walden sat down on his bed. Ripples ran through his sweating body. The muscles in his arms and back tensed as each new wave rolled forward, then back. Small multicolored orbs, like iridescent balloons, appeared in front of his eyes. He looked at his hands and arms. 'I can see every vein. I can see the blood going through them.'

'Don't be frightened by it,' Forrest said. 'Your mind is just open now.'

Jeffers came into the hooch. Walden's eyes locked on the CAR-15 around his neck. Suddenly death, dying, horrible screaming things, were in the hooch.

'Get that thing out of here. Get that away from me,' Walden shouted.

'Wow, it's only me,' Jeffers said.

'Get it away from me,' Walden repeated. *It had to be the weapon. It had to be the weapon.*

'Get the gun out of here, Danny,' Forrest said. 'He may be going on a bummer.'

A strong feeling of déjà vu came to Walden. It was familiar, and so simple. The smallest thing took on great importance and far-reaching meaning. It took a long time to light a cigarette for that reason. Faces appeared in the walls and in the air around him, all looking as if they were out of the twenties. The faces were black and white only. Like a cork bobbing to the surface, the thought of an LRRP ration he had seen earlier in the day, covered with ants, entered his mind. As soon as the image came to him, he felt ants crawling. He looked at his bed, at himself. There were millions of them all over everything. He began

236

to brush them off his legs and arms. 'Ants, ants. They're all over me.'

'There's nothing on you,' Forrest said calmly. 'Believe me.'

'I can see them.'

'You just think you do. There is nothing on you. Think of something pleasant, beautiful. Love, think of love.'

Walden saw the ants were gone. *Love, love*. A warm, soft feeling came over him. The sky opened after a long storm, and the sun appeared. He became a partner with the world. 'It's love. That's the answer,' Walden said. 'The answer, the reason.' He reached out his hands to Forrest. He felt he had to pass on what he had just discovered. He began to talk as though they were children gathered at his feet. He knew then what Jesus knew, what Jesus had tried to tell the world. For the first time in his life he knew, really knew, that he was also the son of God. That they all were. They all had to find out what he had just discovered.

'You can hate,' Walden said. 'But the more you hate, the farther away from the truth you will go. You can kill those things you hate, but they will never go away. The only way to erase hate is to love. For it is only in loving that you will be loved. It is the only way. It is the answer.'

'Wow, man.' Workman chuckled. 'You're really out there.'

'I'm with God. I'm a part of God, just as you are, as Jerry is, as we all are. There is nothing that should frighten us, because there is nothing that can hurt us. We can never die. We can leave our bodies, but that is not dying. Tell Danny to come and be here with me. I want to talk to him.'

A few minutes later Jeffers eased into the room, a doubtful expression on his face. Walden hugged his friend to him. 'I'm sorry I hurt you,' he said. 'There were things that frightened me, that will never frighten me again.' Jeffers lifted his eyebrows. 'You will come to understand.' Walden motioned to him to sit down next to him. 'I just want you to be close to me now.' Jeffers grinned and sat.

By first light the effect of the drug began to wear off. The dazzling light show, the feeling of understanding, became subdued and then were gone.

'I can't believe it,' Walden said to Forrest. 'I'm sober, straight, and serious. I'll never be the same again. I'll never look at things like I did before.'

'You really went on a trip.' Forrest smiled. 'For a while there I was wondering if you were going to get extracted.'

CHAPTER TWENTY-FOUR

'THEY'RE GOING to what?' Walden choked and started to laugh. 'The clerks are going to clean out Marble Mountain? In one day? So they can get CIBs?'

'They're going to do it tomorrow' – Forrest broke into giggles – "cause Sunday is their day off.'

'That goes beyond crazy, right into stupid.' Walden slid the chair away from the desk in the hooch. 'What jerk-off thought up this one?'

'Deacon is in charge of it.' Forrest tried to keep a straight face. He failed, breaking into full laughter. 'He's over in the club now, rallying his troops,' he said between gasps. 'It sounds like a speech from *Sands of Iwo Jima*.'

'They're going to be in for a world of shit. How do they plan on doing it?'

'From what I gathered,' Forrest said, 'they're going to go into the tunnels and flush all those little bastards out into the daylight, while, get this, tactically positioned snipers pick them off.'

'You making this up?'

'I'm not kidding. I was just over at the club listening to it. They're as serious as a goddamn heart attack.'

'Okay.' Walden held up his hand. 'Let me see if I got this right. They're going to crawl into those caves, right, hand-to-hand and all that crap, and run them out?'

'That's the deal, man.'

'Oh, Jesus Christ.' Walden felt real disbelief. 'They think it's going to be a lark or something. Those jerk Remington Raiders have been watching war movies. Honest to God, Jerry, they don't even know what it's like to get shot at. That hand-to-hand-combat shit is beyond the pale.'

'I'm just telling you what I heard,' Forrest said. 'Let's go over and trim the tree. I told Danny we'd be over in a couple of minutes.'

'Let me finish this letter to Hoa.' Walden sat back at the desk. When he was done, he printed FREE (IN COUNTRY) where the stamp would normally go and inserted the pages.

'She writes to you every day?' Forrest asked, standing by the door.

'Yesterday I got three letters from her. One for the morning, one for the afternoon, and one for the night.' Walden smiled.

'Man, you're really different lately,' Forrest said. 'I don't know what changed you more, the LSD trip or Hoa.'

'Hoa,' Walden said without hesitation. 'Without her I wouldn't have been able to figure out the answer.'

The tree-trimming party was in full swing when they got to Jeffers's hooch. The little people from Louisiana Team and Maryland Team bounced around the room, giggling and throwing tinsel on the plastic boughs of the Christmas tree.

'You got lights and everything.' Walden took the joint Jeffers offered and looked at the five-foot, glossy green tree.

'Check it out, man. We've even got snow.' Jeffers picked up an aerosol can from his bunk and shot a spray of white flakes into the air. 'And look at this,' he said excitedly, bounding over to the tree box. 'My mom packed everything in popcorn, and sent along some needles and thread so we can string it. Isn't that far out?'

'Really,' Walden said. The room suddenly smelled of Christmas and flannel Santa Claus.

'I got something special to tell you guys too,' Jeffers said, his eyes going from face to face. 'Mai and I are going to get married as soon as I get back from the next mission.'

'That's great, Danny,' Walden said, shaking his hand. 'We can be neighbors when Hoa comes.'

Jeffers was obviously excited, waving his arms around. 'We're going to Da Lat for our honeymoon. She wants to have a baby right away, but I think we'll wait for a while. I took a couple of green hornets. You guys want to drop?'

'How many, Jerry?' Forrest was starting to give the little people a class on how to string popcorn.

'How many you taking?'

'Three.'

'Same-same.' They washed the pills down with beer. 'Here's to the show of shows tomorrow,' Forrest said.

'What's this?' Jeffers asked.

'A bunch of idiots from Headquarters are going to start some shit tomorrow in the mountain so they can get CIBs,' Walden said.

'To get CIBs?'

Walden saw what he'd looked like when Forrest had told him. 'I couldn't believe it either.'

'What's Easton saying about it?'

'Easton's in Saigon. He probably doesn't know a damn thing about it. It's Deacon's idea. We figure he wants a Silver Star.' At that moment Charlie Horn came through the door.

'I need to borrow a pistol from one of you guys for tomorrow,' Horn said excitedly, looking like a kid about to pee his pants.

'You're not going on this thing tomorrow?' Walden got serious. He liked Charlie.

'Let me borrow your nine mike-mike, Sam,' Charlie said as though he hadn't heard.

'You don't need it because you're not going on this thing tomorrow,' Walden said, realizing that he sounded like his father.

'Sam, everybody in the Head-shed is going,' Horn said, sounding defensive.

'No, not everyone is going. You're not going.'

'Come on, man. I've been sitting up at that goddamn TOC damn near my whole tour. I want to see what it's all about.'

'Look, Charlie,' Walden said quietly. 'I've never steered you wrong before. Forget this thing tomorrow. If you want a CIB so bad, I'll take you with me on a mission. But please forget this thing tomorrow.'

'You'll take me out with you?' Horn's eyes actually got wide.

'I'll take you out, only if you forget this bonehead stunt tomorrow.'

'Okay,' he said, smiling. 'It's a volunteer thing so I guess I don't have to go.'

'By this time tomorrow you're going to be thanking me.' Walden popped another can of beer.

The crump of exploding grenades and small-arms fire woke him. He pulled the pillow over his head, pushing it against his ears with his forearms. After a few minutes of listening to the muffled firefight raging around Marble Mountain, he yanked the pillow off his head and sat up.

'Listen to that already.' Walden looked at his watch. It was half past nine.

'Well, so much for sleeping in.' Forrest sat up and rubbed his eyes.

'It sounds like Deacon's Marauders have run into some resistance,' Walden remarked with a grunt.

'See if you can see anything.'

Walden limped to the door. 'Everything seems to be happening on the south side,' he said after a moment.

'We may as well get cleaned up and get some breakfast,' Forrest said. 'It's a damn cinch we're not going to be able to sleep.'

Half an hour later they joined a group at the mess hall drinking coffee and making bets on how long the fighting would last.

'Are they inside the mountain yet?' Parrish asked.

'Charlie opened up on them as they marched up,' Mike Winston said. 'They're pinned down right now, about thirty meters from the main entrance. Deacon is screaming his damn head off. Wants reinforcements already.'

'This is really going to be something.' Walden swirled the last swallow of coffee around the bottom of his cup.

'Let's pick up some beer, go down to the team hooch, and watch it from there,' Forrest suggested.

'I'll get the PRC-25 we're taking on our mission,' Jeffers said. 'We can listen in on what's happening.'

By the time Walden and Forrest got to the team hooch with the beer, the others were already gathered, scanning the mountaintop with binoculars.

'What are you getting?' Forrest asked, squatting next to Jeffers and the radio.

'They got a few people inside the main chamber. Some American has been hit in there. They're trying to get him out now.'

'Holy Christ, check this one.' Workman pointed out several figures beginning to slide down ropes thrown from the mountain summit. 'I'll bet those guys aren't clerks.'

'Whose teams are on security up there?' Edgewater asked, squinting his eyes, trying to make out the men on the ropes.

'Conner and Talbert,' Walden answered. He borrowed a pair of binoculars from Parrish. 'That's them all right, and Lieutenant Broder.'

He watched as the lieutenant sidestepped over to a cave opening, fumbling with a grenade. A number of shots were heard from inside the cave. A collective groan went up from the group as the lieutenant pitched to the side and toppled over backward. The rappeling rope bound up for a moment in the snaplink, holding the lieutenant upside down. Slowly the body began to slide down the rope. It gradually picked up speed until the form dropped off the running end of the rope and fell to the rocks below.

'Just a Sunday outing to get CIBs, huh?' Walden handed the glasses back to Parrish.

'They just got the wounded American out from inside the main cavern, but they've got another American hit and a Montagnard KIA, and one WIA,' Jeffers said. 'Deacon is heading back for the TOC. He said there's too much noise where he is, and he needs to think.' They watched Conner and Talbert being pulled back to the top of the mountain.

'So much for the rappeling class,' Workman said. He opened another beer.

The fighting continued all morning. By noon plumes of white phosphorus smoke were drifting out of a dozen cave openings, obscuring most of the north wall. Jeffers and Workman picked up hot dogs at the club snack bar and resupplied the beer. By early afternoon the fighting had tapered off, then finally ended.

'I guess the boys figured they earned their CIBs,' Walden said without smiling.

'They're bringing in the casualties at the helipad,' Jeffers said. 'You guys want to check out the damages?' No one spoke, they just started to walk down to the pad. By the time they arrived, a helicopter had already unloaded a number of lightly wounded Montagnards. Another ship was on its way in. The more seriously wounded were Medevaced to the hospital. The dead were taken to the Da Nang morgue. Walden walked among the wounded Montagnards, handing out cigarettes and giving them water. Keegan and other medics shuttled the ambulance and trucks back and forth, carrying the wounded up to the dispensary. Ten of the little people had been killed and more than forty wounded. Two Americans had been killed and six wounded, two seriously. The VC still held the inside of the mountain.

After dark several shots were fired into the camp from the mountain. Walden knew it was Charlie's way of saying they were still there.

CHAPTER TWENTY-FIVE

A FEW DAYS after the Marble Mountain affair Walden and the team were helicoptered to Monkey Mountain for their promised week of training. The mountain was ten kilometers north of Da Nang, along the rocky coast. It gave teams a safe area in which to practise. It had no village or military sites, so the Viet Cong did not venture into it. A Kingbee dropped the team on a patch of white sandy beach, along with enough ammo and food to last a month.

For the team the training consisted of hunting monkeys and wild pigs in the lush jungles that grew almost to the water. They also fished the clear blue ocean with what they called Du Pont lures, grenades and C-4 explosives. The team saw it as a chance to get away from the camp and relax.

After a few days Walden felt the tension leave him. The team took walks on the beach, took naps, took time out. It was a vacation from work.

The afternoon of the day before they were to return, Walden and Forrest sat alone on a high, rocky bluff.

'It's been so nice here I hate to think about it,' Walden said.

'About what?'

'What target they'll have for us when we get back.'

'Don't worry about it,' Forrest said. 'We run a mission, you go down to Saigon and pick up Hoa and live happily ever after.'

'It's ironic, though. For the first time I don't want to run any more targets. But I have to if I want to see Saigon again.'

'Everything has its price.'

Walden looked down the beach at the little people sitting around the campfire. 'Right now I would like to tell them the war is over. That they should go home and make babies or something.'

'Jesus, you're really tired of the fighting.'

'I guess I am.' Walden toyed with a stray strand of thread on his fatigue shirt. 'I've been thinking that I've killed enough people. Too many.'

'You start thinking about that shit and it'll drive you crazy,' Forrest said sternly. 'It's a goddamn war. That's what you do. Kill people.'

'If I thought it had accomplished anything, I might feel differently about it.'

'What do you mean?' Forrest asked.

'We're no closer to winning this thing than we were when I first got here. It's like they don't want to win. Bombing halts. Christmas truces that only we honor. Look at us. We have to pay mercenaries to go on missions with us.'

Forrest didn't answer. Finally they got up and walked back to the campsite.

During the night storm clouds moved in. By morning the clouds hung barely thirty feet off the water. Walden radioed a request for a helicopter, and it began to rain. Half an hour later they were told they couldn't have a ship because of the weather. Walden decided the team would walk out. While they were packing their gear, Pau spotted a sampan moving south toward Da Nang. When shouts and oaths didn't get the lone fisherman's attention, Cuong opened up with a burst of automatic fire across the bow. The boat turned sharply and headed in to the shore.

The expression on the face of the fisherman changed from fear to relief when Hung told him they would pay for the trip to Da Nang. His anxious smile revealed teeth stained by years of chewing betel nut. He spat a stream of the black-and-red juice into the water as he helped them load the rucksacks and gear into his small boat. When everything was stowed on the rickety vessel and everyone was aboard, the gunwales were barely above the water.

Walden had to laugh when a wave broke over the port side of the boat as it turned toward Da Nang. Pau, Cuong, and Forrest all started to bail without a word. Even though it struck Walden as funny, he was glad they stayed within swimming distance of the shore.

They passed the large, rusting hull of a ship driven onto the rocks years before. The superstructure had been removed, leaving only the skeleton to decay in the sea.

It took nearly five hours to reach the Navy docks at Da Nang. Walden called the base camp while a few miles out and requested a truck. It was waiting for them at the dock. They overpaid the papa-san and gave him the food they had left. The old man insisted on helping them load their gear in the truck. Walden walked over to the Vietnamese driver.

'How you doing, Minh?'

'I have bad news,' Minh said, avoiding Walden's eyes.

'What's wrong?'

'Jeffers and team *hết rồi*, *fini*, three days ago,' Minh said softly.

Walden felt the blood leave his head. 'Oh, God, no. Not them, not them.' He leaned against the fender of the truck and put his head in his hands. Bile rose to his throat, and he began to tremble.

Forrest came running over. 'What's wrong?'

Walden looked up at the steel-gray sky. 'Danny and the team got wiped out. They're all dead.'

Forrest looked as if he'd been kicked in the stomach. He staggered back a step.

'Come on, let's go.' Walden climbed into the cab. No one spoke on the drive back to camp. Walden kept thinking of Jeffers and the other Americans on the team, Ronnie Glenn and Gunther Brunn. He half expected to find them at the hooch. For a long time he and Forrest sat inside their room, not moving.

That evening they went to the team hooch. The little people moved about quietly, wrapped in their own silence. Five of their friends had died on the operation. When it became too depressing, Walden and Forrest left and

247

walked back to the American hooches. There were lights on in Parrish's hut, across from Jeffers's place. Workman, Fish, Keegan, Edgewater, and Parrish were inside. They, too, sat around talking in hushed tones, listening to music and smoking joints. Walden tried not to think, but pictures of Jeffers kept appearing in his mind. Memories of the good times would flood in. He forced them back out, leaving nothing but cold emptiness.

Around midnight Walden walked outside. A strong wind blew off the ocean. He looked across the sidewalk at the shuttered windows of Jeffers's hooch. The night was black and cold. *I'll never see Jeffers again.* An ache crawled into his heart. He crossed to the hooch and pulled the door latch. A gust of wind caught the corner of the door and blew it open.

Someone had turned on the Christmas-tree lights. The red-and-green bulbs threw patterns on the walls and beds in the deserted room. The tree stood alone, a long way from home, smelling of spray snow and popcorn strings. Walden looked at the tree, then began to cry. His vision blurred as the first tears of his adult life welled up. Something inside of him broke as the first sob shook through his body. For a moment he tried to check himself, but the gate had opened and he sank to his knees, warm tears coursing down his cheeks. Spasm after spasm wracked his body.

He didn't know how long he knelt in the sand. After the tears were gone, he stayed hunched over, until his breathing became regular again. Rain began to fall as he slowly got to his feet. He closed the door.

CHAPTER TWENTY-SIX

CHRISTMAS CAME and went. Walden wanted to be in Saigon with Hoa, but the team was targeted for a mission after the new year. Nearly every day he received a letter from her. Hung had found a small, comfortable house a short way from the camp, and Walden busied himself with getting it ready. It helped keep his mind occupied.

Two days after the new year began, Walden and Forrest were in the hooch, getting ready to leave for the launch site the following day. Workman came charging into the room.

'Talbert, House, and McKenzie, they've been killed,' he blurted. 'They got the bodies out. The colonel wants everyone in Recon Company to report to the helipad.'

'Sonofabitch.' Walden exploded. 'Enough is goddamn enough.' He threw an empty C-ration box across the room. 'That's enough. That's enough. Sweet Jesus Christ.'

Sergeant Major Pepper and Captain Wells were standing in the company street, talking. Walden and Forrest went to them. Someone had passed the word in the club, and people from Recon Company filed out into the bright sunlight. They also gathered around.

'We're having a company formation down at the pad,' Pepper snapped. 'Five minutes.'

'What the hell happened?' Walden asked.

'What happened? I'll tell you what happened.' Pepper spit, obviously beside himself with anger. 'They fuckin' blew it. That's what happened.'

'Did the whole team get killed?' Forrest asked. The group started down the road toward the helipad.

'Just the Americans,' Wells said.

'Goddammit.' Pepper kicked the ground. 'Goddamn

wise-ass boneheads.' Walden knew then there was something he hadn't been told. Pepper and the three dead men had been old friends.

'What's going on?' Walden asked tensely as they neared the pad. Pepper shook his head, not trusting himself to talk.

'The report we got is that they had taken some booze out with them,' Wells said softly, not wanting the others to hear. 'They were pissed off because they were going to miss the floor show and the New Year's Eve party. The little people said they didn't move at all after they were inserted. They just moved a few meters away from the LZ and started to get drunk. Some Pathet Lao came up. They didn't do anything to the little people. They only shot the Americans.'

Soon after they reached the pad, a Kingbee came in with the three Americans in body bags and the little people. The Vietnamese were quickly taken away on a truck to be interrogated. Colonel Easton drove up in his jeep. The company formed up in front of the bags on the PSP. Roger Tillis, who had escorted the bodies back from the launch site, handed Easton a clear plastic bag containing the notebooks and code pads. He then walked to the formation and squeezed in between Walden and Forrest.

'This is going to be real bad,' he said under his breath, as they watched Easton, Pepper, and Wells go through the notebooks. After a few minutes the colonel walked between the body bags. Long moments passed as he stared at each of them, his hands on his hips. He wore a black ski jacket with the death's head over the right breast; it ruffled in the wind. He smoothed out the faded green beret he wore before he started to speak.

'We lost three today,' he said, pushing the words between his teeth. 'It's bad enough when we lose people because they get detected doing their jobs. But this, this . . . ' He waved his hand at the rubber sacks and shouted, 'This is just a stinking waste.'

No one had ever seen the colonel in such a state. His

features were livid, and he had trouble breathing. He yanked a bloodstained green notebook out of his jacket pocket, and waved it over his head as he stomped back and forth in front of them. His mouth moved, but no words came out. Only the sound of his boots and the drone of the flies swirling around the bags could be heard. When the voice came, Walden flinched.

'Do you want me to read the last entry in House's notebook?' he screamed, glaring at them. 'I'll goddamn read it to you. It says happy fuckin' New Year. That's what it says.' He flung the book across the helipad. 'Real cute, huh?' His voice went flat. 'They went into Laos pissed off because they'd miss a party. Decided to have one of their own. Now they're dead.' He turned his back to the men and looked down at the bags. When he turned around, his voice was very soft.

'Gentlemen, we're not playing games here.' Walden felt a lump begin growing in his throat as he saw the trickle of tears running down the cheeks of the colonel. 'As your commander I feel it is my duty to impress upon you all the gravity of your situation. To make you understand what happens when you get lax on a mission.' He turned to the green bags and unzipped each one.

'Each one of you is going to file past these bodies and look. And the next time you're on a mission and you start to grab-ass, I want you to remember.'

Walden had decided to only pretend to look, but when walking by, he couldn't help himself. Everything from the cheekbones up on Talbert's head was gone. The reddish gray pulp of what was left of his brain was beginning to stiffen as it dried against the rubber lining. McKenzie's lower jaw had been blown away. His upper teeth, cracked and chipped, appeared much too large. House had been hit in the chest and legs. Although his face was unharmed, it was the worst. The glazed eyes stared straight up; the skin was blotchy and gray, stretched taut across his cheekbones. His mouth gaped open, the black lips fused into a leer.

251

Walden heard the colonel behind him. He turned and watched the man kneel next to House.

'They killed you. They killed you,' he said, smoothing the hair on the still head. Pepper helped the colonel back to his feet.

'Let's go now, sir. It's over,' Wells said gently as they led him back to the jeep.

'I'm going to get fucked up.' Walden was breathing heavily.

'You got that right, man.' Forrest pushed his hands down into his pockets and they started back to the company area.

'It's falling apart, Jerry. It's starting to come loose at the edges.'

'You got that right too.'

CHAPTER TWENTY-SEVEN

LONG DAYS passed as the team waited at the launch site for their target area to clear. The skies stayed sullen and gray. It would drizzle, then rain, then drizzle again. The CP tent was cold and miserable. At the end of a week the little people were moody and on edge.

Walden lay on his cot, leafing through a year-old copy of *Time* magazine. A melancholia came over him as he looked at the old pictures and read about things that no longer mattered.

He tossed the magazine away and lit a cigarette. It tasted like mildew. He watched the smoke hang in the damp air. During the waiting he had almost decided that this would be his last mission. What kept him from making a final decision was the question of what would happen to the little people and to Forrest. Walden didn't even want to think of another American taking the team out. It would be like desertion. Yet he felt used up, empty, and the feeling worried him. He could get a job in the TOC like so many others had. He could be with Hoa every night. He could try to find the peace the LSD had touched.

Restless, he got up and walked outside. The rain had momentarily stopped, and the sky looked to be clearing to the east. He gazed across the rain-slick fields of Quang Tri province. Leaving the tent area, he strolled across an open field. A broken artillery box lay open in the wet weeds, making him think of a smashed coffin. Decomposing sand-bags littered the field. The old cloth bags melted into brown lumps, and the woven plastic bags, the type which were not supposed to rot, were also split and decayed.

He kicked at an old C-ration can covered in fine red rust,

moving toward a deserted Marine compound on the far side of the field. A broken barbed wire fence surrounded the camp, rusting on the leaning posts that had once held the wire taut and straight. Walking along the muddy road that led into the compound, Walden saw a plywood sign sagging against a post. The peeling red letters said, CLEAR ALL WEAPONS BEFORE TRAVELLING BEYOND THIS POINT. A cold breeze pushed through the long weeds growing around the sign.

Hunching his shoulders, he walked up the road into the ghost town. The sway-backed billets were dilapidated, stark against the dark clouds. A loose door banged in the wind. He walked into one of the deserted barracks.

A coat of dust covered the floor. The interior smelled dank. A small lizard raced along a wall, then slipped into a crack. Elaborate webs spanned the rafters. The plywood interior was covered with graffiti, and crude drawings. JO JO WAS HERE – ETS JUNE 10, '68. FUCK NAM! KILL A COMMIE FOR CHRIST. A crinkled pinup was fastened to a wall by a rusted thumbtack. Spray-painted on the back wall, reaching from ceiling to warped floor – YOU CAN HAVE IT, UNCLE HO. WE DON'T WANT IT ANYMORE.

When he read the sentence, Walden froze. It was like an LSD insight. His palms began to sweat as his mind folded around the sudden realization. They were leaving. They would all leave. For the first time he knew they were losing the war.

He went to a wall and slowly slid down until he sat on the floor. Far in the distance he could hear the beating of helicopter blades. His hands shook as he took out a cigarette and fumbled for his lighter. It began to rain again. He lit the cigarette and began to gag. He stubbed the cigarette out, folded his arms across his knees, and rested his head. He sat there a very long time.

The following morning dawned bright and clear. The little people sat on their cots, unhappy, emotionally drained after waiting so long. Walden and Forrest went to the operations tent to see if they were going to be inserted.

'Those little dudes are as skittish as spooked cats,' Walden said as they approached the tent. 'If we go in today, they'll be thinking we'll all be going to die.'

'They've been praying since we got up,' Forrest said.

'Pack your gear.' Slader grinned from behind his desk.

Walden felt his heart drop. 'It's a go?' He tried to look stalwart.

'Yup, you're going back to Da Nang.' Slader giggled as their faces flooded with relief.

'You bastard,' Walden exhaled.

'Well, it's clear here, but we just got the report from Covey that your AO is socked in. You guys wouldn't be worth a damn anyhow.'

'You got that right.' Walden grunted. 'My little people saw the sky this morning and started lighting incense.'

'There should be a week's time limit on these things,' Slader said. 'There's a convoy going back to Da Nang in about an hour.'

Walking back to the tent to tell the team, Walden admitted to real relief. Waiting to go on a mission was a grinding thing. Each day the confidence slipped farther and farther away. The longer the mind had to think about the possibilities, the less one wanted to go. Imagination was the worst thing a soldier could have.

An hour later the trucks moved out onto the highway back to Da Nang. The team had piled onto the back of a flatbed with two jeeps chained to it. The air smelled clean and fresh after the rains. The sunshine was warm and the scenery was beautiful along the road. A small boy waved to them from the back of a grazing water buffalo. Walden waved back, remembering when he was small and would wave at passing trains from the field.

'You know,' Forrest said, passing a joint to Walden, 'this war wouldn't be any fun without grass. If I weren't getting stoned right now, this trip would be boring.'

'You must have a point.' Walden looked across fields of

rice. 'It's hard to believe there have been some godawful battles along this road. It looks as peaceful as the countryside back home.'

'This must have been a hell of a beautiful country before the war if it can look like this after thirty or forty years of fighting.'

'In August of sixty-five, when I first got here, we had to travel up Highway 19 to where we were going to build our base camp at An Khe,' Walden said. 'We drove through this pass that the Hundred and first Airborne had secured for us. It was the most beautiful place I had ever seen. There were waterfalls, giant trees, ferns, everything lush and green. Everyone was spellbound by it. A few months later I came back down that same road to visit some of our guys in the hospital at Qui Nhon. They had sprayed the pass with this defoliant. Everything was dead, gray, like the Dismal Forest. The trees just had these empty branches. There was a gray, dusty powder that covered everything. The water was a brown sludge, and the birds were gone.'

'God, what would that shit do to people?' Forrest asked.

'I don't know.' Walden shrugged. 'We had to operate in some of the sprayed areas. We'd be covered with the stuff. A few of the guys asked about it and they told us it was harmless after a couple of hours.'

'That's good,' Forrest said, settling back in the seat.

Passing through Hue, there were still stark reminders of the Tet offensive. There were piles of rubble that had once been buildings; walls carried the scars of bullet holes and shrapnel; burned hulks of tanks and APCs rusted where they had been pushed into ditches along the road. It reaffirmed for Walden the truth he had found in the Marine compound the day before.

Later, leaving the city limits of Phu Bai, the convoy stopped in a traffic jam at a bridge approach. Walden picked up his weapon and walked to the edge of the truck bed to see up the road. A throng of people had formed at the entrance to the bridge and several were yelling. In a few minutes the convoy began to move slowly forward.

Nearing the crowd, Walden could hear the wailing of a woman. The truck crawled up to the crowd, pushing through people and carts. As they pulled up, Walden could see down into the crowd.

'Oh, my God,' he heard himself whisper. There were two tiny legs of a child, and then the grisly smear of the upper torso where a truck tyre had run over it. He stared at the small form on the hot, steaming tar of the highway. An old man from the crowd put his conical straw hat over the upper part of the body. The truck lurched forward. Walden turned away.

'Don't look,' he said when he saw Forrest coming forward. 'It's a dead baby. You don't want to see that.' Walden slumped down, blinking. It had been just one more ugly scene until he'd noticed the child's shorts. The shorts had little smiling whales printed on them. Little red whales on a white-and-blue sea.

CHAPTER TWENTY-EIGHT

THE CONVOY made good time after the bridge. Unloading the trucks outside of camp, Walden saw most of the people from Recon Company standing along the road. Parrish and Workman waved to them as they walked through the gate.

'What's going on?' Walden asked, joining the line of men.

'The colonel is leaving. We've got a new commander,' Parrish said. 'Easton's leaving in a few minutes. We wanted to see him off.'

'When did this happen?' Walden dropped his rucksack to the ground.

'Right after you left for the launch site,' Workman answered. 'A message came in up at the TOC for eyes only. From Chief SOG. Said, "Your private army is now terminated. Report to Saigon for further orders." '

'I suppose this new guy is a real asshole, too.'

'Worse than that,' Parrish said. 'A real paper pusher. He's not even Special Forces qualified. We found out that he only made three parachute jumps, but he still wears jump wings.'

'You should've heard the speech he gave us.' Workman giggled. 'He said he was going to make soldiers out of us. Said that in all the years he had been in the military he had never seen such a ragtag outfit. Said we needed discipline.'

'That's not all of it.' Parrish grunted. 'He said we were going to break the record for insertions in a month. The record is thirty now. He said we were going to run thirty-five, or his name wasn't J. P. DeNair.'

'We're in the shit, and that's a fact,' Workman muttered.

They stopped talking and braced to attention as the colonel's jeep came down the road. They saluted as he drove by. Easton looked tired, dejected, as he passed.

Walden instructed the little people to take their gear down to the hooch while he and Forrest turned in the code books at the TOC. After being cleared into the concrete building they went straight to the mail room.

'Let me have my mail from Hoa,' Walden immediately said to Warner.

'There's only one,' Warner said. 'It came in right after you guys went up to the launch site.'

'You're sure this is it?' Walden asked. He was almost afraid to read it, but felt reassured at the first line. She said she was waiting every day for him to come to her. The last part said she would write again the next day.

'You're positive this is it?' Walden asked again.

'That's all I got, Sam,' Warner said, handing them letters from home.

'I have to get to Saigon. There's something wrong,' Walden said to Forrest as they walked toward the war room. 'She must be sick or something.'

'She's probably busy getting ready to move,' Forrest answered. 'Don't worry about it. She's all right.'

They gave the code books to the S-1 sergeant and were on the way out when the new colonel came in. He was short and fat, with a red face. He looked soft.

'Colonel,' Walden said in greeting.

'You must be Walden,' the colonel said, shaking hands loosely.

'Yes, sir.'

'I'm your new commander, Colonel DeNair. Colonel Easton informed me that you're one of the best one-zeros we have here. I'll be expecting a lot from you.' Major Deacon stood behind the colonel, looking pleased. 'I understand your mission has been cancelled because of bad weather,' DeNair said.

'Yes, sir,' Walden said, wanting to leave, disliking the man because Deacon seemed to like him.

'I'm sure we can find another target for you within the next few days.' DeNair smiled.

'Sir, my people have been up at the launch site for nine days. They're tired. They need some rest.'

'The way I see it, all they've been doing is resting,' DeNair said. 'Major Deacon has been filling me in on the way this camp has been run. There are going to be changes made, Sergeant Walden. I'm not as concerned about popularity polls as the last commander was.'

'Sir, I suggest that you spend a little time talking with the team leaders. Read some of the after-action reports that come out of these areas we operate in.'

'I have been thoroughly briefed, thank you, sergeant,' DeNair said curtly. 'This organization is going to start operating like it was part of the military again. Is that quite clear?'

'Yes, sir,' Walden answered, biting his lower lip.

'However, I've always been a fair man. I think you'll find that if you play ball with me, I'll play ball with you. That's all.' DeNair dismissed Walden and Forrest with a wave of his hand as he walked past them.

Once outside, Walden began to seethe. 'That fat, dumpy little fart,' he hissed. 'He and Deacon are buddies already. That tells me everything I have to know about that bastard.'

'Take it easy,' Forrest said. 'That man looks like he'd court-martial you for spitting.'

'Goddamn, we leave for nine days and the whole world turns upside down,' Walden said. 'Well, screw him. I'm going to Saigon.'

'He's not going to let you go to Saigon,' Forrest said. 'At least, not until we run a mission.'

'I'm going to Saigon. There's something wrong. I can feel it.' Walden stomped toward Recon Company. 'One way or another I'm going.'

After dropping off their weapons and web gear, they went together to the Recon office. Pepper and Wells greeted them as they walked in.

'Charlie, I have to go to Saigon,' Walden blurted. 'There's something wrong with my girl.'

'Oh, Jesus Christ, Walden, this isn't the time for that sort of shit. Have you met the new commander yet?'

'I just did. Screw him, Charlie. I've got to go to Saigon.'

'You're going to have to forget about it for a while,' Pepper said firmly.

'Charlie,' Walden said as calmly as he could, 'I've never gone AWOL, or anything like it, in all the time I've been in the service. But I'll tell you right now, I'm going to Saigon one way or another.' Pepper looked at him. Forrest shuffled his foot around in a circle.

'Can we let him go for a few days?' Pepper looked over at the captain.

'What's the problem, Sam?' Wells asked, toying with a pencil.

'She sends me two, three letters a day. There hasn't been anything except one letter since we left for the launch site,' Walden said.

Wells wrinkled up the side of his face and looked at Pepper, who merely shrugged.

'All right, I'll make up some bullshit. But I want you back here in three days,' Wells said.

'That's all the time I'll need. Thank you, sir.'

'There's a Blackbird flight at nine tomorrow morning. I'll get you on the manifest,' Pepper said.

'Thanks, Top.' Walden smiled.

'You fuck up, Walden, and I'll have your ass.'

CHAPTER TWENTY-NINE

AT THREE in the morning Walden gave up trying to sleep. Each time he closed his eyes, he would see Hoa standing somewhere alone, looking back. The fear that something had happened to her, that she was sick or worse, knotted his stomach. He got up and dressed. Hanging his weapon around his neck, he stepped out into the coolness of the night air. He lit a cigarette and walked toward the corner bunker on the beach. It was deserted, the team standing guard that night having chosen the middle bunker thirty yards away. Climbing on top, he sat down inside the sandbag walls surrounding the tin roof of the rain shelter. The sound of the waves breaking on the beach masked his voice when he started to talk.

'God, I know I don't have the right to ask You for anything. I've spent the last few years of my life killing people. I know if I died right now, I would go to hell. But I'm not asking for anything for myself. You can do to me what you want to; I really don't care anymore. You can even let her love someone else. I'm just asking You to let her be all right. You know I haven't been so happy down here. I guess after that church thing, I figured I deserved anything I got.'

Walden lit another cigarette and remembered the vicious firefight inside the church. He saw again the crumpled bodies between the bullet-splintered pews, the puddles of blood running into the middle aisle, the fallen crucifix with the shrapnel-blasted Christ broken across the altar. It had been a sacrilege, a true sacrilege, but he hadn't thought about it until afterward. His only concern had been staying alive, and keeping his buddies alive.

'Okay, I know it was a desecration of Your home. I'm not asking You to forgive me. But please, God, don't let anything happen to Hoa. Don't punish her because she loves me.' He couldn't think of anything to add. So he murmured, 'Amen,' and walked back to the hooch. He felt better; God had listened and understood.

On the flight to Saigon, Walden was able to get some sleep. Once on his way to Hoa, he was able to relax with the thought that he would soon be with her. It was going to be okay. At Tan Son Nhut he wasted no time in getting off the base and hailing a taxi. The driver seemed to sense Walden's urgency. He used only the gas pedal and the horn as he zigzagged through the congested streets. A number of times Walden was certain they were going to crash, but he didn't say anything, only wishing they could go faster.

When the taxi pulled up in front of the iron gate, Walden knew something was terribly wrong. The guard shack was empty. The chain was off the gate. Panic set in as he tossed a thousand-piastre note to the driver. He rushed through the open gate, his eyes darting over the silent courtyard. The fishpond was empty.

'Hoa,' he screamed. He leaped the three steps to the door, then stopped as it swung open. For a moment he saw Hoa standing on the threshold and felt a soaring sense of relief. Then he realized he was looking into Dominica's sober face. She burst into tears and ran back into the house. Walden was unable to move for a long moment, then rushed into the front room.

The house was empty except for a few packing crates and cardboard boxes. The paintings were gone from the walls, only the light impressions on the stark walls remaining. He stopped, hearing only the sound of Dominica crying. He was out of his own body, watching the scene with someone else's eyes, as he stepped to Dominica, kneeling on the floor, her face resting in her hands. He yanked her to her feet.

'Where's Hoa?' Her mouth opened and closed. She burst into tears again.

263

'Damn you. Where is she?' Walden shook her roughly by her wrists. He could feel her stiffen as she fought to stop crying.

'She die, Sam,' she whispered. His hands dropped from her. His mind began to crack and pop like a dying fluorescent light.

'Hoa go to market. VC bomb blow up. I told by police. I go hospital, but already she be dead.' Dominica began to weep again. 'I go France now, to my parents.'

Walden turned for the door, unable to speak.

He didn't stop when Dominica called out behind him, 'Hoa love you very much. Very much.'

The last he heard was the sobs. He went through the gate, not pausing. He stumbled awkwardly as he stepped into a chuckhole, his body lurching to one side before he regained his balance. The people went by in faceless blurs. He was hypnotized by the sound of his boots on the pavement. Each step was another tick on a clock, and he stepped the ticks off, adding more and more.

A long way and a long time later he began to feel dizzy and weak. He stopped on a shaded side street and looked about him. Only the sound of jet fighters taking off from Tan Son Nhut airbase told him he was near the field. He stepped into a small bar.

Inside the gloom a ceiling fan squeaked each time it revolved. A radio behind the wooden bar played Vietnamese music. He bought a bottle of Export 33 beer from the fat mama-san, then retreated to a table in the back. Instinctively, he lit a cigarette. The smoke was dry and bitter. His hands shook so badly that he almost dropped the beer bottle. In all his life he had never felt so completely alone.

By the third beer he'd begun to feel what had happened. He quickly ordered another to drown his awakening brain. He couldn't bear to think of her, yet he couldn't help it. He began to feel drunk as the beer bloated his stomach. Early evening came, and the bar began to fill with GIs and bar girls. At first the voices and laughter helped distract him, but after a while they became unendurable.

He bought a fifth of Johnnie Walker from the mama-san. Stepping out into the dark, he began to walk aimlessly again, the bottle jostling against his leg in the side pocket of his fatigue pants.

Walden found himself standing next to the French National Cemetery. It was surrounded by a high concrete wall, yet there were holes blasted through by the heavy fighting of Tet sixty-eight. Through one of the jagged gaps Walden saw a portion of the large cemetery, lit by a half-moon.

He stepped over chunks of rubble around the opening and entered the graveyard. The silence was complete. He walked across the clipped, dry crabgrass toward a stone monument centered in an open pavilion. Rows of white tombstones surrounded it, bleached bones in the moonlight. Saplings stood in a row along one side of the monument. He sat down under one of the trees, putting his back against it.

He pulled the bottle out and opened it. Lifting it above his head, he saluted the grave markers before bringing it to his lips. He gagged. The skin on the sides of his face shivered as he tried to hold the liquor down. By the third swallow his system was becoming anaesthetized to it. He lit a joint from the plastic deck, then took another swallow from the bottle.

Half the bottle later, long after the joint was gone, Walden got up and staggered through the tombstones. Then he began running through the rows of graves.

'You all died for nothing,' he screamed, tearing open his fatigue shirt. 'You all died for nothing.' The night air rushed against his sweaty chest. He pointed at the stones accusingly. 'I'm in a graveyard of idiots. Dead fuckin' idiots.' He stepped backward, catching a headstone behind his legs and falling, then lay sprawled in the dirt. He began to laugh as he crawled up to the marker and rested against it. 'And You, You,' he screamed, pointing a finger toward the sky, 'You're the biggest fuckin' idiot of all.' He jerked the bottle up to his lips, swallowing until the liquid ran out the corners of his mouth.

'You're God, and You're so damn unsure of Yourself that You make us go through all this shit to see if we'll still love You when it's all over.' The words disappeared across the field of graves. 'Well, I don't love You, You bastard. I hate You. Do You hear me?' His voice reached a raw screech as he pulled himself to his feet. 'I hate You, and I hate Your priests, and I hate Your nuns, and I hate Your pope, and I'm glad I killed those fuckin' slopehead motherfuckers inside Your house. I wish now I had burned the sonofabitch to the ground.' He slumped to the earth, spittle running down his chin as he glared at the heavens.

'I'm supposed to say, "Take care of her, God"?' Walden sobbed. 'Some shit like "Thy will be done"? Is that it? Answer me!' The moon weakened as a cloud passed below it. 'Come down here. There's no one here to see You but me. Appear to me. You used to do it with Your fuckin' prophets and disciples. Let me see some of Your glowing orbs and shit. Come on down here so I can punch your fuckin' lights out.' He sobbed again. 'At least, come here and tell me why You killed her.'

Only silence came back to him. The far walls of the cemetery pulsed to his breathing.

'Okay, asshole. If You won't come here, I'll go there.' Walden pulled the .22 caliber pistol with the silencer out of his belt. 'The one sin you'll never forgive?' He started to laugh. He set the bottle on the ground, then reared back up. 'I'm going to hell anyway; it don't mean a shit to me.' He put the barrel to his temple. 'Here's to You, You sonofabitch.' He cocked back the hammer, staring across the rows of tombstones, knowing they would be the last thing on earth he would see. His finger rested on the trigger. He drew in a deep breath, held it, then pulled the trigger. There was only a click.

'Shit,' he mumbled. 'You're not going to get out of it that easy.' He ejected the shell with a violent motion and put the

266

gun back to his head. He pulled the trigger again. Again a click.

He began to laugh and cry at the same time, tears running down his cheeks. He fell on his back, then rolled on his side, laughing and coughing, looking at the gun. After a while he sat up, grabbing the bottle and dropping the gun in the dirt. He took another swallow from the bottle, then released it as he wrapped his arms around himself. He began rocking back and forth, repeating her name over and over. He slumped over and the last thing he heard was the whiskey slopping from the overturned bottle.

The sun burning his eyelids woke him. He rolled over and threw up. His nostrils burned as some of the vomit found its way into his nose. His body convulsed. Each time his stomach heaved, his brain exploded. After minutes of twisting on the ground he got to his feet. He had to get back to the team. It was the only thing left. He stood up, his head thundering, and looked up at the bright sky. 'You lucked out, You bastard. You really lucked out,' he whispered.

Retracing his footsteps, he climbed back through the same hole he had used to come in. Several Vietnamese stared at him when he reached the sidewalk. He waved down a taxi.

In the Special Forces Air Liaison office next to the Air America terminal, Walden went straight to the water cooler.

'Goddamn, Sarge, you look like holy hell,' a master sergeant said.

Walden didn't answer. He gulped down two cups of water and for a second felt better; then a spasm made him rush outside as the water came up.

'You okay?' the sergeant asked, when Walden came wobbling back in.

Walden slumped into a metal folding chair next to the man's desk. 'You got anything going to Da Nang today?'

'A Blackbird flight is leaving in about thirty minutes. Who do you belong to?'

'Command and Control North, CCN,' Walden said, trying not to gag.

'Hell.' The sergeant snorted as he shuffled through papers, looking for the manifest. 'If I was going there, I'd be in worse shape than you.'

'That would be hard to do, my friend,' Walden said. *And when you ask them how much should we give, they only answer more, more, more.*

CHAPTER THIRTY

WALDEN WAS walking down the wooden sidewalk past the TOC when he heard his name called. Major Deacon jogged up to him.

'You look terrible,' Deacon said, screwing up his red marshmallow face.

'Thanks,' Walden said, and began walking away.

'Sergeant,' Deacon said indignantly, grabbing Walden's arm. 'I didn't call you to pass the time of day. You're being briefed on a target tomorrow at oh nine hundred. Be there.' Walden yanked his arm out of Deacon's grasp, glaring at him.

'How'd you like to straphang on this one with us?' Walden asked, ridicule in his voice. 'I'll even let you walk point.'

'Are you threatening me?' Deacon hissed, crossing his arms over his chest as he looked Walden up and down. 'There've been some changes around here, Mr Bigshot one-zero. You don't have Easton to hide behind anymore.'

'You're pathetic. You know that?' Walden took a step forward. Deacon took two steps back.

'Just be at the TOC tomorrow, Walden. Just be there.' Deacon continued walking backward. Walden forced himself to turn and walk away.

After checking in with Pepper and hearing again that they were targeted, Walden went to the team hooch. Finding it empty, he walked down to the beach. Forrest and Workman, Parrish and Fish, were on the sand, sunning themselves and drinking beer.

'You back already?' Forrest sat up, shielding his eyes

from the sun. 'What the hell happened?' he asked when he saw Walden.

'I have to talk to you,' Walden said, his voice barely above a whisper. The others didn't say anything as Walden turned and began walking slowly down the beach. Forrest caught up with Walden a little way down, but didn't say anything. He lit a joint and they walked to the cove by the POL dump.

They sat down on the warm sand. Finishing the joint, Forrest pulled a pack of Pall Malls from his pants pocket. He lit two, handing one to Walden.

'So you broke up,' Forrest said, slapping Walden's bent knee lightly. 'It isn't the end of the world. We've still got Nam.'

'She's dead,' Walden said softly, and the tears started again. Forrest stared at him, his mouth open. 'I can't believe it.' Walden wept. 'I can't believe she's gone too.'

Forrest put an arm around Walden's shoulder. 'It'll be all right, buddy. It'll be all right.' Forrest squeezed him close, his eyes blinking rapidly. 'It'll be all right.'

At breakfast the next morning Walden was finally able to keep food down. The news had swept the camp, and the customary mess chatter was gone as Walden picked at his food. No one seemed quite sure what to say to him. Even Coop shunned the front table.

After eating, Walden and Forrest went to the TOC for the mission briefing. Deacon shot a dirty look at Walden but didn't say anything. The colonel waved them over to the map board.

'Major,' DeNair called over his shoulder. 'Would you care to join us?' Turning to the map, he tapped a fat finger against an area that had a red circle crayoned around it. 'Does this look familiar to you, Sergeant?'

Walden studied the solid green inside the circle with brown contour lines heaped on top of each other. 'Can't say that it does.'

'It should,' DeNair said, disappointed. 'It's Tango Five,

the target where you reported the helicopters, and where it's reputed one was shot down.' He looked from Walden to Forrest. 'I want a piece of that helicopter.'

'All right,' Walden found himself saying. 'When do we launch?'

The colonel was taken aback for a moment by Walden's quick acceptance. Deacon cleared his throat.

'Well, when do we launch?' Walden repeated in a bored voice.

'Five days?' DeNair asked, unsure of how to deal with Walden's approach.

'We can be ready in three,' Walden replied. Forrest didn't say anything.

'Well,' DeNair said. 'I guess I had you figured all wrong, Sergeant.'

'I've never weaseled out of a mission before. I don't see why you expect me to start now.' Walden lit a cigarette.

'Let's say I got some reports about you.' The colonel eyed Walden. 'That you're quite outspoken, perhaps?'

'We do our job. That's more than I can say for some around here.' Walden looked directly at Deacon, then leaned over the desk and tapped an ash into an ornate ashtray sitting on the colonel's desk. It was apparent that it was there for looks only. The colonel pretended not to notice.

'Sergeant Nobel will give you the pertinent information on the mission,' DeNair said crisply. Walden crushed the cigarette out in the ashtray.

Outside the TOC, Forrest grabbed Walden by the arm. 'What the hell was that all about? It's the dumbest damn mission I ever heard of. You trying to get us killed?'

'Didn't you see what they were up to?' Walden asked. 'They wanted us to turn it down so that they would have something on us. I wouldn't give the bastards the satisfaction.'

'What the hell was that we-can-go-in-three-days bull-shit?' Forrest growled.

271

'I wanted to see the expression on their faces,' Walden said.

'Sam, remember what you always say about dying stupid. You push this I-don't-give-a-damn game too far and we're all going to buy it dumb.'

That afternoon Pepper called a muster formation for the people in Recon Company.

'Okay, listen up,' Pepper bellowed, walking out in front of the men. 'You're not going to like this, but you might as well get used to it,' he began. 'I got a list of new rules here that have been issued by the new commander. Rule number one, no cutoffs in the mess hall. Rule two, the club will not open until sixteen-thirty hours, except on Sunday when it will open at thirteen hundred.' A rolling groan went up from the formation. 'Knock it off, damn it.' Pepper scowled. 'It gets worse. We have to close down House Ten.' He was referring to Recon Company's private whorehouse in Da Nang. A new wave of curses ran through the formation. 'Dismissed.'

'How do you get out of this chicken-shit outfit?' Workman bitched as the formation broke up.

'It's the old Army trick,' Walden said. 'A new commander comes in and takes away all the old privileges. Then, when he starts to give them back, everyone thinks he's a good guy. How long have you been in the Army anyway?'

'Since the day after I went stupid,' Forrest said.

'Come on, walk me up to supply. I have to get a new twenty-two pistol,' Walden said. 'The firing pin is blunted on mine.'

CHAPTER THIRTY-ONE

WALDEN WOKE in a peculiar mood the morning they were to launch. Walking to the shower with Forrest, he didn't feel the usual prelaunch butterflies banging around his stomach. The nervous tension was completely gone.

The little people were already in the showers. They yelled and giggled as they played in the water. Pau grinned broadly, signalling with his hands that Walden should take his shower.

'*Cám ón, ông,*' Walden said, bowing graciously and stepping into the steaming spray of water. The little people made ribald comments in Vietnamese.

'Very pretty,' Pau laughed, pointing at Walden's white buttocks.

'You think so?' Walden said good-naturedly.

'Same same *cô,*' Lap tittered, raising an eyebrow.

'How'd you like your little lights punched out?' Walden grinned.

'Light punch out?' Lap repeated, looking quizzical.

'Translate for me, Hung.' Walden stuck his head under the shower. He smiled to himself as he listened to the others rib Lap after Hung had explained.

'Why do you guys always shower with your underwear on?' he heard Forrest joke. 'You afraid someone is going to see your pee pee?' The remark quieted them down considerably.

After dressing they joined together for the customary visit to the shrine. Walden accompanied them but stood to one side as the rest went through the ritual. It was the first time he had not joined in. When they walked to the mess hall, Pau fell in alongside Walden.

'Why you no do?' he asked, holding Walden's hand.

'It's taken care of,' Walden said reassuringly, squeezing the small hand in his own.

For the first time before a mission Walden ate heartily. Parrish and Workman had risen early to have breakfast with the team. Coop looked radiant, fawning over Walden as she had in the past. She didn't resist when Walden put his arm around her waist after she'd brought over a second helping of steak and eggs. No one laughed or made snide comments when she leaned over and kissed Walden on the forehead.

Walden was leading the team out of the mess hall when DeNair and Deacon came in. He motioned for the team to go ahead. He stopped in front of the two officers. 'Is there any special piece of this motherfucker you want?' Walden asked, looking down into the colonel's face.

'No, no, just do the best you can,' DeNair said hurriedly, extending his hand.

'I wanted to take the major with me' – Walden looked at Deacon – 'but you know how it is, only the good die young.'

The colonel brought his unshook hand back in, scratching the top of it self-consciously.

Outside on the street Pau was tying the red ribbons to the front of sights and the uniforms of the team. Always before, Pau had waited until just before they boarded the helicopter. He stepped up to Walden and solemnly attached the red strips of cloth.

Master Sergeant Waters pulled up in front of the mess hall in a pickup truck and asked if they wanted a ride or if they would walk down to the pad as usual. Walden motioned to the little people to load onto the truck.

'This is the first time we ever rode down to the pad,' Forrest said.

'There's a first time for everything.'

'Did you get your special goodies?' Forrest asked.

'I never forget that,' Walden said. 'It's the best idea those clowns in Saigon ever came up with. Especially the bad AK rounds. Every time I plant some of them, I get a warm feeling all over. I can just see one of those little bastards banging away and then the whole weapon blows up in his face. The counterfeit money doesn't mean much, but those bullets . . . man, they must be packed with C-4.'

'You really get off on planting this shit,' Forrest said.

'Can you imagine the psychological effect it must have on those little dinks? There you are, assaulting a Marine outpost or something, then wham, the dude next to you blows his own head off. Perfect justice.'

A deuce-and-a-half truck stood in the middle of the pad. Four Seabees sat on the open bed next to mail sacks, talking. Three Montagnards sat against the sand-filled-drum retaining wall, facing the pad, waiting for a helicopter to take them to Mai Loc. The truck drove between the wall and the deuce-and-a-half and stopped near the edge of the pad. The team unloaded the rucksacks, putting them out in a row. They then scrambled on top of the drums to await the ships.

Walden and Parrish leaned against the pickup, talking, and Workman and Forrest walked to the deuce-and-a-half to visit with the Seabees. No one was surprised that the Kingbees were late. The morning sun was warm and pleasant. No one was in a hurry.

Sergeant Waters shouted good luck to Walden and started up the truck. Walden waved, then put his arm around Parrish as they started toward Forrest, Workman, and the Seabees.

The explosion tore Parrish out of Walden's grasp. A blizzard of shrapnel whined past his ears. A shock wave slammed into his back and bent him double. He straightened, turned, and saw the hood of the truck drop end-over-end from the sky and crash between him and the twisted wreckage of the pickup.

Walden blinked. The helipad was devastated, covered with writhing bodies. The first thing that came to his mind was that someone had thrown a satchel charge.

'You motherfucker,' Walden screamed as he ran toward

275

the retaining wall. With his CAR-15 poised to shoot anything that looked as if it were running away, he sprinted through the smoke. He stepped over the smoldering bodies of the three Montagnards that had been caught between the wall and the blast. A glance told him they were all dead. Nothing moved on the road. He turned and ran to where Workman was down on the steel plating.

'Oh, shit. Oh, shit,' Workman moaned, looking down at the front of his tattered and bloody shirt. Walden tore open the shirt, buttons flying. He looked down at the little black holes in Workman's stomach and chest. Thin trickles of blood oozed out.

'Don't move, Mike. Don't move. You'll be okay.' Walden rolled the body of one of the Seabees over. The body convulsed, a gush of blood streaming out of the nose and mouth. Walden looked up to find Forrest bending over him, blood dripping from his right ear.

'You hit, man?' Forrest rasped, holding his hands to the back of his head.

'No. What the hell happened?' Walden moved to where Parrish was staggering to his feet, holding his arm as his hand turned red.

'The goddamn truck ran over one of the rucksacks,' Forrest yelled, kneeling next to Workman.

'Where in the hell is the team?' Walden looked around the smoke-shrouded area. He saw Waters roll out of the wrecked truck and fall to the ground, his legs twisted and shattered. Walden ran back to the retaining wall and looked frantically for the team, but there were only the dead Montagnards bunched up against the wall. The team had vanished.

He climbed the drums and looked on the other side. The entire team lay motionless on the sand road. They began to move feebly. In seconds Walden was on the road, taking in the injuries. Pau was on his back, his eyes rolled into his head, his groin wet with blood. Hung's face was black from the soot of the explosion, making his eyes enormous. Blood, thick and bright, ran out of wounds just above his

276

lips and from his scalp. The black face made the scarlet that much more vivid.

'I okay, I okay,' Hung gurgled, trying to spit the blood out.

Walden reached in his side pocket for a field dressing as he held Hung's head against him. Pau had come around and was moaning words Walden couldn't understand.

'I okay. I okay,' Hung kept saying as Walden pressed the dressing against the partially torn-away lip. He took one of Hung's hands and placed it on the bandage.

'Hold on for a second. I have to check the others.' Hung nodded.

'Walwon, Walwon.' Pau was almost crying as he looked down at his blood-splattered crotch. 'You see. You see,' he said, his face twisted. Walden unbuttoned the fly as Pau pitched in pain and anxiety.

'It's still there,' Walden said. He pushed a dressing against the wound slightly above the penis.

'Ya, ya?' Pau beamed as though forgetting the other matter. 'Okay, okay.' He laughed, holding the dressing.

Lap and Playboy had been hit in the legs with Claymore shot and Cuong had been hit in the right arm and upper left shoulder. Cricket's right kneecap appeared smashed, but the bleeding was not bad. Nha, who had only come down to see them off, was able to get to his feet, although he had been hit in the hip. He hobbled to Cuong and began to apply a dressing to the torn right arm.

Walden jumped back on the retaining wall and yelled to Forrest and Parrish, the only two on their feet, to start loading the others onto the bed of the deuce-and-a-half.

'I'm taking Hung to the dispensary and letting somebody know what happened here.' He lifted Hung in his arms as though he were a child. He looked around at the others. 'I go get *bác sĩ*. You no move.' He headed down the road as Hung protested weakly.

The sun got hotter with each step Walden took through the soft sand. His arm muscles began to burn as Hung's body grew heavier, then became limp. Walden could smell the warm blood.

He remembered when his dog had been hit by a car and he'd carried her home. The blood around her muzzle and the pain in her beautiful brown eyes.

Just as he was sure that he was going to drop Hung, he saw the ambulance come speeding around the corner of the TOC.

'Put him in the back,' Miles Keegan said, braking next to Walden. He leaped out of the ambulance truck and ran around to the back to open the doors. 'I heard the explosion. What the hell happened?'

'I don't really know.' Walden eased Hung onto a stretcher in the back and Keegan drove the ambulance to the pad.

'Holy Christ,' Keegan exclaimed as he pulled up next to the team still lying in the road. 'Get them in the ambulance,' he said, grabbing his medic kit and running for the pad. Two gate guards finally came to help. Walden told them to load the team into the ambulance and went to help Keegan.

Walden and Forrest loaded others onto the flatbed while Keegan worked on the more seriously hurt. Then Walden drove the truck up the road to the Naval Hospital. He was amazed at how quickly the wounded were handled. Within seconds of arrival corpsmen and doctors were starting IVs and categorizing the patients according to severity of the wounds.

Walden went to where Workman was being prepared for surgery. Someone had grease-penciled letters on his forehead in black, making his face appear even whiter.

'Some shit, huh?' Workman smiled weakly. Walden took his hand. He stayed with Workman until he was taken into the OR, then went back to where Parrish and the little people were being readied. Finally, after the last of them had been processed through the swinging doors, he watched Keegan remove a small piece of shrapnel from the

278

bone behind Forrest's right ear. Keegan told Forrest it was a good thing he had a thick skull.

Walden and Forrest drove back to camp. A number of people were standing around the pad. Walden parked the truck and began to load the rucksacks and weapons.

'What happened?' Pepper asked, rubbing his arm.

'Waters drove over a rucksack and it exploded, I guess.' They walked to the wreckage of the truck. The left front tyre had been blown completely off. The undercarriage was ripped and twisted. Looking into the cab, Walden knew Waters should have died. The explosion had come right through the floorboard, twisting the pedals and leaving a large jagged hole. 'That's what it was,' Walden said, picking up the stock of a CAR-15 that had been blown in two. 'He ran over Pau's ruck. One of the M-14 toe-poppers must've gone off, setting everything else off too.'

Pepper intercepted the colonel and began to talk to him before he got to Walden. Captain Wells walked Walden away from the crowd.

'What all went off? It almost blew the windows out of the mess hall.'

'Well' – Walden shrugged – 'He carried two Claymores, four pounds of C-4, six hand grenades, ten to fifteen toe-poppers. I guess it all went up.'

'Jesus,' Wells said. 'Is anybody dead?' He looked ashamed he hadn't asked before.

'Three 'Yards for sure,' Walden said, glancing at where the bodies had been. 'They were caught between the explosion and the drums. A Seabee didn't look like he would make it. Workman caught some Claymore BBs in his chest and stomach; they're operating on him now. Parrish got hit in the arm, but not bad. Water's legs are all screwed up, but I think he'll make it, God knows how. Three other Seabees looked to be in pretty bad shape.' Walden went on reciting the list as Wells's eyes opened wider. 'And my team is completely fucked up,' Walden finished.

'You're not hit, are you?' Wells looked Walden over.

'No, I didn't get hit by anything.'

'Where the hell were you when it went off?'

'I was right next to the truck,' Walden said, and for the first time, he wondered why he hadn't been blown up with everyone else.

'Show me where you were standing when it went off,' Wells said.

Walden walked to the spot and turned to face him. 'Right here,' he said, standing barely ten yards from the truck.

Wells smiled in amazement. 'Hey, Top, check this out,' he called to Pepper. 'Walden was standing right there when the explosion went off, and he didn't get a scratch. You believe that?'

Pepper grunted. 'Walden, Forrest, let's go to my hooch. You two look like you could use a drink.'

CHAPTER THIRTY-TWO

IT WAS apparent that Louisiana Team was through. It turned out that Hung had the least disabling wounds, physically. After his upper lip was sewn back together, and the piece of shrapnel removed from his scalp, he was almost as good as new. Yet he had suffered a psychological wound that was much deeper and more serious. He saw the accident as an omen. Confiding in Walden, he told him that he thought he must stop running missions or for sure he would die.

Cuong's right arm from the elbow up had been shattered and had to be put back together with steel pins. The doctors said he would be able to regain about forty percent of its use, but even that would take time.

They removed Cricket's pulverized kneecap after trying unsuccessfully to fit it back together. Pau had suffered a cracked pelvic bone, plus several small wounds in his thighs and lower legs. Lap was crippled with a severed tendon behind his left knee. Playboy, bored with the hospital, went AWOL. When he came back, two weeks later, the wounds in his legs were so badly infected that he almost lost them.

Nha went home to Saigon to convalesce. Mike Workman was sent to the hospital in Japan. Waters had to be sent all the way to Walter Reed. Parrish was back in action after a couple of weeks. Two of the Seabees died, bringing the death toll to six. Of the twenty-seven people on the pad, Walden had been the only one not wounded.

Two weeks after the incident Walden was told to put together a new team. He was also told that Forrest had too much experience to remain a one-one and would have to lead a team of his own. Walden tried to argue, but from the beginning saw it was hopeless. So many changes were coming so quickly that Walden quit struggling against the current. But one good thing happened.

The night Hung was to leave for his home in Saigon, they had a small party in the old team hooch, and Walden was able to pass on the news.

'Deacon broke,' Walden said with a little of the old glee. 'The bastard finally went out in the field. It was a Slam operation, with a whole Hatchet force, so the creep was hardly alone. And they walked into it.'

'Big fight?' Hung asked.

'Big enough,' Walden said. 'Deacon was on the radio, crying, within an hour. I mean really crying. Know what he said? "I didn't know it was like this. Get me out."'

'What's going to happen to him?' Forrest asked.

'He wasn't back in camp thirty minutes before they shipped him out. The puke will probably be handed his retirement papers when he gets off the plane Stateside.' Everyone nodded approval and started to light up.

'I never expected it to end like this,' Walden said quietly as they sat around the table. 'We pulled some shit, though, huh?' He opened a beer and handed it to Hung. Forrest tried to smile.

They drank and smoked grass far into the night, talking about past deeds and other times. They talked about Hung's finally going back to college after ten years of fighting. They pretended a lot of other things. Finally they couldn't keep their eyes open any longer. When it was time for the Americans to leave, Hung went to his footlocker.

He returned with the fang of a tiger in his palm. 'I want to souvenir you,' he said quietly. 'My father have for long time. He give to me. Now I give to you.' Walden picked up the four-inch tooth. It had a Buddha painstakingly carved into the top.

'It's beautiful, Hung.' Walden turned the fang over in his hand.

'You keep with you. You never die in war,' Hung said,

closing Walden's fingers over it. 'I no need now. Someday, maybe you have son that must go to war. You give to him.'

'Thank you, Hung. I don't know what else to say.'

'You no say anything. You keep.' Hung smiled carefully so as not to tear the fresh scar on his lip. Walden placed the tooth in his top pocket and hugged Hung to him.

'I'll never forget you or the others,' Walden said, feeling his eyes smart.

'We smoke last joint, for, how you say in America? Old time sake?'

'Sure,' Walden replied. 'For old time sake.'

They smoked in silence for a few minutes, then Hung spoke again. 'I feel we be together for very long time, Walden. I remember today how many missions we go on together. We go twenty-four times across fence. Some time, Pau, Cuong, Lap, they no have words to say to you. They no can explain you they be safe with you. They ask me to tell you now.'

They looked at each other across the table. Hung struggled to find some words. Finally he just looked at Walden and said, 'You know.'

'Yeah, I know,' Walden said.

The next morning Hung left camp before Walden or Forrest were up. In the end they all left the same way they had come into Walden's life. With no fanfare, no expectations.

CHAPTER THIRTY-THREE

THE SUNLIGHT made the palm branches far below shine. Walden sat, looking down at the changing countryside, reciting no prayers this time. He thought of Hoa, and kissed the wind as it blew past his face.

At the launch site no one was waiting with a truck, so the new team had to walk to the tent area. Walden told his one-one, Charlie Horn, to get the team settled in, then went to the operations tent. A tall blond-haired first lieutenant sat on the desk that Slader used to have. A master sergeant Walden had never seen before sat behind the desk, fumbling with papers.

Earlier in the month Colonel DeNair had issued an order that no team was to be extracted, even under Prairie Fire conditions, without his personal okay. The launch-site crew argued that if they had to radio back to Da Nang for permission, teams were going to get wiped out. DeNair said there were to be no exceptions. The crew responded that if a team in Laos was in real trouble, they would pull first and ask questions later. In a snit DeNair relieved the entire launch site crew, including Slader and Major Cane.

Cane had sent his good-byes to the camp, along with a warning to watch out for 'arithmetic-and-medal people.'

'What's the story?' Walden snapped at the man behind the desk.

'You Walden?' the sergeant asked.

'Yeah. I have my team here and we're supposed to be running a mission today.'

'Right. Okay,' the sergeant said, getting up from the desk. 'The major is over at the Marine mess getting some

284

breakfast. Ah, I guess the pilots should be here any minute?'

'Are you asking me?' Walden said, his irritation obvious.

'Well, the major is on top of this. I just got here a few days ago.'

'I hope somebody is on top of this. Our target area isn't exactly a dry hole. Is Covey up yet?'

'I'm your Covey,' the lieutenant said, standing up from the desk.

'What the hell are you doing here?' Walden half shouted.

'I'll give the pilots their briefing.'

'Oh, for God's sake.' Walden put his hands over his eyes. After a few seconds he took a deep breath and let his hands down. 'Okay, you're both new. Let's just work this thing out and get on with it. Where's your map of the area?' The lieutenant unrolled his flight map and spread it out over the desk.

Walden pulled out his own map and put it next to the lieutenant's. 'Here's my primary LZ,' he said, pointing at a spot on the map. 'You know about the southern ridgeline here, right?'

'What do you mean, know about it?'

'It's full of antiaircraft positions, and I mean full. Didn't anyone tell you that, for Christ's sake?'

'Look, I don't have to take this,' the lieutenant said indignantly, straightening up. 'I'm an officer, I – '

'Look, you dumb fuck,' Walden said, cutting him off. 'It's my ass on the line. You fly us down that southern ridgeline and we'll get blown right out of the sky.'

'Major,' the lieutenant said as the commander came into the tent. Walden hadn't seen him before either. 'This guy is trying to tell me my job.'

'Somebody'd better,' Walden said.

'Now, hold on, Sergeant. What's the problem?' The major walked to the desk.

'The southern ridgeline is full of thirty-sevens and God knows what else,' Walden said, trying to keep his voice down. 'He didn't even know about it. I'm not going

285

anywhere until I'm sure you people at least know what the hell is going on.'

'Now, come on, we can get this straightened out,' the major said. 'There's no sense in blowing up.'

'Don't fly down the southern ridgeline,' Walden said to the lieutenant.

'Okay. Okay. How many times are you going to tell me that?'

'I just don't intend to die dumb. Got that?'

After they lifted from the pad, Walden busied himself checking the team, then monitored the radio. As they neared the LZ, Walden was listening to Covey direct the helicopters in. He felt Horn shaking his shoulder.

'Sam, there are fires burning down there,' he yelled over the noise of the helicopter. Walden looked down and then out at the sweep of terrain. His gut froze.

'Jesus Christ, he's flying us right over the sonofabitch,' Walden screamed. The fires were the southern ridgeline lit up with 37-millimeter and heavy-machine-gunfire. Black puffs of flak began to explode around the helicopter.

'Goddamn! Goddamn!' Walden roared. He fell against the pilots' seats as the Huey nosedived toward the blur of jungle to evade the fire. The force of the chopper levelling out squeezed him against the floor.

The fury in his chest pulled him off the floor and thrust him between the pilots' seats.

'Take us back to Da Nang. Don't even bother returning to the launch site.' He took care to make sure each word was clear. The ashen-faced pilots didn't look as though they would put up much of an argument, but Walden stuck the CAR-15 between the seats for emphasis.

The helicopter was barely down before Walden was off and running toward the TOC. His rucksack was slowing him up, so he just dropped it as he moved. Horn came running up behind him.

'Sam, Sam, goddammit, calm down a little bit,' he said, grabbing the back of Walden's shirt. Walden stopped just

286

long enough to push Horn away. The Vietnamese guard at the gate to the TOC opened it and asked for ID. Walden stuffed him back into the guard shack and stalked toward the steel door.

'*Dùng lại. Dùng lại,*' the guard shouted. Walden turned and saw the guard pointing a carbine at him. In four steps he was on the guard, grabbing the weapon out of his hand. He threw it onto the roof of the TOC, then walked slowly to the door.

He took a deep breath and calmly told the American guard inside his name. As soon as the door opened, he stepped inside.

'Jesus, what's wrong?' the American asked when he saw Walden's face.

'It's important that I talk to the colonel,' Walden said, forcing himself to speak evenly. The guard pushed the button that opened the second door and Walden was inside.

Colonel DeNair and two other men were sitting around a desk, drinking coffee, when Walden walked into the war room. Their faces registered surprise when they saw Walden.

'Sergeant Walden,'' the colonel said, sitting up straight in his chair. 'You're supposed to be on a mission.'

'I quit. I'm through. I resign. I told you I'm not going to die stupid, especially not for stupid bastard assholes who don't know the difference between games and war. You dumb little jerk-offs can do what you want, but I'm out. I quit. You hear?'

They stared, and he stood there, watching, his weapon not quite dangling from his hand.

'I think that can be arranged, Sergeant,' DeNair finally said, his voice quiet. 'It will take a couple of days, of course.'

'Just get me the hell out of here.'

During the week he waited for his orders Walden was made to build a picket fence around Recon Company. He didn't mind. Before leaving for the Army the first time he had helped his dad build a fence behind the garden. It seemed a fitting circle.

He gave his CAR-15 to Horn, passing along the history of the weapon. Walden had received it from an earlier leader of Louisiana Team, and so far no one who had that weapon had died.

The night before he was to leave he and Forrest walked to the old team hooch. Another team was inside, so they sat on the steps and lit a joint. They talked camp gossip and other unimportant things.

'I don't know how to say good-bye,' Walden finally said.

'Then, don't,' Forrest said, draping an arm across Walden's shoulder. 'Total victory.'

'Unconditional surrender.'

There were no tears left to cry, no fears left to hide. The warm night breeze carried the soft dreams of childhood, memories of love and hands that cared. Hoa had given him a gift of love; his friends gave him reasons for tomorrow.

On the day he left, Walden sat quietly in the back of a three-quarter parked near the headquarters building. Only Forrest and Horn were there to see him off. Before the truck pulled away to take him to the airfield, the colonel came over holding a brown paper sack.

'Here's your plaque. We didn't have time to put your name on it, but you can do that.' He pushed the bag into Walden's hands.

Walden held the wooden plaque tightly as the truck moved down the road leading out of camp. As it jolted onto the tar pavement, he kept his eyes on the bed of the truck. *Don't look back. Don't look back.* Then, unable to stop himself, he lifted and turned his head. The camp was already gone, lost behind a rise. He turned around and looked up the road.

THE END